DISCARDED FROM OLDHAM
LIBRARIES

Deirdre L Heywood

DIVISIONAL HEAD

SHADOWS
OF
POWER

*'... and dreams laid to waste
by shadows of power...'*

PROLOGUE

1962

FROM the doorway the girl stared boldly at the man who sat naked on the blue silk cover of the bed.

She could handle this one. She knew his tastes were... exotic, but she wasn't afraid. And she had been assured that her co-operation would be amply rewarded.

In silence, the man watched the girl enter the dimly-lit room. Her unclothed body was perfect. She was about nineteen, with full, firm breasts and long, strong legs. As she came closer he could smell the musky perfume of her body, the scent of her flowing fair hair.

His cold blue eyes travelled slowly over her. Her beauty had no effect; his penis lay slack and indifferent between his pale spreading thighs.

Still without speaking, he indicated for the girl to join him on the bed. She moved to obey, and lay next to but not touching him, her heavily made-up eyes holding his.

The man stared down into the soft young face and it was then that he felt the first stirring in his loins. He imagined those same eyes stark with fear, those full childlike lips twisted in pain and the thought made his shaft grow firmer.

The man's continuing silence began to unnerve the girl lying on the bed. Hoping for a response, she began to run slim, delicate fingers over the heavy fullness of her breasts, half closing her eyes and moaning softly as she caressed her own flesh.

The man's lips tightened in anger. How many times a night did the bitch indulge in the same insulting performance? Did she think he was so stupid, so gullible?

Beneath her own fingers, the girl's round pink nipples hardened into points. With a furious impatience, the man grabbed the blonde's narrow wrists, forcing both arms tightly against her sides. She grunted in pain as the man's heavy onyx ring dug sharply into her flesh.

His eyes were dark with rage. Only men deserved the pleasure of sex — not women. And now he was ready to take that pleasure.

Roughly, he pushed the girl backwards across the bed and with increasing desire forced her into the powerful leather tongs he had fixed to the bedhead. The girl did not resist. She had known what to expect and glared brazenly into the stony mask of the man's face.

But then, as the thick cotton gag was placed across her mouth, and the soft leather noose wound quickly around her neck, the beginnings of fear glittered in the girl's staring eyes.

The man was excited now, his organ stiff with lust as he felt the growing sense of power, of domination. Slowly, with merciless fingers, he began to squeeze the soft milky skin of the girl's breasts. Heart thudding, he watched with pleasure as tears of pain welled into those wide, terrified eyes. Suddenly, the ache in his cock became unbearable.

Without preamble, the man forced his burning flesh between the girl's smooth thighs, shuddering with desire as he moved roughly and deeply into her.

His thick male fingers eased the noose just a fraction tighter around her straining neck, and at that moment the girl's struggles began in earnest.

The smell of her fear, her desperate struggle, made the blood pound thunderously inside the man's head. So much power... So much pain... The thought drove him into a frenzy.

Several minutes passed before realization dawned.

He recoiled in horror, staring with disbelief at the bruised and swelling flesh, the blank and lifeless eyes. Then a violent trembling began to wrack his pale heavy frame.

The camera lens hidden among the ingenious folds of the tented ceiling caught the sick, desperate panic in the killer's ashen face.

CHAPTER ONE

1987

Out of the corner of her eye, Anthea James could see the floor manager giving her the wind-up signal and with skilful ease she brought the discussion to an end.

'And that's where we have to leave the 'Female Factor' for today. Many thanks to our two very interesting guests.' Here Anthea smiled at the two women sitting on either side of her; one was a plump, curly-haired, best-selling novelist; the other an imposingly elegant member of the Bar. 'And of course thank you too to our studio audience for their very stimulating questions.' This time the smile broadened to include the packed tiers of seats that filled the darkness behind the cameras.

Then the full force of the James warmth and sincerity was directed at camera two. 'To all of you at home – thanks for being with us. I hope you'll join us next week when the 'Female Factor' will be looking at the question of surrogate motherhood, with two more special guests.'

For a further ten seconds, as the credits began to roll, the studio audience applauded with enthusiasm. Then, at last, the show was over.

Shaped along the lines of the 'Donahue' program in the States, the 'Female Factor' presented a forum for women of all backgrounds to discuss the relevant issues of the day. The program had been a hit from the start and had made Anthea James a household name. Now, after two years as the show's presenter, Anthea still felt the incredible surge of adrenalin that came with the completion of another successful program. The challenge to improve was always there and challenges had never frightened Anthea James.

At thirty-nine, Anthea James was a major success story. To her large and devoted female audience she had it all: looks, fame, wealth, success. In the eyes of her adoring fans Anthea could do no wrong. She was the woman they most admired, respected, dreamt of being.

Now, as the audience of excited, chattering women began to file out of the darkened studio, Anthea stood up. As always she knew better than to waste an opportunity where her public image was concerned. With no appearance of haste, she smoothly divested herself of her guests, promising to rejoin them soon in the network's VIP room.

As she picked her way across the cable-littered studio floor, Anthea stopped and chatted with the departing audience, those ordinary Australian women whose lives contrasted so drably with her own. It cost her nothing and in the end could be so worthwhile.

The effect of Anthea's presence on her admirers was electrifying. That a woman as important, as successful, as frantically busy as Anthea James could spare a moment to listen, to laugh, to sympathize with them, made them glow with pleasure and self-importance.

Their eager eyes fed hungrily on the image she presented – the gleaming red-gold hair, the expensive, understated clothes and jewellery, the full, perfect figure. To the women clustered round her, Anthea James exuded the confidence and ease of a woman who has never known rejection.

Yet there was no resentment of their idol's glamour and good fortune. For, in some mysterious way, Anthea James was able to make them feel that she understood, that she knew what it might feel like to live in one of Sydney's dreary satellite suburbs with too many children and not enough money.

What they felt for Anthea was love. Love for her compassion and concern, for her understanding of their problems, and for the escape she offered from their humdrum lives. Through her weekly newspaper column, her radio phone-in program and her television show, Anthea James reached out to each and every one of them. She gave them Hope.

It wasn't until thirty minutes later, suitable quantities of the

James brand of charm and sincerity having been dispensed to all, that Anthea was free to climb into her white Mercedes for the drive to her Double Bay home in Sydney's exclusive Eastern Suburbs.

As she turned out of the network gates and joined the heavy stream of late afternoon traffic, she felt herself begin to relax. Putting a live show to air four days a week took its toll. But she loved it, and the financial rewards were more than ample compensation.

In less than ten years Anthea had become Australia's highest-paid media personality. Yet, of even greater importance was the power and influence she had acquired along the way. Anthea smiled to herself as she tapped a perfectly manicured fingernail on the leather-bound steering wheel, in time to the fast and frantic sound of Mendelssohn's 'Italian Symphony'. Tonight at Julian Crane's cosy little dinner party, she was about to extend that power and influence in an entirely new direction. She was taking the first step towards what had always been her ultimate goal.

TWENTY-FIVE MINUTES LATER, Anthea pressed the electric eye on the dashboard and, as the tall, white iron gates swung slowly open, she headed up the curved pebble driveway of her home.

The house, hidden behind a high clipped hedge overhung with muted green English trees, was Anthea's dream come true. Two storeys high, it was one of Sydney's original sandstone homes with a charm typical of its Georgian design. Anthea loved it. Located at the end of a quiet cul-de-sac, its lush springy lawns running down to the Harbour's edge, the house was her haven, her sanctuary. Here she could relax.

As she opened the heavy oak front door and entered the coolness of the black and white tiled foyer, Anthea smelt the lemon fragrance of furniture polish and saw the gleam on the French marquetry table further down the hallway. She felt a sense of satisfaction. Everything was in order, exactly as she liked it.

After a succession of housekeepers whose standards had failed miserably to match Anthea's own, she had finally found Selena. The twenty-five year-old Filipino woman had managed to polish, scrub and dust with the fastidiousness that Anthea demanded.

But Selena did not live in; Anthea cherished her privacy too much for that.

Dropping her soft leather briefcase on the hall table, Anthea went through to the sunny yellow kitchen at the rear of the house. In the refrigerator she found the jug of iced tea that Selena knew always to leave in readiness. Anthea never touched alcohol, or cigarettes. Drugs of any kind held no interest for her and she worked hard to hide her contempt for those who needed such crutches in order to cope with life.

She poured herself a glass of tea and carried it through to the wide back verandah with its sweeping views of the water. Settling herself into the soft down cushions of the white cane sofa, Anthea sighed, then slipped off her high heels and took a sip of her drink. Although she hated to admit it to herself, she felt tired.

Her schedule would have crushed any normal woman; the television and newspaper commitments, the twice-weekly radio program, the meetings and committees, the endless speaking engagements, the constant demand for her imprimatur by a dozen charitable organizations – and now, her steadily increasing involvement in the political arena.

Politics was the reason for tonight's dinner party at the harbourside mansion of her employer, multi-millionaire media tycoon, Julian Crane. It was to be her formal introduction to those men whom she was counting on to be major supporters in her bid for political office.

The forthcoming by-election for the Federal seat of Elwyn was to be her testing ground. As a marginal seat, it was likely to suffer the usual tendency of electors registering a protest vote against the sitting government. The group of high-powered businessmen she would meet tonight, all friends and associates of Julian Crane's, were fully aware that someone with the electoral appeal of Anthea James would have an excellent chance of retaining the seat for the government.

But Anthea was not so naive as to think her fellow guests were purely disinterested parties. There were certain to be favours expected, trade-offs anticipated, when the time was right. No doubt, Anthea raised a cynical eyebrow, there were those amongst them who thought a woman would be more malleable, more easily influenced.

Her eyes hardened as she swallowed the last of her drink. Well let them keep their illusions. In the meantime she would make full use of their support and assistance. Afterwards, they would find out soon enough that Anthea James was not quite the pliable figurehead for Big Business that they had all hoped.

As she stood up and walked back into the house, something made Anthea remember Nan's advice to her about men, so long ago: 'Use them, my darlin'... use them...'

After a quick catnap Anthea woke refreshed. The short dreamless sleep had revitalized her and she felt in good form for the challenge of the evening ahead.

Naked, she slipped out from between the pale pink sheets and made for the bathroom, but the burr of the telephone halted her.

'Anthea? It's Alex.'

'Darling! Where are you?' Alex Volka's faint Hungarian accent sounded just a little more pronounced over the phone.

'At the airport. The Manila flight's been delayed for half an hour. I thought I'd try to reach you before you went out. Tonight's the night, isn't it?'

'Yes. I feel like I'm about to be assessed for head prefect.' Alex was the only person Anthea had told about the dinner this evening. Her tone was light but Alex knew how much it meant to her.

'I'm not sure that I approve of your company – all those terribly respectable wealthy businessmen.' There was something in the dryness of his tone that put Anthea on the alert.

A well-known barrister with a fearsome reputation, Alex Volka had been secretly seconded onto a government-initiated committee which had had the brief of investigating the alarming growth of organized crime in Australia.

But Alex's increasing frustration with the committee's limited powers to follow through on its investigations had caused him a *crise de conscience*. Soon afterwards he had resigned his position. Now, while still as busy as ever at the Bar, his every spare moment was spent in the research and writing of a book through which he hoped to document the detailed activities of, as he described them to Anthea, 'Australia's most protected criminals'.

Alex was convinced that the only way the government could be forced into action was by the publication of the facts he hoped to reveal in his book.

'At least I feel I can achieve something this way, Anthea,' he had said with passion one evening as he sat in Anthea's sitting room, not long after resigning his position. 'On that committee I felt as if I were supposed to work with both hands tied behind my back.'

Angrily, he shook his head of thick blond hair and his grey eyes darkened. 'No, by the time this book comes out, and if I can make sure the mud sticks, the government will *have* to take some action. The public outcry will make sure of that.'

Alex had confided this much to Anthea but as far as names were concerned he had been much more discreet. Anthea had had no hint – until now.

She frowned into the phone. Was there someone among Julian Crane's dinner guests whom Alex was following up? Anthea knew better than to ask. When Alex wanted to tell her more, he would.

Alex's tone had become more cheerful now and for a few minutes they chatted easily before saying goodbye.

'Kisses, my darling. I'll see you when I get back. Don't run away.'

'Just make sure,' Anthea said teasingly, 'that *you* run away from those very attractive Filipino ladies!' Alex's work occasionally took him out of the country. This time, Anthea knew, it was a quick four or five-day trip to Manila.

Alex's rolling laughter reached her down the line and then he hung up.

Thoughtfully, Anthea replaced the receiver. Alex's earlier words were still on her mind. What had he been getting at? Was there really someone in tonight's company whose activities aroused his suspicions?

She knew Alex was working at a feverish pace on his investigations, as well as coping with his usual Bar commitments. In fact, their dedication to their respective careers meant that sometimes weeks would go by before they could get together. The telephone kept them in touch.

Anthea smiled as she stepped into the warm spray of the shower. It was a relationship that suited them both. There were no unrealistic demands, no distracting complications.

She had met Alex Volka three years ago and they had hit it off right from the start. Although only ten when he and his mother had come to Australia from Hungary, Alex still had the charm of so many European men.

Margo Volka, a divorcee and an accomplished pianist in her native country, had been very ambitious for her only child. Sacrificing her own career, she had worked at various full-time menial jobs to put Alex through the best private schools and university. The contacts she had made while giving piano lessons to the children of some of Sydney's wealthiest and most influential citizens had helped in establishing Alex's career. With her son's talents now fully acknowledged, Margo Volka basked happily in the reflected glory of his success. Her only regret was that Alex had never married.

Tall, handsome and elegant, at forty-three, Alex Volka was one of the country's most eligible bachelors. Women chased him, captivated by his charm, his looks, his power. Yet he had remained unclaimed until his meeting with Anthea James. And then it had been Alex himself who had done the chasing. Anthea's own relentless ambition, her driving desire for success, and the scars of her past had left her convinced that there was little place for a man in her life.

But as she grew in prominence, as her successes piled upon each other, and as her wildest dream seemed more and more as if it might become a reality, Anthea was astute enough to see that an appropriate mate was an inevitable social requirement. She would be enlarged in the public eye, would be seen not only as a professional success, but also as a woman who had been equally successful in her personal life.

Now the Australian press were working hard at making her and Alex an 'item', delighting in photographing them together and in speculating on the possibility of marriage.

But Anthea knew that, despite her very deep fondness for him, she would never marry Alex. He was a passionate, exciting man who demanded the best of himself and of life, yet much as she cherished his friendship, respected his integrity, admired his energy and drive, a husband had never been part of her plans.

For Anthea had soon realized that once a woman became a wife, she very quickly became the secondary partner in the relationship. And this would be particularly true of marriage with Alex. As Alex's wife, she would inevitably be eclipsed, overshadowed, and everything she had worked so hard to achieve would slip away from her.

The thought brought a stubborn light into Anthea's eyes as

she stepped out of the shower. She would never let that happen. Not now. Not when she was so close...

Wrapping herself in a cream silk robe, Anthea sat in front of her dressing table mirror and applied her make-up. She knew exactly how to highlight her best features: her slim, straight nose; her high cheekbones; her wide, dark brown eyes. If her jaw was a little too strong, her mouth a fraction too wide, such imperfections went unnoticed in the overall impression of attractiveness.

The colouring and styling of the rich bright hair that hung in elegant simplicity to her shoulders, she managed easily herself. To Anthea's way of thinking, beauty salons were too often hives of idle gossip and intrusive curiosity. They were certainly no place for someone as disinclined as she was to self-revelation.

For despite her high profile, little was known about Anthea's personal history. To the Sydney media, Anthea James' existence had begun a mere twelve years ago. Before that the details were vague. A country childhood...? An orphan...? Brought up by a friend of her mother...? Everything was merely guesswork. Nothing was known about her family, her education, her childhood friends – or the way in which, almost overnight, Anthea James had taken the Sydney social scene by storm.

As far as the media were able to discover it had all begun with the launch of Anthea's exclusive collection of stunning and innovative jewellery on the conspicuous consumers of Sydney's Eastern Suburbs.

Drawn by the massive publicity in Sydney's leading newspapers and magazines such as *Harpers* and *Vogue*, battalions of eager, wealthy women had descended on the opening party at the plushly appointed Double Bay boutique. Just *how* Anthea James had managed to afford such a bombardment of publicity, no-one had ever been able to discover.

But achieve it she did, and Anthea's jewellery sold with fervent disregard for price to the dedicated, well-heeled shoppers of Sydney.

And Anthea had known exactly how to capitalize on her success and intrigue. In no time at all her name was appearing on all the very best guest lists, her photo featuring in the pages of the Sydney press.

It had all happened exactly as she had planned. Anthea smiled with satisfaction as she clipped on the black opal and platinum necklace that was one of her own designs. The jewellery boutique had served its purpose. It was one of the lesser concerns now. She knew that Roy was perfectly able to look after that side of things. After all, it was really thanks to him that it existed at all.

From those early times, Anthea had become steadily more prominent: first in Sydney itself, and then in Australia as a whole. Anthea James had had a game plan and nothing had been allowed to distract her from it.

Now, at last, she was in sight of her final goal, a goal brought closer she was sure, by her selection eight months ago as Australian Woman of the Year.

And tonight, a sudden excitement lit Anthea's dark eyes, she was to take another major step. The right backing and support would ensure her entry onto the political scene. From there, she had no intention of stopping until Australia had voted in its first female Prime Minister.

A sharp thrill ran through her as she let her mind play with that exciting scenario. She wasn't a fool. She knew it wouldn't happen overnight. But she was patient; she could bide her time.

Of one thing, however, she was sure – nothing was going to stop her now.

Anthea stood up and slipped on a black lace cocktail dress that showed off her full bosom and the smooth curve of her hips, yet at the same time stopped short of provocation. She knew the ropes, knew best how to conquer those who might think themselves immune to her charm and presence. She had worked hard to achieve the ultimate winning combination: femininity and power.

But as she made a final check of her appearance in the mirror, her inner excitement was tempered by the knowledge that once she had changed direction and headed into the maelstrom of a political career, she would be subjected to much closer scrutiny by the media at large. It was inevitable.

Anthea's dark eyes glinted in the mirror. She had conquered that fear long ago. Her tracks were well-covered – she had seen to that. Lenore Hamlyn had been dead and buried a long time ago...

CHAPTER TWO

WITH furious impatience, Maxine Crane ripped off the crimson silk St Laurent and flung it on the floor. Shit! Three thousand dollars worth of dress and she still looked like an overfed heifer.

With blazing eyes she stood in front of the full-length mirror and took in the loathsome sight of her ample body clad only in satin bra and panties. Even in the deliberate softness of her bedroom lighting the puckered sagging flesh was clearly visible around her hips and bum. Hanging low and pendulous like two slowly-leaking balloons, were the large breasts she'd once flaunted so proudly. The sight made her sick.

Having kids was what had ruined her, she decided bitterly. That, and the start of her goddamn menopause. Maxine's scarlet lips tightened. Christ, only forty-seven and already she was losing her sap, drying up like an old bone that had been sucked dry.

Angrily, she turned away from the repulsive sight and rummaged through the rows of designer dresses, in search of something that would perform the miracle of transformation.

Tonight especially, she had wanted to look her best. With Anthea James under her roof, Maxine had wanted to preen, to shine, to establish without a doubt her own status and power. Anthea James hadn't won yet.

Maxine felt the anger seethe inside her. How she loathed the bitch; loathed her success, her smug self-confidence, her air of infallible righteousness.

Who the hell was Anthea James, after all? Where had she crawled from? For all her celebrity, no-one seemed to know the answer to that question. From the moment she'd burst onto the Sydney scene completely unheralded a dozen years ago, from the moment she'd opened that outrageous boutique in Double Bay, her climb had been meteoric.

Maxine's cheeks flushed with anger. God, if she had to read one more word written by Anthea James, see those smug perfect features staring at her yet again from the TV set, hear her make one more expertly-argued pronouncement on yet another 'important current issue', she thought she'd vomit.

A look of pure hatred crossed Maxine's puffy, over made-up face as she struggled into a too tight organza sheath. How dare Julian expect her to endure an evening like this. She knew what she was in for; she had seen Anthea James in action often enough before: herself in the background, the dutiful hostess, while every man in the room flattered and fawned over that sharp-eyed bitch.

Maxine's temper flared again. Christ, how could grown men be so stupid? How could they allow themselves to be so easily manipulated? That self-righteous cow clicked her fingers and they fell over themselves to do what she wanted. And, if simple manipulation wasn't enough, Maxine was as certain as she could be without concrete proof, that Anthea James would have no hesitation in sleeping with whomever she felt could best promote her own interests.

Her lips curled in a sneer. Anthea's relationship with Alex Volka was, no doubt, an excellent means of distracting the press from probing into other, more revealing, aspects of her private life...

Still angry, Maxine sat down at her dressing table and applied another layer of colour to her already gleaming lips. Did Julian think she was a fool? Did he think she hadn't heard the rumours spread gleefully around this incestuous bloody town? That Anthea James' speedy climb to the top of the Crane Corporation – the television show, the newspaper column, the radio program – had been achieved by screwing her own goddamn husband...

A tremor of rage ran through her. The thought of having to sit and watch that condescending, sanctimonious face all evening drove her crazy.

In an effort to distract herself, Maxine opened the green velvet box she had taken earlier from the safe. Inside lay a multi-stranded diamond bracelet that Julian had bought her from Tiffany's in New York.

The sight of it did a lot to help elevate her mood and she gave a small sigh of satisfaction as she clipped the rows of blue ice onto her plump wrist. One of her consolations.

Maxine's thin glossed lips curled in a contented smile. And the other was Barry. Without Barry life would be almost unbearable...

Anthea had timed her arrival to perfection.

The Crane harbourside mansion, featured in the usual spread of international architectural glossies, was renowned for its palatial opulence. To Anthea the house was blatantly vulgar – as vulgar as she found Julian Crane himself. But she put such thoughts to the back of her mind as she was shown into the large formal sitting room where the other guests were already assembled.

Eight perfectly barbered heads turned towards her and eight pairs of appreciative male eyes took in the woman who stood poised and smiling in the doorway. Her face was familiar of course, although as yet none of the eight had met Anthea James in person. But, from the time she had openly expressed interest in the possibility of a political future, her progress had been intently observed, her views and opinions closely monitored, and her phenomenal popularity with the Australian public noted with particular satisfaction.

It hadn't taken long for this powerful coterie, dedicated to the protection of its own interests, to decide that Anthea James was a prospective candidate who deserved their serious consideration. The consensus of opinion was that she was a figurehead who might be put to excellent use.

Smiling smoothly, Julian Crane moved forward to greet her. He was thickset and bull-necked, with pallid indoor skin; not even expert tailoring could give him the patina of elegance.

'Anthea, my sweet.' His dry lips barely touched her cheek.

'How wonderful you look – as always.'

There was the usual cool arrogance in his voice. Julian Crane had always given Anthea the impression that, while as an employee she was a valuable commodity and to be treated accordingly, as a woman she was merely to be tolerated. He never seemed at ease in her company.

Now Julian Crane's mouth curled in a supercilious smile. 'Come in and let me introduce you, Anthea. You have a roomful of very serious admirers here.'

The oily smoothness irked Anthea but she kept the smile fixed on her face. Julian Crane needed her, and for this next step in her career, she needed him. Her employer was a powerful man.

Crane had never made any secret of his success. Abandoning a depressed and gloomy post-war Britain he had arrived in Australia at twenty with fifty pounds in his pocket. With the survival skills learnt as a child on the tough mean streets of a Welsh mining village, he had quickly seized the opportunities afforded him by his adopted country.

Transport and communication he soon saw were the backbone of a land as large as Australia. A desk job with a small trucking firm quickly taught him the ropes. Within six months, while still retaining his office job, he'd put a deposit down on his first truck. It was then a simple enough matter to redirect business from his unwitting employer to himself.

It had started from there and eighteen months later, having finally resigned his job, Julian Crane had three trucks of his own and two-thirds of his ex-boss's business.

By 1964 Julian Crane's trucking empire was the largest in Australia. Borrowing heavily while interest rates were laughably low, he had proceeded to branch out into refrigeration and building materials, tapping into a market swollen by the thousands of post-war immigrants to Australia.

Controversial, flamboyant, and a risk-taker, he had made his first million by the time he was twenty-six and was ripe to cash in on the booming resources and property markets of the seventies. From there Julian Crane's fortune had escalated in a dizzying fashion. It was his acquisition in the early eighties of several major daily newspapers throughout the country, followed by the purchase of a leading Sydney television and radio package, that established him not only as a man of immense wealth but of great personal power as well.

And power, Anthea had realized very quickly after meeting him, was something Julian Crane found immensely exciting. That he could use it with indiscriminate malevolance she was also fully aware. She had heard the rumours about the peremptory sackings of attractive young female journalists who had seen fit to resist their employer's blunt advances. And for the bold and pretty young models who succumbed, there was the assurance of a cover-photo on one of the Crane publications.

Anthea had few illusions about her boss, but their own relationship had never been anything more than a very profitable working arrangement. She knew instinctively that to a man like Julian Crane, an independent powerful woman like herself held no appeal. Submissive, easily-managed young girls would be much more to his taste.

Now, as Anthea was introduced to her fellow guests, all leading figures in the country's major industries, her thoughts were once again focused on her ultimate goal.

Smiling graciously as she shook hands with these prominent wealthy men, Anthea could see the open approval in their eyes and she couldn't help but wonder how differently they might feel about her if they knew where her real interests lay.

Big business, she knew, would always survive whether the government in power made the crossing rough or smooth. Certainly, she would play the role expected of her in that regard. She believed in free enterprise, in a system where those who strive, achieve. But, that women should have a major role to play in the operation of that system was the fundamental belief that drove her.

The rules had started to change but Anthea was impatient. She saw a need to speed up the process, to bring to an end the centuries of exploitation and exclusion from power that women had endured. Women – ordinary women – had to learn how to gain real power; in the home, in the work place, and in schools and universities. To help them achieve this was Anthea's dream and purpose in life.

'And of course,' Julian Crane's voice intruded on her reverie, 'you know my wife, Maxine.'

'Of course.' Anthea's voice maintained its friendliness as Maxine nodded coldly and immediately turned away to continue her conversation with the director of a major mining company.

Anthea shrugged inwardly. Maxine Crane hated her; she knew that. They saw each other seldom but Maxine's animosity never diminished. Despite her general popularity, Anthea was fully aware that there was still a particular strata of Sydney's so-called society which had refused to accept her.

The reasons weren't too hard to fathom. Her popularity? Her power? Or was she merely too much of an unknown factor?

Soon afterwards, the party moved into the dining room where

the long mahogany table gleamed with candles and silver and Waterford crystal. As the chairman of a leading international bank helped her into her seat, letting his cool smooth hand rest a fraction too long on her bare shoulder, a half-smile hovered round Anthea's lips.

Women like Maxine Crane would never get in her way.

It was late when the evening finally ended and as she sat cocooned in the soft leather comfort of the back seat of Julian Crane's gold Rolls Royce for the short drive to her home, Anthea felt a sense of overwhelming satisfaction. She was positive that she had passed whatever test had been presented to her tonight.

Every issue raised she had discussed with perception and understanding, had expertly answered the most penetrating questions on a diverse range of subjects. A wave of elation swept through her. She was supremely confident that she would now have the support that counted.

It was then, as she stared out at the quiet dark side streets of Sydney, that Nan's words once more floated into her mind.

'Use them, Lenore... use them... just like they used you my darlin'.'

CHAPTER THREE

THE call from Matt Kelso came through just three minutes before Anthea was due to go to air.

'A car'll be waiting to pick you up the minute you've finished there, Anthea.' Matt Kelso spoke in his usual rapid-fire manner, as if he had another six calls on the line – which was probably the case.

As Sydney's leading media agent, Matt Kelso handled the biggest list of show-biz and sporting clients in Australia.

Matt knew everyone there was to know in Sydney and, as he had said once to Anthea with sardonic amusement, 'There *is* only Sydney in this bloody country, isn't there, darling?'

Matt Kelso was now almost fifty and still projecting the same boyish charm and enthusiasm that had started him on the road to success. He had begun his working life in the inauspicious tedium of a draftsman's office. It was the sudden mushrooming in the sixties of pop bands imitating the Beatles and other English groups that had set him on the path of his future career.

Ambitious and indefatigable, he had established himself as a manager and promoter, operating with such success that less than a decade later, he was importing the sort of big-name overseas talent that had previously been barely aware of Australia's existence.

Anyone starting to make a name for themselves in the media or sporting worlds, and serious about making money, eventually found their way into the Matt Kelso stable. Matt had approached Anthea right at the beginning when the publicity and success surrounding her jewellery venture had brought her into the limelight.

The big, bluff, clean-shaven man with the dirty blond hair, dazzling smile, and manic energy had impressed Anthea from the start. Through Matt Kelso she knew she would get the entrée, she was looking for. And from the first exposure Matt had arranged for her – a six-week guest appearance on a well-known panel show – the rest had been easy. A weekly column in one of the lesser women's magazines had become a feature article in a leading Sydney daily; her spasmodic radio spots had grown into the one and a half hour twice weekly program; and the occasional TV appearances had evolved into the fantastic success of the 'Female Factor'. Matt Kelso had successfully introduced her into the major media set-up owned by Julian Crane; and now Anthea James was as familiar a face as Paul Hogan to the Australian public.

Matt's voice bellowed down the line. 'So don't hang around, darling. The moment the show's over, fly on down here. This bloke is *big* and the deal he's offering is even bigger.' Matt Kelso chuckled. 'If we pull this off, they'll probably make you honorary ambassador, darling.'

Without waiting for a reply, he hung up. The red light on the studio wall was flashing its warning, so Anthea had no time to ponder just how close to the truth Matt Kelso had come.

An hour and a half later the program was over and despite Matt's admonishment to hurry, Anthea took the time to check her hair and face in the small elegant powder room the studio provided for its leading personalities.

The green silk dress and matching jacket was the exact foil for her red-gold hair, dark eyes and fine clear skin. Around her neck hung a plain, slender gold chain, a perfect match to equally simple gold hoop earrings.

Satisfied that she looked her best, Anthea took the elevator down to the entrance foyer where the black Mercedes limousine awaited her. The driver opened the door and, as she slid into the back seat, Anthea began again to think about the deal that Matt was working on for her.

In keeping with America's continuing fascination with Australia, American Media Network were interested in having a leading local personality do a series of interviews with prominent Australians to mark the Australian Bicentenary. AMN, while not quite the giant that CBS was, still stood out as a major media network in the States. The chance to appear before such a huge American audience was a heaven-sent opportunity as far as Anthea's future plans were concerned. She knew that local publicity about the deal would ensure that she became even more strongly identified in Australian minds as someone with an intrinsic interest and belief in her own country.

Today at lunch she would meet with David Yarrow, the American owner of AMN. For it was Anthea in whom AMN were interested, and Anthea was determined that by the time lunch was over it would be Anthea James they were *desperate* to get.

ELEGANT AND ESTABLISHED, Vedette of Double Bay was not one of the usual haunts of the sometimes rowdy, always conspicuous, media fraternity. That, and the fact that its grey quilted banquettes afforded some degree of privacy, accounted for its choice by Matt Kelso.

The restaurant was only half-full but the gentle hum of conversation was brought to a halt as Anthea followed the maître d' to Matt Kelso's table. Fashionably coiffured heads turned and every woman in the room made a mental note of Anthea James' appearance.

At one table by the large picture window, two middle-aged women, impeccably groomed and made-up, lifted their forks from cholesterol-free salads to watch as Australia's most popular female personality made her way across the room.

'Well, Harriet darling,' the plump brunette leaned towards her companion, 'we're in good company today.' As she spoke she took careful note of Anthea James' plain gold jewellery, and suddenly the two-carat diamond studs that lit up her sagging ear lobes seemed just a bit too much for lunchtime.

She sighed. 'How *does* she keep that figure? I'd kill for it.'

Across the table the dangerously slim woman with the severe ash-blonde hair wasn't listening. Harriet Maddern had turned her attention back to her meal. It often happened that she and Anthea crossed paths but neither made any acknowledgement in public of their friendship. It was a friendship based on a long distant past and the very special person who had changed both their lives.

For a moment, an image of herself at twenty rose in front of Harriet's newly tightened eyes: a naive lonely girl from the bush, fresh to the cold, fast-paced anonymity of Sydney.

So long ago she thought, spearing a perfect slice of tomato. Now, as the fifty-two year-old widow of legendary race horse owner and breeder, Mike Maddern, she was a woman who bought her clothes in Paris, Rome and New York; whose chauffeur-driven Bentley was a familiar sight in Sydney's better streets; whose company was sought in the homes of the country's most prominent and powerful citizens.

Marriage to Mike Maddern had introduced her to a life of consummate ease and luxury and Harriet would be forever grateful for her rescue. Momentarily, a shadow crossed her perfectly made-up face. What a shame Mike was no longer here to share it all with her. They had been such good friends, had found real enjoyment in each other's company.

And Mike had been so generous, so eager to make up for the life she had been leading when they'd met. Nothing, in Mike's opinion, had been too good for his beloved wife. He had pampered her endlessly and missed her dreadfully on the one occasion a year that they spent apart: Harriet's three week shopping excursion, to Europe. She wondered sometimes if Mike had ever guessed...

Harriet Maddern put her fork and knife together in front of her. Well, Mike was dead now, killed eight years ago piloting his own plane to a stud sale in South Australia. It had been a shock and she still missed him but life – the comfortable easy life of a wealthy widow – had to go on.

MATT KELSO, WATCHING for Anthea's arrival, now stood up, a smile of welcome on his broad, high-coloured face.

'Darling,' his full rich voice boomed across the room. 'How *are* you? You're looking wonderful.'

With a smile Anthea acknowledged the compliment, as Matt kissed her effusively on both cheeks. There were occasions, she thought, when Matt could be every bit as theatrical as some of his clients.

The waiter pushed in her chair, flicked open the heavily-starched napkin across her lap, and took her order for a tomato juice.

Anthea arched a quizzical eyebrow at Matt. 'So, I flew here as suggested – where's the American connection?'

'Rang through just as I was leaving the office. Said he'd be a few minutes late.' Matt shrugged his broad shoulders in his impeccably cut, grey wool jacket, 'The mountains will wait for Mahomet, my darling.'

He was in excellent humour. The deal with AMN was as good

as clinched, and his own very generous cut of Anthea's excellent fee would be most gratifying. Particularly, Matt frowned, with Anthea seemingly so hellbent on taking to the less-than-lucrative political stage in the near future. Little joy there for himself, he thought with some irritation.

'And I thought American's were obsessively punctual,' Anthea said flippantly as her drink was placed in front of her.

'You'll have to forgive Yarrow then. Seems he had the good luck to be born right here in Sydney town. He was just a kid when his parents divorced and his mother, a Yank, took him back to the States with her.' Matt grinned over his drink. 'Then, of course, like all indefatigable American divorcées, she managed to pick up husband number two a very short time later – Philip Yarrow no less.'

Anthea raised an amused eyebrow. 'You're far too cynical, Matt – especially for someone who's been picked up pretty smartly three times in a row himself.'

Matt grinned and gave a mock salute. 'Touché!'

They chatted easily as they awaited the third member of their party. Matt seemed to think there would be no last minute hitches. David Yarrow had come to Australia himself to attend to the finer details and today's meeting should see the last of those resolved.

Anthea's contract with the Crane Corporation had presented no problems. 'After all, this is a one-off, Anthea,' Matt had explained at the beginning. 'And Crane will get the rights to show the interviews too – for a much cheaper price than it would have cost him if he'd set the deal up himself. Plus, there's the prestige attached to the fact that it's someone from his stable that a major American network is after.'

Now, Matt Kelso gave Anthea a cocky smile across the table. 'This deal's going to put you way ahead of the local pack, darling.'

Anthea knew the truth of Matt's words. On the financial side she had nothing to complain about. Her fee from AMN would be astronomical. But the dollars weren't what really counted. She had more than enough money to live as comfortably as she desired. No, it was, as Matt had said, the prestige, the cachet, and the enhancing of her already high profile that mattered.

Suddenly Matt's eyes were drawn to the restaurant's entrance – as were the eyes of every woman in the room. It was easy to see why. The tall, broad-shouldered man with his perfectly-groomed pewter-grey hair, his lean, clean-shaven face and startlingly blue eyes was not only immensely attractive, but projected as well that unmistakable air of self-possession that is the universal trademark of the very rich and the very powerful.

As his clear blue eyes scanned the room, he seemed oblivious to the attention he was attracting.

With a murmured, 'David Yarrow' to Anthea, Matt stood up, a welcoming smile on his face.

The man in the entrance smiled in acknowledgement and followed the maître d' across the room.

It was then that his affliction became noticeable. The limp was pronounced. And the specially built-up shoe could be seen beneath the hem of his well-cut trousers. A quick glance downwards, and at once polite eyes turned away.

Except for Anthea's.

Her eyes were riveted on David Yarrow's lean dark features and her face had turned chalk-white. A cold sickness moved through her bowels and she felt as if she were choking on her own breath.

No, God, no! It couldn't be. Not after all these years... Not now...

'DAVID!' MATT WAS reaching out his hand as his guest arrived at the table.

'Matt... forgive me. The meeting ran over and the traffic was hell...'

Matt Kelso waved away his apologies and, turning to Anthea, made the introductions as the two men took their seats.

Heart hammering thunderously in her chest, Anthea was barely able to acknowledge the American's greeting as she fought desperately to control her rising panic. It had been so long ago, she reasoned frantically with herself. More than twenty years. And she was so different now... her name, her looks... there was nothing that could tie her to the young unformed girl whom this man had known for such a short time.

The man opposite her was different too, but Anthea knew with a horrifying certainty that she was not mistaken.

It had been David Kershaw then... And there had been the

wheelchair. But, now, as she forced herself to meet his welcoming smile, she recognized again the same blend of seriousness and warm receptiveness in his strong face, the same alert intensity of manner.

And superimposed on those earlier traits was a sense of judgement, of control and command, that had been lacking in the twenty year-old boy. The boy who had found out the truth about the girl called Lenore Hamlyn...

Terror twisted her stomach as she felt the scrutiny of those eyes that were the colour of deep clear water.

'I've heard a lot about your abilities, Anthea. I'm very much looking forward to working with you on this project.' David Yarrow spoke with the easy familiarity so common to Americans. 'I was born in Australia you know; I still have a great affection for this country.'

Anthea slid her eyes away from his gaze and made a murmured reply, barely aware of what she was saying, as she waited, trembling inwardly, for the flicker of recognition to enter those clear, bright eyes. But Matt was talking now, suggesting a wine, recommending items on the menu, and with David Yarrow's attention momentarily distracted, Anthea felt the breath pouring back into her body.

Lunch was served but she barely touched her food. Terror rendered the simple act of swallowing an enormous effort. Every second that passed seemed like a lifetime. So much was at stake. The present, the promise of the future, could all be swept away in an instant if, suddenly, David Yarrow remembered...

Every nerve in Anthea's body was stretched as tightly as piano wire and the sweat slipped slowly between her shoulder blades, while under the table her nervous fingers plucked furiously at the crumpled linen napkin.

Somehow she made it through the meal, forcing herself to join in the discussion of the project that no longer mattered to her. There was now no way that she could entertain the possibility of working with AMN – and David Yarrow. Her only thought was to escape this nightmare as soon as possible.

Abruptly, with a vague excuse, she brought the discussion to a premature end and, fully aware of the look of surprise, then irritation, on Matt Kelso's face, Anthea stood up and made her farewells.

The two men rose also and this time David Yarrow's eyes seemed to study her with closer attention. He spoke carefully, as if playing something over in his own mind. 'I'm real sorry that you have to rush away, Anthea, but I guess Matt and I can finalize things.' He put out his hand and Anthea was forced to take its cool strength in her own. 'I'm sure,' he added smiling now, 'that we are going to enjoy working together.'

Anthea forced her rigid lips into a smile. 'Thank you... It's... it's an exciting project.' To her own ears her voice sounded strained and breathless. And then, as their hands parted, Anthea felt something else beneath her paralysing fear. It was the sudden stab of a deeper emotion. One she thought had left her long ago...

In an agony of agitation, Anthea headed straight to her only haven, the cool stone house by the water's edge.

There, in the safety and security of her own bedroom, she stripped off the silk dress, now damp with sweat, unclipped her jewellery, and with trembling fingers began to cream off her make-up in front of the Italian silver-framed mirror.

Then, with nervous urgency, she studied the clean and unadorned face that looked back at her.

Firm strong features had replaced the soft undefined contours of youth; stylish red-gold hair hung in place of the long pale-brown tresses of the adolescent girl; and an underdeveloped, awkward body had become the full, ripe figure of a mature woman.

Anthea's pulses raced. Could there be the slightest chance that David Yarrow would remember? Could there be anything left in the face now of the young girl he had known... of the Lenore Hamlyn who had been buried over fifteen years ago...?

CHAPTER FOUR

1963

WIDE-EYED with horror and disbelief, Lenore stared up into the man's red bloated face. His foetid breath, stinking of cheap whiskey, reached her nostrils and in shocked repulsion she struggled for release. But, drunk though he was, the man's grip never slackened on her slim trembling body.

Lenore knew there was no point in screaming. The walls between the old stone houses were thick and impenetrable; and anyway, who would come to her aid? Who would care? In the area where they lived, people kept their noses out of each other's business. It was safer that way.

Her heart went cold and still as the man fumbled with his stained, greasy trousers. And then she could see it – swollen and red and ugly between his legs.

As his hand released his own flesh, the man's rheumy bloodshot eyes seemed to glaze and Lenore could hear the faster pace of his stentorian breathing. Fear and panic quickened her own breath too, while her heart fluttered like a trapped bird in her heaving chest.

Then his rough thick hands were tearing off her cheap cotton panties, and with a deep grunt of satisfaction, he had prised her bare slender legs apart.

He lunged himself hard against her and Lenore made a last desperate effort to escape the ultimate horror. But as she thrashed wildly beneath him, it was already too late. With one quick movement he had torn his way into her, branding her young innocent flesh with his thrusting, unyielding weapon.

Shock and pain made the bile rise in Lenore's throat and hot tears of shame and disgust rolled down her chalk-white cheeks onto the threadbare sheets.

The man took no notice, merely pumping his organ deeper and deeper inside her until, in terror, Lenore felt that she would split in two.

At last, with a long drawn out shudder and a moan like that of a wounded animal, the man's sweaty bloated body collapsed against her.

As his hot, foul-smelling mouth panted close to her ear, Lenore just caught the muttered words: 'Ooh, my little baby... you sure are good to your daddy...'

The nightmare had begun.

There was never any warning. Her father took her as he pleased and very soon her submission was total.

'You belong to me, Lenore. Don't forget that.' Drunkenly, he would mumble the words as he forced himself inside his fourteen year-old daughter. 'You're mine, the same way your mother was...'

As she dragged her newly developing body, bruised and torn to school, Lenore prayed with feverish urgency that somehow, in some way soon, the nightmare might end.

If only her mother were alive. Her mother had been kind and good and wise and Lenore missed her with a terrible longing. She knew too that her father would never have dared to touch her if her mother were still alive.

But Judith Hamlyn was gone, sent to an early grave by poverty and despair. By the time she had seen a doctor it had been too late. The blood disease, aided by long hard hours on a cold factory floor, had already won.

Heartbroken, Lenore had cried for days, unable and unwilling to accept the sudden dreadful fact of her mother's death. It was so unfair, she thought, as she lay in sleepless misery night after night in her narrow bed. Already at fourteen she could understand how little her mother had had from life, tied as she had been to a drunk and a gambler who hated himself and the world.

Once, when she'd asked her mother why she endured it, her mother had smiled wearily, 'That's the way the world is for women like me, Lenore. We can't expect nothin' more.'

To Lenore that had seemed wrong somehow. But it was only later that she had understood – that her mother's traps – a child and poverty – were the same as those of too many women.

The reality of women's powerlessness had been brought home to her with ultimate force less than a month after her mother's death. It was then that her father's advances had started.

Lenore had been too ashamed, too guilty, to tell anyone, or to ask for help. Somehow, she was made to feel that she 'owed' her body to her father. His explanation was simple: she was a woman and he was a man, and men had needs that only a woman could satisfy. But the guilt and the terror she felt every time did not leave her.

The deliverance she had prayed so hard for, came four months later, just when Lenore felt she could bear it no longer.

Late one Friday night her father was knocked down in the street, too drunk and incoherent to see the car that had killed him.

Lenore received the news impassively, her face a mask; but somewhere deep inside her she felt the beginnings of a wild euphoria. Her nightmare was over; she was free.

It was then that Nan Reilly took over her life.

NAN REILLY WALKED slowly away from number forty-three, the dirty crumpled envelope containing the rent money clutched in her age-spotted hand. A frown creased her broad wrinkled face. There was something about the girl in forty-three that worried her.

Poor wee thing. Every week the sight of the poor child's pale blotchy face and red puffy eyes pierced Nan's sentimental Irish heart. It was a hard thing all right to lose a mother – and at fourteen, Nan was sure, it hurt a damn sight more. It must be close to six months now but the poor child still looked so distraught.

Of course, Nan's lips thinned in annoyance, the father couldn't be much comfort. Never there most of the time. Nan Reilly didn't miss much; she knew the type – drink and horses and never a moment for either his poor sufferin' wife or his grievin' child. Probably never noticed that the girl was painin' so much all this time later.

As Nan knocked on the door of forty-five she made up her mind. Next week, if the child was still so forlorn, she was going to make sure they had a chat. Yes, Nan decided resolutely, a chat and a nice long bawl in a pair of comfortin' arms was probably all the poor mite needed.

Five days later, Nan Reilly was arranging for the burial of Thomas Hamlyn.

News of his death, less than a block from his own home, had spread quickly, and Nan's heart had gone out to the poor young girl whose misery, she was sure, must now be beyond bearing. The old man might have been a no-hopin' bastard, she thought to herself, but he was the poor kid's flesh and blood after all.

Nan had known at once what she must do, and Lenore, with no relatives or close friends to turn to, had been only too glad of the landlady's offer of help with the grim details of a funeral. Since she'd learned of her father's death, Lenore's mind had been in a whirl, grappling with both a sense of sweet release and the guilt she felt about the manner of her unexpected deliverance.

Two days after the funeral, she was unpacking her few belongings in the sunny high-ceilinged bedroom in Nan Reilly's rambling two-storeyed home. It was only then that Lenore began to realize just how good this stranger had been to her.

Nan had insisted from the start that Lenore move in with her.

'No point in rattlin' around in that huge almighty place by myself, love. I'll fix everythin' and till you leave school you can stay with me.' Nan's cheerful face crumpled into a smile. 'I'll look after you, darlin'. It's a big bad world out there; you don't want to find that out any sooner than you have to.'

Lenore had never met anyone like Nan Reilly before. Where her mother, at thirty-nine, had already been jaded and beaten by life, Nan, surely in her sixties, was filled with unflagging energy and optimism.

Small and neat, with sharp observant blue eyes and crimped hair dyed an indeterminate shade of brown, Nan Reilly seemed to take a real joy in being alive. As they sat around the pitted pine table in her spacious, stone-flagged kitchen, Nan told Lenore a lot about her life. It didn't seem to matter, Lenore noticed, that she herself offered so little in return.

'1923 it was, love. There I was, fresh from the bogs of Ireland, and up in London town.' Lenore soon learned that Nan heartily enjoyed poking fun at her Irish background. 'Determined to be a dancer I was. And you should have seen me then. Velvet skin, trim full figure, shinin' dark hair. And could I move my feet!'

Nan's pale blue eyes glistened at the memory. 'Keen as mustard I was to learn to dance. My poor mother couldn't say no to the likes of me. Somehow she was findin' the money and off I went to classes. Miss Valmay was her name, the teacher. And no nonsense did that one take; tough as a sergeant major she was with us all. There were twelve of us in that class, but only me, mind you, with the drive and determination to be tryin' for the big time in London.'

Nan turned bright eyes to Lenore. 'What a life I had, love. The admirers, the flowers, the gifts. So many invitations to parties, tea dances, dinners...'

Nan's voice trailed off and she sighed. 'And look at me now.'

'You never married?' Lenore's question was tentative. Maybe it was impolite, but she was curious. Surely with all her admirers Nan must have had lots of proposals?

Nan's face darkened. 'Oh, I married all right, love. Stupidest damn thing I ever did.' Her tone turned sour. 'All charm and attention he was – and with the gift of the gab like I'd never heard before. Could charm the saints into hell could that one. We had a lovely quiet wedding in a charmin' little church in Highgate, then four months later I found myself at t'other end of the world.'

Nan's face had gone hard and tight. 'The police were after him. Fraud and menaces. The first I knew about it was when the ticket for the liner was placed in my hands.' She looked at Lenore. 'I was a fool, Lenore. I should have been gettin' out then. But,' her eyes grew wistful, 'I was in love with the scoundrel. In love...'

Again Nan's voice trailed away and for a moment she seemed lost in thought. Suddenly she sat up straighter and her eyes grew sharp as they held Lenore's. 'It's the worst thing that can ever happen to a woman, Lenore, falling in love... I'm tellin' you that me darlin'.'

Later, when she was alone in her room, Lenore pondered what Nan had said. She thought she understood. After what had happened with her father, Lenore knew she would never fall in love. No man would ever have power over her again in any way. Not over her body, her mind – or her heart. Of that she was determined.

With a shiver, she slipped beneath the covers of the old-fashioned brass bed. It took her a long time that night to fall asleep.

Life with Nan soon fell into a pleasant routine and, as the days passed, Lenore found it easier to turn her thoughts from the trauma of the previous few months.

Her schoolwork improved, as did her appetite. Nan was a good cook and there was always a tempting hot meal waiting for her when she got home from school.

'You're too thin, my girl. You need a bit more meat on those bones. Here, take some more of this.' And Nan would ladle another spoonful of steaming stew onto her plate, cut another slice of juicy roast to tempt her. It was food Lenore had seldom seen at home and she ate it with relish.

There were other differences too in Nan's house. Lenore had noted the gleaming piano and the expensive old fashioned furniture in the front living room, as well as the fresh flowers throughout the house and the fine soaps in the bathroom.

On Saturday afternoons, Lenore would put on one of the pretty new dresses Nan had bought her and they would take a taxi into the city to see one of the latest films. For Lenore, it was a brand new world; she had never known such treats before. With her father so often incapable of work, and her mother's pitiful wages, there had never been anything left over for extras.

Still, Lenore was puzzled. How could Nan afford such luxuries? She didn't go to work, and the properties she owned in this run-down inner suburb of Sydney could hardly be rented for very much. One day, when she felt she knew Nan well enough, Lenore broached the subject.

Nan threw back her wrinkled neck and laughed. Her faded blue eyes crinkled in amusement as she patted Lenore's hand.

'Darlin', you've got to be makin' it however you can in this old world. And I do all right, don't you worry about that.'

It wasn't really an answer, but Lenore didn't ask again. She had assured herself of the one thing that had been worrying her – she wasn't a burden in Nan's home.

*

NAN WAS GENEROUS in other ways as well. Often Lenore would come home from school to find some pretty young girl chatting earnestly with Nan. The girls seemed just a little bit older than herself, and sometimes in Lenore's private opinion, they wore just a little too much make-up.

'They all bring their problems to Nan,' the old lady would explain cheerfully, as if she didn't mind at all.

Lenore soon decided that Nan Reilly was a very special kind of person – a saint in human guise. But, comforting as she found her, Lenore never mentioned what had happened to her after her mother's death. She had drawn a curtain over that part of her mind. Her body was healed and now, once more belonged solely to herself.

Or so she thought.

LENORE LOCKED THE toilet door and quickly pulled down her panties. For a moment she had thought... But nothing. Not a speck, not a smudge; nothing to bring the relief she had been searching for week after week.

She tried to stay calm. It was nothing to worry about really, she told herself. Her periods had always been irregular. There had been no time yet for them to fall into a pattern. Twice before she had missed a month altogether. That's how it was when things were just starting; her mother had told her that. She was not going to worry, although now it had been so long.

Back in her bedroom, Lenore stood in front of the mirrored door of the old carved pine wardrobe. With frightened eyes she forced herself to look at the straining of the white cotton school blouse across her breasts, at the way her belly threw the pleats of the navy wool skirt out of line. She recalled too the dizzy spells at school and the awful lethargy that made her so tired; some afternoons all she wanted to do was to come home and go straight to bed.

With furious determination, she pushed the unthinkable out of her mind. Nothing was wrong. It was Nan's cooking, that was all.

That was all, screamed the voice in her head.

*

'NAN, I'M HOME!'

Dropping her heavy schoolbag in the hallway, Lenore went through to the kitchen at the back of the house. Nan, wearing a flowered apron over her blue cotton dress, was stirring a steaming pot on the stove.

'Smells great, what is it? I'm starving.'

Nan chuckled. 'What do they do to you at that school?'

Lenore helped herself to a glass of cold milk from the refrigerator and sat down at the kitchen table as Nan put the lid on the pot and turned down the flame.

'That can look after itself.' Then as she took off her apron and hung it on the large brass hook behind the kitchen door, she raised a quizzical eyebrow at Lenore.

'Love, I know you're a growing girl,' her tone was jocular, 'but I'm just takin' a close look at you these days in that school uniform. You're burstin' out in all directions.'

Lenore's head shot up. Her face turned ashen, and with a wild desperate sob the tears came at last.

Later, much later, in the darkened bedroom, Lenore lay pale and quiet beneath the covers while Nan, perched beside her, soothed back the damp tangle of hair from her brow.

Lenore felt completely calm now; a strange sort of peace filled her soul. The burden was shared; it was no longer hers alone. Nan's light-hearted words had been the catalyst snapping the fragile threads of her control and forcing her to face at last her frantic self-delusion.

For a long time she had wept uncontrollably, her damp face pressed against the dry papery skin of Nan's warm neck, and in an agony of revelation, had finally gulped out the horror, the shame, the desperation, of the last few months.

Arms wrapped tightly around the sobbing girl, Nan had listened to the tortured muffled words, while the blood boiled in her veins and sickness rose in her stomach.

The bastard! The god-awful bastard! She should have guessed; should have put two and two together weeks ago, when she'd seen the child's face so white, so stricken, time after time...

And now, right under her own damn stupid nose, and she couldn't see the lass was near five months gone.

Nan rose and looked down into Lenore's pale drained face.

She spoke softly and with utter surety. 'Don't you fret, darlin'. Get some sleep now. We'll fix all this, just you see. There'll be nothin' to worry about soon enough.'

DAN FARRELL HAD protested strongly as Nan had known he would, once he'd conducted the examination.

The girl had gone and now he faced Nan Reilly across his large untidy desk. His eyes, under grey unruly eyebrows, avoided Nan's hard gaze. He knew how intractable Nan could be, and he knew how fond she was of the girl, but this time she had to see reason.

'Nan,' his tone was defensive, 'there's not much I haven't been able to manage at some time or t'other for you and your girls, but this one's too late. I don't have to tell you that. It's too dangerous.'

His long spindly fingers played nervously with the old-fashioned fountain pen that lay on the desk in front of him. Dan Farrell was a thin, grey-haired man, his slimness broken only by a soft protruding paunch. Right now there was a very worried look on his bony face.

He leaned against the cracked brown leather of his high-backed swivel chair and this time looked directly at the woman sitting opposite him. 'Nan, you've got to let her have it. Afterwards, I can arrange something. It's the only safe way.'

Unflinchingly, Nan returned his stare. 'No, Dan. That's not possible.' Her voice was as cold as her eyes. 'She's got to be rid of it. Now.'

Picking up her handbag from the chair beside her, Nan stood up and walked to the door. With one hand on the handle, she turned and spoke again, her voice low, her words spaced carefully.

'No lassie ever deserved to bear her father's child.'

Afterwards, they left her alone.

Weakly, Lenore turned her head on the narrow trolley and registered the fact. Nothing but the green insipid walls, the one curtained window, and the tray of gleaming instruments.

'Natural labour,' the doctor had said, looking down at her nervous eyes as she lay beneath the crumpled cotton sheet. 'Just the same as natural labour and,' he'd added in a low emotionless tone that had chilled her, 'the pain'll be every bit the same as well.'

Lenore's heart had hammered crazily in her chest and as the tears of fear and panic started in her eyes, she turned her head from the doctor's pitying gaze. Dear God, she prayed, let me be able to stand it, let it be quick, please God...

It had lasted twelve agonizing hours. The 'natural labour', induced by hourly hormone injections, produced such crucifying peaks of pain that Lenore had felt as if her insides were being ripped from her core.

Now, as she lay, torn and exhausted, the warm stickiness crusting her thighs, her gaze was held by a lumpy bloodied object lying in the cracked porcelain sink.

Surely...? It took a moment – a lifetime – for the realization to dawn. And then, in a rush of horror, she knew. She could see the features that already at nearly five months could be identified as human in this stained and fleshy lump that lay lifeless so close beside her.

A scream of pure terror tore at Lenore's parched throat.

A FEW WEEKS later, when Nan sat her down in the large high-ceilinged sitting room they hardly ever used, Lenore saw a different side to the old lady she had come to know. This was a harder, tougher Nan who looked at the world in a way Lenore did not quite understand.

Since that dreadful day with Dan Farrell, they had never talked about what Lenore's father had done to her. By silent agreement it was implied that that part of Lenore's life was over; a tragic episode that had been dealt with in the only way possible and was best forgotten.

But now, as Nan spoke sitting opposite Lenore on the chintz-covered armchair, Lenore realized that what had happened to her was still uppermost in Nan's mind, as it was in her own.

Nan pursed her lips so that the wrinkles were etched deeper around her mouth, and when she spoke there was an intensity in her voice that Lenore had never heard before.

'The world's a tough place for a woman, Lenore. Always has

been – nothin's changed. But what a girl like you has to learn – and learn well – is that a woman can still have a very special strength.'

On the sofa opposite, Lenore sat quite still, one leg tucked beneath her. She looked at Nan expectantly, sensing that what the older woman had to say was, somehow, going to be very important to her.

Nan leaned forward. 'Lenore, you've been after havin' a hard lesson very early in life. You know now that men are stronger, physically, than a woman will ever be. You've been used in that way, Lenore, and you know that in those situations the boyos will always win.

'But, believe me, there's another sort of strength, another sort of power, that a woman can have. It's the sort of power that comes from bein' able to look after herself completely; the power that means she'll never have to dance to any man's tune. And,' Nan's eyes narrowed, 'you know where that power comes from, Lenore?'

Lenore sat silent as Nan, her face suddenly hard, answered her own question. 'From money. It's only money that makes a woman as strong as a man in this world.'

Nan's old shrewd eyes looked into Lenore's young unknowing ones. 'If things continue as well between us as they've started off, Lenore, that's a power you'll be havin' one day. You'll have freedom, just like I've had freedom. But, you're cleverer than me, love, far and away cleverer than old Nan, that's for sure.'

For a moment Nan's face relaxed, and she chuckled. 'Me, I'm just street-wise, love. Had to be – and that was good enough for me. But you,' her voice became serious again, 'you're quick and bright; even an ol' fool like me can see that, and you're goin' to use that freedom. You're goin' to make it in life. You're goin' to the top. But only if you remember one thing, Lenore.'

Nan's eyes gleamed with a piercing intensity. 'Money's a great thing, love, but there's somethin' else worth rememberin' too.' She placed a triumphant hand on the young girl's knee. 'It's because men are weak in a certain way that you'll be strong, Lenore. Remember that, and use it my darlin'. Be sure to use it...'

CHAPTER FIVE

AS the months stretched into a year since her arrival at Nan's, Lenore became increasingly aware of Nan's growing fondness for her. It was an emotion she found easy to reciprocate. She had so much to be grateful for, in the peace and comfort and kindness that she had found in Nan's home.

'I could never have children, Lenore,' Nan had confided to her one evening as she pulled a comb through the wet tangles of Lenore's long, brown, newly-washed hair. 'It was somethin' I've always regretted. If things had been...'

Her voice trailed off and she put down the comb. Then she turned Lenore round to face her, placing her dry, lined hands on the girl's shoulders.

'You're just like a daughter to me now love. You know that? Havin' your sweetness and innocence in this house has made me very, very happy.'

Lenore looked back into Nan's glistening eyes and saw the force of emotion contained there. With a small moan of happiness she threw her arms around Nan's neck and hugged her.

'I love you, Nan,' she whispered.

LIFE WITH NAN was never boring and Lenore spent most of her spare time in Nan's company. Only on Sunday afternoons would Nan shoo her out of the house, saying that she 'had her paperwork to do.'

It was then, Lenore knew, that Nan shut herself in the big untidy room she called her office.

The room at the back of the old stone house was almost filled by the huge leather-topped desk that stood beside the window overlooking the street. On every available surface lay piles of dusty paper, scribbled on in Nan's small spidery writing.

It was the one room in the house that Nan was not keen for Lenore to enter. Not that she forbade her specifically; she merely pointed out that 'it'd be better an' all if you didn't touch things in there, love. Believe it or not I have a system; I know where everythin' is – sort of. Anyone else'd mess things up.'

Lenore would have liked to help and indeed had offered to give Nan a hand – maths was her best subject at school – but usually Nan declined.

Only occasionally, when she seemed to get herself in a muddle, would Nan ask for Lenore's assistance. And then Lenore would sit down and add together the long columns of figures – so quickly and accurately that Nan would chuckle in amazement.

'You're a genius, Lenore, a bloomin' genius. I wish I had your head.'

Sometimes Lenore wondered at the sums she was adding up. If they represented money, they meant that Nan was a rich woman, far richer than Lenore had ever imagined. And she knew this was the 'freedom' that Nan had spoken about. But how, she wondered yet again, had Nan acquired such a sum?

Lenore didn't always have Nan to herself. There was usually a steady stream of people calling at the house. Most of them, as Lenore had seen soon after moving in, were good-looking young girls whom Nan seemed to enjoy mothering.

'The best-lookers sometimes get into the worst trouble,' Nan would chuckle to Lenore.

Lenore wasn't jealous. She understood how others could be drawn to Nan's kind and wise ways, just as she herself had been. And anyway, the visitors never really impinged on her special relationship with Nan. Nan would introduce them briefly if Lenore was around, then take them off to the privacy of her office. After a short time they would say a pleasant goodbye and be on their way.

The faces were always changing but there was one regular visitor, who came to see Nan every Sunday morning and usually ended up staying for the lunch that Lenore now took it upon herself to cook.

Roy Brennen, in his late twenties and powerfully built with thinning blond hair, was the only man ever invited to the house. Lenore soon decided that he was one of the nicest people she had ever met. She looked forward to the time every Sunday morning – usually around eleven – when the bell would ring and she would open the door to Roy, dressed as always in his well-pressed jeans and snowy white shirt, the same old leather briefcase under his arm, and a grin on his gentle square face.

'Roy! Come in.' Smiling, Lenore would let him in to the long cool hallway of Nan's home and her giggles would start immediately. To Lenore, Roy Brennen was the funniest person she'd ever known.

He had the most amazing way of telling the simplest story, that sent the tears rolling down Lenore's cheeks while her belly ached from laughing.

But first, he and Nan would spend a little time together in Nan's office while Lenore put the finishing touches to their lunch. When Roy was their guest, they ate in the dining room instead of the kitchen where she and Nan usually took their meals.

Lenore would drape one of Nan's heavy lace tablecloths over the round polished oak table, carefully arrange the beautiful old silver cutlery, and then place a cut-glass wine goblet beside each setting.

Lenore hated wine, somehow the smell of any alcohol brought back memories of her father, memories she still had to fight hard to keep at bay. But she liked to drink water from the heavy elegant glass.

Lenore knew what business Nan had to discuss with Roy. Nan had told her briefly that Roy was a tenant in one of her buildings and that, in exchange for a lower rent, he did all the handyman jobs around the place. 'Roy Brennen is good with his hands,' Nan had told her simply.

And often, before lunch, Lenore's eyes would be riveted on those long, slender and amazingly sensitive hands, as Roy played a popular tune on the piano for her and Nan.

Marvelling at their delicate slenderness for a man of Roy's otherwise powerful build, she had said as much one day. Roy roared with laughter. 'Wouldn't be much good as a watchmaker with hands like bunches of bananas now would I, Lenore?'

Lenore joined in his laughter and later, as Roy kissed both her and Nan goodbye, she remembered the time when she had been apprehensive about the touch of this man's flesh against her own, even in such a gentle way. But not now. Roy Brennen was her friend, a man she could trust. She did not fear him as she feared the loud-mouthed, hot-eyed boys at school.

Standing in the doorway, waving as Roy disappeared around the corner, Lenore wondered, not for the first time, why a man as nice as Roy had never married.

She found out not long afterwards, when she and Nan were shelling peas at the kitchen table one cold and gloomy winter's afternoon.

Lenore had been thinking about Roy. She wanted his help. She had visited him in the small jewellery store where he worked and had stared in wonder at some of the fascinating pieces he was re-modelling from the heavy old-fashioned designs people left with him. Roy, it seemed, did a lot more than mend broken watches!

It was then that the idea had come to her. Soon it would be Nan's sixty-second birthday and Lenore wanted to give her something very special. She'd been puzzling over it for a long time and was still undecided – until she saw Roy's work.

Then, with growing excitement, she had known what to do. Amongst the little of any value that she had kept from her mother's pitifully few possessions, was a broken string of pearls and a small ruby ring set in an intricate, over-fussy design. Lenore decided that she would have Roy make up a brooch for Nan, a brooch that Lenore would design herself using the small dark ruby and the pearls. It would be a very special thank you to the woman who had been so generous with her love and kindness.

The ring, Lenore's mother had told her, had been her own mother's engagement ring. With this thought in her head, along with her thoughts of Roy, Lenore was now suddenly prompted to enquire: 'Why hasn't Roy ever married, Nan?'

Nan's busy fingers stopped moving, and she lifted her head from her work to look at Lenore. There was a strange, appraising look on her lined face. Then, with a heavy sigh, she dropped the empty pod onto the pile beside her.

'Oh, my love,' the words came out in a long drawn-out breath, 'I guess you're old enough now to know about these things.'

Nan leaned her elbows on the table and frowned for a moment, as if she were concentrating intently on something.

'Lenore, love,' she said at last, 'people are all different in this world; you know that by now. There are people who pray six times a day, people who'd rather die than eat meat, others who'd never dream of gettin' in an aeroplane, and,' Nan kept her voice matter-of-fact, 'there are men who are different too; men who *like* women, certainly, but... as friends only, not... not in the physical sense, you understand.

'Well, love,' Nan looked closely at the young girl's face, watching for her reaction, 'that's the sort of man Roy is.'

Lenore's smooth brow creased in a confused frown. 'You mean not all men –' she broke off, colouring slightly, unable to say what she meant. She was remembering what her father had said about 'men's needs', the needs that only a woman could satisfy...

Nan understood. 'The sort of men I'm talkin' about love, men like Roy, well – they find comfort among their own sex. It's the way they are, you see, these homosexuals as we call them.

'But,' Nan's voice held a sharp note, 'that's not to say we've got to scorn them or look down on them; it's somethin' they just can't help and you shouldn't let it change the way you feel about Roy.' Abruptly, Nan stood up. 'Come on, love, I'll get on with this. Homework time for you.'

Slowly, Lenore climbed the stairs to her room, trying to digest what Nan had told her. Of course it wouldn't change her feelings towards Roy, but the whole idea took some thinking about.

One thing was sure, she decided, as she closed her bedroom door, she was certainly learning a lot about life while living with Nan.

Lenore spent a long time working out exactly how she wanted Nan's birthday gift to look. Finally, satisfied with her design, she went one afternoon after school to show it to Roy.

'I must say, Lenore, you've got quite an artistic eye.' Roy looked in surprised admiration at the piece of paper that lay on the workbench in front of him; the piece of paper on which, painstakingly, Lenore had detailed her design for Nan's brooch.

'I like it,' Roy nodded approvingly, 'especially the way you've used the different sizes of pearls to balance the weight of the ruby.'

Lenore blushed at the unexpected praise. She had wanted the impression of a spray of flowers, yet something with a modern feel. What pleased her most was that Roy thought the idea would work.

'You can make it then, Roy?' There was a breathless note of

excitement in her voice. 'You'll help me do this for Nan?'

Roy looked gently into Lenore's shining eyes. 'Of course I will, sweetheart. And Nan will love it, I know she will.'

But as Lenore left the shop, now happy and relieved at his acceptance of her design, Roy's face clouded with uneasiness.

The girl loved Nan, adored her – as much as Nan adored Lenore in return. A sudden coldness twisted Roy's stomach at the thought of what could destroy their love.

NAN HAD ALWAYS been an early riser and was inevitably up and in the kitchen long before Lenore put in an appearance. But today, on Nan's birthday, Lenore had been up since first light, barely able to contain her excitement as she waited for a more reasonable hour to awaken Nan and give her her gift.

It lay now, wrapped in silver paper, on the lace-covered wooden tray beside the cup of Earl Grey tea that Nan called her morning 'heart starter'.

'Happy birthday, Nan!' Unable to wait a moment longer, Lenore carried the tray into Nan's big cluttered bedroom and placed it on the small polished bedside table, while she waited for Nan's eyes to blink open.

'Sweet Jesus, love,' Nan muttered sleepily, 'and aren't you the bright and breezy one this mornin'.' Struggling to sit up, she pushed the thinning waves of bracken-coloured hair from her face.

'It's your birthday, Nan.' Lenore grinned happily as she arranged the pillows behind Nan's back and then, with a flourish, set the tray upon her lap.

'There! Happy birthday, Nan.' Bending down, she kissed Nan's dry sleep-warm cheek.

'Well, what have we here?' Fully awake now, Nan's voice was teasing. 'A new set of saucepans maybe?' Cackling at her own joke, she picked up the small wrapped parcel and fumbled with the paper.

Lenore couldn't speak. Her eyes were shining with delight as, finally, Nan drew out the small velvet box in which Roy had placed the finished brooch.

As she opened the lid, Nan's eyes widened in amazement. Delicate and perfect, the brooch lay on its bed of black satin, as beautiful as Lenore had dreamed it would be. Roy had done a wonderful job.

'They were my grandmother's jewels, Nan,' Lenore said softly. 'Roy made them up for me. I... I wanted you to have them... to thank you for everything. Do you,' her voice was hesitant, 'do you like it?'

'Oh, my darlin',' Nan's voice was a whisper and tears glistened in her faded blue eyes, 'it's... it's beautiful...' She turned her wrinkled face up to Lenore's, 'As beautiful as the girl who's made my old age the best time of my life...'

LENORE TURNED SIXTEEN, secure in the even tempo of her life with Nan. The life that lay in front of her seemed happy and inviting. Her final school results had been excellent and now she was eager to begin the search for a job. Nan had never made her feel obliged but Lenore was looking forward to contributing to the household.

Each morning before breakfast, she scanned the employment columns and read out to Nan the more interesting positions.

'Aim high, darlin',' was Nan's firm advice. 'There's no value in being stuck in a typin' pool for the rest of your life. You're made for better things than that.'

Nan spoke with unshakeable conviction; but, as Lenore looked at what was offering for a raw inexperienced sixteen year-old, she wondered just exactly how she would fulfil Nan's ambitious prediction.

And as she searched the newspaper each morning, Lenore was aware too of the worry in the older woman's eyes. She understood what Nan was afraid of: with a job, an income, and some new young friends, there was no doubt in Nan's mind that Lenore would be ready to move out and make a life of her own.

'And that's how it should be, love,' proclaimed Nan. Lenore could see how determined she was to face the issue squarely. 'It was different when you first came here; you were a child then. But now you're a young woman and,' she forced a mirthless laugh, 'you don't want to spend your time with an old fogey like me.'

Lenore looked into Nan's face and saw the effort it cost her to say those words.

For a moment Lenore didn't reply. Then an impish grin lighting her face, she said, 'You're not getting rid of me that easily, Nan Reilly. I like it here – and, what's more, you're the youngest old fogey I know!'

But it was in fact Nan's age, and the frailties accompanying it, that finally brought Lenore face to face with the secret Nan had kept hidden for so long.

Just a few days later, Nan had felt a bit off-colour. 'A touch of cold, love,' she'd assured, as she sipped at the hot lemon infusion Lenore had insisted she drink.

But the 'touch of cold' had become steadily worse, until, giving way to Lenore's pressure, Nan had taken to her bed. Then, despite Nan's protestations, Lenore had called Dan Farrell to the house.

'It's the 'flu all right,' he said, packing away his stethoscope in his battered leather case. 'Just keep an eye on her, Lenore. Lots of fluids – and call me if she gets any worse.' He left the house, avoiding the young girl's eyes, as he remembered with a certain unease the events of more than a year ago.

Lenore was glad now that she had not yet started work; she would be free to stay at home and care for Nan. The sight of that pale drawn face above the bed clothes twisted her heart.

Three days later Lenore had to summon Dan Farrell again. This time he was worried. 'You were right to call me, Lenore. We'll have to get her to hospital. She's not as young as she sometimes likes to behave. This time she needs complete rest; pneumonial pleurisy can have serious complications for a woman Nan's age.'

It was almost three weeks before Nan was well enough to come home. Even then she was weak and tired, her face drawn, her body pitifully thin.

On Roy's first visit after Nan's illness he spent a long time shut up in the privacy of her bedroom, so long in fact that Lenore started to worry. Nan tired very easily now; surely the business Roy had to discuss could wait another week or two. Nothing could be so vital.

When Roy finally emerged his face was white and set. He seemed in a hurry to leave and refused Lenore's invitation to join her in the light lunch she had prepared.

'No, sweetheart, not today thanks. I should have told you earlier I'm sorry, but I've got to get home.' For a moment his eyes held hers in a look that Lenore didn't quite understand. Was it pity, a sort of regretful sadness, she saw in his eyes?

Lenore wondered about it after Roy had gone and suddenly a cold tight knot formed in her stomach. Was there something Roy was keeping from her? Was something still seriously wrong with Nan? The colour drained from Lenore's face. She couldn't bear it if anything happened to Nan; she couldn't bear to lose her now.

It was later that same day that Nan called Lenore into her room. The afternoon sun, shining through the shutters, painted stripes of light on the polished wooden floor.

Nan sat propped up against the pillows, a blue cashmere shawl wrapped around her narrow shoulders.

'Sit down, Lenore.' Nan indicated the straight-backed chair beside the bed. There was an expression of great pain and anguish on her face and suddenly Lenore could see how much older she looked. The lines around her eyes and mouth were etched more deeply, her hair, undyed for the last few weeks, showed a rim of white next to the scalp, but most frightening of all was the terrible fragile brittleness of her thin wasted frame.

'Nan, what's wrong?' There was something about the look on Nan's face that made cold fingers pluck at Lenore's heart.

For a moment Nan said nothing, merely staring into the young girl's frightened eyes. Then, drawing a deep breath into her lungs, she turned her head on the pillow and looked away from Lenore, into the far corner of the room. In a voice that shook only slightly she began to speak, softly and at great length...

Hours later as she lay in the darkness of her own bedroom, Lenore felt the dazed numbness, the strange lightheadedness that comes with shock.

A cold sickness crawled in her stomach as she turned Nan's words over and over in her tortured mind.

Nan had told her everything, had held nothing back. And Lenore had listened, frozen in disbelief, as Nan explained about the strange young women who called so often at the house; about the reason for Roy's regular Sunday visits; about the bundles of money contained in his old leather briefcase.

As the words Nan spoke forced their way relentlessly into her consciousness, a steady droning hum had begun in Lenore's reeling mind: 'It can't be true. It can't be true...'

It was only as the endless night finally greyed into dawn that Lenore at last accepted the reality of what she had been told: that Nan Reilly, the woman who had cared for and loved her as a mother, had been for many years the owner of the most notorious, the most prosperous, brothel in Sydney.

Finally, with acceptance came sleep, and as her eyes closed Lenore had made her decision. She would do what Nan had asked her to do.

No matter how abhorrent she found it, she owed Nan that.

CHAPTER SIX

'Lenore?'

Lenore looked up from her work. She was sitting in the room that had once been Nan's dusty untidy office. Now it was neat and organized and these days it was Lenore who worked at the big leather-covered desk.

Tanya Martin's bright green eyes looked at Lenore from the half-opened doorway and with a small sigh Lenore put down her pen. Whatever Tanya had to say, she knew it would take time. Tanya was long-winded at the best of times.

'Sorry to disturb.' With a smile that held not a shred of apology, the twenty year-old girl came into the room flashing long bare perfect legs in a short blue mini skirt. She pulled up a chair opposite Lenore.

She was stunningly attractive. Her long dark hair, parted in the middle, was worn fashionably straight to her shoulders, her already large eyes were made larger by their fringe of false lashes, and her small shapely bosom was accentuated by the tight ribbed top.

'So, how's life?' Tanya's broad warm smile made her already lovely face even lovelier.

This was going to take a while Lenore could tell. Tanya always had difficulty in coming to the point. But for all that, Lenore couldn't help liking the girl. She knew now that Tanya's outward show of bravado and confidence hid a painful insecurity that stemmed from a childhood full of beatings and abuse suffered at the hands of her mother's endless string of boyfriends.

'Guess they just couldn't stand a whinging kid hanging round,' Tanya had told Lenore more than once, shrugging her narrow shoulders dismissively. 'Must have been a relief the day I was made a ward of the State; she didn't have to worry about me any longer.' Tanya grinned. 'Best thing that ever happened to me.'

Tanya had been eleven then and, from the time she turned

twelve, she'd never heard from her mother again. Now she neither knew nor cared what had happened to the woman who had borne her. She was too busy making sure that her own three year-old daughter knew she had a mother who loved her.

Lenore judged that it was about Mandy, as usual, that Tanya wanted to speak. Nothing important, just someone to listen to her obvious delight in her child.

'She's incredibly bright, Lenore. You should see the way she catches on to those games I buy her. The kid's a whizz!' Warm maternal pride shone in Tanya's big green eyes as she pulled a cigarette from her handbag and lit it with a thin silver lighter.

Lenore knew that Tanya had no idea who Mandy's father was. It was something Tanya had spoken about at length. 'I was crazy then, Lenore. Nuts. Went through men like a bowling ball through skittles.' She gave a short laugh that held no amusement. 'Still don't know why I did it – I didn't give a damn for any of them...'

Lenore had guessed the reason easily enough. Tanya had been driven from body to body, bed to bed, in an endless search for the warmth and affection she had never known from either a mother or a father.

Even at seventeen Lenore could understand that need. Wasn't it love, after all, that had drawn her so strongly to Nan?

No, Lenore didn't look down on these women she always referred to in her own mind as Nan's girls. The word 'prostitute' was one she would never use. She knew now that these girls were not very different from herself; women searching for that freedom, that security, which Nan had spoken of so strongly.

At first, all those months ago, when Nan had revealed the truth to her, Lenore had felt nothing but a sick repulsion, a disbelieving abhorrence, for the world Nan spoke of.

But eventually, as she carried out the reluctant promise she had made to assist Nan with the financial side of the business, Lenore had come to understand. Working for Nan was the only chance these women had to gain real money and real independence in their lives. It made her think again about the sort of world they lived in: where the victimization of women, their lack of real power, could drive them to this extreme. It wasn't right somehow.

Nan had spent a lot of time trying to make Lenore understand.

'The girls are happy, Lenore, they're treated well. And where else in this male-dominated world would they ever get the opportunity to set themselves up so well?'

Nan's tired cynical eyes looked at Lenore. 'It's an honest trade, love. It parts with what it's paid for, to be sure. And it puts my girls on an equal footing with any of those doin' the payin'.' Her voice took on a hard note. 'And don't be fooled, Lenore, there's plenty doin' the payin' who'd never admit to it. Judges, businessmen, politicians... that's who come to my place.'

There had been a hint of pride in Nan's tone that had shocked Lenore then.

As she listened with half an ear to Tanya's endless story about Mandy's latest escapade, she thought to herself how little shocked her these days.

For a year she had been handling Nan's books, sorting out the figures, putting in order what had been a jumble.

At first she had had to fight to keep herself from remembering what the rows of figures represented. But, as the months passed, she had finally come to accept the role she now played. Whatever else Nan had done, she had been good to her. She would never forget that.

That day when Nan had lain so ill and tired on her bed, drained by the effort of her confession, and asked Lenore simply and directly for her help, she had been unable to refuse; '... just till I'm better Lenore that's all. It's too much for Roy with his work too... and afterwards, if you want to go, well... I'll understand.' And her debt, her obligation, and yes, her feelings still for the tired old woman whose pleading eyes held her own, had made it impossible for Lenore to be indifferent to Nan's request.

By the time Nan had made a full recovery, Lenore had organized the whole book-keeping system so effectively that, by silent agreement, she had continued with the work. To Nan's joyous relief, Lenore had said nothing about moving on.

Free now of the need for secrecy, and with Lenore to handle the paperwork, Nan spent more of her time at the two adjoining terrace houses three blocks away where she conducted her business. She liked to be on the spot, attending to the matters that required her attention. As she told Lenore with some amusement, 'For sure, where you've got a houseful of women livin' together, love, there are always problems.'

Nan spoke openly about everything these days and while the

old feeling between them had been restored, Lenore couldn't help the way she still felt about the lifestyle that Nan's girls had been forced to choose. One day, she promised herself, she would do something; she wasn't sure what, but something that would help women free themselves from the different sorts of exploitation forced on them. She thought then of her mother, whose meagre wages and lack of education had sentenced her to a lifetime with a man who had done nothing but degrade and humiliate her.

Lenore brought her attention back to the girl in front of her. Who knew what Tanya might have achieved given the right opportunities, the right environment, a world where women's work was valued as highly as men's.

She interrupted the girl gently. 'Tanya, if you're going back to Nan now, could you give her this?' She handed a paper bag containing two new receipt books across the desk. She had Nan organized now.

It was a strange life Lenore led these days. Without the contact offered by school or a proper job, and with Nan so often out of the house, it was a lonely isolated existence.

She supposed that she could have joined clubs, a sporting group, but how could she let herself form friendships when she was able to reveal so little about herself?

Nan Reilly understood the crippling burden of the secret she had entrusted to the young girl she loved, and sometimes when she saw the loneliness in Lenore's eyes, a terrible feverish guilt overcame her. She had been wrong to take the girl in; wrong to involve her in the sort of life that cut her off so completely from others of her own age.

But then Nan would remember her plan; the plan that would make everything up to Lenore; the plan that would remove her completely from the life she now led.

Nan had it all worked out. As soon as Lenore turned nineteen she would send her away. One of those fancy finishing schools in Europe was what she had in mind. There she would mix with the right people; learn the things that Nan would never be able to teach her. And when she came home, there would be the money to set her up in her own small business. Anything she chose.

Nan smiled in satisfaction at the thought. She had no doubt

that Lenore would make a success of anything she set her mind to. That the girl would make her mark, Nan was utterly confident.

'I'm off now, Nan'.

Lenore put her head into the kitchen where Nan lay dozing in the afternoon sun that streamed through the back window.

They had just said goodbye to Roy who, as usual, had called in with the week's takings and stayed for lunch.

Lenore and Roy were still close. She had coped with that shock too. Much of what Nan had told her about Roy was true. He *did* live in one of Nan's properties – behind the 'business' in fact; and he did attend to the few odd jobs that needed doing. But Roy's real role was to handle the money and provide protection for the girls. 'Not,' said Nan, the same curious note of pride in her voice, 'that there's ever been much trouble, mind you – not with our sort of clientele...' But it made sense, she said, to have someone like Roy on the spot.

Nan stirred and, opening her eyes, smiled at Lenore.

'Fine, love, enjoy yourself now.'

Lenore did enjoy her Sunday afternoons. Her favourite outing was a trip on one of the Harbour ferries. She didn't care where she went. As long as she was on the water with the wind blowing in her face, the sun glinting off the ocean, and the salty tang in her nostrils, she felt free and young and happy.

Today was no different. She took the ferry to the Zoo and spent two fascinating hours staring at the monkeys, the seals, the big, prowling cats. After a cup of tea – where she noted with a sudden stab of loneliness that she was the only person by herself among the crowds of families and young hand-holding couples – she took the ferry back again to Circular Quay.

It was as she stood among the Sunday crowds, waiting to disembark, that Lenore met the boy.

'Bloody goddamn thing.'

She heard the muttered oaths close behind her and turned to frown at the speaker.

It was with guilty surprise that she saw the wheelchair. Its occupant, a good-looking, dark-haired boy in his late teens or early twenties, was having a hard time manoeuvering through the crowds to the gangway.

A moment later the hard rubber tyre of the chair had hit against the back of her shoe.

'Oh, hell! I'm sorry!' The frustration showed in the boy's tight face and his blue eyes were dark with annoyance.

'Can I give you a hand?'

He looked up at her. 'Well, if you can.' His tone was far from gracious but Lenore blamed that on his frustration.

She moved behind him and, after waiting until the bulk of the crowd had departed, steered the wheelchair onto the gangway. The boy said nothing but she could see that his knuckles were white as he gripped the chair.

On the concrete surface of the dock, the chair was easier to push. 'I'll help you up to the turnstiles,' Lenore offered. She could see the chair would have to go through the gap by the ticketseller's booth.

The boy grunted but said nothing. When they were through and on the roadway, Lenore asked, 'Can you manage now?'

'Of course I bloody can.' The boy's mouth was set and he rolled the chair away from Lenore.

She felt the colour wash over her face. The rudeness of it.

'Hey... I'm sorry.'

Still angry, Lenore looked around. The boy had stopped not far away and turned the chair to face her. 'I was a bad-tempered ignoramus – forgive me please. It's just that... sometimes I get so angry with myself and this...' He indicated the chair.

Lenore picked up the trace of an accent. American, she thought.

'I'm David Kershaw.' His bright blue eyes were friendly now. 'If you're not in a hurry to go somewhere will you forgive me by letting me buy you a coffee?'

Lenore looked at him. There was a vitality about his eyes and face that negated the confinement of his body, a warm intensity in his manner that she found strangely compelling.

She walked towards him. 'I'm Lenore Hamlyn.' She smiled down at his lean dark face. 'Okay, I guess a coffee will buy my forgiveness.'

They found a small cafe nearby and, while Lenore pulled up a seat, the boy positioned himself opposite her.

'Were you at the Zoo?' she enquired when the waitress had taken their order.

'No.' The boy's tone was flat. 'Just another place that's out of bounds to me in this.' He hit his hand hard against the chair's rubber tyres. 'I made it to one of those little parks by the water and just sat there taking in the view.' His tone became lighter, 'It's something else, isn't it? Nothing quite like it where I come from.'

'America?'

'Yeah, but I meant L.A. Lots of buzz and action but not a real lot to soothe the soul.'

As they drank their coffee, David Kershaw told her about himself. He was twenty-one and visiting his father who lived in Sydney. 'My parents broke up when I was twelve. Mom was a Yank so she went back home after the divorce and I went with her.'

'Do you miss Australia?'

David Kershaw shrugged. 'I guess I adapted. I get out here every year or so to visit my dad. Although,' his eyes grew dark again, 'that's been tougher since this happened.'

He saw the question in Lenore's eyes. 'A dumb crazy accident. A football game. It happened when I was sixteen. I ended up with severe compression on the spine when someone landed on top of me. The medicos say it'll take a miracle for me to walk again.'

A sudden uncontrollable bitterness twisted his mouth. 'My mother still believes in those miracles. She's spent a fortune taking me to experts all over the place. Canada, Europe... you name it, we've been there.' He gave a choked, bitter laugh. 'You can see how far we've got.'

Lenore felt her heart go out to him. His sense of frustration and despair was almost palpable.

'Sometimes it can happen,' she said gently. 'I've read about it. You mustn't give up hope.'

'No...' The boy's voice was heavy, flat. Then, making a visible effort to change his mood, he said, 'Hey, how about we take in the Botanical Gardens. Sit and watch the sunset? What do you say?'

Lenore looked into those bright, compelling, blue eyes and knew she wasn't going to say no.

As she let herself into the house that evening, a little later than usual, Lenore felt strangely buoyant and light-hearted.

The boy in the wheelchair was interesting; she liked his mind, his sense of humour, his quick wit and animation. Yet she had been surprised to hear herself accept his invitation for the following Sunday.

But then of course – the words emerged with a sudden terrifying force from her subconscious – a boy with David Kershaw's handicap would never be a threat.

THERE WAS A shine in Lenore's dark, velvet eyes and a heightened colour in her cheeks as she hurried down the path through the park to the teahouse near the beach.

In Sydney, to find a bus running to schedule was rare at the best of times; on a Sunday it was a miracle. And now she was running late for her meeting with David.

But he was waiting, watching for her, his wheelchair pulled up at a table overlooking the water.

'Hi, Lenore! You see what we Yanks can manage? The best table in the house!' He grinned at her from under dark silky hair, his perfect white teeth flashing even whiter against his tanned olive skin.

Now that she was here, close again to the force of his personality, his vibrant attractiveness, Lenore felt suddenly nervous.

'Hello, David.' There was a breathlessness in her voice that was not entirely due to haste. 'I'm sorry I'm late. The buses – '

'Hey,' David Kershaw held up a hand to silence her. 'A lady never apologizes – and a gentleman always waits in patient good humour. Didn't anyone ever tell you that?'

Lenore saw the teasing light in his eyes and started to smile. The ice was broken and, as they ate the dainty chicken sandwiches, the pastries and the fat cream cakes, conversation between them was easy.

Only once did David become agitated.

'There's one thing that makes my mother glad I'm in this chair, Lenore: Vietnam. Better a crippled son than a dead one's the way she sees it.' His blue eyes grew dark and hard. 'It's a stinking rotten war, Lenore – a war in which America never should have got involved!!'

As he expressed the fervour of his opposition to the conflict in that far-off Asian land, the strong lines of David Kershaw's face tightened with emotion, and there was something in the force of his passion that suddenly drew Lenore closer to him. She felt a sudden rush of warmth for this man whose feelings could reach so deeply and strongly beyond the confines of his own personal tragedy.

But the strength of her response she found oddly disturbing, and her hand trembled slightly as she raised the coffee cup to her lips. It was, she told herself fiercely, merely compassion, a desperate sympathy for another human who had been denied his full and rightful share in life.

Then, as they were waiting for their bill, David asked the question that brought a sudden heat to Lenore's cheeks.

'Tell me about your work, Lenore – book-keeping you said? Is it a big firm you're with?'

Lenore felt her heart start to beat more quickly and she lowered her gaze, folding with particular exactness the checked cotton napkin that lay on the table in front of her.

'N-no. Just a... small place.'

When it was obvious that she wasn't going to add anything further, David prompted, 'And there're other young staff?'

'A few.' There was a tightness in Lenore's throat as she spoke the lies.

Looking up, she sought to divert his attention from herself.

'What about you – what are you going to do now?' He had told her already of his plan to complete his business studies at Harvard. She knew it was a prestigious college and was impressed by David's cleverness.

'No surprises there. Going into my stepfather's business. He's got his fingers in lots of pies.' He grinned at her. 'I'm sure he'll find something to keep me off the streets.'

Later they sat together in the park, Lenore on one of the faded wooden benches, David beside her in his chair. Around them families were enjoying the fine weather, chasing balls or dogs, bathing in the cool clear water, playing games on the springy grass.

With a smile on her face, Lenore watched the activity. This time, she thought happily to herself, she was not alone; this time she had David by her –

The hand closing over her own made her jump. She looked down at the slim brown fingers then up into the serious, perfect lines of David Kershaw's face.

He spoke, and his tone was casual, but there was nothing casual about the look in those unwavering blue eyes.

'You know, Lenore, I can't think of an awful lot of young attractive girls who'd be interested in wasting a lovely day like this with... someone in my condition. I'm sure they'd rather be at the beach, or playing tennis, doing something more exciting.'

He looked at her in a way that made Lenore's heart beat a little faster and she was all too aware of the touch of his hand on hers.

'You're a special sort of person – you know that, Lenore? As beautiful inside as on the side that the world sees. And you've been kind to a stranger, gentle and understanding to a guy who can offer so little in return. This,' he hit his hand against the chair with the same fury and frustration Lenore had seen before, 'this makes me only half a man, Lenore. And that,' his voice was suddenly harsh, 'is as good as no man at all.'

Lenore sat still and silent, her eyes held by the anguish in David's face as he struggled to regain his composure. When he spoke again, his tone had softened.

'Thank you Lenore, for helping me pretend – for a short time at least.'

Then, his eyes looking into hers, he gently raised her fingers to his lips.

And still Lenore said nothing. The touch of his lips burnt against her skin, and inside her raged a fury of emotions that she had never dreamed existed.

CHAPTER SEVEN

ALL the next week as she waited for Sunday to come round again, Lenore struggled in a haze of conflicting feelings. She was, by turns, excited and frightened by the feelings that had been unleashed inside her.

She wished she could have confided in Nan, asked her advice; but a stronger force made her want to keep this secret to herself, to ponder it alone, to hug it close to herself in the privacy of her room.

She was unnerved by her sudden turmoil. What had happened to affect her so strongly? A few kind words? A touch of flesh against flesh? The sharing of jokes and laughter? Lenore felt confused – and afraid. But in two days time she would be seeing David Kershaw again...

He opened the door at once to her ring.

'Hi, Lenore! Come on through, tea's laid out on the back verandah.'

His smile put her immediately at ease and she followed as he wheeled his way down the broad cool hallway.

It was his father's house. An old stately freestanding Federation home where the grandeur and elegance, Lenore could see, had been meticulously maintained.

'This place is really too big for the old man by himself,' David spoke over his shoulder, 'but he can't bring himself to sell it. Loves the place too much.'

Lenore could see why, as she walked past open doorways that revealed beautifully proportioned rooms, elegant marble fireplaces, and deep rich cedar woodwork.

She was captivated by the aura, the style of a bygone age, and, as her eyes took in the formal beauty of the house, she made a silent, determined promise to herself. One day she would own a house like this. She would work for it and she would achieve it.

Tea was waiting on a small wrought iron table on the wide shaded back verandah. As she settled on the rattan divan, Lenore was as much enchanted by the house's setting as she had been by its interior.

The sweeping splendour of a native garden afforded total privacy from neighbours and a series of stone terraces led from the closely clipped lawn to a bush reserve below. Beyond that stretched the silken blueness of the ocean.

'How wonderful,' Lenore's eyes were bright with pleasure, 'to have so much garden... all these beautiful growing things... It's so different from Nan's.'

In her eagerness, the words had slipped out before she was aware of them and Lenore stopped abruptly. She had, in answer to David's questions, told him only that she lived with her 'guardian', Nan Reilly. She had elaborated no further.

David raised an inquiring eyebrow as he poured their tea from the stoneware pot. 'No garden?'

'No.' Lenore shook her head, staring intently into her cup as she stirred in the sugar.

'Where do you live then, that you don't have a garden?'

Lenore hesitated. David Kershaw would be back in America soon; there could be no harm in telling him.

'Surry Hills – it's an inner city suburb.'

'Sure. I've been past there,' David nodded. 'I know what you mean, not much room for big back gardens so close to the city.'

The uncomfortable moment passed and as they talked and laughed together, Lenore felt herself relax. Her eyes wandered to David's strong handsome face as he pointed out a brightly-coloured rosella in a nearby tree. She felt again the same stirring begin inside her. He was so attractive, so gentle, such good fun. She would miss him when he left.

She forced the thought from her mind.

'Isn't your father going to join us, David?'

'No, he's away for a couple of days. Some business interstate. He tries to avoid that happening when I'm here such a short time, but it couldn't be helped. He's a busy man.'

After they had eaten, they moved into the garden and Lenore delighted in the various colours and aromas that charmed her senses.

'Look,' she brushed a gentle finger over a red-veined leaf.

'What do you call this? It's so pretty.'

'Beats me,' David laughed. 'Roses, daisies, cactus and gum trees – that's my limit.'

'And look at this one.' Lenore swooped on a large glossy shrub hung with small purple flowers. She turned to him with a shy smile.

'One day I'm going to have a garden like this... just as beautiful... and I'm going to know the names of everything in it.'

He looked at her silently for a moment, and when he spoke his voice was gentle. 'You know, Lenore, I think you will.'

Later, with the sky showing signs of an approaching storm, they returned to the house and were washing up their tea things, when David suddenly said, 'Hey, I've got just the thing for you. I've just remembered. Come on.' He threw down the tea towel and gestured to Lenore, 'Come and look at this.'

With a mixture of hesitation and curiosity, she followed him down the hallway and into a room that was cluttered with the sort of paraphernalia that told her it was the bedroom reserved for David's visits. A big old Turkish carpet covered the floor, and books and records lay untidily on shelves and on the large polished desk. In one corner, on an upholstered divan, lay an open suitcase. French windows led onto the verandah that surrounded the house, but its broad roof kept the room dim and cool.

'Here,' David manoeuvred his chair close to the bookcase that lined one wall and pulled out a large hardback book. He showed its cover to Lenore and she saw it was an illustrated botanical guide. 'Just what we need,' he said with satisfaction. 'It belongs to my father. As old as the hills, but I'll bet it'll tell you everything you want to know. Take a seat and we'll have a look.'

Lenore looked around. The wooden chair at the desk was covered by clothes, the bed was cluttered with records and a small portable record player.

David laughed. 'I guess I'm a slob. Dad's housekeeper has strict instructions to stay clear of here while I'm in town.'

He wheeled towards the divan and dragged the half-empty suitcase onto the floor. 'This'll do.' He switched on the gold shaded lamp that stood on the desk.

Lenore sat down and, to her utter surprise, in one quick movement David had slid out of his chair onto the divan beside her.

He smiled at the look on her face. 'I figured it was time I did myself the favour of sitting next to you properly. I don't mind at home, it's all the fuss when I go out that I hate – pulling out tables, shuffling chairs around...'

He opened the book and spread it across their knees. Lenore felt the cool touch of his arm, the faint contact of his body against her own and, as he bent to examine the pages, there was something in the sight of his slender brown neck that made her pulse beat faster. His closeness was overwhelming.

'Here, Lenore – this is it,' he exclaimed triumphantly, touching her arm. 'It's –' Suddenly he stopped, his hand still resting on Lenore's soft skin, his clear blue eyes staring into hers. The book fell to the floor, and for a long moment it was as if both had ceased to breathe.

Then, with a soft drawn-out sigh, he brought his lips to hers and, as if in a trance, Lenore felt the gentle touch of his mouth, his warm quickened breath against her cheek.

She made no movement, but her heart was racing as David drew back and looked again into her wide nervous eyes.

'I've wanted to do that for so long.' His voice was a whisper. 'I've dreamt of it.' He moved closer again and rested his lips against the softness of her hair, close to her ear. 'You could be so easy to love, Lenore... so dangerously easy.'

Those words seemed suddenly to bring Lenore out of her trance; seemed, in a sweeping instant, to set her fears at rest and close her mind to the painful, savage memory of another man, another place.

And then David's mouth was once more on hers and now, softly, tentatively, she began to kiss him back. A shudder passed through her as she inhaled his clean manly scent, felt the hardening pressure of his mouth against her own.

Slowly, he drew his body further onto the divan and as he pressed close against her, Lenore felt herself grow curiously fluid in his arms. She could feel the thudding of his heart in rhythm with her own as the length of his body stretched out beside her.

Now his tongue was gently tracing the fullness of her lips, probing gently at her teeth until, in instinctive response, she opened her mouth to his.

It was like a shock wave through her entire body, the unexpected fury of her response. With trembling limbs she clung to him until at last he drew back, leaving her lips burning, her heart hammering in her chest. Their eyes met and she saw the force of her own emotion reflected in that piercing blueness.

'Oh, Lenore... I want you so much... so much.'

She buried her face against his chest, breathing heavily through parted lips. She felt unable to answer, unable to control her reeling senses. All she knew was that in so short a time, David Kershaw had managed to shatter the hard shell that she had built so carefully around herself. Her pulse pounded, and the touch of his hand against her cheek, her neck, her hair, sent an almost physical ache through her.

'Lenore... Lenore...' He whispered her name over and over again and she felt as if she could have listened to the sound for ever.

Then a soft shuddering sigh escaped her lips as David's fingers slipped tentatively beneath her blouse to find the swell of her breasts. Her pleasure was pure and explosive, her nipples firming instantly at his touch.

A moment later, shirt and blouse discarded, they were flesh against flesh and she heard his harsh uneven breathing, his groan of pleasure, as his searching fingers outlined the circle of her breasts and stroked the surging nipples to a point.

He lowered his head and his mouth moved to where his fingers had been and Lenore felt her body roar in response. His lips traced a burning path down her neck, her shoulders, her breasts, as he whispered his love, his need – and his vulnerability.

'Can you bear me as I am, Lenore? Am I asking too much of you?'

The agony, the hopelessness in his voice made her love him all the more. She could barely supress the cry of delight that rose inside her. She wanted him. She wanted him.

Her eyes shone brightly into his. 'Oh, please, David... please.'

He stared at her then, lips dry, voice unsteady.

'I'm... this will be my first time, Lenore. I'm not sure –'

She stopped him with a kiss, closing herself around his warm pulsing body. Nothing else mattered, just the feel and the touch and the taste of him.

She helped him with her skirt, and then to ease the trousers from his useless legs. As he slid his hands down her slim nakedness he whispered, 'I'll be gentle, my darling... It's the first time for both of us, but trust me... Don't be afraid.'

Lenore closed her eyes, her face buried in his neck. He was right. It *was* the first time. His love and tenderness, his youth and beauty, would wipe out what had gone before.

Instantly, instinctively, their bodies found the tempo that bound them together and moments later, in a release of liquid fire, David called out, 'I love you, Lenore... I love you, my darling...'

The thunder woke them where they lay close and warm in each other's arms. With the rain falling heavily through the trees, their bodies found each other again and, as the ecstasy throbbed through her for a second time, David's whispered words were scored on her mind.

'I'll never forget you, Lenore... no-one ever forgets the woman who makes him a man.'

'I love you David,' she moaned aloud. 'I'll always love you.'

CHAPTER EIGHT

LENORE looked at her watch and frowned. Forty minutes had passed now. What could have held David up?

This was their last weekend together before his return to the States. 'Let's not be sad, Lenore,' he'd said to her as she'd left the house late that last Sunday afternoon. That glorious afternoon when her heart and soul had felt as if at last they had been unlocked. 'Let's be happy knowing that someone special exists for each of us. We'll write, keep in touch, and I'll get back to Sydney just as soon as I can.'

He'd paused then, looking up at her where she stood by the open front door. 'You'll never know how much meeting you has meant to me, Lenore.' Then, gesturing for her to bend down to him, he'd kissed her gently. The love and wonder she'd seen in his eyes had made Lenore's heart sing. 'Till next Sunday,' he'd said softly.

Lenore felt uncomfortable sitting at a table by herself while others waited to be seated. The skinny overworked waitress had asked twice already if she was ready to order.

'I'm waiting for someone,' Lenore had replied, nervously keeping her eyes from the waiting queue of people at this popular weekend spot.

Now, with a shudder, she finished her second cup of coffee; she had sat with it so long that it was stone cold.

The waitress was beside her once again. 'Look, love, I'm going to have to ask you to leave. I can't keep asking people to wait while you sit here dawdlin' over one lousy cup of coffee.' She gave Lenore a spiteful smile. 'Looks like he's stood you up, don't it?'

The waitress moved away and, with her cheeks burning, Lenore pulled some money from her purse, left it on the table, and hurried out.

What *could* have happened to David? They had made their

plans so exactly. His father was at home now so they had decided to have a quick bite to eat and then find a place in the sun to talk, to kiss, to be together. To make the most of their last afternoon.

Lenore's heart ached that so much of their precious time was now being wasted. They still had so much to say to each other; so much to confide and discover.

Dejected and irresolute, Lenore stood on the footpath outside the cafe. What should she do now?

Then, her eyes searching up and down the street for David, she spied the empty telephone box. She hesitated only a moment. She didn't like to do it, but what other option did she have?

At the third ring, a man's voice, quiet and refined, answered.

'Hello, Brian Kershaw speaking.'

Lenore's throat felt dry. She forced herself to speak.

'Yes... I'm Lenore Hamlyn, a... a friend of David's. I was wondering if I could speak to him please.'

There was a pause at the other end of the line.

Then Brian Kershaw spoke the words that turned Lenore's heart to ice. 'I'm sorry, my son isn't here any longer. He returned to the States rather earlier than he intended. Can I – '

But Lenore had replaced the receiver, her face chalk-white, a cold sickness churning her stomach.

NAN FROWNED AS she watched Lenore's back at the stove.

There was something wrong with the girl to be sure. For the past couple of months she had not been herself, moping around, saying little, not even venturing out of the house on weekends like she used to.

Could it be a boy? Nan wondered as Lenore put the plate of lamb chops in front of her. But Lenore hadn't seemed interested in that sort of thing. And little wonder, thought Nan with bitterness; her father had cured her of that.

Whatever it was, it upset Nan to see Lenore's unhappiness. She wished the girl would say something, tell her what was wrong. She'd asked once, but Lenore's flat, toneless 'nothing' had been the only reply.

Well, Nan thought, she wasn't going to interfere; she knew better than that at her age. The girl'd tell her when she was good and ready.

As they ate together in silence, Nan let her mind wander to happier thoughts. This morning she had received a letter of reply from the school in Kent; it sounded just the thing. Languages – French and German; a well-designed business course; and an emphasis on the 'finishing' that produced refined young ladies skilled in various social accomplishments. Yes, Bartham Hall sounded exactly what she'd had in mind. Lenore was only seventeen but Nan felt pleased to have all the information at her fingertips.

She chewed thoughtfully on a piece of minted chop. Maybe it might be just as well to send Lenore there sooner than she'd planned. At eighteen the girl could surely look after herself; Nan had no doubt about that. She sighed. It was, she knew, only her own selfish delight in Lenore's company that made her want to keep the girl beside her for as long as possible.

Nan pondered the issue. What difference was twelve months going to make? She'd miss Lenore whenever she went. She had to put the girl's interests first; and, even more importantly, she had to remove Lenore from the world she had come to know in the last few years.

She cast a sidelong glance at the silent girl beside her. She wanted the best for Lenore; wanted her to make the most of herself, to move in the top circles, to meet the right people. Nothing, Nan thought with determination, was going to stop Lenore achieving it all. Money would help – and there would be plenty of that, enough to ensure that Lenore would never be forced to pay the price so many women paid. No, Lenore would never need to answer to any man.

LENORE FOUND IT difficult to concentrate on anything in the weeks following the shock of David Kershaw's abrupt departure.

Her thoughts churned endlessly as she fought to make sense of what had occurred between them. Surely if David had been taken ill his father would have told her?

She tried to find excuses. Perhaps there had been some sort of emergency at home? With his mother? His stepfather? But then couldn't he have left a note for her with his father? He must have realized that eventually she would have got in touch?

Her feverish mind swung between the ache of love for David and the pain of his betrayal. And in the end that was the conclusion

Lenore was forced to accept. She had been used. The words of love had been meaningless, the look on David's face and in his eyes, nothing but a sham. It had been a trap, a means of enticing her to do what all along, she now realized, had been his plan.

Lenore fought fiercely against the bitterness and humiliation that might have crushed her. She had been stupid and blind – but it would never happen again. Never again would she trust her heart to any man.

The experience with David had lacked the brutality of her father's advances, but it had been, just the same, another sort of violation.

It was when the second month came around and her period had again failed to arrive, that Lenore knew for sure she was pregnant. Her breasts were swollen, her nipples tingling and tender, and most mornings on waking, she was gripped by a wretched, tearing nausea.

When her condition was confirmed by a doctor chosen at random from the telephone directory, Lenore took the news impassively.

'What do you intend to do?' the doctor asked coldly, aloof and removed in his well-cut suit, his pink scrubbed hands folded in front of him on the uncluttered desk.

Lenore stood up and looked steadily down into his reproachful eyes. 'Nothing,' she answered in a tone as cold as his own.

As she took the train back to Nan's, Lenore was sure of only one thing. She would keep this from Nan until it was too late – for she knew what Nan would try to make her do. A sick taste filled her mouth as, in her mind's eye, she saw with dreadful clarity the lifeless bloodied lump that had lain discarded in Dan Farrell's sink two years ago. It was a sight she would never forget.

Lenore clenched her fists. Not again. She would not be responsible for the death of yet another human being. This time she would have the baby. She would keep it and bring it up and love it. And everytime she looked at it, she would be reminded of how love was meant to be between a man and a woman. But so rarely ever was.

With blank eyes Lenore looked out of the window at the passing rows of redbrick suburban houses, at their cramped backyards and their ugly soul-destroying sameness.

Yes, she would have this child, and if the dreams and ambitions that Nan had aroused in her could never be fulfilled, then that was how it was meant to be.

In time she learned to act in front of Nan as if she were still the old Lenore. But it was a different Lenore now who laughed at Nan's jokes, who discussed her investments, who chatted with Roy and Tanya. Her innocence and hope were gone, and in their place a sour and heavy cynicism poisoned her heart and mind.

The weeks passed, and as she grew larger, Lenore dressed carefully to hide her condition from Nan. The nausea had passed, but each day as she worked at her desk she ate nothing so that in the evening with Nan she could do justice to her meal. The sight of the full plate made her stomach churn but Lenore was determined not to arouse Nan's suspicions.

Once a month she attended an out-patients' clinic at a large public hospital where the baby's progress was monitored. She refused to bow to the subterfuge of a cheap gold band on her left hand; boldly and defiantly she announced herself as Miss Hamlyn among the group of waiting, bulging women.

But the deception she was practising with Nan was harder to bear. There were times when Lenore felt the best thing to do would be to go away, to leave Nan's home and put an end to the lies and evasions that filled her with guilt.

But to do that would mean the loss not only of her home and the income she now so desperately needed, but the loss too of her best friend. For to keep her secret would mean she would have to leave without explanation, cut off all contact – and Lenore knew she could never bring herself to treat Nan that way.

No, she thought grimly, she must keep her condition hidden for as long as possible and then hope that Nan would understand. Understand and help her. Once the baby came and was accepted, life, Lenore was sure, would go on as before.

She managed to keep her secret until halfway through the sixth month of her pregnancy.

Then, one afternoon, disturbed by the ever-increasing strength of the baby's kicks, she left her desk and went into her own bedroom. There, overcome by a curious fascination, she stripped off her clothes to stare at her misshapen body.

Running her fingers gently over the large spongy softness of her breasts, Lenore wondered at the web of fine blue veins that mottled her milky skin; with a sense of awe she smoothed her hands over the exaggerated curve of her belly. It seemed beyond belief that skin could stretch to accommodate such a change in shape.

Then her fingers felt the small bump of a scar near her navel, the result of a fall on the rough concrete edges of a garden bed when she was four. And with a sharp stab of pain she remembered how David's fingers too had found the flaw on her young body; recalled his gentle enquiry and her murmured explanation.

Trapped by the memory, Lenore stared blankly into the mirror. Every detail of that rainy afternoon was burned into her mind. She had given herself completely, held nothing in reserve, and in the joy of their intimacy she had felt herself renewed, restored to the purity and innocence of which she had been so cruelly cheated.

But there had been so little time to savour that sweetness, so little...

Turning from the mirror, Lenore sat naked on the bed, burying her face in her hands as the hot angry tears rolled down her cheeks. Why... Why...?

She didn't hear the door opening and was unaware that Nan, home earlier than usual, had come into the room and was now staring ashen-faced at the sight of Lenore's nakedness.

It was the whimper Nan gave as her hand flew to her mouth that made Lenore lift her tear-stained face in shocked surprise.

Nan's voice was a disbelieving whisper. 'Sweet Jesus, Lenore... What have you done? What have you *done*?'

Nothing Nan said could change Lenore's mind. All her pleas that Lenore see reason were met with quiet, but total resistance. She couldn't understand why the child of someone Lenore had known such a short time, someone who in all likelihood she would never hear from again, should mean so much to her.

'Lenore, listen to me.' There was a note of desperation in Nan's voice. 'You're ruinin' your life. You mightn't see that now, but it's true. There's not many ready to forgive – never mind give a chance to – an unwed mother. Keepin' that child will mean

CHAPTER NINE

PATTING herself dry on the white satin-edged towel, Harriet Maddern admired the curve of her breasts in the full-length mirror. At thirty-two, she decided happily, her bosom was still magnificent.

She wrapped the Italian silk gown around her nakedness as she thought about what she would wear to Nan's that afternoon.

They didn't get together a lot these days, but when they did the same feeling was always there and they never failed to enjoy each other's company. Right from the start, Harriet thought, she'd got on well with Nan. Nan had been kind to her when she'd been young and frightened and alone.

Of course, she'd ended up in the 'business'... But then, as she thought so often to herself, if she hadn't she would never have met Mike, never been living the sort of life she did now. Harriet was aware too that, in a curious way, Nan was proud of her, proud that she had adapted so easily to the world to which Mike Maddern had introduced her.

One afternoon a few months ago, Nan had had reason, it seemed, to dwell on the success Harriet had made of her life.

'Of course I never miss a word about you in the papers, Harriet love, but,' Nan chuckled and her eyes grew brighter, 'the newspapers only ever give half the story, don't they?'

And with a smile, Harriet would tell Nan all the gossip, fill her in on the bitchiness, the extravagance, the infidelities, of the very rich. Nan loved it.

Harriet's own marriage, however, had been a success.

'You were lucky with Mike, love,' Nan had told her more than once. 'Men like him aren't there for the pickin'. Too many bastards among the rest of 'em.' Nan's eyes grew fierce. 'That's why I want Lenore to be free of 'em, free to live her life the way she wants.'

Harriet heard the determination in Nan's voice, felt her concern for the girl who shared her life and home.

the end of everythin' you've dreamed of, Lenore, don't you understand that?'

Her tired blue eyes looked pleadingly into the young girl's set face. 'Listen to reason, my darlin'. Adoption's the only way out, the only way to put all this behind you and go on to make somethin' of yourself. You must see that.'

'No.' Lenore's mouth was a tight, determined line and there was a stubbornness to her tone that Nan had never heard before.

'No, Nan, much as I love you and am grateful for what you've done for me, I'm keeping this child, giving it life. And do you know why?' She looked with tragic eyes into Nan's lined, despairing face. 'Because Nan, I've realised that once you're gone, it'll be the only thing left in this whole dirty world that I'll ever trust myself to love.'

'That child's meant the world to me, Harriet,' Nan continued. 'And I want the best for her. At seventeen, she's got everythin' in front of her.'

Nan paused, then shot Harriet a penetrating look. 'I'd like to think, Harriet, that if Lenore ever needed help after I'm gone, she could turn to you.'

Harriet hid her surprise. She barely knew the girl; had met her only a couple of times in Nan's home. But she saw the plea in Nan's eyes.

'Of course, Nan. If there's anything I can do.'

She made the promise easily, humouring an old woman.

Since that time almost a year ago, Harriet had seen little of Nan; Mike's business had kept them out of the country a great deal. Now, as she moved through to her bedroom with its off-white carpet, its oyster silk walls, its uninterrupted view of the Harbour, Harriet realized just how much she was looking forward to the afternoon in front of her. She and Nan had a lot of catching up to do.

Sitting down at her dressing table, she sprayed Chanel Number 5 in her cleavage and around the silky paleness of her hair. It wasn't her favourite perfume but the one Mike always bought her. It had been his first gift to her and the fragrance he'd been convinced ever since that she preferred. Harriet had never had the heart to tell him otherwise.

In the same way, she thought, putting the top back on the heavy glass bottle, she would never tell him he was a lousy lover. Once a fortnight, three or four minutes, and that was it. Not that she was complaining; it suited her well enough. Men hadn't appealed to her in bed for a long time.

That was why, when they'd first met, she'd liked Mike so much. He'd come in regularly, once a month, and after the preliminaries were out of the way, they would lie together talking for hours. Mike was a great talker.

Of course, in that time she could have been handling another half a dozen clients, but Mike paid well for her exclusive company. He could afford it. Mike Maddern was one of the country's richest men, yet he had none of the arrogance and self-importance Harriet had come to expect from men of his type.

She had realized at once, of course, who he was. His face had been a familiar sight in Sydney's social pages when his wife had been alive. But Vivien Maddern had died seven years ago and, despite his demanding active life as a leading racehorse owner and breeder, Mike Maddern was a lonely man.

Harriet had understood that pretty early on. The sex was just an excuse. Mike Maddern wasn't particularly interested in sleeping with a woman. What he wanted was company – and, after a short time, it was always Harriet's company.

Still, it had come as a complete shock the day he'd made his proposal.

'Harriet, you and I've known each other eight months or so now, isn't that right?'

Harriet had nodded, puzzled by the earnest tone in his voice. Mike was usually fun and light-hearted, glad of a laugh and a bit of banter.

'I like you, Harriet,' he continued with the same seriousness. 'I like you a lot. And I need someone special in my life.' He paused for a moment as if expecting Harriet to say something. When she didn't he went on. 'Vivien's been dead for seven years now and I still miss her, I'll always miss her. We didn't have kids but we had one hell of a great marriage.'

He gave a nervous cough and sat up higher in the bed. 'What I'm trying to say, Harriet, is that I think you're a woman I could spend the rest of my life with.'

Her shocked face stared up into his and he smiled. 'Oh, I know you're working here and all, but I think I can understand that. I know that circumstances can sometimes drive a woman to desperate measures.' The smile became a chuckle. 'The same way things can drive a man to come to a place like this.'

His tone grew serious again. 'I'm not asking how you ended up here, Harriet; that's your own business. No,' he shook his head, 'there's only one thing I want an answer to.' He looked down at her, his eyes searching hers. 'Will you marry me, my dear?'

Harriet was totally and utterly incapable of answering. Dazed, she stared wide-eyed into Mike Maddern's weather-beaten face. This kind, unassuming, rich and worldly man wanted her, Harriet Wallace, to be his wife. Never in a million years would she have dreamed of such a wonder. What Mike Maddern was offering her was not merely an escape but an elevation to the sort of life she could barely begin to imagine...

His eyes still held hers, waiting anxiously for her reply. Harriet released a long drawn-out breath. 'Yes, Mike... Oh, yes...'

OF COURSE FOR appearances sake they'd had to make certain arrangements. Harriet flew to London where Mike had booked her a room at the Dorchester. Two days later he joined her there and a week after that they were married by special licence in the Chelsea registry office. Afterwards, they celebrated at a small luncheon party at the Cafe Royal with the senior staff of Mike's English stud farm.

On a wonderful two-week honeymoon in Paris, Mike had spent lavishly on a wardrobe and jewellery for his new bride and Harriet had begun to get an inkling of the sort of life she had entered. She felt happily certain that she would have little trouble adapting.

The news of the marriage was leaked with perfect timing to the Australian press, so that on their arrival at Sydney airport they were met by a barrage of photographers and newsmen, and later Harriet read about herself as the 'lucky Australian model working in swinging London who had stolen Mike Maddern's heart'.

For nine years now Harriet had enjoyed a warm and loving companionship – and minimal sex – with her devoted husband, and a lifestyle among the rich and famous on three continents.

Yet sometimes, only sometimes, she felt oppressed at being surrounded by people who lived entirely for themselves and their own indulgence.

It was at these times that Harriet felt the need to see Nan, to talk with the woman who could always restore her perspective on life and keep her feet firmly on the ground...

Make-up completed, Harriet slipped the cream silk blouse carefully over her head. Yes, it would be good to see Nan. With Nan she could relax, drop her facade.

That afternoon, Harriet spent much longer than she had anticipated with Nan Reilly.

CHAPTER TEN

ROY was in the house when Lenore's labour began and Nan sent him to fetch Dan Farrell. By the time the doctor arrived she had everything ready in Lenore's bedroom: clean sheets, towels, hot water, and the baby's white cane crib.

'Steady now, love,' Dan Farrell looked down into Lenore's pale sweating face. 'You'll manage.' He pushed aside an overpowering sense of *déjà vu* as he scrubbed his hands and made ready.

Nan held Lenore's hand and mopped her brow as Roy hurried off to fetch more hot water. To Lenore, the pain was every bit as bad as it had been before and she prayed that this time it would be over quickly.

Half an hour later, when the contractions had become excruciatingly intense, Dan Farrell leaned over her and said, 'I'm going to give you something, Lenore, to ease the pain. The baby's much bigger this time.'

Lenore panted harshly through dry parted lips, barely able to nod her head. Anything to relieve the piercing agony that was ripping her apart.

Dazed, she felt Dan Farrell's hand take her own, the quick sharp sting of a needle, and then blissful darkness took away the pain.

Nan bit her lip as she looked down into Lenore's shocked, ashen face.

'Wha... what did you say?' Lenore's voice was a harsh incredulous whisper. The drug had worn off and there was a painful throbbing between her legs but Lenore hardly noticed as she tried to grasp the reality of Nan's words.

'Oh, my poor, poor darlin'.' Nan's face, heavy with despair and pity, looked down at Lenore, tears trembling in her pale blue eyes.

'Nan... what did you just tell me?' Lenore's voice was weak and low but the anguish was clearly audible.

'The... the baby's... dead, love.' Nan's voice broke and the tears fell without restraint down her face. 'The cord – it was wrapped around its neck, my darlin'; the poor thing was blue and gone by the time Dan Farrell drew it from you.'

She brushed away her tears and clutched Lenore's hand, the stone-cold fingers limp in her own. 'Oh, my sweetheart, my heart's bleedin' for you... I know how much you wanted that wee babe...'

With a stab of fear, Nan looked at Lenore's blank eyes and the awful mask-like pallor of her face. 'There'll be other children, Lenore... when the time is right, my sweet love, there'll be others.'

An icy stillness gripped Lenore's heart and the blood seemed frozen in her veins. Nan was wrong. There would be no more children. There would be no more risk of love.

CHAPTER ELEVEN

ENGLAND 1967

THE school was set among five acres of parkland just an hour's train journey from London.

With pupils drawn from wealthy and powerful families in the New World and the Middle and Far East, no expense had been spared in renovating the two hundred year-old grey stone building to include every modern convenience.

After two months at Bartham Hall, Lenore had settled into the daily routine – formal lessons in the morning: languages, art, musical appreciation, business principles, and in the afternoon: horse-riding, ballet, tennis and instruction in the social skills that would ensure immediate acceptance in the most esteemed of company.

After the baby's death, Nan had insisted that Lenore 'get away' at once.

'Make a fresh start, love; forget what's happened and get on with your life,' she'd said, helping to pack Lenore's two brand-new suitcases. 'It's sooner than I wanted to lose you, but it's you I've got to be thinkin' of, not my greedy Irish self.'

For a moment she stopped her frantic packing and folding to turn to Lenore. She took the girl's hands in her own and stared into those dark, impassive eyes. 'What's done's done, love. Always remember that in life. Never have regrets. Look in front of you and forget what's left behind.'

Lenore heard Nan's words, knew the wisdom that lay behind them – but she also knew with utter conviction that she would never forget. Something deep inside her had changed. She was different now.

*

AS SHE PICKED up her books at the end of the morning's lessons, Lenore thought how different she was too from the girls around her.

Their ceaseless chatter about clothes and boys, about the husbands they expected eventually to snare, and about the wealthy lives they expected to lead, sparked an angry incredulity in Lenore. How *could* they be prepared to exist as second-rate partners to all-powerful, authoritative husbands who would view them primarily as the breeders of their heirs? How *could* they waste their lives in a mindless round of social events and shopping sprees when there were so many more important things to do in the world?

Lenore never joined in those conversations in which the girls, giggling or earnest, outlined the dreamed-of futures. If, as sometimes happened, she was asked a direct question about her own plans, Lenore would merely smile evasively. 'Who knows?' she would shrug. 'At our age plans change so easily.'

It was a lie. With precise and deliberate calculation Lenore had planned exactly what she would do with her life.

'... SO LENORE, DARLING,' Nan wrote in her shaky spidery hand, 'happy nineteenth, birthday. I only wish I could have been there to share it with you, but you know, my love, you were in my heart and thoughts just the same. The idea you wrote of sounds wonderful. I told Roy about it of course and he's sure you'd be doing the right thing. The grand piece you put together for my birthday that time showed you've got the talent he says.

'So, my dear, make sure you give me all the details, then I can see to the fees and anything else you might be needing...'

The idea had been forming in Lenore's head for quite some time now. It was all part of her long-term plan, exactly what she needed to make her mark, to set her on her way. If, as Roy said, she did have the talent, then with his help she knew she could succeed.

The year at Bartham Hall was almost over and she had made the most of what the school had to offer. There had been trips to London to the ballet, the opera, the theatre and Lenore felt a new confidence in herself, a growing sophistication that had come with the skills she had acquired, the people she had met.

Her German was good, her French even better, and the business skills she'd been taught had been practical and relevant; although Lenore was sure she would be one of the very few at Bartham Hall to put them to any use.

Her mind had been opened in other ways too. London in the late sixties was the focus of unprecedented social upheaval. A cultural revolution had been brought about by a bold and enlightened younger generation derisive of the restrictions and conservatism of the established class system. Through their blatantly sexual music, their outrageous fashions and their new economic power, young people were demanding, loudly and assertively, a change in the old order.

Lenore too was swept up in the tempo of the era. She realized that for women, in particular, the changes were fundamental. The ready availability of the contraceptive pill had given them, for the first time, control over their bodies. Released from the threat of unwanted pregnancy, women were like caged birds let loose in the world – free at last to determine their own destiny.

And it was, Lenore noted with a certain pride, a fellow Australian called Germaine Greer who was providing the focus for women's issues. Lenore found much to absorb and wonder about in the creed of that outspoken woman.

WITH TIME TO spare before beginning the three year course at the Metropolitan School of Fine Art and Design, England's most prestigious college of jewellery design, Lenore accepted an invitation from Lisette Joulet, a fellow pupil at Bartham Hall. Lisette, the daughter of a wealthy industrialist, lived with her family in Paris. Her stay with the Joulet family would, Lenore hoped, provide an excellent opportunity to further improve her French, to visit the museums and art galleries and to taste for herself the magic that was Paris.

The six weeks she spent in France added to Lenore's education in every way. She loved the passionate conversations that were the norm each evening around the Joulet dinner table, when the issues of the day were discussed among the family. On one such occasion Madame Joulet's aunt was present and the fifty-six year-old woman made an immediate and lasting impression on Lenore.

Madame Lafert was a Deputy in the French government. Since her work with the Resistance during the war, politics had been the passion of her life.

Not slim, but elegant and impeccably groomed, Madame Lafert expressed her views articulately and forcefully on French and international affairs. She was, Lenore was quick to note, also a staunch supporter of equal rights for women.

'Women need to learn to be independent, to stop seeing men as their fathers who will always look after them. They must take charge of their own lives.' Noting Lenore's keen interest, she directed her remarks to the young Australian. 'Not that one must exclude men as partners in this difficult world, certainly not,' she gave a rumbling laugh. 'Look at me – married thirty-five years, two children, but never, *never* have I felt that my role was restricted to only that of wife and mother. No,' she shook her thick silvery hair, 'there are no obstacles women cannot overcome with perseverance and determination.'

That night Lenore went to bed inspired by Madame Lafert's words and achievements.

THE SHORT TIME in France changed Lenore in many ways. There was a style, an elegance, a forthrightness about the French that she began to realize had been lacking on the other side of the Channel – and unconsciously she began to develop many of those same qualities.

There were physical changes too. In the last twelve months her figure had filled out; she had grown another inch and at Lisette's persuasion, she now put herself in the hands of a skilled *coiffeuse*.

The long brown tresses disappeared and in their place a smooth curve of red-gold hair bobbed gently on her shoulders, the colour highlighting her creamy skin and huge, velvet eyes.

Lenore liked the change and was impressed too by the way Lisette showed her how to colour her eyes, her cheeks, her lips. Suddenly in the mirror Lenore saw a very different image; it was a sophisticated young woman who stared back at her.

Boys noticed the changes too. The eyes of Jean-Luc, Lisette's twenty-two year-old brother, lit up every time Lenore came into a room, and he was unfailingly charming and attentive to her.

But from Lenore there was no response. She was polite but always distant, ignoring his flattery and flirting. Boys did not interest her. That part of her was dead and sealed off; it would never distract her again from the pursuit of her ambitions.

One night, however, she reluctantly allowed herself to be talked into accompanying Lisette, her fiancé André, and Jean-Luc to the Opera.

'You must come with us, Lenore,' Lisette widened her big green eyes in encouragement at her friend. 'This is something not to miss in Paris.'

And so she had gone – sitting as far away as possible from Jean-Luc when all four of them bundled into a taxi, not allowing his arm ever to touch hers as they sat side by side on the red velvet seats with the spectacle of *Aida* unfolding before them.

Lisette was right, Lenore had enjoyed the performance, but still, she was glad when it was over. It was difficult to ignore Jean-Luc's attempts to flatter and touch her, remembering all the while that she was a guest in his father's house.

But the worst part of the evening occurred on the drive home.

'Hey, André,' Jean-Luc turned bright eyes to his sister's fiancé – they had gone to a nearby cafe after the performance and the two men had drunk cognac – 'Let's show Lenore the girls in the Bois. That will be interesting for her I'm sure. She can't leave Paris before she sees that!'

'Oh no, Jean-Luc! That's not –' Lisette started to protest, but Jean-Luc ignored her.

'Come on, André, what do you say?' Jean-Luc encouraged. He would show this cold bitch something; make the colour come to her face. The tarts in the Bois de Boulogne would bring her to life.

André shrugged, giving in to his friend. Next moment, following Jean-Luc's instructions, the taxi was heading for the park which in daytime was so beautiful but at night become a place of ugliness and degradation.

Jean-Luc glanced sideways at Lenore as the taxi moved slowly past the girls standing in the shadows of the trees. There was no expression on her cool pale face as they passed the prostitutes with their garishly painted faces, their long leather boots, their near naked bosoms and their short skin-tight skirts.

'Come on, Jean-Luc, this is enough! Take us home!' Lisette was protesting loudly now as they followed the cars moving slowly in front of them – the customers making their careful choice.

With a shrug, Jean-Luc leaned back against the seat. He was disappointed that the girl beside him had shown no response, no embarrassment. She was a frigid, sexless bitch.

'Okay,' he said sulkily, 'let's go.'

Later that night, as she lay in her bed, Lenore recalled what she had seen. The images, seared on her mind, made her shiver with repulsion – repulsion at the animal delight she observed in Jean-Luc's face as he'd leered at the pitiful figures under the trees.

AT THE SCHOOL of Fine Art and Design, Lenore discovered the joy that comes from artistic expression. Her teachers inspired and encouraged her, and she spent every vacation studying the work of some of Europe's most skilled craftsmen in Belgium, Germany, France and Switzerland.

It was only as her second Christmas abroad came round that she realized how long she'd been away from home. With another two years of college yet to finish, she felt a sudden, painful longing to see Nan and Roy; to feel the touch of the Australian summer sun against her pale indoor skin. But a short visit home was, Lenore knew, out of the question. It was such a long way to go and would be so expensive. Nan had done so much for her already. But while Lenore's fees and accommodation were taken care of by Nan – an undreamt of situation for the majority of struggling students – Lenore had insisted on providing her own spending money.

She had found a Saturday job – as counter assistant at Mashadi, an exclusive jewellers in Knightsbridge. There, from her two Egyptian bosses, she had learned a lot, not only about design and retailing, but about the nature and tastes of the very rich. Lenore saw soon enough that the possession of wealth did not necessarily equate with good manners and contentment.

She arrived back at her flat one Saturday evening, exhausted after dealing with a particularly demanding American actress, and found the letter.

At first the handwriting on the envelope had made Lenore think it was from Nan. But on opening the letter she had found merely a brief note from Nan and another folded envelope. Her name was written on it but no address – just an instruction scribbled in pencil: Please Forward.

Puzzled, she read Nan's note first.

My dear Lenore,

This arrived for you and I have sent it on as asked. I suppose it must be from a pal of yours here. Hope all is well, my love. I'll be in touch soon.

                All love,
                Nan.

Frowning, Lenore opened the other envelope. As she saw the signature, the blood drained from her face and her knees felt as if they would give way beneath her.

She sat down on the nearest chair, the words swimming in front of her eyes as she read:

Dear Lenore,

I hope you receive this. I have thought about you so much in the last two and a half years. It is only now that I have managed to get back to Sydney. The last eighteen months I have spent on my back in a hospital bed but, finally, my mother's prayers have been answered. I can walk. With a limp – but I can walk.

After you left me that afternoon so long ago now, I thought very deeply about what had happened between us. It seemed to me I had no choice but to come to the very painful conclusion that it would be impossible for me to see you again. There was no way that I wanted you to be saddled with a cripple. Because, Lenore, something told me that you would have taken me on – I could see it in your eyes, or so I thought, as we lay in each other's arms. And for me, that would have been a dreadful waste of two lives.

Not to see you again, Lenore, to pretend that we had never met, was the hardest decision I've ever had to make.

It wasn't until the treatment looked as if it might actually be a success that I dared to think of finding you again. It was only as a fully functioning male that I felt I could offer you what I thought you deserved.

Well, I found you Lenore.

I remembered Nan Reilly's name, remembered the name of the suburb, Surry Hills, where you told me you lived. As it turned out all I had to do was ask at the local hotel one evening and, to my delight, everyone knew Nan Reilly's 'place'.

I found out why soon enough.

Why didn't you tell me, Lenore? Why did you let me torment myself all those years with the thought of what I had lost?

What we shared that afternoon meant so much to me. But for the girl I had longed for, dreamt of so often, it had been nothing more than a day's work – a moment of pity perhaps for a deprived, pathetic cripple?

And all you got was my grateful thanks, Lenore.

Wasn't I man enough to pay for it like the rest?

D.

Lenore let the letter drop from her icy fingers. For a long time she sat perfectly still as the words of that last sentence played over and over in her paralysed mind.

And when the tears finally came, they tore at the core of her, for the horror, the futility, the unspeakable depravity of it all.

CHAPTER TWELVE

THE phone call from Roy came just a day after Lenore's final exam. She felt sure she'd done well but it would be another fortnight before the results would be known.

She had never intended to remain in London and was flying out in another four days, eager to return home. She had been away from Australia for over four years and was longing to see Nan and Roy again, longing to tell them all she had seen and done and learned.

But a deeper need was also driving Lenore home. She was filled with a restless impatience to set in motion the plans she had deliberated over for so long. And she was determined that, no matter how long it might take her, no matter how many obstacles might be placed in her path, she would make her voice heard, would acquire the power to ensure that other women too were offered the chance to achieve the independence and freedom that men expected as their God-given right.

This struggle, she knew in her heart, would be her driving force; already it was her obsession.

Now, surrounded by piles of books and open suitcases, Lenore was interrupted by the shrill ring of the telephone.

The voice of the British operator told her that a call was being put through from Sydney, Australia. Lenore barely had time to register this fact, before Roy's voice, distant but clear, came over the line.

'Roy!' Lenore was thrilled to hear the long rolling vowels of his Australian accent, an accent that sounded stronger than ever, accustomed as she had become to the sound of English voices.

The next moment, Roy's words turned her joy to apprehension, and then fear.

'Yes, Roy, I understand.' She heard her own voice, strained and unnatural. 'I'll come at once.'

Six hours later, having worked with desperate urgency to finish her packing and clean up the flat, Lenore was at Heathrow airport awaiting the departure of a Qantas flight to Sydney. To alter her flight at such short notice had not been easy, but in the circumstances a seat had been found for her.

As she waited for her boarding call, Lenore found it impossible to sit still. She paced around the packed departure lounge, willing herself already on the plane, in the air, back in Sydney – and at Nan's bedside.

Two weeks, Roy had told her on the phone. The stroke had happened two weeks ago. But Nan had refused to let her know, not wanting to disrupt her during that vital last exam.

Lenore remembered Roy's words. 'She took a turn for the worse two days ago, Lenore, but it wasn't till she was sure your exams were over and done with that she'd give me your phone number, despite my pleading.'

Lenore heard the desperate intensity in Roy's voice.

'Hurry, Lenore. There's not much time. She'll go happy if she sees you here.'

Fighting hard to hold back her tears, to hide the despair in her heart, Lenore looked down into Nan's pallid face, the skin as crumpled as old parchment.

She forced her dry lips apart. 'Nan... it's me. Lenore. I'm here.' Her voice was hoarse with emotion as she took Nan's cold thin hand in her own.

Slowly, Nan lifted tired heavy eyes to look at the young woman who stood beside her hospital bed. In a sudden flash of energy, a smile touched those eyes in their nests of wrinkles.

'Lenore, my love... oh, I'm so glad you're here.' The words came out in a harsh broken whisper and she clutched weakly at Lenore's hand.

Lenore sat down on the uncomfortable metal chair and, bending closer, heard Nan's thick heavy breathing. 'You're going to be fine, Nan... You're... you're going to get better and when you come home, I'm going to take care of you.'

Nan's colourless lips smiled weakly. 'That's not true, love; you and I both know that. But I've no regrets. Not now.'

Her watery blue eyes travelled slowly over Lenore, taking in the woman who had emerged from the girl she'd sent away.

'You've made me proud, Lenore. You're everythin' I knew you'd be, and more.' Her voice faded, and as she closed her eyes Lenore's heart leapt in sudden alarm. Then, with an almost palpable effort, Nan went on, her voice barely audible now, her eyelids flickering. 'I've fixed everythin', Lenore. Roy knows all about it. It's all yours. You'll never want for anythin' my darlin'.'

She forced her eyes open and looked lovingly into Lenore's tear-stained anguished face. 'Never have regrets, love; remember what I told you. You're strong, Lenore – you'll do anythin' you put your mind to.' Nan took a long shuddering breath. 'You're a survivor, my darlin'...'

At the private funeral service Lenore was taken aback when Roy arrived at the chapel in the company of a tall, very slim blonde woman in a severely-cut dark suit.

Before Roy could explain, Harriet Maddern spoke.

'Lenore?' She hid her surprise as she held out her hand. She would barely have recognized the girl she had once known; it was an elegant young woman who now stood before her: the discreet make-up, the brightly glowing hair, the unmistakable French cut of the simple black dress. The years in Europe had transformed Lenore into a poised and sophisticated young woman.

'Forgive me please, Lenore,' Harriet said in a low voice. 'We have met before – I'm an old friend of Nan's. I-I just had to come today. Roy was worried that it might upset you but –'

Roy interrupted. 'Harriet was a good friend of Nan's for many years, Lenore. I hoped you wouldn't mind.'

Lenore looked at the older woman. Yes, she remembered Harriet Maddern now. Nan had often pointed out Harriet's photo to her in newspapers and magazines and, although she had never explained how their friendship had come into being, Lenore had had her own suspicions.

After the short, simple service, Roy had to return to work, and when Harriet suggested that perhaps Lenore would like to have a drink with her, Lenore's first instinct was to refuse. But, she reconsidered, why not? This woman had known Nan; why shouldn't they spend some time reminiscing together on a day like today?

It was over drinks in the pre-lunch privacy of an inner-city cocktail bar that Lenore felt herself warming to Harriet Maddern, as the older woman spoke with affection of the friend they had both lost. Here was someone, Lenore thought, who had cared for Nan every bit as much as she herself had.

'We were very good friends, Lenore. I'd known Nan a...long time.' Harriet reached out a long slim hand for her drink and Lenore noticed with professional interest the diamonds and emeralds that encircled her perfectly manicured fingers. 'It was always good to talk to Nan,' Harriet continued, 'to listen to some of that no-nonsense Irish wisdom when it seemed that everyone else I knew was just too out of touch with the world.'

Harriet took a sip of her drink, then put down her glass and gave Lenore an appraising look. 'Nan worried about you, Lenore. She was concerned that once she was gone you'd have no-one to turn to.' Harriet gave a very small sigh, she knew that sometimes no matter how much we seem in control of our lives, it's nice to know that there's someone who'll give us good advice, comfort us, listen without judging.'

Harriet leaned forward and laid a cool soft hand on one of Lenore's.

'I hope we can be that sort of friend to each other, Lenore. We've both lost Nan – and women need each other.'

THE WEEKS FOLLOWING Nan's funeral passed in a blur for Lenore. She felt numbed, dazed, unable to accept the finality of Nan's death. She'd had so much to share with Nan, so much to thank her for, and to give her in return...

It was Roy who made her realize how much had changed since she'd gone away.

'Not long after you left, Lenore, Nan started winding things down, and then six months ago she finished up the business completely. She wanted it, and everyone concerned with it, all cleared away before you returned. She was fair to the girls; she gave them enough to see them through, get them started in something else.' Roy held Lenore's eyes with his own. 'What she wanted was a fresh start for you, Lenore; a clean background from which to launch you...'

They were sitting in the living room of the large airy apartment Nan had bought herself in the leafy suburban privacy of Sydney's exclusive North Shore. This was a world of upper-class tranquility and complacent wealth – Nan had moved herself far away from the close-knit community of her old working-class suburb.

'She missed Surry Hills you know, Lenore,' Roy went on, 'but she did it for you. You meant everything to her.'

His voice was gentle and the tears glistened in Lenore's eyes as she sat in Nan's favourite old armchair, covered now in a brand-new chintz print.

'You're a rich woman, Lenore,' Roy went on. 'Prices for inner-city real estate have sky-rocketed in the last year or so. Nan sold up at just the right time.' He looked at Lenore, so still and quiet across from him. 'Have you any idea what you're going to do now?'

Slowly Lenore raised her eyes to meet his and once again Roy was struck by the new poise and confidence of the young woman sitting opposite him.

In a voice filled with utter conviction, Lenore said, 'I know exactly what I'm going to do, Roy, and I'll need your help.'

It took them eighteen months to pull it all together.

Lenore stayed on in Nan's apartment for a few more weeks, then sold it to move closer to the city and to Roy. She bought a pretty bluestone cottage in Paddington, one of the first of the inner-city suburbs to be taken over by the young and stylish and made their own. The house was small and charming with ivy-covered walls and a tiny fragrant courtyard. But best of all, Roy was only five minutes away. Now running his own small jewellery business, he had agreed to help Lenore in any way possible with what she had in mind. Together they spent long hours working on their designs and planning the campaign that would launch the most original, the most spectacular jewellery collection Australia had ever seen.

With the designs finally decided on, Lenore and Roy made a whirlwind buying trip – Bangkok for rubies, Hong Kong and Tokyo for pearls, Rome for gold and platinum.

But it was in Australia itself that Lenore found the gems that most excited her imagination: the splendid black opals, unique to Australia, from the hot desert region of Lightning Ridge; and the wonderful Australian sapphires, not only the familiar blues, but the rarer greens and golds with their mysterious hearts of fire.

Then for weeks, she and Roy worked far into the night, putting together pieces of such workmanship and style that Lenore knew without a doubt her plan would work.

When the necklace that was to be their centrepiece lay finished on its white velvet pad, Lenore's heart skipped a beat. Ten black opals each of eight carats were set in plain heavy gold and alternated with exquisitely cut five carat diamonds. The beauty of the creation took her breath away.

The lease of the shop set right in the heart of Sydney's shopping mecca of Double Bay, was taken out in the name of Anthea James.

It was a name that Sydney was to become familiar with in the two months leading up to the opening of the Anthea James boutique. It was the name heading full-page advertisements in *Vogue* and *Harpers*, advertisements featuring such exquisite and outstanding jewellery that tantalized readers made sure to note the opening date of the boutique.

And it was an opening like no other Sydney had ever seen. No free champagne, no waiters or trays of canapés – and no price tags on the sensational works of art on display.

In the silver and grey interior of the Double Bay shop, ceiling spotlights illuminated each individual piece of jewellery where it lay brilliant in its cage of glass, like some museum display of fragments from a rare and ancient civilization. POA was printed in silver on the small black card that described each piece.

Sydney's matrons bristled. Price on application? How presumptuous... But as the room filled with eager curious women, the mood changed. A buzz of excitement ran through the stifling air, as first one, and then another, of the magnificent unique designs was marked as sold. Word of the astronomical prices asked and received, spread like wildfire, adding to the excitement, the intrigue, and finally, the overwhelming desire to own, to have for oneself, at least one of these stunning masterpieces.

The breathtaking black opal necklace was snapped up by a visiting American businesswoman, the owner of a chain of luxury hotels. The press became frenzied in their attempts to elicit the asking price from the joyful purchaser. When guessed-at sums were put to the immaculately-groomed, copper-haired woman in her forties, she laughed, delighted at the fuss.

'Is that U.S. or Aussie dollars?' she teased in a heavy Texan drawl.

By the following day, the name of Anthea James was on all the lips that counted. Her telephone never stopped ringing as requests rolled in for interviews from all sections of the media.

Vogue begged to be allowed to feature Anthea and her 'wonderful, stunning work' in their forthcoming issue. Anthea was happy to agree. It was a commercial opportunity she would make the most of; but of her private life the press would learn only as much as she intended them to know.

Anthea's name was already appearing on the best guest lists in town. Following the spectacular opening success of her enterprise, and the attendant press attention, it came as no surprise just four weeks later when she was approached by the producer of the 'Peter Wyatt Afternoon Show'. It was the highest rating daytime television program in Sydney.

As she sat with Roy in the living room of her home outlining the offer she had received, Anthea's eyes shone. 'It's just the occasional guest spot to start with. Maybe three times a month. But,' she leaned forward in excitement, 'it's enough to keep my name in front of the public, enough to launch me towards the sort of exposure I'm aiming for.'

Roy smiled and raised his half-full glass of whiskey. 'You're on your way, Anthea, my dear.' He almost never made a mistake now with her name. 'I wish you all the very very best.' He was genuinely happy for her. He knew where Anthea's long-term ambitions lay; knew what drove her so hard to succeed. And Roy understood. After all, he knew exactly what it was like to exist as a member of a persecuted minority in an aggressive male world.

Sitting back, Anthea tapped perfectly oval, unvarnished nails on the arm of the white linen sofa. 'And this is just the beginning Roy,' she said quietly. 'Just the beginning...'

And it was.

The enormous media fuss following the opening of the Anthea

James boutique proved to be just the springboard Anthea had aimed for.

The occasional TV spots soon became regular appearances and her comments were sought on various topical issues – frivolous 'female issues' certainly, but Anthea didn't care. It was a beginning, the foothold she had sought.

Eighteen months later, Anthea's classic looks, her warm and articulate personality, along with the media's growing interest in her, brought her into Matt Kelso's stable. It was then that her career really took off. The name of Anthea James could be assured of attracting a huge female audience and it was from the security of that knowledge that Matt Kelso negotiated a spectacular deal for her with the Crane Corporation.

Anthea was ecstatic. The only thing spoiling her joy was Roy's strange lack of enthusiasm for this major step forward in her career. He had never articulated his feelings, but Anthea knew him too well not to notice his reserve at her success.

Was he afraid, she wondered, that with the pressures and distractions of the world in which she would now move, she would forget him? Anthea did her best to reassure Roy, to make him realize that he held a unique place in her life and in her heart. He had done so much to help her in her ambitions, had so generously allowed all the glory associated with the jewellery business to be hers alone.

And Roy was her last link with Nan, her last link with the past. The past she had buried so effectively. Or so she had thought...

CHAPTER THIRTEEN

1987

'BUT, *why* for Christ's sake, Anthea?' Matt Kelso demanded fiercely into the phone. 'The money's bloody incredible. We're all set to sign on the dotted line. Why, for Christ's sake do you want to pull out now? Are you trying to commit professional suicide?'

At the other end of the line Anthea could hear the effort it took for Matt Kelso not to lose complete control. Charming and urbane when all was going smoothly, he was renowned for the force of his fury, the strength of his language, when someone or something blocked his way.

This was the first time Anthea had been given a glimpse of that famous temper. But she would not be intimidated by caveman tactics from Matt Kelso.

'No, Matt.' The flatness and finality of her tone reached him clearly at the other end of the line. 'I've changed my mind, that's all. I'm too busy, I'm afraid. It's too big an undertaking when I've got this political business on my plate. Please apologize for me to Mr Yarrow. I'm sure he'll find someone else perfectly capable.' Quietly, she replaced the receiver.

Matt Kelso swore loudly and effusively as he threw down the phone. Busy! It would only take six weeks of the bitch's time – nothing. And the bucks... He thumped the desk hard with his fist as he thought of the size of the commission Anthea James' withdrawal would cost him. Not to mention making him look an unprofessional hick in front of fuckin' Yarrow. Jesus!

He stood up and marched over to the broad picture window of his fortieth floor office. Hands thrust in his trouser pockets he stared grimly at the panorama of Sydney below.

*

Anthea put down the phone with a sense of relief. It had been the only way. David – his name alone was enough to send a shiver through her – would have no trouble finding someone else. Any one of Sydney's hot-shot media types would jump at the chance – the money, the kudos, the exposure to a mass American audience. And with luck, David Yarrow would be out of the country in a couple of months and she would have nothing more to fear.

Anthea closed her eyes as the stab of pain shot through her. Only the memories he had so startlingly awakened would remain to haunt her.

THREE DAYS LATER, having failed twice more to persuade Anthea to change her mind, Matt Kelso was finally forced to put David Yarrow in the picture.

When the American came on the line he listened quietly to Matt Kelso's mellifluous voice giving its carefully-worded explanation for Anthea James' last-minute withdrawal. He didn't interrupt. When Kelso had finished he asked succinctly, 'Is it money?'

'It doesn't seem so, David. I'm her agent and she certainly didn't indicate that to me. No, I can only say again how –'

David Yarrow cut short his apologies. 'Sure. Listen, Matt, give me time to think about this. I'll get back to you. Or,' the idea came to him, 'would you have any objection to giving me Anthea's private number? I'd like to discuss this further before I do anything else at this stage.'

Matt Kelso felt a moment's hesitation. Normally he never allowed customers to deal directly with his clients. And especially where the client was as big as Anthea James. There was always the very faint possibility that his services as an agent might be redundant in the future.

But this deal was a virtual *fait accompli*; and if Anthea came back into the picture, so did his commission.

'Sure, David,' Matt said helpfully, 'I only want to make sure you get the person who'll do the job best for you.'

David Yarrow put down the receiver, a thoughtful look on his face. Why, he wondered? Anthea James had seemed pleased with the deal her agent had negotiated. Why was she pulling out now?

Turning the problem over in his mind, he stood up and walked across to the gleaming mahogany table to choose a bottle of Scotch from the others on the tray. He poured a couple of inches of the rich amber liquid into a glass, added a splash of water and carried the drink out onto the back verandah. As he leaned back into the creaking rattan divan he was distracted from his thoughts by the sight of the overgrown garden. It was a shame. He'd been so goddamn busy; but he must get someone to see to it. The place had been so splendid when his father was alive.

David recalled the last time he had seen his father. It had been four weeks after that final operation, when he had taken his first steps in eight years. Thanks to the commitment and support of a surgeon willing to experiment with a radical new treatment, David had learned to walk again. Intensive physiotherapy, coupled with a series of delicate operations to ease the pressure on his spinal cord, had brought about the miracle his mother had prayed for.

His father had been delighted. Despite the geographical distance, they had always been close. Brian Kershaw had even understood when, at his step-father's insistence, David had dropped his father's name.

They had been sitting here just as he was now, in the dusk, talking quietly together, when David had finally forced himself to bring up the subject. He had been dreading it. But his father had understood. 'It's a great chance you've been offered, David. Yarrow has an enormous business empire and you're his only heir. It's only natural he'd want you to take his name when it will all eventually come to you.'

His father had turned then and looked at him in the gathering shadows. 'I'll have little enough to leave you. This house, a small sum of money, some stocks. But know one thing son – whatever happened between your mother and myself, I've always loved you. It was a terrible blow to me when your mother made her decision – a natural enough one – to go back to the States. I've missed you a lot all these years.'

David remembered the words well. That was the last time he had seen his father alive. For the next four years he'd been busy finishing college and catching up on the years he'd missed while in hospital. Then, immediately after graduation, he had started working for his stepfather. He had just made plans to spend his first proper vacation with his father, when the news came of his death. Brian Kershaw had died on the golf course of a massive heart attack.

David had flown to Sydney for the funeral, and to attend to his father's affairs. The lawyers had tried to encourage him to sell the house. 'That style of place is very much in vogue these days, Mr Yarrow,' the pink-faced, sartorially elegant lawyer had advised. 'With a block that size plus its ocean views, you'll get a good price for it.'

But David could not be persuaded. Somehow, despite the problems that would no doubt ensue, he wanted to hold on to the house. This time he could only be away from the States for a week; it was all too quick. But later, he promised himself, he would come back to Sydney and stay for longer. Then he would live in the house and remember his childhood and the gentle wisdom of the man he had seen too little of.

Now, as he finished his drink and watched the dying rays of the sun gleam golden on the trees, David wondered why it had taken him so long. Fifteen years. Time, and a steady stream of tenants had taken their toll on the house and the garden. Well, he stood up, he would attend to that now. If all went as planned he would be here quite a while. He was glad he had hung on to the place. It held so many bitter-sweet memories.

For a moment he had completely forgotten the problem of Anthea James.

CHAPTER FOURTEEN

BARRY Francis had always found it easy enough to hide his distaste for the soft and sagging middle-aged female flesh that fell with such ease and regularity into his bed.

Maxine Crane might be no softer or saggier than most – but she was certainly richer. Much richer. A small satisfied smile played on his lips as, poised above him, Maxine's flushed and puffy face looked into his. She mistook the reason for his smile.

'You love it don't you, darling?' She panted the words from between smeared red lips. 'An older woman knows all the tricks.'

Beneath her, Barry Francis' smile grew wider. 'I love the way you love it, baby. You're so deliciously randy.' His voice was a silky murmur.

And why not, thought Maxine in delight, with a virile hunk of twenty-nine year-old male like you beneath me? She sucked her stomach in and ground herself harder against him. God, she loved young men. The smooth, firm hardness of them, the ceaseless appetite, the total abandon.

For a moment she let her concentration wander. Barry turned her on so much, she wondered why she had resisted so long. Not, she thought, that Barry had pushed; he'd been the perfect gentleman. It was she who had ached for him, wanted him so much, from the moment they'd met. Only her paranoia that Julian might find out had held her back. If he ever guessed... Maxine pushed the awful thought from her mind.

But later, as she sat behind the wheel of her silver-grey BMW, a flush of sexual contentment still colouring her re-done face, the fear stabbed at her again.

She knew what Julian was capable of where his ego was at stake. She knew his desire for revenge would stem, not from any sense of moral outrage or possessive jealousy, but from his fury at having been made a cuckold. That another man, a young and handsome man, was making a fool of him, would drive him into a demonic rage. Maxine shuddered at the thought.

That was why there had never been anyone in Australia before. She had never dared.

It had been easier in London and in Europe. Maxine's gleaming red lips curled as memory returned: the eager, energetic barman at the Savoy – they'd spent all his off-duty hours in her bed until Julian had arrived to join her; the young, divinely handsome cab-driver in Rome – there, she'd had two glorious weeks of freedom with shopping as the perfect excuse.

As she fought her way through the late afternoon traffic, a series of faces, hands, mouths, and other memorable parts of young men's anatomies, filtered through her mind.

But, she fast-forwarded to the present stud, Barry Francis was the best of them all. So gentle and tender, so concerned for *her* pleasure. So different, she thought darkly, from the increasingly spasmodic ravages of her husband whose swift and violent assaults left her sore and dissatisfied.

She tightened her diamond-thick fingers around the steering wheel. It was risky, but she wasn't going to give Barry up. What she and Barry had together was something special.

Five minutes after Maxine Crane had left there was no sign of her ever having been in Barry Francis' apartment. He had quickly washed the sticky stain of lipstick off the long-stemmed glass, removed a strand of frosted blonde hair from the quilted bedhead, and changed the rumpled cotton sheets on the king-size bed.

Wrapped in a blue and gold kimono, joint in one hand, a glass of Chivas Regal in the other, Barry could now concentrate on the positive side of his acquaintance with his departed guest.

He had known Maxine Crane almost five months. They had met at a gallery opening – the latest over-priced crap by the current whizz-kid of the Big Money set. Openings were Barry's favourite hunting grounds. Rich randy women thick on the ground, all aching for flattery, attention... and sex.

It was their eyes that gave them away, never fixed on the person being talked to, never still for a moment, but darting greedily around the room, looking through the gays and concretely married men as if they didn't exist, to settle on men like himself: good-looking, sexy – and unattached.

Then followed their pathetic attempts to chat him up, to assure themselves at close quarters of his worthiness. Nine times out of ten, Barry passed the test. They inevitably forgave the slight limpness of last season's dinner shirt, the non-Italian cut of a well-filled suit.

Charming, responsive, and witty, Barry watched the light start to shine in their hard, rapacious eyes and a cosy feeling crept over him at the thought of the treats and gifts to come. Meals in expensive restaurants; a dozen new shirts; an outrageously priced table lamp he'd 'admired for so long'; and, if he was really lucky, a week or two at some Pacific hideaway.

But in Maxine Crane, Barry knew, he had cracked the jackpot. It was thanks to her that he was now living thirty floors up in one of Sydney's most expensive apartment blocks, able to take his breakfast in full view of the Bridge and Harbour.

Less than a month after they'd met, she'd found him this place. 'Much more discreet, darling,' she'd smiled, the day they'd visited it together. 'No-one but no-one I know lives on the North Shore.'

Barry hadn't complained. For one thing, the place was a great improvement on his cramped if well-addressed previous apartment. And he was every bit as keen as Maxine to keep their affair under wraps. After all, he gave a dope-lazy smile, why kill the oh-so-golden goose?

For a moment, he frowned. Yes, it would pay to be careful. For if Maxine's paranoia had taught him anything, it was that Julian Crane would be much less inclined than a lot of other husbands to turn a blind eye to his wife's extramarital activities – despite, according to Maxine, Crane's own predilections in that department. But, Barry raised an eyebrow, Anthea James? Maxine had to be wrong there. He couldn't quite picture Australia's number one female paragon in that situation.

THE PHONE CALL to her home that evening took Anthea completely by surprise.

'I hope you don't mind my calling you like this, Anthea. I managed to persuade Matt to give me your private number.' The voice was as calm and precise as it had been over their lunch together.

Anthea's breath caught in her lungs. 'I – I – Of course not,' she finally managed, her hand suddenly clammy around the receiver.

Vaguely, she was aware of David's voice, of his attempts to win her back to the Bicentennial project. But now her shock was mingled with an overwhelming fury. How dare Matt give out her private number! How dare he put her in this position! She had a good mind to –

Abruptly, she cut David off in mid-sentence.

'No! I'm very sorry but...' As quickly and forcefully as she could, she explained: her political interests, the heavy work schedule she envisaged...

When she'd finished, David was silent for a moment. Then, in a voice as mild and courteous as before, he said, 'Well, I'm real sorry I can't persuade you to change your mind this time, Anthea. Perhaps when your other commitments are less pressing I'll be able to tempt you into doing something with us.' There was a query in his tone, a hint of something else in his mind, but Anthea barely noticed. She murmured a non-committal reply, her hand trembling as she replaced the receiver. Her relief was enormous. What she would never have admitted to herself was the overwhelming sense of loss and despair that tinged that relief.

THEIR MEAL WAS simple – omelette and salad, followed by cheese and fresh fruit. Anthea knew that after days spent eating hotel food, Alex would be more than ready for something plain and unadorned.

'Delicious.' Alex kissed the back of her neck as he helped carry their empty plates through to the kitchen. Anthea smiled. 'I'll make the coffee. You go and sit down, darling.'

She had seen the fatigue in Alex's face while they were eating. He'd been back from Manila only twenty-four hours, after a week away. As yet they hadn't talked about his trip. Anthea knew only that he had been looking for further leads on Asian links with Australian organized crime.

She never pushed Alex to tell her anything. By its very nature Alex's investigation had to be as covert as possible. His right-hand man was Ted Raynor, a retired Special Branch detective, upon whose network of contacts on both sides of the law, Alex relied heavily. Anthea respected the privacy of the work on which both men were engaged.

Yet now, as she carried the pot of freshly-brewed coffee through to the living room, Anthea sensed Alex's need to talk. He had been vague and preoccupied all evening; his tension was obvious.

Replacing the cup of too-hot coffee on the table by his elbow, Alex turned to her and frowned.

'You know, Anthea, I'm so close, so close to cracking this whole set-up.' His voice was low and intense. 'And the Asian racket's the dirtiest of the lot. Bloody slavery in the twentieth century, that's what I found in Manila, Anthea.'

Anthea listened in silence, her eyes fixed on Alex's tight, troubled face.

'They're bringing young Filipino girls out here,' Alex went on, 'innocent naive girls, totally unaware of what they're getting themselves into. They're well enough educated – computer workers, hairdressers, that sort of thing; and what gets them in is the money. Seven or eight hundred dollars a week they're told they can earn in Australia. Well, they jump at it, don't they? And who can blame them – coming from families with five or six kids all scratching for enough to eat?'

In exasperation, he ran a hand through his thick blond hair.

'The organizers at the Manila end arrange the lot – passports, visas, false references, airline tickets – and always for a group of girls at a time. They come in as tourist groups, you see, cultural clubs. It costs, of course – maybe three or four thousand dollars each. But if a girl doesn't have the money – and most of them don't – then she's told it can be arranged on credit; she can pay it back from her earnings.'

Alex shook his head. 'Nothing's left to chance, Anthea. Nothing. The girls arrive in Sydney as a "consignment", always on specific days, and they're told exactly which entrance gates to use for passport clearance. Then, as soon as they're through, they're made to surrender all travel documents, passports, airline tickets, and are taken to the apartment where they're going to live.

'But,' Alex's eyes had gone hard, 'they're not here to work in their usual professions, Anthea. Oh no... These girls end up working as prostitutes in the various establishments of Australia's major crime bosses.'

Abruptly, he picked up his cup and took a mouthful of coffee before going on. 'And there's no hope of escape. The girls are told that if they attempt to break their "contract" with the organization, they face prosecution as illegal immigrants because they've entered Australia on forged documents. And the threat of their families at home finding out the nature of their activities is enough to silence them. For girls like these, such exposure would be an unbearable shame.'

Alex sighed in frustration and leaned his big frame back against the sofa. 'It all works by fear, Anthea. The girls are prisoners, they never get out, it's just work and sleep. Some of them work fifteen hours a day, and are beaten up if they don't make their quota of clients. And you know what else?' Alex turned bitter eyes to Anthea who sat motionless beside him, her face pale except for two bright red spots on either cheek. 'They go home broke after all that, Anthea – the organization rakes it in and these poor bitches go home with barely a cent.'

For a moment Alex said nothing. When he spoke again his voice was cold and exact. 'I'm going to nail them, Anthea. I'm going to nail the bastards behind all this.'

Later, with Alex sleeping peacefully beside her, the images he had evoked returned to torment Anthea. She thought of the girls he had spoken of, imprisoned and helpless, forced through fear of violence and disclosure to be sexual slaves.

And she thought too of Nan. Of the justifications she had offered for the highly lucrative business she had run for so long. *Her* girls, Nan had said, had *chosen* to do what they did; for them it was an escape rather than an imprisonment, a chance to gain the security and independence they would never otherwise have found.

But, as she lay next to a lover whom she met on free and equal terms, Anthea knew, as she had always known, that no justification was possible for such exploitation. Without self-respect, security and independence would never be enough.

Just before midnight, Alex awoke and dressed. He kissed Anthea warmly and left to return to his own apartment. He had never stayed a full night with her; she had never extended the invitation and he had never asked. Their relationship had unwritten rules, agreed to by silent mutual consent.

They were good friends, there for each other when the need arose. But Anthea had no intention of ever again stepping over the bounds of friendship into the dark destructive territory of love. And even sex, she found, could be kept exempt from deeper implications. Alex was a skilled, considerate lover, and she took pleasure in the weight of his body upon hers, the feel of his skin against her own; it fulfilled the elemental need of making contact with another human being in a tough and lonely world.

But tonight there had been too many distractions; not merely Alex's disturbing disclosures, but the torment of memory that recalled a time when sex had released something hidden deep within her soul, when it had been more than an elemental fusion of two bodies.

As she heard the sound of Alex's car fade into the night, Anthea was glad to be alone.

IT WAS AFTER 10p.m. when David got home. The smell of fresh paint greeted him as he opened the front door and he smiled in silent approval. The painters were almost finished; and outside, the garden was slowly being restored to its former splendour. His father's house was again becoming the place he remembered.

He threw his briefcase and the handful of mail on the living room sofa and, shrugging off his jacket, went through to the kitchen to get himself a drink. God he needed it, he thought, pouring the cold frothy beer into a long fluted glass. He'd had one hell of a month. First, the rearranging of the Bicentennial project made necessary by Anthea James' abrupt withdrawal, and then, on top of that, the frantic workload required to finalize his takeover of the Lewis Armand media network.

About three years ago David had had the first hint of Armand's desire to sell. Feelers had been put out and, mainly because of his own Australian connection, David had been interested. Not, he thought, taking a grateful swallow of beer, that Philip Yarrow would have been. His stepfather had been dead now for over three years, but the older he'd become, the less Philip Yarrow had been able to grasp the growing global nature of the media structure. For Yarrow senior, America had been the only territory of interest.

But, David mused, loosening his tie, media concerns these days were no longer mere national affairs. Look at Rupert Murdoch's empire. Not that he had the acquisitive drive of a Murdoch; it had been the chance to establish himself in the country of his birth that had attracted him to the Armand deal.

The negotiations for the sale had dragged on and on, but now, at last, and for a price that suited him, he had acquired Armand's set-up: a national television network, major newspapers in three States, and a handful of low circulation magazines. No matter how hard Armand's lawyers had tried to dress it up, the company had been ailing on all fronts. But it was exactly that challenge that David was looking forward to. The deal would be made public in a week's time and then he could settle down to a closer review of the whole set-up. He would cut back where necessary, establish more aggressive marketing techniques, search for more viable options.

He sipped happily at his beer. Everything had worked out as he'd hoped. And now he had organized it so that for the next three or four months at least, he could focus his attention on consolidating his newly acquired Australian interests. This was the opportunity he'd been looking for. A reason – beyond merely emotional ones – to entice him into spending more time in his home town.

He went through to the sitting room and, putting down his glass, placed an early Carly Simon record on the stereo. As the strong sensual voice filled the room, David sat down on the long blue sofa and leant back, his eyes closed. The sound of the music was infinitely soothing.

But still his thoughts kept straying back to the business at hand. It was a shame, he mused, that he hadn't been able to persuade Anthea James to work with him. She was the name, the personality, he needed to add power and punch to a revamped network. He knew from Kelso that she was not tied in to the Crane organization; her contract there seemed deliberately flexible. Exactly what he would have expected of a woman of Anthea James' acumen. Maybe there was still a chance that he might be able to woo her...

The image of those dark intelligent eyes, that shining golden hair, came into his mind – not for the first time. Their meeting had been short and businesslike, but Anthea James had made a lasting impression on him. He had sensed her strength and reserve; the beguiling blend of power and femininity had struck him with an overwhelming force. And the same disturbing reaction had been there even during their brief telephone conversation. Later, trying to analyse it, he had found it difficult to say just what chord in himself Anthea James had managed to touch.

For it was a long time since any woman had evoked such a powerful response in him. He was aware that his own reserve and aloofness was off-putting, if not downright insulting, to a lot of women. A few had been brave enough – or angry enough – to tell him as much. Yet while he could sympathise with their reactions, David knew that he was powerless to change. Somehow he found it safer to avoid the emotional chaos, the vulnerability, that went with any developing relationship between a man and a woman.

Expressionless, David sipped at his drink. He had loved once, completely and deeply, but the memory of that time, that person, was something he had ruthlessly repressed. No longer could he conjure in his mind the face of the girl he had loved; he had worked hard to blank out the bitterness and sense of betrayal...

The music came to an end and suddenly David caught sight of the mail he had tossed beside his briefcase. With one quick swallow he finished his drink and reached to the far end of the sofa to pick up the four envelopes he had thrown aside earlier.

It was the pale grey envelope that brought a frown to his face. It carried American postage and was addressed in a bold familiar scrawl.

Kelly...

Slowly, and without enthusiasm, he slit open the envelope.

'DAD, YOU'RE HOPELESS!' Kelly Delamar's laugh rang out across the court as her powerful serve easily evaded the desperate lunge of the thick-set, balding man at the opposite side of the net.

Oscar Delamar grinned as he wiped the sweat from his brow.

'You're just too good for me, honey. Or *I'm* just too old for you.' His daughter had won and he followed her off the court.

It was a typical Californian day – blue sky and warm – and all around them could be heard the soft plunk of tennis balls as the designer-dressed members of the Bel Air Country Club spent Sunday morning worshipping in their own special way. But, Oscar Delamar noted with his usual pride, even the most dedicated male player was momentarily distracted from his game by the sight of Oscar's tawny-haired daughter.

As they sat in companionable silence, shaded by a pink cabana and sipping long glasses of freshly-squeezed fruit juice, Oscar stole a sidelong look at his twenty-year old only child. He took in the mist of toffee-coloured hair curling softly to her shoulders, the wide intelligent hazel eyes, the strong slim body in the short tennis dress that showed off her long tanned legs to perfection.

There was no doubt about it, he thought, the older Kelly got, the more beautiful she became. Yet, more and more these days, Oscar's paternal pride and delight were tempered with a sense of fear. He worried a lot about Kelly's future; the path she would end up taking in life. He wanted the best for his only child; he wanted her to find the same depth of love and security that he and Eve had shared.

For the hundredth time, Oscar cursed the accident that had so prematurely robbed him of his adored wife. A drunken driver had changed all their lives forever. Kelly had been just ten at the time, and her grief at the sudden tragic loss of her mother had been heartbreaking to see.

In trying to make it up to her, Oscar knew he had spoilt her, indulged her too much and too often. He sighed inwardly. Eve would have been stronger he was sure. Much as she had loved their long-awaited daughter, she had been strict and uncompromising when the occasion had demanded. And a child needed that sort of discipline. Oscar knew there would be times, as Kelly grew older, when life would fail to go exactly as she wished. A prickle of unease ran through him as he raised his glass to his lips. How then, would his wilful headstrong child cope with the normal obstacles and setbacks of life, from which he had been guilty of shielding her for so long?

Oscar had been well able to indulge his daughter's every whim. In the twenty-five years since the shaky launch of Ensemble Publishing, the company had grown into a massive publishing conglomerate. He had worked hard; his gambles had paid off, and he had been amply rewarded for his efforts. When at last he and Eve had had a child on whom to bestow their good fortune, they had been ecstatic.

Pampered and fussed over since she was a baby, educated at exclusive private schools, her vacations spent in Europe, Aspen, or Hawaii, Kelly Delamar had led a privileged existence.

Eve's sudden death had been a terrible tragedy, but Oscar had done everything in his power to help his young daughter come to terms with her loss.

Kelly was the centre of Oscar's life and in the eight months since she'd started college, he'd missed her very much. So today was a special pleasure. With Kelly at home for the short Easter break, Oscar was determined to make the most of her company.

'Dad,' Kelly's voice interrupted his rambling thoughts, 'did you know that David was going to be away *all* this time?' Her voice was casual but her eyes didn't meet her father's; they stayed fixed on the straw she was stirring round and round in her empty glass.

Oscar answered carefully. 'I guess he's got a lot to keep him busy, honey. And it's a long time too since he's been back in Australia. Not since his father died.' Oscar always found it difficult to think of David as anything but Philip Yarrow's natural son. He had so many of Philip's traits – the same strength of character, the same sense of purpose and determination to succeed.

But these thoughts were at the back of his mind now as he kept his eyes on his daughter's strangely withdrawn face. It was a long time before Kelly spoke; then, eyes still avoiding his, she said with studied nonchalance, 'I thought he might have been home for Easter.'

Oscar Delamar knew then that she still hadn't got David out of her system.

Later, at home, immersed in the warm pulsing froth of his spa bath, Oscar couldn't quite relax. He thought again of Kelly. He didn't want her to make a fool of herself with David. Or to waste her life yearning after a man she could never have. For certainly, Oscar thought, David had done nothing to encourage the girl. Her attentions, he was sure, made David uncomfortable.

Oscar sighed as he stepped out of the tub and dried his nut-brown aging body on the thick white towel. His daughter's continuing obsession with David disturbed him more than he cared to admit.

Kelly had known David all her life, ever since Oscar's business relationship with Philip Yarrow had developed into a close personal friendship. But Kelly had been a baby while David had already been in college, and as she had grown up none of them had seen the danger.

'Next to daddy, you're my very very favourite man, David,' she would exclaim as she climbed on his knee and looked with wide devoted nine year-old eyes into the fond, amused face of her father's friend. 'I'm going to marry you when I grow up.'

It was a comment she was to repeat often as the years passed, and Oscar blamed himself for not seeing what was happening.

In the pastel peacefulness of her own bedroom, Kelly was finding it difficult to concentrate on the book she held in her hands. It was John Updike's *Couples*, a set text for her Lit. 2 course and, much as she normally enjoyed Updike's work, this afternoon it couldn't hold her attention.

Still restless, she stood up from her bed and walked out onto the wrought iron balcony that overlooked the lush green lawns of her father's Bel Air estate. She had been looking forward to these few days at home; to see her father of course, but hoping too that David would be back. She had written to him – twice. Short, friendly notes 'just to say hi'. But the one noncommittal postcard she'd received in reply had been disappointing.

With a deep sigh, Kelly turned back into the room and disconsolately threw herself across the bed. She worshipped David. She always had. No-one else could match him in her eyes.

She'd had boyfriends of course but their bragging, their uncouthness, their lack of sophistication soon irritated her.

There was the call yesterday from Greg Altmann. They'd dated each other for a short time before she'd left for college. Greg had wasted no time in getting in touch with her once he'd known she was back home for the Easter vacation.

Tall, blond, and handsome, Greg was the twenty-two year-old over-indulged son of one of Hollywood's leading producers. He had done his best to coax her into accepting his dinner invitation.

'C'mon, Kelly. Just a nice quiet table for two at Le Dome and later we can catch up with the gang at Roxy's.'

The gang. Kelly shuddered as she remembered one of her last dates with Greg Altmann. They had driven up the coast to Pacific Palisades and the multi-million dollar home belonging to the father of one of Greg's friends. The party had been well underway. On a stage set up next to the enormous free-form swimming pool a well-known rock band had been belting out its latest hit while close to a hundred doped-out kids did their best to destroy the exquisite home and gardens.

Recalling that occasion it had been easy for Kelly to knock back Greg Altmann's invitation.

Kelly knew that her father worried about the dangers that the Californian youth culture presented to his only daughter. It was one of the reasons he had been particularly pleased when Kelly had been accepted into the prestigious college in Boston. But while California had its own particular problems, it was the stifling snobbery of the East Coast that Kelly found hard to handle.

Boston boys, once they had managed to overlook her Californian origins, took her home to stately houses in Beacon Hill to be vetted by Mother. Over sherry, or a fine porcelain cup of Darjeeling, these elegantly dressed Daughters of the Revolution would look her sharply up and down. Did the girl in front of them have the necessary qualifications to be allowed an introduction to the clan? For it was obvious that Mother made the final choice; and the blue-blazered sons watched anxiously for her response.

No, Kelly shook her head, there had been nothing in those young men either to compare with David.

She was aware of her father's unspoken opposition to her infatuation with David. She realized her father was hoping that at college she would be distracted by someone nearer her own age. But, Kelly sighed again rolling over onto her back, it was David and David alone she wanted.

She smiled to herself as she remembered the last time she'd seen him. They had dined together at Chasens the evening before her return to college after the short Christmas vacation. Her father had meant to be there too, but an unscheduled meeting had delayed him in Chicago. So it had been just the two of them.

She'd felt like a princess, walking into the foyer on David's arm. As they made their way to the table, she'd been only too aware of the envious looks in other women's eyes. It had been wonderful to have David all to herself; a rare enough occurrence over these last few months. Nearly always it was the three of them: David, her father, herself. On other occasions she had to share him with big noisy groups at the Marina Club or at tennis parties.

But that night – Kelly's eyes shone at the memory – David's attention had been focused entirely on her. As they'd eaten the chilli steaks for which the restaurant was rightly famous, the conversation had been general: college, David's business, his imminent trip to Australia. It was only when Kelly had tried to broach more personal matters that David's reticence had been obvious.

Kelly sighed. She was certain it was merely the difference in their ages that accounted for David's reluctance to take their relationship further. Hadn't the kiss she'd given him when he'd dropped her home that night, proved that she was a grown-up woman, available and ready to share his life in every way?

CHAPTER FIFTEEN

WITH a sigh of fatigue, Anthea switched off her typewriter. The article hadn't been easy to write; she was treading in dangerous waters and had to be careful of her facts. But she had been determined to put a feature together as soon as possible. Now, before giving it to her editors, she would check it with Alex. What she had written was based on the information he had given her and she wanted to be extra sure that she had distorted none of the facts.

Perhaps they might get together this evening, Anthea thought, putting the finished article in a plain Manila folder. The subject was too important for there to be any delays. She wanted this piece published as soon as possible.

She stood up, pulled the blue wool dressing gown tighter around her and moved to the window that overlooked her back garden and the water beyond. She loved this time of day. The streets silent, the dew fresh on the lawn, and the chorus of hungry birds as the pale blush of dawn edged over the pewter sky.

She had written some of her best articles early in the morning. And the piece she had just finished, on the Asian prostitute racket in Australia, was among the very best of her efforts. And, why not? thought Anthea cynically, turning away from the window. Her passionate views on prostitution had been formed long ago and at disquietingly close quarters...

Downstairs in the kitchen she switched on the coffee maker and made herself toast. As she buttered the crisp warm bread, Anthea's thoughts turned to the more immediate future.

In less than two months she would be facing the Action Party pre-selection committee in preparation for the forthcoming by-election. Given the weight of support promised her by some of Sydney's most prominent figures, she was fairly certain that her candidature was assured. She wasted little time contemplating the machinery of support and influence; the system, she was sure, was no dirtier or cleaner than most. The seat to be contested was a marginal one but once her selection was confirmed, Anthea was determined to put every effort into winning.

A sense of power and anticipation gripped her as she sat in the silent kitchen. She was about to get the chance she'd been waiting for. The encounter with David had been a close call but she had side-stepped the immediate danger. Soon – a tremor ran through her at the thought – David would be out of the country and the last possible threat to her ambitions removed. David Yarrow would be out of her life.

Just for a moment, emotions so long unacknowledged fluttered into life. Then, abruptly, Anthea stood up and let herself out of the house. Shivering in the crisp autumn air, she picked up the pile of newspapers from the glistening lawn. Her cover-to-cover survey of the day's news was a ritual – and a necessary one – for someone in her profession.

The item received a brief mention on the front page of the *Sydney Morning Herald* and detailed coverage in the business section.

Anthea's breath quickened as she read: 'American Giant Buys Up Armand in Major Media Deal... Rumours of a takeover bid for the Armand media network were confirmed late last night by Mr David Yarrow, managing director of the major American media company AMN. Mr Yarrow, at present in Australia, has completed negotiations for the purchase of Armand Australia, and has plans for a major shake-up of the ailing network...'

Later, as she stood under the warm spray of the shower, Anthea finally felt released from the turmoil that had gripped her since she'd read the morning's newspapers.

Drawing on those inner reserves which had never yet failed her, she accepted the facts calmly. She would waste no more time worrying about David's continuing presence in Sydney. They had met once; he had shown no sign of recognition. She would not let groundless fears sap her energies or distract her from attaining the dream she had carried inside herself for so long.

SELENA, ANTHEA'S HOUSEKEEPER, arrived just as Anthea was leaving the house.

'Can you put together one of your wonderful paellas, Selena? I may have company this evening.'

'Yes, Miz James,' the petite dark-eyed girl answered quietly. 'I will do that.'

But, as Anthea zipped up her briefcase, the girl did not move away. Sensing Selena's hesitation, Anthea raised an enquiring eyebrow. 'Is there anything else, Selena?'

The girl fixed dark, troubled eyes on Anthea. 'Oh, Miz James, I do not know who else to talk to about my problem. I – ' She broke off, lips quivering, the tears brimming in her eyes. With a puzzled frown, Anthea put down her briefcase and led the unhappy girl back through to the kitchen and sat her at the table.

As she pulled up a chair opposite, she could see the girl struggling for control. 'Now, Selena,' Anthea's voice was low and reassuring, 'tell me the problem.'

An unwanted pregnancy was her immediate thought. She knew that Selena had come to Australia four years ago, after her marriage to an Australian. But since then the relationship had ended. If Selena *was* pregnant, it was a serious problem for a staunchly Catholic Filipino.

But Anthea was way off target.

'Miz James, it is my cousin, Beatrice, I am worrying about.' Selena's voice shook as she spoke and her hands twisted nervously in her lap. 'We are very close, very good friends. She – she was to come to Australia and I was very happy. But,' she turned fearful eyes to Anthea, 'it is now eight weeks since she has left the Philippines and I have no word that she is here. And her family at home, they have had no letters. It is as if – as if Beatrice has disappeared into the air.

'Please Miz James,' Selena's worried eyes held a plea as they looked at Anthea, 'you can help me to find my cousin?'

As she reassured the frightened girl, a cold knot of alarm tightened in Anthea's stomach.

'ALEX, IT ALL points in the same direction.' Anthea's tone was insistent as they sat together after dinner, on her living room sofa. 'From what Selena could tell me – and it wasn't a lot – it seems almost certain that the cousin has been trapped into the same sort of deal you've been investigating.'

Anthea counted the facts off on her fingers. 'Landing herself a "very well paid job" as she told her family; everything – airline tickets, visas, references – organized for her; and now, eight weeks later, not a word of the girl's whereabouts.'

Anthea spoke with conviction. 'The facts fit, Alex.'

Slowly, Alex nodded his blond head. 'I think you're right, Anthea. And I also think that the time has come to blow the top off all this. What you've done here,' he tapped the typed sheets that lay on the coffee table in front of him, 'is going to be our opening volley.' His grey eyes narrowed and met Anthea's dark ones. 'Maybe this sort of up-front attack is just what we need to scare the bastards into making their first false move.'

WITH A SATISFIED smile, Barry Francis replaced the receiver and checked the time on the brand new Rolex he wore on his left wrist – a present from Maxine.

9.55 p.m. Half an hour they'd said. By this time of night the traffic on the Bridge shouldn't be a problem. But still, he couldn't waste time. Finding a park at the Cross was always a bastard. Still, Barry grinned to himself, business was business.

In his bedroom, he picked up the heavy pottery lamp that stood on the small bedside table and, carefully unscrewing the base, pulled out the tightly wrapped parcel. He'd already cut the stuff to buggery and now, twice its original weight, it lay wrapped and waiting – ten grams in each separate plastic envelope.

It was one of these that he slipped into the inside pocket of his jacket. Then, wrapping up the parcel again, he replaced it in its hiding place.

Dealing – nothing too big – was Barry's sideline. It kept the wolf from the door between women. He'd had only one conviction recorded against him, and that was four years ago for a shitty little hunk of hash. A quick court appearance, a fine, and he was free to keep servicing his regular customers.

He'd got into coke two years ago. A much more lucrative affair. Tonight's bit of business for instance would put two thousand bucks in his pocket.

Barry smiled again as he switched off the lights and left the apartment. One hundred percent profit. Not a bad margin for half an hour's work.

*

Barry felt a moment's nervousness as he followed the man into the darkness of the lane behind the busy main street and its glaring neon lights. The Cross never slept. Pimps, prostitutes, pushers, and the hordes of gaping tourists, kept the main strip jumping at all hours.

'Not here,' the thickset, well-dressed man with the blond corrugated hair had said, after they'd met as arranged in a booth at the local McDonalds. Fair enough, Barry had thought, the bloke's being extra careful. But it wasn't until he was out of the door and following his customer – not one of his regulars – into a dark side street, that he'd felt a flicker of fear. Christ, he wasn't about to be rolled, was he?

But, even as the thought occurred to him, the blond man had stopped and was waiting for him not ten steps ahead. Barry relaxed.

He was within spitting distance of the man when he felt the first blow. It came from behind, a cruel thump to the right kidney. Then the three of them were on him, and Barry screamed as he fell to the hard cold bitumen under a rain of blows. Leather smacked savagely into his ribs, crunched his nose, filled his mouth with blood.

Feeling as if every bone in his body had been broken simultaneously, Barry was vaguely aware of a hand hauling him up by the collar of his jacket, of another reaching for his inside pocket. Then a voice hissed in his ear: 'Keep right away from Maxine Crane, pal, or next time you'll really have something to scream about.'

The hand released him suddenly and Barry fell backwards with a head-splitting thud. It was all over in two minutes.

'NO, ANTHEA!' JULIAN Crane glared at her, eyes blazing. 'I said drop it, and I *mean* drop it.' Breathing heavily, he tapped the large onyx ring on his left hand against the rich polished surface of the desk that separated them. 'We've published the one article; you've dealt with the same goddamn topic on the air – and that's enough. The whole of bloody Australia isn't interested in what happens to a handful of money-hungry Asian birds.'

A dangerous light filled Anthea's eyes. 'What you call a handful Julian is closer to a thousand women. And, as I've tried to make clear through the means available to me, these women are nothing less than prisoners. They're *forced* into this game.'

Her lips tightened. 'I want to follow up on this, Julian. It's something I feel very strongly about. And besides, whoever's behind this racket is involved in all the other aspects of organized crime in this country. They've got to be, to run something as massive as this. Drugs, police, customs, judicial corruption – they're all part of it.'

Anthea stood up, her face pale, and looked down at her employer. 'Harassing and exposing is what the press is all about, Julian. It can't be seen to be muzzled in cases like this.'

She waited for Julian Crane to reply but for a long time he merely held her eyes with a hard appraising look. When at last he spoke his temper was once more under control, his voice low and intense.

'What you have to remember, Anthea, is that you're dealing with dangerous people, powerful people, who could stamp on you, get rid of you, more quickly than you'd believe possible.' He paused, his eyes still fixed on hers. 'You're aiming for a political career, Anthea – this isn't the way to go about it.'

Slowly spinning the green leather chair around so that his back was to her, the view of Sydney before him, he pronounced firmly and unambiguously, 'Drop it, Anthea. It's a dead duck.'

Face set, Anthea strode down the corridor to her own office. She closed the door, something she rarely did, and sat down at her desk to master the emotions aroused by the encounter with Julian. She was seething with fury. Fury at her impotence in the face of Julian's adamant refusal to allow her to follow up on a subject about which she felt so strongly.

They had had their share of disagreements in the past over editorial policy, but never before had Julian been so utterly intractable on an issue. Why he was being so stubborn, Anthea could not imagine. There was, contrary to Julian's opinion, very strong public interest in the topic. Both her newspaper article and the radio segment she'd done, had elicited a wide-ranging response. As a result she had planned to invite the Consul-General for the Philippines to appear on the *'Female Factor'*. But, Anthea's eyes darkened, Julian had vetoed that.

And then, beneath her feelings of rage and impotence, Anthea became aware of another response to the encounter with her employer. A sense of wariness, of unease. Was she imagining it or had there been a threat implied, some sort of insidious menace behind Julian's seemingly artless words of warning?

For the first time Anthea felt a flicker of doubt about her future.

Disturbed and preoccupied, she was in no mood for her lunch with Matt Kelso. Matt had already apologized for having given David Yarrow her private number, and for Anthea the matter was closed. Now, as the coffee was served, she realized with a small shock that Matt had brought the conversation round to another offer by David Yarrow.

'Look, Anthea,' Matt's tone was earnest, cajoling, 'the bloke's keener than ever for you now that he's taken over the Armand set-up. He knows that he needs a name, a face, to get him rolling. And you're the one he wants.'

Anthea said nothing. Today Matt was affecting the role of country squire in tweed jacket and woollen tie. Leaning on his leather elbow patches, he frowned at her across the table.

'The deal's even better than last time, Anthea. This isn't just a one-off. This time Yarrow wants a personality to get his whole show on the road – and he's prepared to pay heaps to get Anthea James. He understands your political aspirations and he's willing to work around that; as well he's offering you *carte blanche* to follow up on those issues that are so important to you.' Matt leaned closer and lowered his voice conspiratorily, 'Think what a platform that offers you, Anthea. Think of it.'

Watching her face carefully, he leaned back in his chair and added, 'The bloke's bending over backwards to get you, sweetheart.'

Anthea could see the self-interest written all over Matt Kelso's broad, ruddy face. And why not, she thought, it was all a matter of business – and Matt gave value for money. She knew that any contract he'd arrange would ensure her of an excellent deal.

Only there could be no deal, despite the inducements which, in normal circumstances, she'd be crazy to refuse. The offer of complete control, after today's clash with Julian, was hard to resist. But she had no choice.

'No, Matt, I'm sorry. I'm just not interested.'

*

JUST A LITTLE bit drunk from the champagne she'd had at lunch, Maxine parked her car in the visitor's space under Barry's apartment block. She hadn't rung, but it was unlikely that Barry'd be out. He was a late sleeper, and usually spent the day fiddling with his 'work'.

Poor Barry, Maxine thought, pushing the lift button for the thirtieth floor. The two or three canvases she'd seen showed that he had a long way to go before he'd set the art world on fire. Still, she smiled charitably, she admired his perseverance.

She was looking forward to seeing him. The lunch party at Harriet Maddern's had provided her with a fund of amusing gossip that she knew Barry would relish every bit as much as she had. Maxine smiled as the lift hummed upwards. She'd never have dreamt that one of the Bench's most distinguished incumbents might actually be gay...!

The lift doors opened at Barry's floor and as she stepped out Maxine saw with amazement the pile of cardboard boxes, the bulging suitcases, and the stack of stereo equipment that cluttered the entrance to Barry's apartment.

Puzzled and alarmed, she squeezed her way past the assortment of household items and through the open front door. In a far corner of the living room Barry was bent over a carton, filling it with records.

'Barry, what –' With a gasp of horror she broke off as Barry stood up and turned around. His face was a mass of vivid purple bruises, his lips raw and crusted, and his eyes so black and puffy that she could barely see between his lids.

'Barry...' She breathed his name in shock. 'What – what happened?' At the same time she moved towards him, her hand outstretched in an instinctive gesture of comfort.

He swung away from her and Maxine stopped dead.

'Ask your fuckin' husband.' The words came out as a dry rasp from between his swollen lips.

A dreadful coldness gripped Maxine's heart. Her mouth moved but no sound came. At last she croaked, 'You're – you're leaving...?'

A horrible parody of a laugh escaped Barry's lips. 'I can take a hint, baby. Now,' he edged past her, dragging the carton of records into the open doorway, 'will you piss off and let me get on with this.'

CHAPTER SIXTEEN

THE young Asian boy blinked nervously under the burning glare of the arc lights. He had never in his life been in a television studio. But the lady – Miz James – had assured him that his story was very important. She wanted him to tell again – this time in front of the television cameras – how he had come from Manila to search for his sister, Philomena.

Joseph remembered how excited Philomena had been the day she had left for her new job in Australia. She would earn 'very very much money' she had said, and the whole family had been happy. For his father had TB and had not been able to work for a long time. His mother did the laundry for a rich family in a big beautiful house, but they paid her very little. And he, Joseph, stood for long hours in the local market selling cassettes to the tourists – the few who came these days to the Philippines. With another three children at home to be fed and clothed, Philomena's money would help them all.

But, after four months without a word from Philomena, his mother had become very worried. It was then that she had begged and pleaded for a loan from the local moneylender in order to send Joseph to Australia.

Now, ten days later, he had little money left and still had not found his sister. But the Filipino's he had met up with here had made contact for him with the important lady who was, it seemed, also worried about girls like Philomena. 'You must talk to this lady, Joseph,' his new friends had said, 'she can help you.'

But could she? It seemed that she too knew little.

'But you can help, Joseph,' Miz James had said to him at their first meeting. 'If you tell this story on television it will mean that pressure is kept on our government to look for Philomena and all the other Filipino girls who have come here.'

Joseph had been very nervous about doing this, but he had agreed. He had to do everything he could to help find his sister.

'Don't be nervous, Joseph.' Anthea smiled at the skinny dark-haired youth who sat waiting in one of the two chairs set up in readiness for the interview. There was no audience. This was something that Anthea had arranged privately. Her plan was to tape the interview then show it to Julian in the hope that he would see its value and allow her to put it to air.

She felt sure that the audience appeal of this boy's story would convince Julian of its worth even if, ethically, he had little commitment to the subject.

While reluctant to fill the boy in on the details as she knew them, Anthea had urged him to tell his story. As soon as he had agreed, she had booked a studio and a production crew. It was the crew who were now causing the delay. Surely, Anthea frowned as she looked at her watch, they hadn't mistaken the time. They had kept her waiting for fifteen minutes now.

She glanced at Joseph who sat, sweating and ill at ease, under the glare of the lights. He'd be a wreck before they even began.

Her patience at an end, Anthea strode to the wall telephone and called through to Bob Heely, the production manager.

'Bob – it's Anthea. I'm in studio three.' She didn't bother to hide her irritation. 'Look, I had a crew booked to join me here almost twenty minutes ago now and I'm still waiting – what's the hold-up?'

There was a silence at the other end of the line before Bob Heely replied.

'Sorry, Anthea,' the production manager sounded acutely embarrassed. 'They're not available... boss's orders.'

IN A COLD fury Anthea let herself into the house.

The hour she had spent with Julian Crane had drained her both emotionally and physically. Deeply resentful of his undermining not only of her professional integrity but also now of her authority within the network, she had attacked him with passion.

Julian Crane hadn't given an inch.

'Look, Anthea, you seem to forget that I'm the boss here. I employ you and I decide what we follow up and what we don't.'

Pale with rage, the words had slipped spontaneously from Anthea's lips: 'Just what are you scared of, Julian? Who are you protecting?'

Julian Crane's watery blue eyes had gone as hard as chips of ice.

'Be careful, Anthea,' his voice was steely and exact. 'Be very careful... you may not be quite as invulnerable in this town as you'd like to think.'

This time there was no mistaking the threat in both his tone and his words.

A menacing silence fell between them and it was Anthea who broke it, her voice calmer now, her eyes scornful.

'I'm quitting, Julian. Giving notice as from this moment. Freedom of the press is still a viable option outside the Crane Corporation, I'm sure.'

Julian Crane gave a short bark of laughter that contained no trace of humour. 'Oh no, Anthea – you're not quitting. You've got a contract, baby. Walk out of here and you won't be working anywhere in this city for a long, long time. I'll see to that.'

His eyes held hers like a snake watching its prey. 'No, baby, you'll do what I say. And from now on you're on suspension. All programs cancelled until I see fit to run them again.'

For a long moment they stared at each other. Then triumph twisted Julian Crane's pale lips as, without a word, Anthea turned on her heel and left the room.

Now, recalling the scene, Anthea felt the same impotent rage she'd felt in Julian's office.

MATT KELSO THREW his head back and laughed loudly. His bulk seemed to fill Anthea's elegant sofa where he sat, hand clasped round a heavy glass of Scotch.

'Matt,' Anthea's voice was icy, 'I fail to see anything amusing in all this. All I want to know is, can Crane do this to me?'

Amusement still lighting his face Matt Kelso shook his well-groomed head. 'Course he can't, Anthea. Not the way *I* fix contracts. Your contract now has less than six months to run. The way it's set up, it can be broken by either party if negotiations for its renewal have not commenced prior to that final six months.'

Matt grinned cheekily at her over the rim of his glass. 'And from the time David Yarrow started making expensive noises about you, sweetheart, I quietly forgot all about implementing those negotiations, didn't I?'

*

It was late by the time Matt left but Anthea was too agitated to think of sleep.

She had given Matt the go-ahead to draw up a contract between herself and AMN. Predictably, Matt had been delighted. But now, alone in the quiet shadows of her sitting room, Anthea wondered if perhaps she had acted too rashly.

Of course she was getting out of the Crane set-up immediately, but was she crazy to be accepting a job with David's organization?

Forcing her doubts aside she turned her thoughts instead to her fortuitous release from the strictures of Julian Crane's authority. Thank God for Matt – he was worth every cent he made out of her. The restrictions Julian had tried to impose were anathema to her professional and personal integrity. Anthea was convinced that the press had a moral obligation to maintain its focus on the subject of organized crime in Australia; to ensure government reaction by continued investigative reporting.

Why, she wondered again, had Julian leaned so forcibly on her to drop the issue? The rich, she knew, were notorious for protecting their own; but could Julian really be shielding someone involved in something as vile, as incriminating, as this? Or – a sudden chill ran through her as she sat alone in the semi-darkness – was it Julian Crane himself who had something to hide...?

THE DEFECTION OF Anthea James to the newly acquired Australian arm of AMN caused a sensation in the Australian media.

The brief statement released by Anthea did little to explain the mystery of her sudden departure from the Crane Corporation.

'I am looking forward,' Anthea stated simply, 'to the challenge of something new, and to increasing the market share of the network I have joined.'

Her peers and competitors were in little doubt that money had had a lot to do with that 'challenge'.

But in the weeks that followed, other reasons were proposed for Anthea James' change of direction. Over the last couple of years Anthea had never made any secret of her desire for political office. And now the plans were revealed for her new prime time television show, 'Open To Comment', with its focus on topics more politically provocative than those dealt with on the 'Female Factor'. It seemed that Anthea James would be working hard to broaden the base of her electoral appeal.

Among those who analyzed such things it was agreed that Australia's most powerful media personality was still every bit as keen to follow up on her avowed aspirations.

That was of course Anthea's plan – a plan she saw in no way disrupted by Julian Crane's certain withdrawal of support for her bid for office. After all, her political future did not rely entirely on her former employer's patronage. She had, she was sure, other equally influential supporters more than eager to back her.

Meanwhile, ignoring the rumours that raged around her, Anthea directed her energies towards establishing herself at AMN.

At initial executive meetings with David and other senior staff, it was agreed that Anthea, while still contributing a weekly column to AMN's newly acquired daily tabloid, should concentrate on making a strong grab for the ratings with 'Open To Comment'.

As well, David was still keen for her input on the Bicentennial project. Although in the interim, a young up-and-coming male presenter had been signed on for the series, David was eager to adapt the concept to allow for an introduction to the program by Anthea.

He explained his ideas to her at one of their early production meetings.

'With the series being shown internationally, I'd like to use as broad a choice of backgrounds as possible, Anthea. I had thought that maybe your introduction could be shot in Cooktown – it'd be a pleasant change from the over-use of places like Botany Bay and Sydney Harbour which I'm sure will be the popular focus. What do you think?'

He'd looked straight at her then with those intense, clear blue eyes and Anthea had felt something happen in the pit of her stomach.

'I – I think that's a great idea, David.' Through sheer strength of will she kept her voice steady. But there was nothing she could do to still the quickened beating of her heart.

Anthea put her most urgent fears to rest after her second meeting with David. It was obvious that she had nothing to be afraid of. David Yarrow, she was sure, had forgotten that Lenore Hamlyn had ever existed. In his mind, she had done nothing more than fulfil a pressing sexual need. Any deeper feelings their brief affair might have aroused in him would certainly have disappeared with his discovery of the 'truth' – as he saw it – of Lenore's past. And even now, after all these years, the thought of David's impetuous misjudgement of that young innocent girl, sent a wave of bitter sadness through Anthea.

But thoughts like these, Anthea pushed forcibly from her mind as she and David worked more and more closely together. And slowly, as her fears subsided, other feelings took their place.

Observing David at such close quarters, Anthea came to admire and respect his professionalism, his speedy grasp of the Australian media scene, and his easy rapport with staff at all levels. It was the sort of professionalism she had worked hard to cultivate in herself, and found rarely in others.

If other, less distinct, emotions sometimes underlaid this admiration and respect for the man who was now her employer, Anthea fought hard to repress them.

She worked long hard hours to adjust to her new position but relished the freedom she enjoyed at AMN. Released from restrictions placed on her by Julian Crane she was free now to pursue the topic that obsessed her so strongly.

In another scorching article on the extent of organized crime in Australia, Anthea dealt this time with the overwhelming evidence of corruption at all levels within the police and judiciary. The expected fiery rebuttal from the Minister for Police – and the silence from the Bench – only served to give the topic greater impact in the press.

For the opening story of 'Open To Comment' she was able to line up not only the Consul-General for the Philippines, but also the irate Minister for Police, as well as a senior representative of the Customs Department. Anthea knew already that she was guaranteed a red-hot start to her new program when it went to air.

Deeply involved as she was in this change of direction in her career, Anthea had not, however, lost sight of her primary aim.

The only real and effective power, she knew, was to be found in the political arena. And, in the long run, what Anthea wanted was the greatest power of all – the highest office in the land.

But with the time of the pre-selection ballot fast approaching, the continuing silence from those whose support she had been promised, made Anthea uneasy.

She expected to have heard by now from those men she had last met at Crane's dinner party. She was sure that on that evening she had dispelled any lingering doubts they might have held about her value as a candidate. She had demonstrated her comprehensive knowledge of topical issues, as well as a solid understanding of the political process. They had assured her of their enthusiastic support – so why now had she received no further communication?

Eventually, Anthea had no other option but to initiate the contact herself. And it was Harvey Minton who she telephoned. As the Action Party's Federal President Minton had been among those who had attended the dinner at Crane's that evening.

Their telephone conversation was brief and formal. It made Anthea's blood run cold.

'To tell you the truth, Anthea, there's a lot of doubt within the ranks as to the value of this on-going campaign of yours. You've sensationalised a most unsavoury issue, made the government seem incompetent and lax. There's the proper machinery to deal with these things, but it takes time to put into action. I must say Anthea, your repeated demands for an instant response from the government make you look rather politically naive.'

Anthea found it hard to believe what she was hearing. Through gritted teeth she said, 'Harvey, the government has quashed or ignored the findings of two special investigative committees. The only way to force some positive action out of them is via the press. It's my job, Harvey – the only means I have of drawing attention to a very important issue. If I'm fortunate enough to gain office I can use different – hopefully more effective – means of combating a problem of this magnitude. As far as I can see, the whole system needs shaking up.'

There was silence at the other end of the line. Then Harvey Minton gave a long drawn-out sigh, and when he spoke again it was as if he'd already lost all interest in the conversation.

'It was a very ill-judged move, Anthea.'

Struggling to control her temper, Anthea asked bluntly, 'Look, Harvey – just one question: Can I still count on your support?'

Harvey Minton's answer was equally blunt. 'Not while you're so strongly identified with this campaign, Anthea.'

*

Roy had never seen Anthea so angry.

It was Sunday afternoon and they were sitting together on her back verandah catching the last of the sunlight. Roy listened in silence as Anthea told him all that had happened.

'Something smells in all this, Roy.' Her face was tight with anger. 'I'm getting warned off, and I have no doubt it's on Julian Crane's instructions. The message is loud and clear: drop this campaign or the Action Party dumps me.'

Eyes blazing, Anthea turned to Roy. 'Crane is one of the biggest contributors to Party funds, Roy – and that gives him a lot of power. Just the way he likes it. But this time he's using that power in an attempt to destroy me.' Her voice was cold and precise. 'Julian Crane is out to stop me in any way he can.'

Roy looked at Anthea and then said quietly and with utter conviction, 'Crane won't be a problem, Anthea. I'll see to that.'

Roy left soon after but Anthea sat on in the gathering dusk, a frown drawing her brows together as she pondered Roy's enigmatic words. What had he meant? What lever could Roy possibly use against Julian Crane's immense power and influence?

She hadn't expected any practical assistance from Roy. He was merely her confidante – as he had been so often over the years. There was one secret, however, she had never revealed...

Roy was over fifty now and their friendship had lasted the distance. From the time of Nan's death he had always been there when she'd needed him.

His help had been invaluable in establishing the jewellery business that had launched her with such impact on the Sydney scene. Roy had been content to stay quietly and unobtrusively in the background, to allow Anthea alone the glory of the venture's amazing success. Only much later, when Anthea's media career was safely established, had he emerged as the 'new owner' of the Anthea James boutique.

With a sigh Anthea rose, picked up the tea tray and walked back into the dark and empty house. Roy had helped her then; he could do nothing for her now.

Later that evening, as she lay in bed far from sleep, Anthea's thoughts turned again and again to the sudden and unforeseen setback to her plans.

SHADOWS OF POWER

It was now too late to seek support elsewhere. What she had to do – and fast – was win back the confidence of her original backers. Somehow, she and Alex had to make a breakthrough in their investigations; they had to find proof of the connection they were now more and more sure existed between Crane and organized criminal activity in Australia.

AS HE DROVE away from Anthea's that afternoon, Roy knew exactly what he must do. He gave a small humourless smile. Nan, as usual, had been right.

Roy had always been aware of the shrewdness and toughness beneath Nan Reilly's disarmingly amiable exterior. In all the years he had known her, he had never seen Nan come off second best to those ignorant or presumptuous enough to underestimate her. From somewhere up her sleeve, Nan Reilly had always been able to pull an extra ace.

A certain smug satisfaction appeared on Roy's face as he drove slowly through the Sunday afternoon traffic. Now, even from beyond the grave, Nan's canniness was going to ensure that there would be no further setbacks to Anthea's long-held ambitions.

Roy wasted no time. Five minutes after his bank opened on Monday morning, he was in the basement, turning the key that unlocked his safety deposit box.

There, on top of the small pile of essential documents – insurances, leases, deeds, his last will and testament – lay a brown paper parcel securely bound with strong strips of tape.

Roy slipped the parcel into his briefcase, relocked the box and replaced it in its slot. Less than three minutes later he was out on the footpath in the warm autumn sunshine.

It wasn't far to walk to the small block of offices just near Chinatown. He had called Sean earlier and explained what he needed. Sean owed him a favour and Roy knew he would ask no questions.

Trusting himself to the shuddering, antiquated lift, Roy alighted at the fourth floor and knocked on the door displaying the grimy plastic sign – *Favourite Film and Video Services.*

'It's open!'

With a sudden stab of bitterness, Roy recognized the voice of his ex-lover. He pushed open the door and stepped into the two cramped rooms that housed Sean Russell's business.

Film cannisters and video boxes lay in piles on the desktops and chairs in the front room. But Roy barely noticed the disarray. He had eyes only for Sean Russell himself who had risen from behind one of the cluttered desks.

'Roy! Hi...' Holding out his hand, Sean grinned the warm cheeky grin that Roy remembered. It was more than a year now since he'd seen Sean, but the young man's beauty still had the power to affect him.

Sean Russell was in his early thirties with silky, darkish hair and green eyes with long, curling lashes. In his tight-fitting jeans and clinging sweatshirt the perfection of his slim strong body was tauntingly displayed. Roy's heart thudded painfully as he took the younger man's hand in his own. They had been close once; but that was over now.

Studiously avoiding Sean's teasingly flirtatious eyes, Roy sat the briefcase on top of a pile of dusty film catalogues and removed the brown paper package.

'You can have this ready for me today? You're sure?'

'Anything for you, Roy. No hassles.' Sean grinned again, well aware of Roy's discomfort.

At that moment a young man appeared through the doorway leading to the other room. He was in his mid-twenties, shortish, wiry, with thick curly blond hair and smooth pink skin.

'G'day.' He nodded at Roy with casual indifference and Roy understood immediately: the boy's glance implied only too well that he was no competition.

Sean's amusement was obvious. 'Roy, this is Pete. He – ' a perfectly timed hesitation, ' – works with me.'

Roy didn't hang around.

'Call me when it's ready,' he said stiffly, as he closed the door behind him.

CHAPTER SEVENTEEN

ANTHEA saw less of David Yarrow at work than she might have expected – and for that she was grateful. Although she tried hard to ignore the fact, she had to admit to herself that David's presence had a dangerously unsettling effect upon her.

There was, of course, no hint of this agitation in her efficient handling of her daily affairs. But sometimes late at night, when she was alone at home after a day spent in David's presence, a sense of terrible loss would engulf her. Loss of youth, loss of innocence, loss of love. At the same time too she would become conscious of how lonely her life had been; it was a loneliness she had not felt, or admitted to, for many years.

She could not discuss it with Roy or Alex. This was something private, indefinable, and troubling.

Often in these lonely musings, she would allow herself to wonder why David had never married. In all the newspaper profiles that had appeared following his takeover of the Armand organization, there had been no mention of a marriage in his past.

Was it the years he'd spent in a wheelchair, Anthea wondered, that had kept him single? David was a late starter in the cutthroat arena of corporate business – was it the need to prove himself first, which had left no time for women?

Women, Anthea had no doubt, would have found plenty of time for David Yarrow. Surely an enviable prize. And yet, she had been around David long enough to understand the obstacles that might have daunted even the boldest, the most tenacious, of these pursuers.

For pleasant and approachable as he might be with those around him, David was at the same time strangely reserved. He projected a sense of detachment that Anthea could see made both men and women keep their distance. David Yarrow gave the impression that intimacy with another human being was among the least of his requirements.

*

Around 5 p.m. on a cold and dreary Sunday afternoon, Anthea found herself again in a restless, troubled frame of mind. But this time she was driven to do something she hadn't done for over twenty years...

All of a sudden the house seemed oppressively claustrophobic. Those things which could normally distract her – work, books, music – were today of no use in alleviating the heaviness of her mood. The muted ticking of the French engraved clock on the mantelpiece and the moan of the wind through the trees were the only sounds she heard as she sat in the uneasy solitude of her living room.

With a sigh Anthea put down the novel which had failed to hold her attention. She stood up slowly and moved to the window. With a frown, she stared out at the crisp, wrinkled leaves that had drifted across the lawn. What was it that was troubling her, disturbing her so deeply?

In the distance, she caught sight of a ferry buffeting its way through the swell of the Harbour waters and, almost with relief, Anthea realized the source of her agitation. Somewhere in her subconscious had been floating the memory of those Sunday afternoons on the Harbour all those years ago.

Turning abruptly from the window, she went through to her bedroom and pulled on a pair of warm, low-heeled boots and threw a navy cashmere coat over her shoulders.

This was something she had to do, she told herself, her breath quickening at the thought. This would be a catharsis; it would drive away once and for all the demons which, she now was forced to admit, still haunted her; it would banish the memories which for too long she had suppressed and been so afraid to face.

The house was not far away and Anthea decided to walk – as if by physical exertion she could help to purge herself of the madness that raged within her.

She didn't see the car until it was too late. It pulled up not a dozen steps in front of her and Anthea's eyes widened in shocked disbelief as she recognized the man at the wheel.

Before she could move a muscle to flee, David called out: 'Anthea! What a surprise! Are you looking for me?'

She stood as if rooted to the spot, her face ashen; her lips moved but no sound came. She had never dreamt for a moment that David still had any connection with the house.

He was out of the car now and walking towards her. She stammered out an explanation. 'I – no – I was just walking...'

David didn't seem to notice her confusion. 'Well, come on in for a moment. It's too cold to stand out here.'

He held the gate open for her and, in a daze, Anthea found herself doing as he had invited.

As he unlocked the front door David smiled and indicated his damp hair and the salt-stained spray jacket he was wearing.

'Couldn't resist this wind – I'm a sailing freak.' He gave a dismissive shrug. 'It's one of the few sports where my leg's not a handicap.'

He switched on the hall light and led the way to the rear of the house. Feeling as if she were sleepwalking, Anthea followed slowly, her pulse racing as images of her last visit to this house filled her mind.

In the small sunroom off the kitchen, Anthea finally forced herself to speak. 'You – live here?' Her tone was incredulous.

David shot her a curious look. 'Yes, it was my father's home. I lived here as a child. After my father's death I found that I didn't want to sell the place. It needed some work, of course, when I moved in – it had been let for a long time – but it's certainly more pleasant than living in a hotel.'

Anthea's mind went blank; she could think of absolutely nothing to say. For a moment as they stood facing each other in that newly-decorated room, still smelling faintly of fresh paint, an awkward silence fell between them.

It was David who broke it. 'Look, why don't you take a seat, Anthea. Let me get you a drink of something, then if you don't mind I'll take a quick shower before I freeze to death. You don't have to rush away do you?'

Through pale, stiff lips Anthea replied, 'No...'

Later, Anthea sat alone while David was in the shower; the coffee he had made her remained cold and untouched on the table beside her. She felt paralyzed in a limbo of indecision.

Although her overwhelming desire was to stand up and leave the house immediately, at the same time she felt incapable of movement – a barrage of all too vivid memories assaulted her, as the scene of that afternoon so many years ago played over and over in her mind.

Hands trembling, she forced herself to pick up the cup and sip at the stone-cold liquid. This was something she could never have foreseen in her wildest dreams; a staggering impossible perversion of the past.

David reappeared, his hair damp and his face flushed from the shower. Dressed casually in a soft yellow pullover and faded blue jeans, he smiled at her as he sat down on the sofa opposite.

'This sure is a pleasant surprise, Anthea. I've been meaning to get us together – informally, out of office hours, I mean – for quite a while. It's something I like to do regularly with all my senior staff. It's just that getting this whole show on the road has kept me so goddamn busy.'

Anthea heard herself murmur the conventional replies but, alone with the man whom she had once loved so wildly, so desperately, her emotions ran riot.

But, with a superhuman effort, she gave no sign of her inner turmoil. They spoke of her plans for 'Open To Comment,' then discussed their competitors and David's impressions of Sydney.

But Anthea had no wish to push her luck. As soon as it was politely possible, she stood up to leave.

She refused David's offer of a lift and insisted on walking. By now she was in an agony of impatience to be alone, to restore some balance to her chaotic emotions.

'Well, next time we mustn't leave our meetings quite so dependent on chance, Anthea.' David smiled as he picked up the coat she had flung across one end of the sofa. 'Here, let me help you.'

For hours afterwards, Anthea's body burned where his hand had brushed carelessly against her.

'THIS CAME A few minutes ago, Mr Crane – special delivery.'

Julian Crane's secretary, a brusque, grey-haired woman in her late forties, handed the package to her boss. It bore his name and was marked 'Urgent and Strictly Confidential'.

With a frown, Julian took the parcel as he strode into his own office. From its shape he could guess at the contents – a video cassette – and he cursed under his breath.

Shit, this is precisely what he overpaid a whole army of fat-arsed executives to look after: the review of new material. Who the hell had been stupid enough to direct this stuff to him?

He was about to toss the package aside when his fingers felt an added thickness under the paper wrapping.

His frown deepened as his curiosity got the better of him. He picked up the jade-handled paper knife and slit through the broad strips of tape that bound the package.

The envelope, also addressed to himself, was attached to a side of the container. Impatiently Julian tore if off and removed the folded, typewritten note inside.

The message was brief but explicit: 'The evidence contained on this tape should give you very strong reason to restore support for Anthea James' political ambitions, Mr Crane.'

A flicker of alarm crossed Julian's face. What the hell...? Roughly, he ripped the cassette from its container; there was no clue to its contents. Suddenly nervous, he crossed the room and pushed the cassette into the recorder that sat on the long polished teak shelf. What sort of game was some prick playing...?

Julian Crane, white-faced and trembling, soon saw that it was no game.

'*Who* did you say delivered this?' Julian Crane hissed as he stood over the frightened, wide-eyed receptionist.

The girl had never spoken a word to her boss before and to have him confront her now in a raging temper, left her virtually speechless.

'I – it wasn't one of the usual firms,' she stammered in reply. 'No firm at all ac – actually, Mr Crane. He just told me it was urgent that you receive the package as – as soon as possible.'

Three minutes later, the plump brunette reduced almost to tears, Julian Crane had a description of the man who had delivered the cassette. It didn't help at all.

IT WASN'T YET 5.30 p.m. and Maxine was already halfway through her third vodka and lime. Leaning back into the sofa, the television set flickering noiselessly in front of her, Maxine felt the warm, luxuriant heaviness in her limbs as the liquor took its effect.

Thank God for booze. By dinnertime she'd be well and truly loaded, but who gave a shit.

And anyway, she blinked her heavy eyelids slowly, if Julian came home in the same white hot rage he'd turned up in last night, she'd be glad of the protective glow that alcohol provided.

It could never be argued, Maxine brooded, that Julian had the sweetest of tempers, but last night he'd been the angriest she'd ever seen him in all the too long years they'd been married. Whoever or whatever had upset him had done a first class job... and the thought brought her no small degree of satisfaction.

Not, of course, that he'd told her a word about it; Julian barely spoke to her these days if he could avoid it. A sudden bitterness twisted Maxine's flushed, puffy face. Julian Crane was too busy, too important, too powerful, to have time for his pathetic, insignificant wife.

Warm tears of self-pity gathered in the corners of her bloodshot eyes. Christ, why couldn't he have left Barry alone? Why the hell did he have to screw that up for her? Through a drunken haze Maxine could still recall the look on Julian's face when for once she'd stood up to him, dared to defy him.

'What the fuck does it matter to you, Julian! You don't care a shit about me... Why should it matter if I can get it somewhere else!' She'd screamed the words at him, tears pouring down her face.

He'd looked at her then with contempt and loathing, his icy self-control in sharp contrast to her frenzied outburst.

'You're Mrs Julian Crane in this town, Maxine. Remember that. And no bloody toy boy makes a fool out of me.'

The menace in his tone had been unmistakable. 'Go near the bastard again and I'll make sure he's set-up and busted so quickly he'll lose all that pretty charm that sucked you in, baby. It won't last too long behind bars.'

Julian had told her about the drugs of course. But Maxine hadn't cared. That was no concern of hers; all she wanted was to feel Barry's strong young arms around her again, to feel the warm glow of sexual release with someone who'd provided a short moment of pleasure in her shit of a life...

But, Maxine finished her drink with one quick swallow, she

was too frightened of Julian ever to make contact again with Barry. A little shiver ran down Maxine's spine. There was something about Julian that had *always* frightened her.

JULIAN CRANE MADE the call on his private line. It was after seven and his personal staff had left the office. There was no chance he'd be overheard.

As he punched out the number his blood pounded with the same fury that had assailed him for the past twenty-four hours. He wanted time to think, to figure something out. But for the time being at least, the bitch had him where she wanted him.

He cursed the role he had played in Anthea James' climb to the top. It was he who had made her a star, a name, given her the power and influence she now exerted. And, he swore again, it was thanks to him too that Anthea had made the political connections she'd been so openly seeking. He clenched his jaw in rage. That had been the biggest fucking mistake of all.

At the time it had seemed the ideal set-up. Anthea's popularity and widespread appeal had virtually assured her of a speedy climb up the political ladder. He'd been convinced that in Anthea James they'd have the perfect talking head: a passive grateful female who could be manipulated, subtly and expertly from behind the scenes.

Julian Crane's eyes blazed with anger at the extent of his self-deception.

And now he'd have to convince Harvey Minton that Anthea James was back in the running. What a fucking idiot that'd make him look. But, he swore fiercely, the bitch hadn't won yet...

'Hello, Anthea James speaking.' The sound of those warm, modulated tones in his ear made Julian Crane's fury explode.

He spat out the words: 'Okay, Anthea, if you want to play dirty...we all play dirty. I don't know how or where you got it, but sure, that tape puts you back in the race. But remember this, Anthea, as soon as I get my hands on every fucking copy of the thing – and count on it, baby, I will – you'll rue the bloody day you ever took me on!'

He'd slammed down the phone before Anthea could begin to understand what he was talking about.

*

It was the only connection Anthea could think of. That *had* to be it. Something Roy had done was behind that astonishing call from Julian Crane; whatever Roy had done to 'help' had somehow provoked this extraordinary reaction in her ex-boss.

She glanced at her watch. Almost 7.30 Roy would be home from work and preparing one of the Asian meals he enjoyed so much. Unless he had a lover, his routine rarely varied.

Hurriedly she picked up her coat and car keys. She had to know what was going on.

As she backed the white Mercedes into the street, Anthea realized with a sudden chilling flash of intuition that, in some as yet unexplained way, Julian Crane had become a much more dangerous opponent.

For a long moment after the screen in front of her had blanked out to a haze of wavy lines, Anthea sat frozen in horror.

The images she had just seen had lacked clarity and sharpness, but there could be no mistaking what had taken place. The sight of the girl's head lolling lifelessly against the pillow and of Julian Crane's stricken face – younger, plumper, but clearly identifiable – was burned into her memory.

Deathly pale, she turned to Roy who sat motionless beside her, his troubled fearful eyes never leaving her face.

'Did you...' Anthea's voice faltered and she began again. 'You – you knew about this when I began to work with Crane?'

Roy nodded. 'Yes,' he said quietly. 'But that was your first big break, Anthea. I – I didn't want to take that away from you.'

Anthea said nothing. She was remembering Roy's strange lack of enthusiasm at the time when she herself had been so delighted with the offer from the Crane Corporation. Now she understood.

Roy broke the silence. 'Crane came to Nan's place on a number of occasions, Anthea. He was in his twenties, loud-mouthed, rowdy, just starting to make real money. He roughed up the girls and they complained to Nan. Nan warned Crane off, told him to stay away from the place. But Crane just laughed and told her that if she started laying down the rules, he'd tip off the police about her business.

'Well, of course Nan had things under control at the local station.

But there was the danger that Crane would take it higher – anonymously, of course. So Nan couldn't make a fuss. But next time Crane came to the place she gave him the room where she had the camera set up. What Nan wanted to do was catch him in the act – literally – then if he was still up to his old tricks, she meant to produce the film as a threat to keep him away from the place for good.'

Roy's voice became even lower. 'What she hadn't foreseen was that a girl would die before she could get rid of Crane.'

'What – what did Nan do?' Anthea found it almost impossible to dispel the numbness of shock.

'She – well, it was in everyone's interests that the whole thing be hushed up. The girl had just started with Nan – Sheila was her name. She came from somewhere interstate, and if any family ever bothered looking for her we never heard about it. Nan arranged for... the disposal of the body.'

Anthea felt as if her breath had been cut off. She didn't dare speak, couldn't bear to hear herself ask the shocking question that hovered on her lips. How Nan – her Nan – had been able to 'arrange' for something like that.

Roy continued, his eyes turned away from Anthea now as if unable to face the knowledge dawning in her shocked face.

'Crane never knew about the film. Nan kept that; that was her way. She left it with me for safekeeping. Maybe she felt that someday it might be... useful.' Roy's voice faded away.

For a long moment they sat in silence then, abruptly, Anthea stood up. Without looking at Roy she pulled on her coat. 'I have to think about what this means, Roy – alone.'

He followed her to the door, and as he said goodbye his voice held a note of appeal. 'I was trying to help, Anthea. I hoped that this would stop Crane from getting in your way. I never dreamed he'd contact you about it.'

Anthea turned to him. 'You did what you thought best, Roy. I know that.' The pallor still showed on her face but her voice was steady again. 'Only I'm not naive enough to think for one moment that Julian Crane is finished with me. Not now he knows what I've got on him.'

CHAPTER EIGHTEEN

IT was cold in the car without the heater running and Barry Francis pulled up the collar on his leather jacket. He was determined to sit it out. He'd been tailing Crane for days now, waiting every evening – as he was now – across the street from the central city office block that was the headquarters of the Crane business empire. He had still to come up with something; but he'd made a vow to himself that somehow, in some way, he would make Crane pay for what his hatchetmen had done. And Barry knew there was only one way to do that.

The sweet irony of his chosen method of revenge brought a gleam to Barry's eye. He would get back at Crane through the very means by which Crane himself held power: the press.

If you could take Maxine's word for it, Crane was running round all over town. What Barry was after was some scrap of real evidence he could dangle in front of one of the less salubrious tabloids. Even if they might be too wary of libel to actually print Crane's name, the hints could be heavy-handed enough. Crane himself would certainly get the message. Barry grinned. He'd not only get his own back, but a fistful of bucks thrown in for good measure.

He didn't think evidence would be too hard to come by; Maxine had always been sounding off about Crane's affairs. Not, of course, that she'd gone looking for proof herself. In Maxine's position it didn't do to look too closely into such matters. A divorce after all, was not what she had in mind; not when it meant the loss of the wealth, prestige, and social kudos that went with being the wife of one of Australia's richest, most powerful individuals.

No, the way Barry read it, Maxine's game had been to make a lot of noise about Crane's affairs as justification for her own amorous wanderings. Barry's smile widened; he understood perfectly.

When he thought about it, it was really only Anthea James who had got under Maxine's skin, become her real obsession. Maxine had been so sure that Crane had had something going with his biggest star.

But Barry wasn't quite so convinced. Anthea James didn't even work for Crane any longer – not, of course, that that couldn't be a smoke screen for an affair that was still going strong. But Barry didn't think so.

Sure, Australia's media queen was good-looking, sexy even, for a bird on the wrong side of thirty. Yet, somehow, he figured, that wouldn't be Crane's scene. A nice piece of fresh young arse, Barry decided, would be more Crane's style. One of those baby-faced models, perhaps, who would kill to make the cover of a Crane publication.

He grinned to himself in the darkness; an underage sex charge would be just the thing to hang on Julian bloody Crane.

He felt the cramp beginning in his left leg and checked his watch. 7.25. Jesus, it was cold. And he was bloody hungry. He'd give the bastard another ten minutes and then call it a night. He'd had enough.

As he settled back in his seat, Barry thought back over the last couple of weeks. He hadn't come up with a lot. After a couple of days checking out Crane's usual daily routine – departure from home, 8.15; lunch at various expensive establishments; back to the office till late evening – Barry figured that his best bet was to keep an eye on his prey's after-hours movements. Hence his daily vigil. So far he'd found little to excite him.

Only once had he thought he was on to something. One evening around eight he'd followed Crane – who was driving himself this time – to a small, smartish terrace house in one of the back lanes of Woolloomooloo. But the next day when Barry returned to the address he was confronted with a tall, very slim, dark-haired girl in her early twenties, the receptionist it seemed for Anson and Lambert: Importers. At least that's what the sign on the office wall said.

The bird had eyed him with a casual indifference Barry found disconcerting – he was used to a much more enthusiastic reaction from the opposite sex. She answered his questions curtly. – 'Yeah, importers... we don't sell to the public,' – before returning to the magazine that lay open on the desk in front of her.

Barry left. There was no reason to disbelieve her. He only wished later that he'd asked what it was that the firm imported...

Suddenly alert, Barry sat up as Crane's driver pulled up in front of the building. He turned the key in his own ignition as Crane appeared from the revolving doors and slid into the back seat of the Rolls.

But they'd been driving for less than five minutes before Barry saw that Crane was headed for home.

Cursing, he turned out of the traffic in the direction of Bondi where he now lived. Quite a come down from the North Shore exclusiveness provided by Maxine Crane's generosity.

Barry let himself into his cramped two-bedroom flat with its utilitarian brown carpet and its rusty wrought iron balcony that gave no glimpse of the sea. Tired and disgruntled, he went straight to the fridge and poured himself a beer. He was carrying it through to the living room when he caught sight of himself in the dusty hall mirror.

The last smudge of purple was fading from beneath his eyes, but he could see quite plainly the recently acquired bump that spoilt what had been a perfectly shaped nose.

The sight made Barry grit his teeth. Fuck Crane! He was going to hang in there. Sooner or later, he'd come up with something on the bastard.

CHAPTER NINETEEN

'YOU are taking these too, Miz James?' Selena held up a pair of green high-heeled sandals.

'Yes, Selena, put them in – they'll go with that green and white suit.'

The two women were in Anthea's bedroom packing the garments and accessories Anthea would need for her trip to Cooktown.

'It is very hot in Cooktown, yes, Miz James?' Selena asked as she looked at the things Anthea had laid out on the bed.

Anthea smiled as she tucked a small box of electric rollers into her cosmetic case. 'It certainly is, Selena – endless summer.'

'The same as in my country,' Selena answered, and Anthea caught the wistfulness in the young Filipino's voice. She knew that Selena would love to return to the Philippines now that her marriage was over. But the girl realized the sense in staying in Australia as long as possible; that way she could save the money to send to her family in Cebu.

A hardness glinted momentarily in Anthea's eyes. Just as those other girls had been trying to do...

She glanced at Selena as the girl folded the last of the dresses into the almost full suitcase.

'You know don't you Selena, that I am still trying to find out what happened to your cousin? That I haven't given up?'

Selena looked up from her work, her dark sad eyes staring into Anthea's. 'I know this, Miz James,' she answered softly. 'But I don't think we ever find Beatrice.'

Later as she sat in the comfort of her first class seat for the flight north, Selena's words came back to Anthea. She felt a sudden illogical sense of guilt that so far she had been unable to do anything about finding that girl... any of those girls.

She frowned as she looked out the window at the brown and empty landscape so far below. She and Alex still had no real proof of Julian Crane's connection with the prostitution racket, or the blackmailing and corruption of Custom's officials and the police. It was instinct and sheer coincidence they were going on, nothing else. But they were still hoping for a breakthrough, for some positive evidence that would link Crane to the whole business.

Then, from the back of her mind, emerged the nagging thought that had been with Anthea since she'd first learned of the existence of the video cassette. As she had watched the gruesome images played out in front of her she'd known instantly that she should tell Alex about it.

The film revealed a lot about the man who was Julian Crane. The fact that she had kept that knowledge to herself played heavily on Anthea's conscience, she was forced to question her own integrity. Her eyes gazed unseeingly now at the vast emptiness below. To tell Alex about the tape would mean revealing the truth about her past...

THE HEAT HIT her like a damp heavy blanket as she stepped out onto the tarmac of Cooktown's small airstrip. Anthea was glad of the air-conditioned comfort of the car that was waiting to take her the short distance to her hotel.

The Cooktown Embassy was exactly what she might have expected in this small remote Australian township. It was a two-storeyed wooden building of typical tropical construction: wide verandahs overhung by a bull-nosed corrugated iron roof.

Outside the public bar in the shade of the verandah, groups of men, scantily clad in shorts and sweat-stained T-shirts, sat around rusty tables laden with glasses. They stared at Anthea as she alighted from the car and entered the hotel's deserted foyer. Green linoleum floors, a vase of dusty plastic roses on the unattended reception desk, the all-pervading smell of stale beer – this was Cooktown's best. Anthea smiled to herself as she pushed the rusty bell for service. Sydney seemed a long way away.

A plump, rosy-cheeked girl wearing a shapeless blue and white checked dress that showed large damp patches under each overfleshed sunburnt arm came through from the back room.

She greeted Anthea effusively. 'G'day. You must be the lady from the big smoke. How was the trip up? You must be pretty buggered. We're a bloody long way from Sydney, aren't we? Come on, I'll show you your room. Best in the house seein' youse are a TV star and all.'

Barely stopping for breath, she hooked a key off the rack, came round from behind the counter and picked up Anthea's suitcase with seemingly little effort. She kept up the machine-gun fire commentary as she led a bemused Anthea up the broad flight of wooden stairs and down a chocolate-brown corridor to a room at the end.

'Here y'are. It's quieter this end away from the bars.' She deposited Anthea's luggage on the bed, a suspiciously uncomfortable-looking affair covered by a green chenille bedspread.

'It's air-conditioned too,' the girl announced proudly, twiddling a dial on the rusty apparatus that was wedged under one of the windows. The roar as the machine burst into life made Anthea wince; it would be a toss-up between the heat or the chance of a decent night's sleep.

'Dinner's at 6.30 sharp. There's drinks in the fridge there if you're needin' one.' The girl pointed to the small bar fridge beside the laminated dressing table.

She turned to Anthea. 'Everythin' okay then?' She gave the impression that amid such luxury, the question could only be superfluous.

Anthea smiled. 'I'm sure I'll be just fine.'

As the girl shut the door behind her, Anthea tested the bed and rolled at once into the hollow in the middle. It was then that she began to giggle.

Anthea and the crew worked long hard hours to get the footage they wanted. The locations already decided on by production manager, Ron Brothers, were spot-on, Anthea had thought as he'd driven her around that first afternoon.

The next day as they set-up for filming on the banks of the historic Endeavour river – named after Cook's ship that had been beached there for repairs – Anthea realized again how right David had been to choose this spot for the introduction to the series.

But the heat and the flies did not make for comfortable conditions; to escape the worst of the noonday sun filming began early in the morning. As the make-up girl patted the sweat from her face for the umpteenth time, Anthea had to admit she was glad that the shooting schedule was only four days. She was looking forward to the weekend she'd planned in Cairns before returning to Sydney. It would be her first visit to the popular north Queensland resort.

'A good idea, Anthea,' David had said when she'd mentioned it to him as they were going over the final details of her trip. 'Probably your last chance for a break before 'Open To Comment' gets underway.' He'd leaned back then in his green leather chair and stifled a small sigh. 'I must say I only wish I had more time to do the same thing myself. I'd love to see more of this beautiful country.' Then casually, in an off hand manner, he'd added, 'Where were you thinking of staying in Cairns?'

Heads turned and whispers were exchanged as Anthea entered the cool, spacious foyer of her Cairns hotel. She could not fail to notice the signs of recognition among the Australian holiday-makers, and for a moment her thoughts turned wistfully to Cooktown.

Despite the physical discomforts there had been something infinitely soothing about the sleepy casualness of the place. The townsfolk, deprived of the questionable blessings of commercial television, had neither known nor particularly cared who she was.

Aware of the stares as she followed the bellboy into the lift, Anthea now recalled the relief that mere anonymity can bring. But, she watched the numbers flash as the lift moved upwards, this was the path she had chosen and loss of privacy was just one of the many sacrifices she'd had to make in pursuit of her ambitions.

Her room on the fourteenth floor provided sweeping views over lush tropical foliage to the ocean beyond, while beneath her she could see the bright blue curve of a swimming pool surrounded by gardens riotous with colour.

It was late afternoon and Anthea decided that a shower then a nap were in order. Later, she thought in pleasant anticipation, a meal of first-class Queensland seafood in the warm tropical air of the terrace restaurant would be a perfect end to the day.

AS HE SAT in the taxi that took him from the airport to his hotel, David felt his body rigid with tension.

Was he crazy? Had he taken leave of his senses to do what

he was doing? For it was, he knew, a sort of madness. A madness which had driven him to get on a plane and come here like this.

During the flight he'd been unable to relax at all, and as they'd come closer to their destination he'd told himself he could still stop this; he could return to Sydney the moment he arrived if he liked, or change hotels and never run any risk of seeing her. The choice was his.

But even as the various possibilities for escape presented themselves to his feverish mind, David knew he would heed none of them. At last he had admitted his obsession, faced up to the overwhelming force that had pulled him from the beginning towards Anthea James. From their very first meeting he had been aware of the strength of his response; he'd known that in some strange compelling way Anthea had awakened in him emotions that had lain dormant for too long.

For as long as he could he had tried to deny what was happening inside him. When he'd been successful in luring her to the network, he'd told himself that his elation was due merely to the acquisition of her talents and her kudos for his new enterprise.

But as their work drew them together, in the end it had been impossible to ignore the increasingly disturbing effect of her presence.

The afternoon she'd come into his home had been the catalyst that had finally brought him face to face with his feelings. On that cold grey winter's day as they'd sat, just the two of them together, in the quiet warmth of the house, David had known for the first time in many, many years, a sense of total connection – yes, that was the only word that properly expressed how he'd felt – with another human being.

And now, his heart pounded wildly in his chest, he was here to tell her how he felt...

He showered, changed, and came down to the cocktail bar early. He wanted to secure a table that would give him an all-encompassing view of the foyer yet at the same time afford him the privacy of the bar's dim lighting and bamboo partitions.

As he waited for his drink his eyes roamed around the large hotel foyer with its shining marble floors. Groups of casually dressed tourists moved to and fro, some towards the restaurants, others into the small shopping arcade; still others joined him in the dim intimacy of the cocktail lounge.

There was no sign of Anthea.

She did not appear until he was well into his second drink and his heart lurched as he saw her emerge from the lift. She was wearing a white flowing dress that left her shoulders bare.

With a trembling hand he put down his glass, while Anthea, seemingly oblivious to the reaction she was causing, made her way towards the terrace restaurant.

Moving his chair slightly, he was able to watch as the maître d' sat her at a table by herself at the edge of the terrace.

For the hour and twenty minutes that Anthea took to eat her meal, David sat in an agony of restlessness. He had no intention of approaching her in such a public place. Perhaps when she had finished she would come into the now almost deserted bar or take a stroll in the gardens.

He was right. As soon as she signed her check, Anthea stood up and left the restaurant, taking the broad stone steps to the pool and gardens below.

David was on his feet immediately, his drink forgotten, as he hurried out in the same direction. From the top of the steps he could see her. Avoiding the brightly-lit pool, deserted now at nearly 10 p.m., she had turned along the pebbled path that led, he guessed, through the gardens to the beach.

Slowly David started after her, trying to quiet the thumping of his heart. Lamps set low along the path and throughout the well-tended gardens meant he could not lose her.

As he made his way past hibiscus, oleander, and the thick twining boughs of purple and white bougainvillea, David realized with a flash of objectivity, just how crazy his behaviour was. She'd think he was mad. She'd be polite but find a quick excuse to get away; would never mention it again, but always think him a fool nonetheless.

He knew. He knew it could happen like that – but reason could not stop him now.

She was standing facing the ocean not three yards in front of him, just where the thick tropical lawns gave way to the dimpled white sand. The lights from the garden were behind him now, but in her white dress and with the soft silver gleam of the moon dappling the waves, Anthea was plainly visible.

It was then as he stood motionless, watching this woman to whom he was so powerfully attracted, that the terrifying thought froze him to the spot. It was a possibility that, in his mad driving need, had never occurred to him.

He knew nothing about Anthea's private life. Perhaps this was a weekend she would be sharing with a lover, someone she was committed to or deeply in love with.

The thought tore at him; a black giddiness descended on his brain. Why had the idea never struck him before? Had he merely blocked out that intolerable possibility?

As the realization played havoc with his whole being, David was still conscious that it was not yet too late to turn away, to leave all as it was, to continue the daily battle against the need within himself.

It was then that Anthea made a slight movement, her body curving sensuously in the soft white fabric of her dress as she placed a hand on her hip.

He spoke.

'Anthea.' His voice just reached her above the hiss and murmur of the sea.

She spun round and in a fleeting second her face registered a myriad of emotions: surprise, shock, alarm, disbelief...

'David!'

For one incredible moment it seemed to Anthea as if her very thoughts had conjured up the man who stood before her. 'What are –'

David walked over to her. It took a superhuman effort to keep his voice steady.

'Figured you had the right idea. And this seemed like the perfect weekend after all to avoid executive burn-out.' He forced the lightness into his tone and smiled down at her. 'Surprised?'

Anthea's bewilderment was obvious. 'Well, I –'

Again David cut her off. 'A million miles from Sydney, isn't it?' He turned his face up to the clear, sparkling night sky.

Anthea said nothing and he brought his eyes back to hers.

'Shall we walk a little...?'

Any hesitation Anthea might have felt was dispelled a moment later as David's cool firm hand slipped easily into her own. Her instant physical response and the sense of unreality were overwhelming as they fell into step together, their bodies bumping gently against each other in the darkness.

And then as David spoke, asking about her plans for the weekend, Anthea, still stunned, began to understand. David was trying to discover if she was here alone, free of other commitments.

She moved like a sleepwalker, barely aware of the low growl of the surf, the distant echoes of music and laughter. Then she heard herself reply that yes, she was alone... was expecting no-one. And all the while her mind screamed that she'd been alone, so utterly alone, from that day so many years ago when the man beside her had gone away and left her...

For a while longer they walked in silence until, as if in silent agreement, they came to a stop further up the deserted beach. With his hand still clasped around hers, David looked out to the softly murmuring ocean. When he spoke his voice was deceptively calm.

'Have you ever felt like... doing something crazy, Anthea? Really crazy, I mean... that you just can't stop yourself from doing? You know you're probably making a mistake, jarring things out of order that might never again fall back into place – but you just can't help it. You have to take that step, take that risk. Or,' there was a new intensity now in his lowered voice, 'regret it for the rest of your life...'

He said nothing more and standing beside him, Anthea could feel her heart thumping almost painfully in her chest as she began to grasp the astonishing significance of David's words.

And then the breath seemed to catch in her throat when next moment she felt herself drawn into the fold of David's arms and heard the words he was whispering into her hair.

'I want you, Anthea... I've wanted you from the very first moment I saw you.'

For Anthea the world suddenly turned upside down.

'David...' The word was barely audible but the naked need it expressed was the trigger that at last released everything they had both fought so long to control.

There, in the warm salty air, David's lips crushed down on hers and in that moment it suddenly seemed to Anthea's reeling mind that the past and the present had been fused into one. The man who held her now was the same David she had known and loved so long ago. It was as if in the space of a heartbeat more than twenty years had been swept away...

And then all thought stopped as pure sensation took its place. Anthea was drowning, spinning crazily in the touch, the taste, the sheer physical presence of the man whose arms enfolded her. In the thrill and shock of the moment all fear, resistance and indecision were swept away.

Then they were lying against the cool soft sand and as David's lips seared a path down her neck and across her bare shoulders, Anthea arched instinctively towards the source of her pleasure.

Through a mist of desire she was aware of the harsh uneven rhythm of David's breathing as his hand slowly eased up her dress and traced the soft swell of her burning flesh to arrive at her core. There, her heat and moistness left him in no doubt that her need was every bit as great as his own.

Breathless with desire, their bodies locked together, they found at once that feverish urgent rhythm which made the blood roar in their veins.

Moments later, their need too urgent for restraint, each in quick succession soared to that piercing ultimate pleasure. A moan of uninhibited joy burst from Anthea's lips and her heart pounded thunderously against the man who was crying out her name again and again...

It was a lifetime later that their pulsing bodies calmed and they lay in the anonymous darkness, wordlessly stroking, kissing and clinging to each other. Like two people ravenous for love, Anthea marvelled silently, the tears still damp upon her cheeks.

Later, they made their separate ways back to the hotel. The decision was mutual and unspoken. The rest of the night they knew would be spent in each other's arms.

In Anthea's room they stood for a long time under the fine cool spray of the shower, holding each other's smooth slipperiness their eyes reflecting the strength of their joy and wonder.

Then, still damp, they threw back the crisp white sheets of the bed, this time to savour at length what they had shared so hungrily, so hastily on the beach.

Like blind people they explored each other's bodies, touching, stroking, caressing, until at last they were ready for that long spiralling climb to the ultimate pleasure.

As he entered her warm damp softness, David whispered, 'No woman has made me feel like this for a long long time, Anthea. I thought it was all over for me... that I'd never feel this way again.'

She clung to him then, breathing in the smell of his freshly showered skin, feeling his cool strength enfolding her, and drowning in that perfect pulsing rhythm that made nothing else exist.

AFTERWARDS, SATED AND content, they lay cradled together in the darkness while David struggled to explain his crazy impulsiveness.

'From the very first moment, Anthea, there was something that drew me towards you, something so powerful it was impossible to ignore. Then, later, as I saw more and more of you, this sense of... connection, grew stronger every time. It was the afternoon you came into my home that I finally realized my feelings weren't going to go away – that somehow, soon, I would have to do something about them.'

He bent his head and kissed Anthea's tumbled hair. 'I told myself that I was crazy, that by confronting you with this madness I could lose you entirely... but in the end that was a risk I had to take.'

Anthea rubbed her face gently against David's naked chest listening to his heart beating calmly now. Her whispered reply was barely audible. 'Sometimes, David, we all have to take risks...'

For a long time after David's warm steady breath against her neck told her he was asleep, Anthea lay wide awake. She needed this peace and stillness to help her come to terms with the events of the whole explosive evening.

First and foremost she knew that she was as deeply, as completely, in love with David as she had been more than twenty years ago. The force of her response had shocked her, yet at the same time made her piercingly aware of the extent of the void that had existed inside her. Much as she cared for Alex it was nothing like this; it had never been and never could be.

The same dangers and fears still existed, but she knew that nothing now was going to keep her from this precious second chance at love. Even if, the pulse beat more quickly in her temple, to accept that love was going to take a very special sort of courage.

For Anthea realized that to enter completely into a relationship with David now, would mean a denial that that other time had ever existed. It would mean a wiping of the slate, a new beginning, a total blocking out of that earlier time with its betrayals and illusions, its agonies and aftermath. And, most important of all, its connection with the life she had worked so hard to conceal. David must never know. The burden of the past must be hers alone.

A sudden chill ran through her. Did she have that strength? *Could* she sever herself so completely from all memory of that first time and accept the present as her only reality?

She turned her head on the pillow and in the first pale glimmering of the dawn that slipped through the half-closed blinds, saw David's sleeping face next to her. She looked at the fine lines on his forehead, the deeper ones around his strong mouth, the long dark lashes resting gently against his cheeks flushed with sleep. She breathed a long drawn-out sigh. She would find that strength...

David's kisses on her eyelids awoke her. The blinds were open fully now and the room was flooded with bright sunshine. Instantly Anthea was awake. Despite her lack of sleep she felt wonderfully alive.

'You know what? Today the sun's come up just for you and me.' David, propped up on one elbow beside her, smiled as she opened her eyes, blinked in the strong light, then saw him watching her.

The memories and the emotions of the previous night flooded back to her.

'Oh, David...' Anthea reached out and put her arms around his neck and he moved closer, kissing her ears, her throat, her mouth.

'This is a dream I don't intend ever waking from,' he whispered as he ran his hands lightly over her naked, warm body under the crumpled sheet.

Anthea's response was immediate; the touch of his hand made

her nipples spring to life, the milkiness start between her legs. Her lips parted as her breath quickened.

Bending his head to her breasts, David explored their soft fullness with his tongue and lips until Anthea could bear it no longer.

Sensing her readiness, he moved his body over hers and sunk himself, eager and erect, deep inside her.

They were a single entity joined in heart and mind and body, as they slowly entered that black spinning force that lifted them moment by moment, breath by panting breath, to a shattering explosion of completeness.

'I love you, Anthea... I love you...'

Trembling, David clung to her and Anthea knew that nothing in her life would ever be the same again.

CHAPTER TWENTY

TO those who worked with Anthea the changes were clearly visible. Alongside the unflagging professionalism, the drive and the commitment, her staff were quick to note their boss's greater gentleness and tolerance as she coped with the day to day pressures of her hectic schedule.

Alex also noticed the changes in Anthea when they got together three days after her return from North Queensland.

'You look great, darling,' he smiled in greeting as Anthea opened the door to him. And she did. There was a glow and vitality about her that was impossible to miss. The break had done her good, Alex decided.

But inside the living room, as he drew her towards him, and kissed her warmly, he sensed at once the tenseness, the new reserve in her response.

Withdrawing from his embrace, Anthea busied herself preparing his drink, at the same time launching into an amusing description of her Cooktown accommodation. But as he sat down Alex was aware that beneath the flippancy was a nervousness he had never observed in Anthea before.

Ignoring his quizzical look, she handed him his drink and settled herself in the sofa opposite.

'Now, Alex – bring me up-to-date.' She looked at him expectantly; on the phone he had said merely that there'd been a 'very promising' breakthrough in their investigations.

For a moment Alex studied Anthea without speaking. Something had happened to her since she'd been away; and only now was it beginning to dawn on him exactly what might be the reason for the change.

Trying to ignore the churning in his stomach, he told her what had occurred in her absence. And it was to Ted Raynor, the retired Special Branch detective with whom he was working so closely, that Alex gave the credit.

'Ted's got us our first real break, Anthea. His contacts have turned up Neil Leard. Leard was dismissed a month ago from the Customs branch at Sydney airport and it seems as if he really might know something about the Asian immigration racket.

'My guess is that somewhere along the line Leard's put the bite on someone for a bigger slice of the action, and not only was it refused but Leard was given the boot as well. "Insubordination" was the reason given for dismissal... But,' Alex's grey eyes narrowed, 'Leard's got a real bee in his bonnet. He wants revenge. Only he's not quite sure just how far he can go in blowing the whistle without getting himself in too deep. What I'm trying to do is get him to go public with what he knows.'

'And how much is that?' Anthea was watching Alex intently.

Alex raised an eyebrow. 'Well, from what he's hinting at, it seems he knows how the whole operation is set up – and the names involved.' Alex frowned. 'I'm sure if we can just convince Leard that we can guarantee him immunity from prosecution, he'll talk. Then we can start following the rope until we see how far it goes...'

For the next half-hour they discussed the matter, then Alex finished his drink and stood up to leave. As he pulled on his jacket he added: 'This is a huge operation, Anthea. It's needed massive backing to set it up and keep it running so smoothly... and that keeps someone like Crane right in the line of fire.'

As she walked with Alex to the door Anthea knew she couldn't let him go without explaining why, from now on, their relationship had to be different. For despite the deliberate casualness of their friendship, they had cared a lot for each other – and it was never easy to withdraw from the intimacy that sleeping together inevitably creates.

But, Anthea assured herself, Alex would understand; it had never been his desire to tie her down.

'Alex...' She put a hand on his arm as he made to go. 'There's... something I have to tell you.' As he turned towards her she saw the oddly blank look on his face.

'Alex...' Now that the moment had come she found the words difficult to say. 'We've always been straight with each other and I –'

Briskly, Alex interrupted her. 'I know, Anthea... it's written all over you.' Something happened behind his grey eyes. 'I have no right to ask this, I know, but... will you tell me who it is?'

Anthea's heart beat quickly. There was a coldness in Alex's response she had not been prepared for.

'It's...David Yarrow.'

Alex stiffened and for a long moment he said nothing. Then, turning abruptly, he buttoned his jacket and felt in his pockets for his car keys. When he faced her again, the blank look was back in position and his voice was carefully neutral.

'I've never told you this before, Anthea, and maybe I shouldn't be telling you now but... I'd always hoped there might be... a future for us one day. We both have our goals, our obsessions I know, but I could see a time –.' He broke off and when he spoke again there was an edge to his voice. 'I hope you're not making a mistake, Anthea, that you're not going to let this get in the way of everything you've worked so hard to achieve. I'd hate to think –'

With an effort, Alex swallowed the rest of his words but his obvious anguish and confusion left Anthea badly shaken.

Fighting to recover his composure, Alex added: 'All I want is your happiness Anthea – and I have no right to interfere. But,' he spoke the words evenly and with intensity, 'I love you too much to walk out of your life quite so easily.'

He kissed her then, quickly and gently on the forehead, and the next moment Anthea was alone.

The memory of Alex's reaction disturbed Anthea for a long time afterwards. She'd had no inkling of the depth of his feelings, or of his hopes for a more committed relationship.

Or had she? With a sense of guilty unease Anthea forced herself to face that possibility. Had she in fact refused to acknowledge the evidence that must always have been staring her in the face?

It was a question that plagued her yet at the same time couldn't distract her from the fact that, through the miracle of being reunited with David, her soul was alive with a joy she hadn't experienced in over twenty years.

Since their return from Cairns they had managed to spend just one night together and Anthea was aching for the feel of David's arms around her, the taste of his lips against her own. The past was at rest; she had nothing more to fear. Only the future mattered now.

*

The tap on her office door came as she was working on the feature for her weekly newspaper column. Following her conversation with Alex, Anthea was focusing on corruption in the Public Service; although as yet she had not pinpointed the Customs department in particular.

Looking up, she saw David smiling at her from the doorway.

'I'm dead sure I'm disturbing you,' he said, coming into the room and shutting the door behind him. He moved behind her chair and, placing his hands on her shoulders, bent his head to kiss her hair.

'I'm going crazy,' he whispered close to her ear. 'All I can think of is being next to you, touching you, having you with me night after night...'

A hot wave of desire swept through her, but before she could reply David had moved to perch on the desk beside her.

His tone changed as he smiled down into her upturned face. 'As your employer, Miss James, I hereby order you to take leave of absence for one whole weekend – with the said employer, of course.'

His teasing blue eyes made Anthea's heart turn over. 'I hear and obey,' she answered solemnly.

The drive from Sydney to the Southern Tablelands took almost three hours.

It was just after two p.m. when David, after checking with the rough, hand-drawn map that lay on his lap, turned off the main highway and up a long twisting driveway bordered by thick leafy trees.

There, standing on a grassy knoll with views over the rolling countryside, was the cottage. Lowset, built of the sandstone used by the early settlers, the inscription etched into the stone under the eave was proof of its authenticity: 1887.

'David! How in the world did you know about this?' Anthea exclaimed in delight, as she stepped out of the car and took in the ivy-covered walls and the polished cedar door with its heavy brass knocker. 'It's gorgeous.'

'National Trust I'm assured,' he answered, pleased at her reaction. 'The original gatehouse to a homestead which was destroyed by fire.'

Anthea smiled and shook her head. 'Why does it always take a visitor to discover a country's nicest secrets?'

'C'mon,' David lifted their suitcases from the car, 'let's see if the inside lives up to the exterior.'

Without a doubt it did. A warm, cosy ambiance was created by the polished wooden floors strewn with woollen rugs in muted colours, by the open fireplaces already stacked with logs, and by the antique cedar bed with its lacy white linen.

In the tiny stone-flagged kitchen a gleaming array of brass pots and pans hung above the modern cooking range.

'History with all the mod cons,' grinned David as with a flourish he opened the refrigerator door.

Anthea shook her head in delighted surprise at the sight of the tins of caviar, the bowls of prepared salad and assorted cheeses.

'And here,' David tapped the pantry door, 'coffee, tea, fresh bread, crackers. No need to put a foot outside the door for thirty-six hours. If you get my meaning.'

Anthea moved towards him and slowly slid her arms around his neck. 'Loud and clear,' she said softly, her lips finding his.

Just after six p.m. they forced themselves to get out of bed and, after a long hot shower together, Anthea made a pot of tea and arranged a tray of assorted goodies from the refrigerator. She carried it through to the living room where David had lit the fire. The mist had come down and it was cold outside but the glow from the fire and the one low lamp gave the room a comfortable cosiness.

Dressed in their bathrobes, they sat close together on the deeply-sprung sofa, helping themselves from the tray on the low table in front of them.

'No television, no newspapers, no telephones... heaven on earth,' sighed David contentedly as he put down his empty plate.

Anthea smiled, pleased to see him so relaxed. She knew that this instant in time, this warm cosy room, the look on David's face, would stay with her always.

There was an old-fashioned radio on a shelf in the corner of the room and, as they tidied up, they listened to a medley of blues numbers.

'New Orleans wasn't always the home of the blues, you know,'

David told her, as they curled up on the sofa again. 'For a short time in the twenties, Chicago took over the role. It was the closing down of the Storyville district in New Orleans that caused the blacks to go north to Chicago.'

Leaning against David's chest, Anthea listened in silent contentment as he told her of some of the fine blues singers he'd listened to in clubs all over the States.

'You know, the thing that strikes me most about the blues sound,' David was saying, his mouth close to her ear, 'is its lazy, rolling sensuality... its eroticism.'

Then his hand was moving down the open neck of her robe and Anthea felt the warm throb of desire start in her veins. Her heart danced in excitement as his stroking became more urgent.

'Anthea...' He was slipping the robe off her shoulders and discarding his own, as he drew her down to the soft thick rug in front of the glowing fire.

'I want you, Anthea... I want you all my life,' he said breathlessly as their bodies joined in ecstasy.

It happened just before midnight when the fire was a mere glow of dying embers.

The chill in the room woke them from the sleep that follows total sexual fulfilment. David stirred first and with a shiver moved gently away from his sleeping lover. Getting to his feet, he found his bathrobe and tied it tightly around him. Anthea's warm woollen robe was still lying on the sofa where they'd dropped it. He picked it up, then knelt on the rug again and ran his fingers down Anthea's sleeping body.

'Wake up, my darling,' he said softly.

With a small sigh Anthea opened her eyes. It took her a moment to realize where she was, and then she smiled sleepily up at David.

'I don't want you catching a chill, darling... put this on and we'll go to bed.'

'Only if you promise to start all over again.' Anthea whispered back, only half in jest, her skin tingling at the gentle touch of his fingers on her skin. Yawning, she stretched out a hand for David to help her to her feet.

But David didn't seem to notice. Still kneeling beside her, he was staring at her nakedness, at the small scar that flawed the otherwise smooth pale flesh of her abdomen.

With a puzzled frown he reached out and touched the tiny puckered imperfection.

Anthea stopped breathing. Suddenly wide awake, she was immediately alert to the danger.

'How long have you had this, Anthea?'

Something in David's tone made a black giddiness descend on her; panic clamped her throat. Surely David wouldn't remember...

He was waiting, silent and motionless, for her reply.

Time passed endlessly until Anthea breathed out the words: 'Since childhood...'

David drew back, a strange look on his face as he stared at her in the shadowy room.

Anthea dared not meet his gaze. Averting her face, she fumbled for her robe. She prayed for the moment to pass. Please God... please... Her heart hammered thunderously in her chest.

But, with icy fingers, David brought her face back to his and Anthea knew it was too late. White-faced and wide-eyed, she saw the look of sheer incredulity on his strong dark features.

Unable to bear his scrutiny any longer, Anthea closed her eyes as if, by some miracle, she could shut the nightmare out.

But she knew she had lost. She had taken the risk and she had lost.

She heard the long shuddering sigh that escaped David's bloodless lips. 'Oh God... it's Lenore... it's Lenore, isn't it?'

CHAPTER TWENTY-ONE

For what seemed like an eternity neither of them moved or said a word.

Then David got to his feet and Anthea, stricken, opened her eyes to look at the man who now held such total power over her. The power of love. And the power to destroy...

He had turned away; his back was to Anthea as he stood facing the dying glow of the fire.

Even from behind Anthea could see the desperate tension in his body and a choking bitterness and despair engulfed her.

Whom did he most detest, she wondered? The Lenore Hamlyn of all those years ago – the 'prostitute' who had done him such a pitiful 'favour'? Or Anthea James, the liar and deceiver who had cheated not only him but the thousands who admired and looked up to her?

Frustration tore at her for the ugliness, the unjustness, of it all...

At last, unable to bear the tension a moment longer, Anthea got to her feet and wrapped the robe tightly around her. In the atmosphere which engulfed them her nakedness seemed suddenly, horribly, obscene.

David must have heard her, but he made no move to turn around. Desperately afraid that he would cut her off, refuse to listen, Anthea knew nevertheless that she must at least try to make him understand, to make him listen to the truth.

Struggling to maintain her fragile control, she broke the dreadful silence. 'David, I –' Her breath was ragged, choking off her words. Swallowing, she tried again. 'Oh, David what –'

Suddenly he turned to face her and instead of the contempt, the shattering disdain, she had been dreading, there was a look of sheer agony on David's ashen face.

But it was his voice that shocked her even more.

'Tell me about it, Anthea... Tell me about Lenore...'

A sob caught in her throat. Never before had she heard such utter gentleness in a man's voice...

She stared at him across the room, saw the tightness around his mouth, the flicker of something she didn't understand in the depths of his searching blue eyes.

And then, finally, the significance of his words sunk in.

David wanted to know... wanted to hear the truth.

That realization made the breath suddenly pour back into her body. Trembling, she took a step backwards and sat down on the edge of the sofa.

'All right, David.' Her voice was a whisper. 'I'll tell you. I'll tell you everything.'

And she did, stumbling a little at first, but soon the words came pouring out as if having been dammed for so long, there was relief in their release...

Quietly and dispassionately, she told him what had happened with her father; she told him about Nan and about the old woman's kindness to her; she explained her ignorance of Nan's business until the day when, ill and weak, Nan had asked for her help. In a voice growing steadily stronger, Anthea described how her work with Nan had helped open her eyes to the needs and problems of women in a society that offered them little chance of equality. Such insights, she continued, had given her the drive, the ambition, to choose the path she had taken.

'I never 'worked' for Nan in the way you believed, David. When we made love that very first time you showed me that there could be a different face to love. Something far removed from the vicious abuse of my father and the coldly exploitive sex that occurred in the brothel. What we shared together wiped out that ugliness for me...'

She looked at him, begging him to believe her.

'I loved you, David... nothing else mattered. And then, when you left without a word, all I could think was that for you it had meant nothing – that I had meant nothing. So I blocked it out, tried to put it all behind me. Then, that letter –'

Suddenly David was beside her and she saw the torment of guilt in his eyes as his arms went around her. Burying his face in her hair he moaned: 'God, Anthea how can you ever forgive me...? How can I ever forgive myself...?"

They went to bed then and the rest of that long night was charged with raw emotion that spilled over in explanation, consolation, forgiveness and love. In short erratic bursts they filled in for each other the years they had lost.

'It was the hardest thing I ever had to do, Anthea, leaving you like that.' David's voice was filled with anguish as he held her in his arms. 'I needed your love for the whole man, not your pity for the cripple. I couldn't let you confuse the two.

'It wasn't until I saw that there really was a chance that I might walk again that I dared let myself think of finding you. Because, Anthea, I never forgot you. Even after I... found out, I couldn't get you out of my mind. There were women of course, later; but somehow it was never right. Something I could never really understand held me back.'

He turned her face up to his. 'Until I met you. With you I felt instantly, completely, alive. As if I'd been waiting for you all my life... You were a stranger, but right from the start I felt that uncanny connection with you. Now I understand...'

As she stared up into David's tired but happy face, Anthea felt drained and lightheaded from the purging of emotions that had lain dormant for so long.

They had told their stories, each in their own way trying to make sense, for the other, of the years they had lost. This is why I am this way, their words implied: Anthea driven to succeed, never again giving any man the power to hurt her as she had once been hurt; David aloof and removed, yet forever searching for the woman who would remind him of the girl he could not forget...

And now Anthea was filled with euphoria as David drew her closer. They had found each other, explained the past, and held nothing back.

Except, a shadow crossed Anthea's face, the fact that she had conceived a child. A child who had been stillborn. That pain she would carry alone.

CHAPTER TWENTY-TWO

'SO, congratulations again, Anthea... we're very pleased, of course, that you'll be contesting the seat for us.'

It was Harvey Minton, the Party Federal President, who had telephoned with the good news; and this time there was no hint of the dryness of tone, or the provocative manner that had existed in their conversation of a few weeks earlier.

Anthea's eyes shone as she replaced the receiver. She had done it – what Julian Crane had done his best to prevent. She had faced the pre-selection committee and won Party nomination. In the end, Harvey Minton and the others had given her the backing she needed.

Restless with delight, Anthea stood up from her desk and moved to the window; but she saw nothing of the view in front of her. Her thoughts were on the work to come. She knew she had taken on a formidable load. The first series of 'Open To Comment' was ready to go to air in just three nights time. And now, in addition, there was the full force of her political campaign to be launched: agendas to draw up, details to finalize, plans to be made for speeches, appearances, debates.

With a surge of excitement Anthea knew that at last she was within sight of gaining the sort of power that would – in time – change the lives of countless numbers of women.

Her dark eyes blazed. *Her* power would be *their* power...

David shared her delight when she told him the good news.

'That's wonderful, Anthea. Now you must give yourself every chance of being elected.' Amusement flickered in his eyes, 'I guess this means I'll be learning a lot more about the Australian political system over the next few weeks.'

They were sitting together in David's cheerful kitchen, enjoying the late supper Anthea had prepared. The house felt different to her now; it seemed warm and welcoming, now that the memories it evoked could be savoured with the sweetness of nostalgia. David slept in what had been his father's bedroom; but on their first night in the house together they returned to the bedroom where they had lain all those years ago. In an emotionally-charged evening they recaptured the essence of that pure young love...

Anthea glanced at David across the table. As she prepared to launch her campaign, the time they had together was more precious than ever. But she knew that David understood those things in her past that drove her so relentlessly, that made her so determined to empower women at the grass roots level.

Her eyes softened as she watched him eating the meal she had prepared. This is how the relationship between a man and woman is meant to be, she thought. The sharing of roles, traditional and non-traditional, between two equals. She was committed to a man with whom she could be her own person; between herself and David there existed no threat of two inflated egos jostling for position. He had respect for her needs and ambitions and would not stand in her way.

As she turned back to her meal, Anthea felt infused with a new strength and confidence. She felt certain she could achieve her goals and still have the man she loved by her side.

ANTHEA WAS SPEAKING to a jam-packed room. Her audience, mainly women, sat crammed into the rows of seats, stood four deep around the walls, crowding into the aisles and stairways.

'... and these are serious matters that need to be looked at – and corrected – in this country today. The growing trade deficit, youth unemployment, the erosion of the rural economy...all need urgent attention by those who are our elected representatives.

'But to this list must be added also those issues that affect women in particular.' Anthea paused, her dark eyes travelling slowly over the hushed audience. 'I know there are many of you here today who want to work, *need* to work, but are sick and tired of the battle to find affordable, accessible child care. I wish to state here and now, that the provision of adequate child care centres is one of my major priorities.

A roar of spontaneous applause interrupted her and Anthea waited till it died away before going on.

'One of the greatest threats women face in today's society is that of physical violence and abuse – a threat directed not only at themselves but, more terrifyingly, towards their children. Women and children have the right to live their lives free of the fear of domestic violence, of incest, of sexual abuse. No longer must they be the passive victims of male aggression. They –'

But again her words were drowned in a storm of applause; and on the faces of the assembled women – old lined and knowing faces, young fresh and idealistic faces – Anthea saw the glow of hope and belief.

'I am dedicated to creating an environment of safety, of freedom, of equal opportunity at every level – for you, your children, your children's children... All human beings deserve that right. It –'

Once more her listeners interrupted the flow of Anthea's speech. It was a scenario repeated a dozen times during the full forty minutes that she spoke of women's rights in marriage, in education, in employment, of the need for job-sharing and enforceable maintenance payments.

And when she was finished the crowd as one rose to its feet, applauding wildly as, under the glare of the hot television lights, Anthea smiled her thanks. She had made an outstanding political debut.

It wasn't until the late night television news that Anthea had a chance to watch herself and judge her own performance. She was home alone, weary after a day of relentless pressures.

The press – the Crane Corporation conspicuous by its absence – had been out in force for the launch of the electoral campaign of one of the country's best-known faces. No other first-time candidate, Anthea knew, would have received such massive attention. And, she watched as the cameras scanned the enthusiastic audience, if her speech had dealt with much broader issues than might be expected in one seeking election as a backbencher, then that was the way she had planned it all along.

Now, thanks to the inspiring response to the opening of her campaign, she had every reason to count on ultimate success.

Anthea sighed as she leaned back against the sofa, pulling the soft fleecy dressing gown around her. With love as a bonus, she had never felt happier in her life than at this moment.

CHAPTER TWENTY-THREE

'SO I thought it best to give you some warning, Dave – cause I know she means it to be a "surprise".' The edge of irritation in Oscar Delamar's voice was not dulled by distance.

'I'd have tried to ring her, talk her out of it, but by now she's traipsin' round the backwoods of old Kyoto somewhere...' He sighed heavily into the phone. 'Goddamn it, Dave, if only I'd known... but the trip was part of Kelly's media course... a party of fellow students in the art history department. She was mad keen to go... I didn't dream there was an ulterior motive. Then two days ago I get a letter saying she'd "just decided" – now that she was so close – "to go on Down Under".'

Oscar paused then added grimly, 'This has gotta stop, Dave. She's too old to listen to me and too young to see that she's screwin' up her life. This time you don't pull no punches. Give it to her straight. For all our sakes.'

Hiding his own dismay at the news, David tried to pacify his old friend.

'Stay cool, Oscar. Maybe it's for the best this way. If Kelly does turn up in Sydney, she might just decide for herself that there's not much point in hanging round... That going home and getting on with her own life is a better option.'

For a second the enigmatic words hung between the two men, but David didn't elaborate and Oscar was too polite to enquire further. But moments later as he replaced the receiver there was a puzzled frown on his suntanned face.

Back in the kitchen David poured himself a second cup of coffee. It was seven a.m. and the call from Oscar had got his day off to a bad start.

Mechanically he stirred sugar into the steaming liquid. So, the problem with Kelly was still not at an end; his absence, it seemed, had done nothing to resolve the situation.

Cup in hand, he walked to the window and looked out at the

lawn wet with dew, and at the weak winter sun struggling through the trees. Sipping at his coffee, he pondered the problem. Well, what he'd told Oscar was true; maybe it *was* all for the best. This might bring things to a long overdue head. But, his brows drew together, it meant too that he would have to put Anthea in the picture.

David looked approvingly at the food set out on the small polished table pulled up between the two comfortable chairs. Terrine and crackers, smoked salmon on rye, fresh fruit. Undeniably healthy, he smiled to himself as he checked his watch. 12.35. Anthea should arrive any moment. Despite what he had to tell her, he was impatient for her company. He was glad that she'd agreed to come at such short notice. Their busy schedules usually meant that, formal meetings aside, they saw little of each other during working hours.

As he paced around the small private annexe to his main office, once again the feeling of happiness he had never thought possible welled up inside him. To have found, so unexpectedly, the woman he now realized he'd been searching for all his adult life, was a miracle he still hardly dared to believe.

It was clear to him now why, right from the start, he had been drawn so compulsively towards Anthea. Somewhere, deep in his subconscious, there had been recognition of the girl he had known so long ago. The girl whom, despite his hasty misjudgement, he had never been able to forget.

In Anthea's appearance there was little to remind him of Lenore. But beneath the well-groomed sophistication, the careful public image of the mature woman, lay the same warmth and spontaneity, the same gentleness and concern, which he had loved in the seventeen year-old girl.

It felt sometimes to David as if there were two women he loved; two fused into one, rather like those wooden Russian dolls that fitted one inside the other. Inside Anthea there was Lenore, and on top of Lenore there existed Anthea.

He knew now as he waited, that if Anthea had not come back into his life, it would have been a life cruelly wasted...

There was a tap on the door and he turned as Anthea entered the room. For a second he neither moved nor spoke, as he drank in the sight of her.

*

They ate, and Anthea listened without interruption as David told her the whole story.

'It's awkward, Anthea – has been for years. Our families were so close. Even though my mother barely moves from Carmel these days she never fails to see Oscar if she's in L.A.'

David turned troubled eyes to Anthea. 'I saw a lot of Kelly Delamar while she was growing up. But she was just a kid and that's the only way I ever thought of her. She was always saying she was going to marry me when she grew up.' He shook his head. 'We all treated it like a joke, but,' David stood up and moved restlessly round the room, 'it's not a joke any longer. It's become a serious obsession. And the fact that I haven't married has merely convinced Kelly that I'm waiting for her...'

He turned on his heel and looked down into Anthea's dark eyes.

'God, Anthea, I don't want to hurt the girl, or humiliate her, but she's got to be made to see that she's putting her life on hold for no good reason. She should be going out with boys her own age, falling in love...'

Exasperated, he sat down heavily again. 'I'm hoping that when she sees me for the first time in a committed relationship it might open her eyes to the truth – that there never was and never will be room for her in my life.'

David sighed and leaned back in his chair. 'What really worries me is the fact that I'm living in that big house alone. Kelly's not shy, Anthea. Whatever arrangements she might have made, once she finds out about the house, she'll make it very obvious that she expects to be my house guest.' He shook his head. 'That's just impossible.'

Anthea thought quickly.

'Maybe I can help...'

THE ELATION SHOWED in Kelly Delamar's eyes as she looked out the aircraft window at the curved azure bays of the Australian coastline below.

They were only ten minutes away from Sydney airport and she could hardly contain her excitement. If, as she hoped, her father had kept the news to himself, her arrival would be a complete surprise for David.

Checking that her passport was handy in her soft Gucci holdall, Kelly congratulated herself yet again on the shrewdness of her plan. From the moment she had signed up for the trip to Japan she knew what she was going to do. It had been easy to arrange the flight on to Australia – and that way there had been no risk of her father trying to stop her.

She was sure that after three months alone in a strange country, David would be delighted to see a familiar face. And, Kelly's smile broadened, in a different place, away from everything that was familiar to them both, he would see her in a completely new light. Her father would not be in the background to inhibit them; David would be more relaxed; he would see her at last as the grown-up woman she was.

The plane banked and suddenly Kelly saw below her what she realized was Sydney Harbour. The beauty of the huge inlet with its graceful arching bridge, its soaring Opera House, the dozens of smaller bays and coves dotted with small craft, took her breath away. She was really there!

Kelly was used to the admiring glances that followed her as she made her way through Customs and Immigration. Tired as she was, the tall athletic-looking girl with her tumble of tawny hair and striking looks, drew the attention of both men and women; there was something so attractively buoyant and confident in her carriage.

The queues were long and the processing took forever. A little American efficiency was what the Aussies needed, Kelly thought impatiently.

But at last she was through. Pushing the luggage trolley out into the bright sunshine, she saw the row of cabs.

'Where to, love?' the cabbie asked as he stowed her suitcase in the back.

'I have a reservation at the – uh – Intercontinental. I guess you know it?'

The cabbie, stocky and freckled, grinned as he pulled out from the kerb. 'I think we'll find it for ya.'

It wasn't a long trip to the city but the traffic was heavy, despite the fact that, at 10.00 a.m., the morning peak hour had passed.

'I guess you guys need a few more freeways,' Kelly commented as they stopped for yet another red light.

The cabbie grinned as the dollars clocked up on the meter.

Her room was fine – on the eighteenth floor with a great view of the Bridge and Harbour. Although weary, Kelly knew that her jet lag would be all the worse if she tried to sleep now. Anyway, the idea of a look around the city appealed to her.

She unpacked, took a quick shower and changed. But before leaving her room, she made sure the operator had found her the telephone number of AMN Australia. As she carefully wrote it down Kelly smiled happily to herself. She now had the perfect opportunity to show David that the difference in their ages didn't matter. She was a woman now, not a child any longer. Didn't the way she felt about David prove that?

Back in her room just before four, Kelly knew she could resist the impulse no longer. She picked up the phone, got an outside line and dialled David's business number. As she waited for an answer, a nervous thrill of anticipation ran through her. Tomorrow, after a good night's sleep so she would look her best, she would see David, have him all to herself at last.

Finally she got through to David's secretary and gave her name.

'I'll see if Mr Yarrow is available,' the woman said, her accent sounding pleasantly quaint to Kelly's ears.

'Kelly?'

Her breath quickened as she heard David's voice.

'David – surprise! I'm in town!'

'I know – Oscar told me you were due in.'

The disappointment in Kelly's voice was obvious. 'Oh... I wanted... Still,' she brightened again, 'it doesn't really matter, does it? Just figured that with Australia so close it'd be a great idea to drop in on you. I thought you'd be back in the States before this... you must be missing home, huh?'

'Almost too busy to think about it. I've taken on something big here and have to see it set up and running.' There was a reserve and formality in David's tone which Kelly put down to the fact that he was speaking from his office.

'Yeah, Dad told me. I want to hear all about it.' Her voice softened. 'When can we see each other, David? Lunch – tomorrow?'

For a moment there was a silence at the other end of the line. Then: 'Sure, Kelly. Where are you staying? I'll send a car to pick you up around one.'

Later, Kelly wondered again about the flatness of his tone.

DAVID TRIED TO put the problem of Kelly out of his mind as he stared at the papers in front of him. But it wasn't easy. He was remembering the last time he had seen her, that night at Chasens. Oscar had been delayed in Chicago or somewhere and there had been just the two of them – a situation David had been trying more and more to avoid. He'd made a deliberate effort to steer the conversation to safe topics: the courses Kelly was doing, the ideas she had about her career.

Kelly had spoken enthusiastically about her studies. She had a keen mind and David knew Oscar had been delighted when the East Coast college, noted for the excellence of its Media and Communications courses, had accepted his little girl.

Little girl... As their meal was placed in front of them he had stolen a glance at the sophisticated young woman sitting opposite him. Kelly Delamar was no longer a little girl. It was a fact David had become increasingly – and uncomfortably – aware of in recent months. There were times when something in the way Kelly looked at him, touched his hand, his arm at the slightest excuse... well, it seemed downright seductive.

Adding to his discomfort had been the certain knowledge that Oscar too had noted his daughter's increasingly overt behaviour towards his friend.

Eventually, alone with Oscar over a drink one evening, David had brought the subject into the open.

'I'm completely at a loss, Oscar. I've done absolutely nothing to encourage her. I –'

Oscar interrupted him, his tanned face serious. 'I know that Dave. I've got eyes in my head and I can see where the blame lies. To tell you the God's truth I blame myself. I shoulda seen this coming a long time ago.' Grimly, he looked into David's troubled eyes. 'Let's just hope it's something she'll grow out of...'

Kelly's arrival in Sydney made David realize that hadn't happened.

KELLY WAS ON edge with excitement the next afternoon as she sat in the back of the grey Mercedes that drove her along the twisting road with its glimpses of the water.

It was a clear bright winter's day, but with enough warmth in the sun to make heavy clothes unnecessary. Kelly had chosen her outfit carefully: a pale pink suede calf-length skirt with matching toggled jacket. Sexy but smart, she decided.

Now the car was driving into a cul de sac that ended at the harbour's edge, and as they came to a stop she could see a seafood restaurant to her right, its outdoor tables set almost on the sand. It looked delightful with its view over the water back to the city and the famous bridge.

'They're waiting for you there, Miss Delamar.' The driver nodded towards the restaurant as he opened the door for her.

A frown creased Kelly's face. 'They'? Surely she and David would be alone? She had come all this way to be with him and him alone – didn't he realize that?

Flustered and upset she walked along the path to the restaurant's entrance where the maître d' seemed to know immediately who she was.

'Miss Delamar?' He smiled at her. 'Come this way please.'

He led her though the umbrella-topped tables to one set a little apart from the rest. And there at last was David, standing up to greet her, tall and handsome as ever. But Kelly's eyes were drawn immediately to the attractive, elegant, older woman who sat smiling at his side.

'...so you've been involved in the media a long time, Miss James?' There was just a shade of emphasis on the 'long' as Kelly lifted the glass of chilled white wine to her lips.

'It's an ever-challenging area, Kelly – and please, let me remind you again – call me Anthea. We're very informal in this country.'

Kelly kept her irritation under control as she watched Anthea James resume her meal. Why in heaven had David brought this woman along? Why couldn't it have just been the two of them as she had imagined?

As if in answer to her unspoken question David said: 'I wanted you to meet Anthea, Kelly. Not only because of her experience in the media, but also she knows everyone worth knowing in this city. I'm sure she'll introduce you to some very interesting people while you're here.'

To hell with 'very interesting people', Kelly countered angrily in her mind. I came here to be with you...

Then her heart kicked sickeningly in her chest as the idea suddenly occurred to her. Could it be possible that this woman was David's lover? Could *she* be the reason that David had stayed so long in Australia?

It was a thought Kelly at once dismissed. Of course not. David had stayed because he wanted to make sure that AMN was soundly established here. And this woman was merely an employee – although an important one it seemed.

Kelly cast a surreptitious glance at the older woman across the table. She knew the type; she'd seen it often enough before. Anthea James had no time for a man, a family, an ordinary lifestyle. Her career would always be of paramount importance... Not the sort of woman, Kelly concluded, who was likely to attract David...

'How long do you intend staying in Australia, Kelly?' Her thoughts were interrupted by Anthea's question.

Kelly leaned back in her seat and, turning away from Anthea, looked out over the water. 'School doesn't go back till September... I guess I might stay a month or two.'

She missed the fleeting look that passed between David and Anthea.

'Yeah,' she turned back to face them, 'there's no rush to get back. I'm going to take a good look round while I'm here. Though it's a long time to hang about in an hotel.'

She left the words dangling in the air. Hopefully David would get the hint. It wasn't the money, David would know that – she could have afforded to stay in the hotel for a year if she had to.

'Hotels are so impersonal, aren't they?' she added, raising an expectant eyebrow. David must have an apartment of his own; she was sure he would invite her to stay.

David crossed the cutlery on his empty plate. 'Exactly what I thought when Oscar told me you were coming, Kelly. I've discussed it with Anthea and she's been kind enough to suggest you be her house guest during your stay here.'

The young girl's face was a mask of confusion and dismay, and for a moment Anthea's heart went out to her. She added gently: 'Yes, you're more than welcome to stay with me, Kelly. I have a very spacious home, and with the hours I keep you'd virtually have the place to yourself a lot of the time. I'd be very glad to have you.'

Kelly stared at the woman opposite her, noting again the perfectly-groomed hair, the discreet but obviously expensive jewellery, the French cut of her fine wool dress. Her face flushed. She knew she could not now rescind her earlier comments without looking a fool – nor could she question David bluntly about his own living arrangements. She had no alternative but to accept Anthea's offer.

'You're very kind,' she said through stiff lips.

IT WAS TWO days later that Kelly moved into Anthea's Double Bay home. In the meantime she had called David twice, attempting to wriggle out of the arrangement.

When at last she had asked him point-blank why she couldn't stay with him he made it very clear why that was out of the question.

'Look, Kelly,' he said evenly into the telephone, 'Sydney isn't L.A. It's a small town really. Everybody knows everybody else's business. It wouldn't take twenty-four hours for the word to get around that I was entertaining a single young woman in my home.

'Trying to explain the "family friend" bit would only add to the gossip columnists' amusement. And even if you and I didn't mind, Oscar would be most unhappy about that sort of rumour.'

Kelly had too much pride to plead and, as well, she knew that what David said about her father was the truth. His reaction to gutter press innuendo would be fierce.

Why did it have to be so complicated she wondered now as she helped Selena hang up her clothes in the sunny, spacious bedroom in Anthea James' home.

'Have you been with Miss James a long time?' she asked the petite, dark-haired maid.

'Maybe four years now. Miz James is a very important lady but is also very nice. I like to work for her.'

'She's not – never been – married?'

Selena smiled. 'No, Miz James, she never marry. Her work is always most important for her.'

Kelly said nothing but, despite herself, she felt the beginnings of real curiosity about her well-known, 'very important' hostess.

CHAPTER TWENTY-FOUR

THE girl froze in fear.

For a moment she thought she had heard a car, which would mean the man was returning. But no, she let out her breath in relief, she had been mistaken. There was no sound but the birds in the trees, the distant drone of an aircraft – although she could see nothing of these from the shuttered windows.

Her moment of alarm drove her even more frantically to her task. This was the only way she could think of that held any possibility of escape. For she could bear it no longer – the pain, the humiliation, the degradation. She had to get away from here.

For another hour Beatrice scraped at the slight gap in the door jamb with the small pair of nail scissors she always carried in her purse. Finally, the pain of her scratched and bleeding fingers became too intense and she was forced to stop.

In the small dank bathroom off the main room, she washed her hands and dried them gently on the one dirty towel. Back in the sparsely-furnished room – a bed, a dusty table and chair, a grimy hot-plate and an old battered refrigerator – she sat down and fought back the panic that threatened as always to overwhelm her.

How long now had she been here? She couldn't remember. At first she had counted the days – judging night and day only by the threads of light admitted by the shutters – but then, some time in the third week, she had become confused.

And now time had no meaning. All that mattered was to get out before the man returned, before she was again forced to ... Beatrice blanked out the dreadful thought from her mind.

The man had chosen her from among all the other girls just a week after their arrival in Australia. At first she had been grateful, thinking that she at least had been rescued from the 'work' they had all been forced to do.

Beatrice's almond-shaped eyes grew darker. How often had she wished that she had never listened to those who spoke of the money she could make in Australia. How stupid she had been to believe such tales... but she had not been alone in her stupidity. Others like herself had also been eager to make money to send back to their families at home. Like her, they had been trapped. And what she had thought was a rescue by the man was not a rescue at all...

He had brought her here – put her in his large expensive car and driven for a long time to this house that stood all alone in the trees. She was frightened then, when she realized that he meant to leave her here, locked up and alone. But her fear had become far greater when she found out the reason she'd been brought to the house...

Involuntarily, Beatrice's eyes were drawn to the bed – to the heavy leather tongs attached to the sturdy wooden bedposts – and a shiver ran through her. She knew too that in the cupboard which he locked every time, lay the stinging leather whip, the dark suffocating hood... all the things the man used to hurt and terrify her.

She had realized soon enough that it was her fear which excited him. When she struggled and fought she saw the eagerness in his eyes, the lust in his face, as he debased her in every ugly, animal way.

Tears gathered in Beatrice's eyes. She couldn't bear it a moment longer. She had to escape. But she knew that even if she managed that, she would still be trapped by the dense surrounding bush.

It was on the man's last visit that she had been given a ray of hope. He was about to go, leaving her bruised and sickened in the locked room, when suddenly through her pain and terror she heard the ringing of a telephone, then the murmur of the man's voice.

Forcing her battered body from the bed she crept to the door and pressed her ear against it. Yes, it was true! There was a telephone – that worked – in the house.

Excitement lessened her pain. This was the answer to her prayers. For in the one small case she had been permitted to bring, lay the letter from Selena. It was the last letter her cousin had written to her before Beatrice had left Manila. Selena had said how very happy and excited she was that at last Beatrice was going to be with her. And in the letter she had included the telephone numbers of both her home and where she worked.

In her prison, Beatrice had read and re-read that letter many times, crying over the dreams she had had about her new life.

The telephone she knew was her only hope. If she could get out of this room she would be able to make contact with Selena, beg her to come at once and save her from this nightmare.

Beatrice stood up and, knotting back her long hair, set again to her task.

At any moment the man might return.

FROM BEHIND HER outsize, aqua-framed sunglasses, Harriet Maddern viewed her surroundings with satisfaction. Stretched out beside the pool, she took in the green silk waters of the lake, the rugged soaring mountains dotted with sun-faded stone houses, the distant snow-capped alps.

Harriet smiled in utter contentment. Why hadn't God made everywhere like Italy, she mused, feeling the sun warm against her skin. In Australia she'd never have dared expose herself for hours like this to the sun. In no time at all it would suck a woman's skin dry; in contrast the European sunshine was gentle and caressing.

She sipped at her juice and leaned back, totally relaxed. This was her third visit to the Villa Marissa. An American friend, Janie Furst, heiress to an immense construction fortune, had told her about it. Even better than the Golden Door, Janie had enthused. And she'd been right. Not only were there the treatments, but the scenery, the musical evenings... a total sybaritic experience. Harriet now ensured that her annual pilgrimage to Europe always included a luxurious, revitalizing three weeks at the Villa Marissa.

Her eyes moved slowly over the other prone forms surrounding the pool. What she particularly liked was that the Villa catered only for women. Here with no need for the rigours of dressing up, competing, looking one's best, a woman could completely relax.

Her gaze came to rest on a petite, dark-haired woman on the opposite side of the pool. Cara Peruggi was applying liberal amounts of lotion to an already gleaming mahogany skin and her soft high bosom was revealed in all its glory to the burnishing sun. Short glossy hair sat like a wet cap on her neat small head and she had the high-boned aristocratic haughtiness found in some Northern Italian women.

Harriet had already made it her business to become acquainted with Cara Peruggi. The thirty-five year-old wife of a Milanese businessman – furnishings, she had told Harriet with a deprecatory smile – had arrived at the Villa on the same day as Harriet herself. Cara was the type of woman Harriet had always found attractive. The Italian's firm, compact body, her natural arrogance, her icy wit with its suggestion that the only purpose of male existence was to provide for women's pleasure and enjoyment: it was a combination Harriet found immensely appealing.

As she studied Cara Peruggi from behind her glasses Harriet felt the warmth start between her legs. She no longer fought her desires. Why should she, when the opportunity for fulfilment came so irregularly?

Mike, she felt sure, had never guessed and for that she was thankful. For unlike Cara, she had never felt disdain or contempt for the man who had loved her and been so instrumental in elevating her to a position and standard of living she would never have dreamed possible.

She had loved Mike, respected him and wanted only to make him happy. Mike had rescued her and she owed him so much. But, despite her performances to the contrary, he had never satisfied her sexually. Only a woman could do that.

Harriet's hand trembled as she picked up her glass. She wanted Cara Peruggi...

'Allora,' there was a suggestion of humour in Cara Peruggi's voice, 'I think maybe Australian men are not so boring as Italian men, yes, Harriet?'

Harriet smiled. The two women were sitting on the stone balcony of Harriet's room, watching the indigo evening sky fade to darker night. Between them, on a low wrought iron table, stood an almost empty bottle of white wine. Villa Marissa might be a health resort but there was no taboo on the beverage that, to Italians, was the healthiest drink of all. Harriet had invited Cara to sit with her at dinner; it had been natural after that to suggest a nightcap in her room.

'It sometimes seems to me,' Harriet spoke with deliberate casualness, her eyes turned towards the darkening lake, 'that no man could ever be as interesting as a woman...'

Cara Peruggi raised a sardonic eyebrow. Her face, devoid of make-up was startling in its loveliness, Harriet thought as she looked across now at the other woman.

'I think maybe you are right, Harriet... it is certainly more pleasure for me to sit here and speak with you than with Alessandro.' Harriet didn't miss the faint note of contempt with which Cara spoke her husband's name.

'Alessandro speaks of nothing but work, business, the company,' Cara continued, irritation drawing her thick dark brows together. 'I think sometimes I will go crazy if I have to listen once more to the price of fabrics, the problems with employees...' She turned to Harriet and sighed in frustration. 'A woman needs more than that, Harriet. She needs flattery, compliments, teasing, to feel appreciated.'

Harriet tilted the wine around inside her glass and again her tone was light. 'Surely a woman like yourself, Cara, could find appreciation... elsewhere?'

Her companion raised one slim, tanned shoulder in a gesture of dismissal. 'Ha... lovers... they too become boring, Harriet. And the young ones, they are the worst. With them it is always – tell me I am the best, the biggest, the most adventurous...'

A sudden glint of humour lit Cara Peruggi's large velvet eyes as she became aware of the irony contained in her words. 'It is I, remember Harriet, who need the compliments.'

Heart hammering in her chest, Harriet put out a perfectly manicured hand and laid it on Cara's smooth, soft arm. 'Then let me tell you, Cara – you are a very beautiful woman. Even when you are my age you will be beautiful...'

The younger woman looked down at the hand that lay motionless against her skin. Slowly she brought her eyes up to meet Harriet's and with a sudden rush of relief and desire, Harriet saw the interest that flickered there.

A half smile twitched at the corners of Cara Peruggi's full lips. 'You are more interesting than I have thought, Harriet...'

Yet neither made the mistake too often made by men. The build-up, the anticipation, was to be relished, drawn out, not rushed and squandered too soon.

Harriet ordered a bottle of Tattinger and when the champagne was brought and opened, the two women sipped at it slowly, enjoying its cold dryness in their warm mouths.

'I like champagne,' Cara stated. 'But,' putting down her half empty glass, she stretched for her handbag which she'd tossed on the seat beside her, 'this I like even better.'

With a smile she drew from her purse a small white cigarette. 'You permit, Harriet, yes?'

Harriet, already floating from the effects of the wine and champagne, and breathless from anticipation, merely nodded.

With a slender gold lighter, Cara lit the joint, took a long deep drag, then held it elegantly between scarlet nails.

'Perhaps,' Harriet's voice sounded thick and uneven to her own ears, 'it would be more discreet to go back inside. On the night air...'

Cara Peruggi looked amused. 'If it troubles you, Harriet.'

Five minutes later they were in bed, Harriet's pulses racing as her tongue circled the younger woman's dark, jutting nipples.

Through her own soaring pleasure she could hear the harsh uneven rhythm of Cara's breathing, punctuated by small animal-like moans of delight. As her hands roamed over the silky softness of Cara Peruggi's body, Harriet thrust back into her subconscious the memory of all those rough male bodies all those years ago...

'BUT, DAVID, I'VE been here almost two weeks and apart from that first lunch and cocktails one evening, we haven't had a moment together. Not a private moment, I mean.'

At the other end of the line, David could hear the plaintive note in Kelly's voice and he suppressed a sigh, as well as his usual twinge of guilt.

Kelly had called him nearly every day. Eventually he'd had to agree to meet her for a quick drink one evening; but he had ensured that the meeting took place in a crowded, noisy cocktail lounge where the chance of any intimate exchange would be minimal.

Now, it was after ten at night and he was very tired.

'Kelly,' he kept the exasperation from his voice, 'I'm a very busy man – you must realize that. Any time I have for socializing is extremely limited. I don't think you should count too much on my company if you're going to be in Sydney for a while. My advice is to get out and meet people nearer your own age, see something of the place and enjoy yourself before you go back home.'

Tears of frustration filled Kelly's eyes. Why was David being so cold and evasive? She had expected that here, away from their usual background, he would be more relaxed, more responsive. Yet still he was avoiding her, harping again on the difference in their ages. Couldn't he see that it didn't matter? That she wanted no-one else but *him*?

Fighting back tears, she forced herself to speak evenly.

'I'm patient, David. I'll wait until we can get together.'

HIS MOUTH TIGHT with annoyance, David put down the phone, poured himself a stiff Scotch and carried it through to his bedroom. As he undressed, his mind grappled with the problems created by Kelly's arrival.

Worst of all was the fact that he saw even less of Anthea than previously. While she might be doing him a favour in keeping Kelly out of his hair, the upshot was that they had little time for their own relationship.

'But it's not fair to leave the girl sitting alone in the house every evening, David. The nights I am free I really feel an obligation to be there with her. She's upset and she must be lonely.'

They were discussing the problem of Kelly at the end of a brief meeting in his office and for once David wished that Anthea was less understanding.

'Then it's her own goddamn fault, Anthea – you've done your best by offering to introduce her around.' He spoke sharply, guilt adding to his frustration.

Anthea sighed. 'I know, David. A new pretty face is as welcome in Sydney as anywhere... but Kelly shows no inclination to get out and about. She's polite enough about it but...'

David shook his head. 'Maybe I'm being too soft Anthea, treating the whole situation with kid gloves. Perhaps Oscar was right. This time I should tell her to her face that there's no hope and never has been. And now that there's someone in my life she'd better finally believe it.'

Anthea's response was emphatic. 'Oh no, David – you can't do that. Not while Kelly's living with me. She'd feel so humiliated, betrayed.' Her voice softened. 'Let's be patient a little longer, my darling. Eventually Kelly will go home and, given time, I'm sure she'll find someone special. Someone who'll make her forget that she ever had this... crazy obsession with you.'

Anthea looked at him with a troubled expression. 'She's a very warm, intelligent girl, you know, David. I like her. We've talked a little about what she wants to do once she's finished college, and she seems very interested in the sort of field that I'm in. Investigative journalism appeals to her. Maybe,' the idea suddenly occurred to Anthea, 'I should invite her into the office with me sometime – involve her in some research or something. At least she'd be doing things that interested her. What do you say?'

Without giving David a chance to reply, she continued, 'I know – the AMN party next weekend. Why not ask Kelly to that?' A smile came to Anthea's face. 'I'm sure there'd be no shortage of young male staff eager to answer her questions.'

From the look on David's face Anthea could see the idea held appeal. The luncheon party at David's home was to celebrate AMN's success in the first ratings' period. It was the ideal opportunity to introduce Kelly into a milieu that interested her.

David raised a wry eyebrow, his good humour restored. 'I can only hope Anthea, that your matchmaking abilities are equal to your professional abilities.'

ANTHEA WASTED NO time in suggesting her idea to Kelly. Her sympathy was with this bright, striking girl who was so obviously troubled and confused. No-one could understand better than herself how a young girl, hopelessly in love, could feel...

The flicker of interest in Kelly's hazel eyes as Anthea extended her invitation told her she was on the right track. The party might be just what Kelly needed to distract her from her preoccupation with David.

'David thought you'd enjoy meeting the team he's put together,

Kelly. They're the best at what they do and you'll be able to learn a lot about the business at firsthand. Would you be interested in coming?'

The opportunity to see David's home was what struck Kelly first. But Anthea was right, this was a group of people she really would like to meet.

'Sure,' she answered, 'why not?' Then, fearing she might have sounded ungracious, she added, 'It's very nice of you to bother about me, Anthea. Thanks, I'd love to come.'

LATER, AS SHE undressed for bed, Kelly thought again about the woman under whose roof she was living. In the couple of weeks she'd been with her, Kelly had found Anthea easy company. She listened, was interested in her ideas and concerns, and didn't treat her like a child as her father was so often inclined to do. Of course, Kelly thought, she would still have preferred to be with David, sharing every precious moment of this short time together; but at least with Anthea she felt comfortable. A friendship was growing between them that Kelly was no longer resisting.

In fact, she sighed, slipping into bed, she wished she could discuss the problem of David with Anthea. An older woman would surely be able to advise on how to break down the barriers David still insisted on maintaining.

But, Kelly turned over and snapped off the bedside light, she had decided to handle this situation in her own way, to make David see that it was only his own inhibitions that stood in the way of happiness for both of them.

THE NEXT DAY Anthea called Paul Shelton into her office. He was a tall, well-built young man with a healthy rugged face, thick sandy hair and riveting green eyes. Possessed of irrepressible good humour, at twenty-five, Paul Shelton was also one of Sydney's brightest young journalists.

He listened with interest as Anthea explained Kelly's interest in their work.

'She'll be at the party at David's next week, Paul. I'll introduce you and maybe you could take her under your wing for the time she's here.'

'Sure, be glad to, Anthea. Young, single, female *and* interested in my work – shouldn't be too much of a hardship.'

Anthea smiled to herself as Paul left her office. Paul Shelton didn't know the half of it.

The phone call from Alex came just ten minutes later. They hadn't spoken since the night she had told him about David.

Now, as Alex told her his news, there was no time for awkwardness between them.

He spoke quickly, his voice strained, 'It'll be on the noon news, Anthea. It's Leard – the ex-Customs employee. His body was found an hour ago at the foot of The Gap. The police can't decide whether it's suicide or accidental death.' Alex heard Anthea's quick intake of breath. 'Leard had an appointment to see me this Friday, Anthea.' He paused. 'Now we know just how desperate they're getting.'

They both knew better than to discuss the matter further on the telephone and, after arranging to meet with her later that afternoon, Alex rang off. For a long moment Anthea sat motionless, taking in the shock of his news.

Neil Leard was dead. The Gap, a sheer cliff near the entrance to Sydney Harbour, was a notorious location for suicides; but, like Alex, Anthea had no doubt that Neil Leard had been murdered.

Later that afternoon as she left Alex's office where she, Alex and ex-Special Branch detective Ted Raynor had discussed the ramifications of Leard's death, Anthea felt the familiar churning of guilt in her stomach. Again she had mentioned nothing to Alex about the videocassette. As before, the morality of that decision stabbed at her conscience. To protect herself she was withholding what could be damning evidence against Julian Crane... But, Anthea persuaded herself, the cassette could not possibly be the linchpin of their case. At least she hoped to God it couldn't be.

KELLY LOVED THE house. It was marvellous, so much atmosphere, its character meticulously retained. While most of the thirty or so guests from AMN were grouped together in the back garden congratulating themselves on their initial impact on the ratings, Kelly had taken herself on a tour of David's lovely Federation home. Now, in the kitchen, she was chatting with David's housekeeper, Mrs Vincent.

'Even with a house this size, Mrs Vincent, you don't live in?'

'Oh no, love,' the woman answered, clearly enjoying her role as director of the small team of caterers. 'No need to really, not with just Mr Yarrow to do for. I come in for a couple of hours each morning and see that there's something made up for the nights Mr Yarrow tells me he'll be home for dinner.' They were interrupted then by a query from one of the caterers and as Mrs Vincent turned away, the idea suddenly took root in Kelly's mind.

As she left the house and joined the other guests on the back lawn, a delighted smile lit Kelly's face. It was a great idea! A terrific way to prove to David what an asset she could be in his business life... but she'd need Mrs Vincent's help.

'Hi.' A tall sandy-haired man with wonderful green eyes and a friendly smile interrupted her thoughts. 'I'm Paul Shelton. I work with Anthea James... Can I freshen up your drink?'

CHAPTER TWENTY-FIVE

HEART thumping wildly in her chest, Beatrice knew she was going to make it. Her fingertips were raw and bleeding but at last her efforts were about to be rewarded.

Grunting with the strain, Beatrice dug the now blunt point of the scissors again and again into the splintering wood. She was so close now, so close to the telephone that would link her to Selena and save her from this nightmare.

She had no way of knowing, of course, if it was a working day or the weekend; nor did she know anything of her cousin's working habits. She would try both numbers and pray that Selena answered. Not for a moment did she think that her cousin would fail her. Selena had lived a long time in Australia; she must know people who would be able to help. And once she was free, thought Beatrice in grim determination, she would tell everything she knew about what had happened to the other girls like herself who had been tricked, cheated...

'Jesu!' The word escaped from her lips as she suddenly realized she had made it. She was through! She had broken away enough of the wood from around the lock to force it back and allow her to flee!

Shivering in anticipation, Beatrice stopped only to loop her battered white handbag around her wrist before thrusting the damaged door completely open.

For a moment she stood breathless with joy in the sunshine outside her prison. She was in a wide, tiled hallway, dusty and devoid of furniture except for – Beatrice's eyes shone with delight – the grimy yellow telephone on the floor next to the main door.

Forcing herself to think clearly, the girl crossed to the telephone. Trembling with dread lest it now be disconnected, she lifted the receiver to her ear. A wave of warm relief swept through her as she heard the welcome burring sound of a line in working order.

She had made a decision to try Selena's place of work first.

Praying to the Virgin under her breath, she waited, terrified, as the ringing tone sounded in her ear. 'Mother of Jesus, please let her be there, please...'

'Good afternoon. Miz James' residence.'

Selena's clear, calm voice was suddenly too much for Beatrice.

'Selena! It is I... Beatrice!' She spoke in their native Tagalog and the few words were all she could manage before bursting into deep gulping sobs of relief.

'Beatrice?'

Through her tears, Beatrice could hear the utter astonishment in her cousin's voice. 'Beatrice – it is really you?'

Struggling for control, the frightened girl forced herself to speak. 'Yes, yes Selena. – it is I! Please... please... you must help me! Save me from this nightmare...' Then, garbled and chaotic, the words tumbled out as she tried to make Selena understand the hell she had been through...

'... and then afterwards, the man... he took me here, Selena. Only me. And he... he comes to me... does terrible things to me that...' Her voice broke in a strangled sob. 'Oh, Selena, please – you must get me away, help me to –'

'Beatrice!' Selena's voice was sharp. 'Listen to me – stay calm You will be safe soon – I promise you that. Miz James, she will help me. But you must tell me now everything you remember when the man drove you in his car – anything you saw that will help us to find you.'

Realizing the wisdom of her cousin's words, Beatrice fought back her tears, searching her memory for anything that might lead Selena to her.

At first on that long drive she had paid little attention for, despite the man's silence, his impassivity, she had been happy in the thought that at last she was free. How wrong she had been...

Now, screwing up her face, Beatrice tried desperately to think of anything that had stood out on that journey to the house. Then something clicked in her mind. Yes! She remembered the large church made of pink stones they had passed just as the houses began to thin out. She recalled it in particular because it was built in the Spanish style – so like the churches at home. As they passed it she had even been tempted to cross herself, but the mood of the man beside her had stopped her.

But now, thought Beatrice with mounting excitement, the church might save her after all. She began to describe it to Selena...

The first blow caught her on the back of the neck and at the same time the receiver fell from her hands as she screamed in pain.

'Bitch! Fucking bitch!'

Eyes wide with terror, Beatrice whirled around as the man, his face twisted in fury, lashed out again with the heavy metal wrench.

This time the blow crunched terribly against the arm she had raised in instinctive protection of her ashen face.

'No!...' Her scream was one of pure terror. 'No!... Please!'

'Fucking Asian bitch!' The man spat out the words as he grappled with the struggling girl.

Reeling with pain and trembling in terror, Beatrice knew her only chance was to get outside, to make a run for the thick scrub that surrounded the house.

With a superhuman effort she dragged herself clear of the man's grasp, feeling the sleeve rip from her pullover as she flung herself out of the open door and down the steps.

But it was too late. She could hear the man's breath right behind her; a second later, he had a vicious grip on her long thick hair. Beatrice howled in agony as she was flung to the ground, her head cracking against the sharp edge of the concrete drive. For an instant through a red mist of excruciating pain and horror, she caught sight of the frenzied rage that glittered in the man's bulging, evil eyes.

'You-shouldn't-have-done-that, bitch!' His face a glowering mask of fury, the man grunted out the words as he brought the wrench down again and again on the girl's skull.

Her face drained of blood, Selena listened, frozen in horror, as her cousin's terrified screams reached her faintly down the still connected line.

BARRY HAD A five feet four inch blond with a voracious sexual appetite to thank for his stumbling on what might have been a major flaw in his continuing observation of Julian Crane.

If that randy hot-mouthed little Mandy hadn't called at the flat and blown his usual schedule that morning he would never have been in a position to notice Crane drive out from the network's basement carpark at the wheel of a late model white Alfa.

By the time he'd satisfied the rapacious Mandy – not to mention himself – he'd been running late to take up his usual position near the front of the Crane H.Q.

His favourite observation post gone, he was swearing under his breath as he crawled around the block looking for somewhere else to keep watch. To his amazement, he spotted Crane emerging from the rear carpark exit at a time when Barry had always imagined him safely inside.

Cursing even louder, Barry pulled off a screeching three point turn and set off after his prey. Shit! He banged his palm hard against the steering wheel. He couldn't believe his own stupidity. While he'd been sitting at the front, waiting like a bloody moron for the Rolls to appear, Crane had been slipping out – God knows how many times – in the much less conspicuous Alfa.

As he followed Crane's car in the stream of traffic heading north across the Bridge, Barry consoled himself with the thought that perhaps, after all, he was finally going to get the breakthrough he'd been waiting for. The thought sent a ripple of mirth through him as he imagined for the hundredth time getting his own back on Crane.

Just a whiff of scandal, something to tempt the gutter press – that would do nicely. Just enough to plump out his own pockets.

A grin spread over Barry's face. And to think he'd been about to toss it all in. He'd started to figure that Maxine and all the other rumour-mongers had got it wrong, that the gossip about Citizen Crane had been a heap of bullshit – or that Crane had become a monk overnight.

Barry put his foot down and shot up the freeway, keeping one car distance between himself and the white Alfa. It wouldn't do to lose the bastard now.

From his hiding place in the scrub the bile rose in Barry Francis' stomach as he watched Julian Crane strike again and again at the defenceless girl.

For almost an hour he'd followed Crane at what he hoped was a safe distance. He'd begun to wonder if it was just a wild goose chase – how often did the Eastern Suburbs elite venture *this* far north of the Harbour – when, at the next intersection, he saw Crane turn off the main highway.

Barry's puzzlement grew as, fifteen minutes later, the Alfa left the bitumen for a rough winding track. They were deep in the bush when he spotted the house through the trees. The white Alfa was parked outside.

Sharply he'd pulled off the narrow gravel track and driven far enough into the scrub to hide his car completely from view. Then, aware of the sudden thumping of his heart, he'd moved cautiously through the trees towards the house. What in hell had brought Julian Crane to a place like this?

It was then that Barry heard a woman's terrified screams and, ducking behind the peeling trunk of a large silver gum, he watched stupified with shock as the incredible scene was played out in front of him.

In a matter of seconds it was all over. The girl hadn't a chance. With beads of sweat breaking out on his forehead and upper lip, the sickening realization came to Barry – he was the only witness to a murder in cold blood committed by one of Australia's wealthiest, most powerful citizens...

Breathing heavily, Julian Crane looked with distaste at the spatters of blood on his clothes and shoes. Taking a clean white handkerchief from his pocket he tried to wipe off the worst of it. He'd lost control, he knew, but hadn't the bitch realized she was his slave, his possession? A piece of Asian scum with no rights, no claim to freedom any longer?

The mist of rage rose again before his eyes and, shaking his head, he sought to clear his mind. Now, he had to think straight.

There was only the remotest chance that anyone would be able to find the place, no matter what the bitch had told them – but he could take no chances.

Bending down, he took hold of the girl's thin ankles and, carelessly bumping her shattered skull against the path, he dragged her back into the house.

Then he crossed to the phone, snatched it up and dialed a

number. When it answered, Julian Crane spoke carefully.

'Frank – it's me. I've got a package for you to pick up... my place in the country...

The moment Julian Crane disappeared inside the house, Barry turned and ran back through the trees to his car. With shaking hands he gripped the steering wheel and reversed out of the bush back onto the track. Driving as fast as he dared on the loose stony surface, his mind replayed the scene of horror over and over again...

CHAPTER TWENTY-SIX

THE first thing Anthea saw as she turned into her driveway was Selena, wide-eyed and obviously distraught, running towards her across the lawn.

She brought the car to a halt and slipped hurriedly from the driver's seat just as the flushed and agitated girl reached her.

'Selena! What's the matter?' Alarmed, Anthea laid a steadying hand on her overwrought housekeeper.

Selena turned red-rimmed eyes up to Anthea. 'Oh, Miz James, I try to call you... Everywhere I try. You must help me – please!'

'What is it Selena? What's the matter? Tell me!'

Breathlessly Selena gulped out the words. 'It is Beatrice. We must find her... before it is too late!'

Back in the house it took Anthea a further few minutes to make sense of what Selena was trying to tell her. In her distressed condition Selena's English let her down. Then, as she began to understand, Anthea's face paled.

'... and then... suddenly she is no longer speaking... it – it sounded as if the phone had fell to the ground. And after that,' a shudder ran through Selena's light frame, 'there were only screams... terrible screams, Miz James... as if – as if...' Selena broke off and burst into tears.

Crouching down in front of her, Anthea took hold of Selena's slender arms. 'Listen to me, Selena. We must act quickly. You must tell me again, very clearly now, *exactly* what Beatrice said about this church... then I will call Alex. Together we will try to find your cousin.'

Alex arrived less than ten minutes after Anthea's call. She had been fortunate to find him in his office after a busy morning in court and he had left at once in answer to Anthea's guarded but obviously urgent call.

Selena was perched tensely on the edge of a kitchen chair. The tears were dry now on her strained and pale face and her hand clutched an untouched glass of brandy. Anthea quickly told Alex what had happened.

Tight-lipped, he listened without interruption until Anthea had finished. Then, anger and frustration glinting clearly in his eyes, he murmured so that Selena couldn't hear: 'It's damn all to go on to find the girl, Anthea. We –'

He was interrupted by the ringing of the telephone.

At once Anthea was across the room, the receiver at her ear.

'Anthea James speaking.' Out of the corner of her eye she could see Selena staring at her, a tense and frightened look on her face.

As Anthea listened, the others could faintly hear the caller's voice – a male voice, speaking roughly and without pause.

At last, her heart cold and still within her, Anthea replaced the receiver. Keeping her eyes on the phone, she spoke in a hushed tone. 'I know exactly where to look for Beatrice.'

She heard Selena's sharp intake of breath and, fighting to hide her shock and pity, Anthea forced herself to look at the frightened, wide-eyed girl.

'You must stay here, Selena,' she said gently, wishing that Kelly had been at home. 'Alex and I will go.'

Ted was waiting for them at the road junction that the caller had described and, as the well-built, ex-policeman joined them in Alex's car, Anthea quickly filled him in on what she and Alex already knew.

'... wouldn't give his name. Sounded pretty close to dead drunk to me – and if it hadn't been for the incredible call to Selena I probably wouldn't have even begun to believe his story. He *swears* he saw a girl – "Asian chick" was the way he put it – bludgeoned to death.' Anthea looked at Ted. Her face was pale and drawn. 'Murdered by Julian Crane.'

A rapid blink of his eyes was Ted Raynor's only reaction. 'And he told you exactly where it happened?'

'If we've got it right – not half an hour from here.'

BARRY FRANCIS HAD stopped his car at the first pub he'd come to on his drive back to the city. There, in the grass at the back of the carpark, his body had responded to the scene he had so recently witnessed. He had vomited until there was no more to bring up.

Now, as he sat in the almost empty public bar, his clammy hands clasped around a double shot of Johnny Walker, he began to wonder if he'd imagined the whole thing.

But Jesus no, it had been Crane he'd seen leave the city; it was Crane he'd followed north through the beachside suburbs until he'd turned onto that rough winding bush track. And it'd been Crane he'd seen smash the heavy tyre wrench again and again against that poor chick's skull.

As that memory returned, the trembling began again. Barry tossed back his drink, and re-ordered. Another double.

He didn't have to be a genius to understand the implications of what he had seen. There was a choice. Either he could nail Julian Crane in a way he'd never have dreamed possible, or he could end up in the biggest heap of shit he'd ever been in in his life.

Barry gulped down his drink and felt the liquor burn the back of his throat. Stuff it, he was too young to die. He was staying well bloody clear of this. It was too big for him. Small time drug stuff – that was his limit. He raised a shaky finger at the thin brassy blonde barmaid.

'Same again, love.'

The girl raised an eyebrow. Three doubles in less than five minutes? Barry didn't notice.

As he paid for his drink a dozen questions churned in Barry's head. Who the hell had the poor bitch been? She'd looked a slant-eye to him. And what the hell was she doing in a house in the middle of nowhere waiting for Crane? Barry was certain that Crane had been alone in the car. And he was certain that the poor bitch was as dead as dead can be. What, he wondered fearfully had she done to deserve that?

It was after his fourth double Scotch that Barry Francis slid – almost fell – off his barstool and headed for the gents.

He looked at his face in the mirror and the anger that had kept him on Crane's tail for so long returned with a vengeance.

Through bloodshot eyes he took in his misshapen nose, the red and mottled scar that ran from the side of his left eye almost to the lobe of his ear. The legacy of his night with Crane's thugs.

Leaning closer to the mirror, Barry touched the puckered ugly flesh with unsteady fingers. 'Cunts! Fuckin' cunts!' He spoke the words aloud. Spoilt his bloody face the bastards had; robbed him of the near perfect looks that had earned him an easy living.

He turned from the sight and pushed his way angrily through the door back into the bar. He had his bloody chance now, didn't he?

One drink later, Barry Francis was doing his best to convince the operator at AMN Australia that it was a matter of utmost urgency that he be given Anthea James' private number. Right to the top, thought Barry smugly as, through a warm haze of alcohol, he waited for the phone to ring.

'NOT THE SORT of place you'd stumble on if you weren't lookin' for it,' commented Ted as the car lurched and bumped its way along the stony overgrown track. He leaned forward from the back seat. 'Followed Crane here, the bloke said?'

'Yes', Anthea answered over her shoulder. 'He said Crane was alone, driving a white Alfa.'

'I'm just wonderin' what reason he had to be on Crane's tail. And for dobbin' him in to the press – instead of the cops.'

'Someone Crane's stood on once too often is my guess,' said Alex over his shoulder, at the same time swerving to avoid a large pothole in the middle of the track. 'And I for one am damned glad that neither he, whoever he is, nor your housekeeper Anthea, got in touch with the police. Once the police are involved they'll do nothing but scare away the people who might otherwise talk to us. And there's something even more important. I don't want this story to break before we get right to the top of the heap. Up till now all the cops have done is pull in the small fish while the big boys romp free and keep their dirty business rolling on without a hitch. This time,' Alex's voice was coldly determined, 'it's going to be different.'

Less than five minutes later they spotted the house through the trees ahead – just as the caller had described.

'Looks deserted enough now,' commented Alex as he pulled off the track and got out of the car.

Anthea had to agree as she took in the faded shabby exterior of the solitary house. Could Beatrice really have been killed here? For she was certain by now that the girl the caller had seen murdered had to be Selena's cousin.

'Hey – look at this.' Ted pointed to some patches of rough grass near the edge of the driveway. 'Hasn't rained in a week – someone's had a hose to this driveway not long ago, I'll bet.'

Alex met his glance and nodded in silent agreement. Then, his face grim, he turned and walked up to the front door. Without much hope he tried the handle.

'Locked, of course,' he grunted. 'Come prepared, Ted?'

Ted grinned as he drew a heavy bunch of keys from his inside pocket. On the third attempt the door swung open. By now it was late afternoon and inside the house it was dim and shadowy.

Alex felt around for a light switch in the hallway.

'Don't bother, mate.' Ted pointed to the bare socket in the ceiling. 'Won't work even if it's connected.'

'I've got a torch in the car, Ted. Let's get it out and have a better look.'

As they waited for Ted to return, Anthea pointed out the telephone socket in the dusty skirting board near the front door. 'Well, if there was a telephone here, there isn't one now,' she noted.

With the aid of the torch they moved further into the darkened house and Anthea's heart began to beat more rapidly at the thought of what they might find.

But if a recent murder had indeed been committed here, the house showed no obvious sign of it. Every room bar one was empty; the exception contained the bare necessities: bed, chair, table, as well as a stack of dirty plates and cutlery, and a small hot-plate plugged into the wall.

With a puzzled frown, Alex again tried a switch. To his surprise a weak glow lit the fusty-smelling room.

'I thought this room seemed darker than the rest. Look.' He pointed to the heavy shutters over the window-frame and watched as Ted crossed the room and tried to slide the window open.

'Nailed shut,' Ted murmured.

The light from the single bulb barely reached the small grimy alcove that served as a bathroom and Anthea called Ted to come closer with the torch.

A tap dripped with monotonous regularity into the cracked dirty sink. There was an uncurtained shower recess with rusty taps, and a bare, stained toilet. The thought that a human being might have been shut up here alone in such filth and squalor made Anthea sick with anger.

It was when they were turning to leave the tiny stifling alcove that Anthea caught a faint glimmer of something in the beam of the torch.

'Wait a moment, Ted,' she put a hand on his arm. 'Flash the torch this way again.' Guiding Ted's hand she directed the light squarely onto the cracked and peeling windowsill beside the sink.

Next moment the breath froze in her throat as she stared at the object that lay gleaming in the circle of light.

'It's Julian Crane's, Alex... I can swear to that.'

The three of them were standing under the glow of the feeble light bulb and in her open palm Anthea was holding the black onyx ring in its unusual gold setting.

'How can you be so certain, Anthea?' There was a quiver of excitement in Alex's voice as he asked the question. He hardly dared believe that they had been lucky enough to find such positive identification of Crane's presence in the house.

'Because,' Anthea looked up staring straight into Alex's grey eyes, 'a year ago he had it reset – to my design.'

In the fading light, even with the aid of the torch, there was little more they could do. On the long drive back to the city they discussed what their next step should be.

'There're the usual follow-ups of course,' observed Ted. 'A search into the ownership of the property and in whose name the electricity and water have been connected. Also,' he added, 'I'd like to take a closer look at the place tomorrow, in the daylight. There's just a chance the body might have been buried somewhere close by and there could be evidence of skin, hair... caught under the fingernails. Something like that coupled with the ring...' He trailed off, contemplating the possibilities.

'Whatever happens from now on,' put in Alex, 'we're going to keep all knowledge of that ring strictly amongst the three of us. Crane'll know he's lost it, and he'll know where – what he won't know is who's got it. He might just panic and end up doing something very very stupid...'

They dropped Ted back at his own car and, alone now with Alex, Anthea raised the issue she'd been silently brooding upon. She spoke quietly, her gaze focused on the road ahead. 'Alex, I hope you'll agree with me – I think it's time we filled David in on what we know. He's backed me all the way on this anti-crime issue and I think it's time he was alerted to just how dangerous the stakes are getting. Julian Crane is rich, he's powerful and he's got all the right people in his pocket. I think David should be told everything we know.'

For a long moment Alex said nothing until Anthea began to think he had no intention of answering. Then in a carefully neutral tone he said, 'I think you're right, Anthea.'

BEFORE ALEX DROPPED her home, they agreed that if David was free that evening they should get together.

'I'll call him and then let you know, Alex,' Anthea said as she got out of the car.

Alex gave a stiff nod of his head. 'Are you sure you don't want me to come in with you, Anthea?'

'No, Alex, really. It's very kind of you but it'll be better if I speak to Selena alone first. I'm not relishing the thought but it's got to be done.'

They had decided to tell Selena the bare outline of the truth: that there was a strong possibility her cousin had met with foul play, but that while there was no body, there might still be hope. They would say nothing of the fact that a witness had attested to having seen the killing.

'Anthea!' Kelly's voice was high-pitched with alarm and confusion as she opened the front door. 'What on earth's been going on? Selena's –'

Anthea pushed her hand through her hair in a weary gesture.

'Look, Kelly, I really can't go into it all at this stage. It's – it's all rather complicated.'

At that moment Selena emerged, wide-eyed and fearful, from the kitchen. 'Miz James, you – you have found Beatrice?' The hope that still existed in her voice, stabbed at Anthea's heart.

Leaving Kelly standing alone in the hallway, she ushered Selena gently into her study. With a sinking heart, Anthea knew that she was about to erode even further the last vestiges of that hope.

THE ONLY AWKWARD moment came when, at close to one a.m., Alex stood up to leave. They had spent four hours in David's home filling him in on their investigations which had culminated in the astounding allegation made by their anonymous caller.

'You'll have to excuse me,' Alex reached for the coat he'd thrown on a nearby chair. 'It's late and I'm due in court at nine-thirty sharp tomorrow.'

'Of course.' David stood up and held out his hand. 'It's been a real pleasure to meet with you, Alex... I have a much better idea now of what's really going on in this country. And I must say I very much admire the action you're taking personally on these issues.'

Alex took the proferred hand but only momentarily. 'Well this is the closest we've come yet to any real evidence; evidence that can convict, and that connects the man at the top to the whole ugly set-up.' He fastened the buttons on his coat. 'If we land Crane – and I'll be doing everything in my power to ensure we do – it'll be through his own depravities and vices. It isn't enough that he has to deal in these girls for profit; now it seems he's using them to indulge his own private tastes as well. The girl didn't go into detail on the phone but it appears obvious that he'd been giving her a hard time.'

'I'm backing you all the way,' David was emphatic. 'The press has an immense responsibility in the face of such a situation.'

'Thank you.' Alex nodded briefly then looked down at Anthea who sat uneasily on the sofa, her eyes avoiding his.

'Well – I'll leave you two alone then.' He hated the acid tone in his voice, but he couldn't help himself. He was walking out and leaving the woman he loved alone with his rival; and it hurt. But, Alex reminded himself, Yarrow was still only that – a rival. Not yet a victor.

'Good night, Alex.' Anthea met his eyes and flushed slightly. For a second too long Alex held her gaze then turned and left the room, accompanied by David.

David was aware of the tension and when he returned to the

living room was silent as he sat down and picked up his half-finished drink.

Taking a sip, he looked at Anthea over the rim of his glass.

'Alex and you had... something going, I guess? Something important?' he asked quietly.

Anthea nodded. 'We – we were good friends, yes.'

She made no attempt to elaborate and David changed the subject. What had happened in the past no longer mattered; only the future was important now.

'You know Anthea, if Crane realizes he's being closed in on he's going to be a very dangerous adversary. There are people in high places certain to cover up for him and that could put you and Alex in a very unpleasant position.'

Anthea nodded, 'We're both well aware of that, David. Believe me, I've already been confronted with the very special sort of power that Crane wields in this city.'

She told him then how sure she was that it had been Crane behind the attempts to damage her political credibility and to bring pressure to bear on the Party to dismiss her as a candidate.

As she spoke, David listened carefully, his brows drawn together in a deep frown. When she had finished his eyes looked steadily into hers. 'You surely realize, Anthea, that there's a very real danger to your personal safety – and Alex's – in this whole business?' His tone was deadly serious.

It was then, taking a deep breath, that Anthea told him about the videocassette...

It was very early in the morning before they finally got to bed. But there Anthea forgot everything as the length of David's strong naked body pressed against hers, as his hands caressed her gently, slowly, making the fire spread through her veins until finally she was filled with a sense of utter peace and completeness.

'Oh, I love you, David... I love you so much...' Her warm breath carried the message into his hair, his neck, his chest.

Holding her close against him, David sighed into the darkness. 'I want to spend every spare moment with you. If only Kelly weren't around. It's so restrictive, keeping everything hidden, not knowing when we can meet... Why the hell don't you just let me tell her?'

'Sh-h-h' Anthea stroked a finger gently along his neck. 'Be patient just a little longer, darling. My way is better and I'm sure it'll work if we give it time. He's trying his best not to show it, but Paul Shelton is absolutely besotted; a blind person could see that. And Kelly, like any young girl – or old one for that matter –' she grinned into the darkness, 'is not averse to a little flattery and attention.'

Anthea had explained to David her hopes for Paul Shelton but he was far from convinced.

'Yes – but that was never the problem,' he protested now. 'There was never a shortage of interested men. It was Kelly who –'

Anthea interrupted him. 'Ah – but this time, David, she's attracting a man she *respects*. She's well aware of Paul's reputation as a first-rate journalist and that's what attracts him. Here is a man from whom she can learn something, be stimulated by; and from what I can gather she's never found that before in anyone of her own age. It's been a very important eye-opener, David, believe me. But it needs time... just a little more time, darling.'

David was still sceptical but for the moment at least, Anthea knew he'd been mollified. 'I am forced to bow to your superior judgement in all matters relating to the inscrutable opposite sex, my darling.'

Then, with a final kiss to the top of her head, he relaxed and was soon asleep. But, restlessly tossing beside him, it was close to dawn before Anthea's own eyes closed in sleep. Her thoughts were still on Kelly. Despite the confidence with which she'd spoken to David, she hoped she was right about the girl.

In the short time they had been together, Anthea had got to know Kelly quite well and, although the girl had done her best to conceal the fact, the extent of her obsession with David had been made disturbingly clear to Anthea.

When David had first mentioned the problem of Kelly, Anthea had to admit she'd underestimated its seriousness. He was exaggerating she'd felt sure; a case of childish infatuation was not a major problem. But she had been wrong. She could see for herself now that Kelly was hopelessly, dangerously, in love with David.

Anthea sighed as she turned her head against the pillow. She sincerely hoped that Paul Shelton would be the one to break this terrible spell, this fixation of Kelly's. Not that she expected anything permanent to come of a relationship between Paul and Kelly. Her hope was merely for Kelly to discover that she *could* be attracted to boys of her own age group. Kelly had too much to offer to waste her life yearning after something that could never be.

Anthea had begun to realize that there was a lot more to Kelly Delamar than was immediately obvious. Certainly, as the only child of a doting wealthy father, she had been indulged – that was clear enough. But there was another side to Kelly too, a gentle, soft and understanding side. She had a well-developed social conscience, a real concern for those less privileged than herself; it was the basis, Anthea strongly suspected, for her interest in the form of justice and equality provided by the media. And Kelly's concern and feeling for others took a practical form too. Tonight for instance.

While the issues involved had remained a puzzle to her, Kelly, refraining from further questions, sought instead to comfort and console Selena in her obvious unhappiness.

Kelly had a good heart, Anthea thought as at last her eyes grew heavy. While it was true that Kelly's presence caused a certain amount of inconvenience in her personal life, she somehow couldn't help finding herself drawn more and more to the young girl.

CHAPTER TWENTY-SEVEN

THE first light was just beginning to break over the flat, metal-grey sea as Julian Crane, with complete disregard for the speed limit, raced north through the still sleeping beachside suburbs.

He'd first noticed the ring was missing last night when undressing for bed. As was his usual routine he removed his watch and ring together, placing them in the small leather box on his chest of drawers.

For a moment he'd stared in stupefication at the bare third finger of his left hand. Then his stomach gave a sickening lurch. He remembered why the ring wasn't there and where it had been removed.

Alarm raced through him and he cursed his own stupidity and carelessness – but he knew it was useless to do anything about it at this time of night. He'd have to –

Christ! Something clicked in his brain and warm relief poured back into his body. Of course! Frank! Frank would surely have found it.

He crossed to the bedroom door and shut it carefully before sitting down on the bed and reaching for the phone. No doubt Maxine was still downstairs watching her nightly dose of American crap. She'd be putting away yet another of his best reds that she was no doubt too pissed to appreciate. But he wasn't taking any chances.

He punched the numbers. Frank answered right away.

'You're alone?' Frank always knew his voice.

'Sure – and don't worry mate, it's all taken care of.'

'That's not what's worrying me – it's something else.' The sick feeling came back into his belly when Frank made no mention of the ring. Anyway, wouldn't he have called already if he'd found it?

Through gritted teeth he told Frank what had happened.

'Christ, mate, I never set eyes on it. But it's gotta be there. Look, I can go –'

Julian Crane cut him off. If Frank had overlooked this, what else might he have missed? 'Don't bother!' His voice was icy. 'I'll go myself.'

Now, as he sped along the near-deserted streets Julian Crane began to allow himself to relax. The house was too remote, too well hidden, for anyone to merely 'stumble upon' it. That was why he'd chosen it, after all. The ring would be exactly where he'd left it. No harm would be done.

He yawned as he got closer to the turn-off into the bush. He'd had hardly a wink of sleep. Up at five a.m., he'd driven the Rolls into the city, where he'd swapped to the Alfa. He glanced at the Rolex on his left wrist. 6.15 a.m. He'd be back in plenty of time for his regular 8.30 editorial meeting.

The blood drained away from his face as he stared at the empty window sill. Dropping to his knees he felt over every inch of the cracked and grimy tiled floor.

'Fuck!' Standing up, Julian Crane dusted off his hands and felt the beginning of real fear inside him. Where the hell was it?

For a moment his thoughts went to Frank. What if Frank had done the dirty on him and decided to pocket the ring?

But no, he dismissed the idea as soon as it occurred. He and Frank Carter had been mates since they were kids playing on the slag heaps of the Welsh village where they'd grown up; they'd pinched milk-money together from the bruisers on the hill, before graduating to motorbikes and cars. No, Frank wouldn't do that to him. He'd looked after Frank.

When he'd moved to Australia they'd kept in touch. But he'd been the one to make it while Frank, never a big thinker, had stuffed around getting himself a sort of name in the ring – but making little enough to live on. So when he'd sent for Frank, Frank had come. He'd seen pretty early on that he'd have a need for someone like Frank. Frank had his own special way of being 'persuasive', of getting rid of troublemakers and asking no questions. In return Julian had taken good care of his old mate. No, he thought again, Frank had no need to queer his pitch – Frank had it sweet. He'd even trusted Frank to come here to feed the bitch. Frank would never dare touch what didn't belong to him.

Julian Crane clenched his fists. What had happened to the ring? For another twenty minutes he searched the rest of the house, then the front driveway, just in case.

But Julian Crane didn't find what he was looking for.

'YOU MEAN TO to say that even though the drug was thought dangerous enough to be banned over three years ago in the States it's still selling here?' Kelly raised a disbelieving eyebrow at Paul who sat on the opposite side of the littered desk.

'Yeah – we thought it was crazy too. Especially,' he tapped the plain Manila folder in front of him, 'with the sort of local evidence we've come up with against it.'

'And now one of the original American researchers is really going to appear on Anthea's program?' There was a note of incredulity now in Kelly's voice.

Paul nodded. 'You bet – that's the beauty of having a real budget to work with. Doctor Edwin Meerhaus agreed to speak to us on this – and when you hear what he's got to say,' Paul made a soundless whistle, 'more than one head'll hit the ground with a thud in Canberra.'

He leaned back in his chair, looking pleased at the thought. 'What this reeked of right from the start, Kelly, was a pay-off. Sure, the drug company agreed to a re-testing after the U.S. withdrawal but,' he smiled wryly and shook his head, 'three years to complete the tests? No way. We decided to take a closer look.'

'So, tell me,' Kelly sat up straighter in her seat, 'how did you go about it.'

Paul grinned. He'd begun to realize that Kelly Delamar liked the details; the whole *modus operandi* and nothing less. A bloke couldn't resist such genuine interest.

'Read it.' He tossed the folder across the table at her. 'I'll trust your discretion.'

With a glance at his watch he stood up. 'Look, I've got to dash to a meeting. But it should be finished around one. Want to join me for a bite then?' He worked hard at sounding casual.

Kelly looked up from the file that had already begun to hold her attention. She gave him a distracted smile. 'Sure. Sounds good to me.'

As he hurried down the corridor for his meeting with Anthea and the rest of the production team, Paul's heart was still feeling the effects of Kelly's smile. Hell, that girl was beginning to wreak real damage inside him. What, he wondered with a wry smile, was happening to the famous Shelton cool? On the days he knew Kelly was at the network with Anthea, he found himself waiting impatiently for that lovely head to poke around his office door and smile, 'Hi.' Then in she'd come, all long luscious legs and thick shiny hair, trailing some wonderful scent so that, even sitting down, he felt himself go weak at the knees.

He opened a door at the end of the corridor. 'Hi everyone! Sorry I'm late.'

IT WAS THE first thing Anthea heard when she sat up in bed, and switched on the 6.30 a.m. news bulletin.

An iciness snaked through her veins as she listened to the announcer's unemphatic voice.

'... on the rocks near Narrabeen late yesterday. The body appears to be that of an Asian woman in her early twenties and had been in the water a number of days. Police believe the nature of the injuries to the body may indicate that death occurred before the body was dumped into the ocean... At a meeting of the Australian Federation of...'

The voice droned on but Anthea wasn't listening. Every instinct told her that the police had found Beatrice's body.

The ringing of the phone at her elbow made her jump. It was Alex. He too had been listening to the news and now they discussed what the discovery of the body would mean to their own investigations.

'If it does turn out to be who we think it is, there's no doubt that your connection with this – no matter how minimal, Anthea – is going to come out,' Alex said. 'And that, after all, might not be a bad thing – if it turns the screw on our – friend. He'll get a very nasty taste in his mouth, I'll bet, when he finds out how close to home he's come this time.' Alex spoke with a certain grim satisfaction.

They both agreed, however, not to show their hand to the police just yet. Evidence of police corruption was too strong to allow them to be totally open – at this stage at least – with the law.

'If a positive identification is made, Anthea, Selena has to be warned.' Alex was emphatic. 'She'll be called on to make a statement of course, but you must make her understand that it is absolutely essential she mentions nothing of our anonymous caller – nor the fact that you and I ever followed up on his call. If the police go looking for him and find him before we do, we just might end up losing a very valuable witness. Not to mention the fact that we'll all be had up for withholding vital information.'

No sooner had Anthea replaced the receiver than she dialled the number of the Sydney CIB and asked to be put through to the officer in charge of the case that had headed the morning's news bulletin. A moment later she was identifying herself to Detective Inspector John Willard and could sense his double-take as he realized he was talking to *the* Anthea James. As briefly as possible she explained that her Filipino housekeeper might be able to assist in identification of the body.

'Well, to do that Miss James, your uh – housekeeper will have to view the body. Hardly a pretty sight. Will she be prepared to do that?'

Anthea's hand tightened around the receiver. 'Yes... she'll do that,' she said hollowly.

Anthea broke the news to Selena when she arrived at the house just before eight.

'There is a chance – a very real chance, Selena – that it is Beatrice. You understand that?' She looked with compassion into the girl's blank face. 'And,' she continued softly, 'the only way we'll know for sure is for you to look at the body, and tell us.' There was something in Selena's stoical acceptance of the news that told Anthea this was merely what she had been expecting, preparing herself for, ever since Beatrice's desperate call.

'I must do this then,' she said in a quiet, steady voice. 'For Beatrice's family as well as for myself.'

Then, pale and silent, the girl listened as Anthea explained why it was necessary for the police to know something, but not everything.

*

JUST AS ANTHEA was about to leave the house, Kelly poked a sleepy head around her bedroom door.

'Anthea – what's going on? I heard the phone. What time is it?'

Anthea picked up her briefcase and, crossing to where Kelly stood with a puzzled look on her lovely sleep-flushed face, she put a hand on her arm.

'You've been very patient, my dear. I promise, when I get back I'll tell you what's been going on.' She gave a distracted smile and patted Kelly's arm as she made for the stairs. 'But now there are things I have to do.'

It was obvious by the time they arrived at Police headquarters, that the press had got on to the story.

'Anthea! What's your involvement in all this?'

'Your housekeeper, Anthea, is she –'

'Miss James! Is it true that the discovery of the body may be linked to your investigations into the so-called Asian prostitution racket in Australia?'

The dozen or so reporters swarmed after Anthea and Selena as they hurried up the steps into the building.

Anthea allowed Selena to enter through the sliding glass doors before her, then turned and faced the noisy press group.

'At this moment I am not making any statement other than to say that yes, the discovery of the girl's body is linked to my own investigations and' – she gazed evenly at her attentive listeners – 'this can only mean that it's a matter of time before there will be clear-cut evidence to ensure the bringing of a case in this affair.' It was a provocative statement, but neither the press nor the police, Anthea thought, could find anything to object to in her words...

Then, ignoring the immediate clamour of reaction, she turned on her heel and followed Selena into the building.

IN ALL HER professional career, Anthea had been to the morgue only once before and her second visit was no less of an ordeal.

She knew that Selena, while she would never have insisted on it, would be praying for Anthea's presence and support as she went through the ordeal of identification.

Bracing herself, Anthea took a firm hold of the girl's hand as the body was rolled out on its tray.

And there, for a moment, was the face; white as marble, bloated and distorted, but visible for long enough for Selena to whisper 'Yes.' Feeling the hand in her own grow tighter and suddenly clammy, Anthea turned to see the girl begin to sway.

'Come on, Selena. It's over, my dear.' She put an arm around the trembling girl and led her out of that dreadful place and up the stairs to the ladies room where, while Anthea held her head, Selena vomited away the terrible sight.

There followed a lengthy session with Detective Inspector John Willard. Selena, still shaken, was forced to repeat over and over again, everything Beatrice had said to her during that last telephone conversation.

Anthea hoped that in her distraught condition, Selena would make no mistakes. They wanted no slip-ups about the anonymous caller or the fact that she and Alex had been directed to what was certainly the scene of the crime.

Anthea had tried to explain to Selena that even in Australia it was not always for the best to tell the police everything. For the involvement of crooked police in this case was, she felt sure, beyond doubt.

Why else had Crane's operation been unhindered for so long? Why else had a verdict of accidental death been recorded in the case of Neil Leard, despite – as Ted had discovered through his more trustworthy contacts in the force – the appearance of several suspicious marks on Leard's body? No, she and Alex had agreed that, not until they had what could only be seen as irrefutable evidence which would indict Crane himself, could they tell everything they knew to the police.

Half way through Selena's testimony – made more difficult by her problems with the exacting language of the law – Anthea excused herself. She found a telephone and put a call through to David at the office.

'Anthea! Thank God you've called. Are you still with the police? The news report said –'

'Darling,' Anthea broke in but kept her voice low. She was speaking from a vacant office but there was always a chance of being overheard. 'I'm still with the police. I had to stay with Selena but won't be here for much longer, I'm sure. Then I'm going to take her home. She's pretty shaken up, as you can well imagine. Just having to talk to the police,' Anthea gave a mirthless laugh, 'is something to avoid where Selena comes from.' She paused. 'And David, I'm going to have to fill Kelly in on some of this. I'm going to offer Selena the chance to live-in for a while if she'll take it, and it'll help if Kelly's around to keep an eye on her. She'll need to know some of what's been going on.'

For a moment there was a silence at the other end of the line. Then David said evenly. 'Darling, you must be emotionally wrung-out as it is. Let *me* speak to Kelly. I can spare the time this morning...I'll go over there right away. Then, when you drop Selena home you can leave her with peace of mind.'

'Oh, David, thank you. I'd appreciate that so much.'

At the sound of the sheer relief and weariness in her voice, David realized just how emotionally drained Anthea actually was.

Kelly was making a fresh pot of coffee when the doorbell rang.

'David!' Amazement and pleasure showed in her face as she opened the door. 'Come in. Are you looking for Anthea? If you are –'

'No, Kelly.' David walked into the hallway. 'I know where Anthea is – at the police station. And that's why I'm here – to put you in the picture about what's been going on.'

Two cups of coffee later, David had told Kelly only as much as he felt she needed to know of the whole story. He made no mention of Crane or the discovery of the ring.

Facing him across the kitchen table, Kelly asked the obvious question, a frown drawing her fine brows together. 'But you must have your suspicions about who's behind all this. Whoever it is has to be someone very powerful.'

'At this stage,' David avoided her eyes as he spoke the lie, 'we've no real leads. It'll take time I guess...'

'Well,' Kelly's hazel eyes lit up, 'I think Anthea's commitment in following through on all this is terrific.' She looked steadily across at David. 'She's a doer, you know, David, not just a talker. That's what I like about her. Instead of mouthing off from the sidelines like so many of these high-profile females who seem to be more interested in ego-gratification than anything else, Anthea really gets her ass into gear to achieve her goals. Paul – Paul Shelton, you know, he's on her staff – has told me a lot about her.' Kelly nodded knowingly. 'She's a pretty special lady.'

'I know,' David said quietly as he stood up to leave.

Alone in the house once more, now that David had gone, Kelly turned over in her mind everything he had told her.

Poor Selena. Kelly's heart went out to the polite and charming Filipino. Now she understood why the poor woman had seemed so distressed these last few days. She must do what she could to comfort her.

She wondered too about those responsible for the whole sordid prostitution racket that trapped naive unsuspecting girls like Selena's cousin. Who would have the sort of power necessary to buy off both Customs and the law? Whoever it was, Kelly decided, must be near the top of the heap for the operation to run for so long and so smoothly. She knew too little about the Australian scene to even hazard a guess about who might conceivably be involved.

She mulled over David's unexpected visit. He had considered her important enough to be told; had been willing to share with her what was obviously dangerous and vital information.

Kelly felt a warm glow start inside her. At last David was treating her as a woman instead of a child. And, she smiled to herself, what she had in mind would convince him once and for all that she was the perfect partner with whom to share his busy and important life.

CHAPTER TWENTY-EIGHT

THE press had a field day over Anthea James' tenuous association with the murder of the young Filipino.

The reports in the country's leading newspapers were accompanied not only by photographs of Selena leaving police headquarters after giving her statement, but of Anthea's home and of Anthea herself.

Somehow too, the details of the girl's fatal phone call to her cousin with its suggestions of forced prostitution, and sexual abuse at the hands of her unknown captor, were acquired by the press and used to whip up even greater public fury.

Anthea had few objections to the furore on the front pages of most of Australia's major newspapers.

It made sure that the whole issue – of the fate awaiting so many unsuspecting girls – was kept squarely in front of the public.

Following up with a number of articles of her own – not only for AMN, as might have been expected, but also for two national women's magazines – Anthea further emphasized the urgency of bringing those responsible for all aspects of organized crime in the country to justice. And such publicity provided the perfect platform for extending her political support.

It was of particular interest to both Alex and Anthea that Julian Crane's publications took a particularly reserved and low-key approach in commenting on the issues involved – and after the initial report, killed the story dead.

'We've got him running scared, Anthea.' Alex couldn't hide his elation. 'He'll be desperate about that ring – not knowing who's got it or where it might turn up and mean trouble for him.' His eyes gleamed. 'We'll flush him out, Anthea. I know we will.'

It was past midnight and they were both tired as they sat alone in Anthea's living room. Their busy daily schedules left little time for contact at a more civilized hour.

'Has Ted come up with anything on the house?'

'That dump was bought in a company name: a $2 float which was nothing but a front. Services put on in the same name too, of course. Ted's still trying to trace it through.'

'And the caller? – Anything on that yet?'

Alex hid a yawn. 'We're still working on it – someone with a grudge against Crane is what springs to mind, of course. Doesn't seem likely that it'd be a business rival. That doesn't square with frightened, drunken calls from a public phone box. No, it's someone small, Ted feels sure. A disgruntled employee, a –' He broke off suddenly and sat up. 'Hey! Crane's wife. *There's* an avenue we hadn't considered!' He looked at Anthea, his excitement evident. 'What do you know about her – Maxine Crane, isn't it? Enemies? Lovers?'

Anthea shook her head. 'Nothing – though that doesn't mean much.'

'Well, do you know anyone who might?' Alex was alert now.

Anthea thought of Harriet. If anyone knew anything it'd be Harriet. Would she be back yet from her annual summer pilgrimage to Europe? 'Maybe...' she replied, getting up from the sofa. She was too tired just now to think about Maxine Crane.

'Alex, you'll have to excuse me. I'm wiped out – and I've got a hectic day again tomorrow. Plus,' she looked at him, 'I'm going to have to find a spare moment to fill David in on all this.' Weariness made her irritation more obvious than it might otherwise have been.

She was upset with Alex on this point. He had made it clear after that first occasion that in future, if Anthea wanted David to be informed of their progress, she'd have to meet with him alone. It was a time consuming complication she resented.

A flush of colour spread over Alex's cheeks as he stared back at her. 'I didn't ask for it to be this way, Anthea – remember that.' And, standing up he turned on his heel and left the room.

Guilt adding to her irritation and tiredness, Anthea winced as the front door closed loudly behind him.

It wasn't till late the next day that Anthea was able to find a spare moment for a private word with David.

The morning had been taken up with the usual round of production meetings; at noon she'd made a quick dash out of the office to address a luncheon gathering arranged by the organizing committee of her electoral campaign; phone calls and paper work had taken up the rest of the afternoon. And now, close to five, she put a call through to David's office. Was he free to see her?

'Darling, I've been looking forward to it all day.' The eagerness in his voice brought a smile of pleasure to her face.

He greeted her warmly as she came into his office. David closed the door behind her and sat her down in one of the two large comfortable armchairs facing the desk. His lips found the back of her neck.

'That's another thing I've been looking forward to all day,' he murmured in her hair.

He broke away and picked up the phone to instruct his secretary to hold all calls.

Anthea watched him, pleasure and contentment dispelling her weariness. She felt revived in David's presence. What a wonderful thing to happen to them both – to be given a second chance at love. All they needed now, she thought as she relaxed back into her seat, was time. Time to be together, to laugh, to talk, to make love.

But there were so many obstacles at present to such simple pleasures. The pressure was on them to bring a case against Julian Crane as soon as possible, while the momentum of public opinion was still so strong. If they could provide incontrovertible evidence of Crane's activities they'd be in a position to force immediate and positive government action.

Then, too, there was the problem of Kelly. When –

'Anthea?'

With a start, Anthea opened her eyes to see David's frowning face. 'Oh, darling...' She blinked. 'Please forgive me. I'm sorry... everything's been so frantic lately.'

From his seat opposite David looked closely at her. 'You're driving yourself too hard, Anthea. It worries me. And,' he resolved to tell her what else had been on his mind, 'I'm worried too about the amount of personal publicity you've received in relation to that girl's murder. What's been spotlighted, Anthea, is the fact that you're campaigning as hard as ever to force action on the whole issue.' His voice grew deadly serious. 'You're making yourself a very tempting target, you know that, don't you?'

The concern on David's face warmed Anthea's soul, yet he knew how important it was to her to break this case; he knew she couldn't step aside now.

She nodded in reply. 'Darling, as I've told you before, I have no illusions about the danger in facing Crane. But,' she said earnestly, 'I can't stop now. I've got to help Alex see this through to the end. Until we've got a watertight case against Crane. You understand that, don't you?'

David gave a sigh of resignation. 'Yes – I know that.' His voice grew gentler. 'It's just that I love you too much to be able to bear it if anything should happen to you, Anthea.'

'I know darling,' Anthea nodded. 'I promise I'll be careful.' Then, as quickly as possible, Anthea brought David up-to-date on the line of their investigations. 'Alex even had the idea that the anonymous caller might be someone connected with Crane's wife. Someone with a grudge against both or either of them. It's an idea of course. We can't close off any avenues at this stage.'

They discussed the whole situation for another twenty minutes then, as Anthea stood up to go, David put a hand on her shoulder.

'So what's the score between Kelly and our whizz kid reporter?' His voice carried its usual tone of cynicism on that subject.

'Well, she's had at least a couple of dates that I know of,' Anthea replied. Not,' she added with a laugh, 'that Kelly sees them like that. "Meetings" is her word for them. Just another opportunity to pick poor Paul's brain about his work.'

'Any word about when she's going home?'

Anthea raised an eyebrow and looked apologetic. 'Nothing. But it's got to be soon. School starts next month doesn't it?'

ANTHEA HAD BEEN back in her office for only ten minutes when David rang through.

'Talk about telepathy – Oscar's just been on the line. And he wasn't beating round the bush. Seems that every time Kelly's rung home he's never been able to pin her down on a return date. With school starting in less than three weeks he wants her home, pronto. Told me to put her on a plane forcibly if need be.' At the other end of the line a smile crossed David's face. 'I'd have tried that already, I told him, if I'd thought it might have worked.'

'I'm sure she won't be silly enough to drop out of school at this stage, David.' Anthea did her best to reassure him. 'Do you want me to –'

'No, Anthea. This time I'll talk to her myself. She has to realize that for Oscar's sake as well as her own, she's got to go home.'

JULIAN CRANE'S FACE contorted with rage as he skimmed through Anthea James' regular weekly column.

The bitch! She still hadn't left it alone; she was succeeding in keeping the topic fair and square in the public eye! He clenched his teeth. What fucking bastard luck that the Asian slut had some link with Anthea James. Something that should have been a minor news item worth three or four lines had been blown up into front page news.

Frustrated and furious, Julian Crane beat his fist against the newspaper that lay on the desk top in front of him. Christ! There had to be some way he could shut Anthea James' filthy mouth once and for all.

The article was just one of many that had appeared in the press in recent days after the discovery of the girl's body. Only this time, Crane swore viciously under his breath, James was writing openly about the possibility of a link between the Asian whore's death and that of Neil Leard.

Breathing heavily, he forced himself to read the article again:

'... a coincidence, considering the repeated rumors of a tie-up between the Customs department and the Asian prostitution trade, that is perhaps just a little too obvious to be ignored. It is to be hoped that despite a verdict of accidental death in the case of former Customs employee, Leard, investigations may be extended to include a much closer look at the reasons for Leard's dismissal from his position at Sydney's international airport.'

Enraged, Julian Crane threw the newspaper aside. The bitch was getting too close to the mark. There had to be some way of fixing her, shutting her up. There *had* to be.

Pushing back from his desk, he stood up and, hands in pockets, paced restlessly around his office. Somehow he had to find a way of setting up James, of compromising her to the extent that she'd be forced to drop the whole thing. If there was no possibility of digging up the dirt he needed, then he'd manufacture it easily enough.

Julian Crane clenched his fists. But he couldn't do anything until he got his hands on that tape.

DAVID'S INVITATION TO a lunch for just the two of them had come as a delightful surprise. Of course, Kelly thought as she got ready, she would have preferred dinner, but lunch was a start. She had seen far less of David during her stay here than she'd expected, and the time they had spent alone had been minimal. Today would be a pleasant change.

Kelly enjoyed their meal in the small busy bistro, although, she thought David seemed a little tense. The trouble was, she concluded, he worked too hard, worried too much – and had no-one to come home to who could help him relax.

Kelly took a deep breath. Given courage by the wine they had shared over lunch, she reached across the table and laid her hand over his. 'How much longer are you going to have to stay here, David? When are you coming back home?'

'I'm not real sure, Kelly. Things are more complicated here than I'd anticipated. Everything's running more or less smoothly at home. I have an excellent management team and we're in daily contact. I want to set up things here the same way.'

Even as he spoke he wondered why he didn't just tell her the truth – that it was Anthea, more than anything else, who was keeping him here. Kelly was old enough to face the truth.

But as he saw the disappointment, the fading hope in those beautiful hazel eyes, the words stuck in his throat. Later, he promised to himself, while cursing his weakness, he would write and tell her how everything in his life had changed, how he had found the woman he was going to marry. He would keep the letter light and casual, as if any overtones between himself and Kelly had never existed...

Now, he folded his napkin carefully and laid it by his empty plate while he told Kelly the real reason for their meeting.

'Oscar rang me a couple of days ago, Kelly. The new college term starts soon, as I'm sure you know, and he's very anxious to have a return date for you. He wants you to call, to let him know when to expect you.'

Avoiding his eyes, Kelly didn't answer.

'You know, Kelly, that you must go home.' He made it a statement rather than a question.

With eyes still lowered, Kelly nodded, but her mouth had set in a stubborn line. Then she lifted her head and her bright glistening eyes looked into his. 'Sure... I've got to go home,' she said.

There was something in her tone that David didn't like.

As she sat in the cab on the way home from the restaurant, Kelly knew it was time. She must put her plan into action at once. It had to work, she told herself. Even if David wasn't yet in love with her, he'd be forced to see that he needed her. And that was a beginning...

THAT SAME EVENING Kelly had agreed to join Paul Shelton for a drink. She drove herself to their rendezvous in her rented, unpretentious Ford, glad once again that Paul had made no protest when she'd refused to let him pick her up at Anthea's. That, Kelly thought, would have given too formal a definition to their meeting, something she wanted to avoid.

Now, as she waited for the light to turn green, she had to admit that she enjoyed Paul's company. He was a refreshing change from most of the young men she'd mixed with at home. In the short time she'd known him he had influenced her views on a number of issues, given her a new slant on the world.

What struck her most was that, far from having acquired the cynicism apparently innate to his profession, Paul Shelton had maintained a balanced, optimistic outlook on life which Kelly found particularly infectious.

He was looking out for her as she entered the pleasant, laid-back bar. Its clientele, Kelly noted wryly, consisted of trendy young executive types.

'Hi!' She joined Paul at his table near the open glowing fireplace. A bottle of white wine sat in the ice bucket at his elbow.

He smiled in greeting as he filled their glasses, a teasing light in his startlingly green eyes. 'I hope you're becoming duly appreciative of the fruit of the vine of my native country?'

Kelly grinned. 'Oh, I've managed to force down the odd glass or three.' Unless he was referring to his work, Paul was rarely serious and Kelly enjoyed his light, cheerful banter.

They spent a pleasant hour discussing – discreetly – Paul's most recent project, and then teased each other over the pros and cons of their respective countries until: 'Do you think you could ever live in Australia, Kelly? Permanently I mean.'

Paul's question was innocuous enough but there was something in his tone that made Kelly look up. He was watching her closely across the table.

She raised one shoulder. 'Sure, it's fine here. The people, the climate, the mood of the place – yeah, I could live here.' With David, she thought, she could be happy anywhere.

Paul said nothing further on the subject. When the bottle of wine was empty, he made a suggestion. 'What about a coffee?'

'Fine.' Kelly looked around for a waiter.

But Paul had other ideas. 'No, not here.' He was on his feet and pulling out her chair. 'My place is just a block away. Let's go there.'

Kelly frowned but before she could think of a polite way to decline the invitation, Paul's hand was at her elbow and they were out on the street.

Paul's apartment was in a small block of six just five minutes away. As they left the sharp night air for the warmth of the foyer, Kelly told herself she had nothing to be up-tight about. Paul wasn't going to come on heavy, she was sure.

Rejecting her offer of help, he left her in the living room and went through to the kitchen. Soon he appeared with two steaming mugs of coffee.

He made an apologetic face. 'Just instant, I'm afraid. Can you bear it?'

Handing her the mug, he crossed to the stereo and played the record that already lay on the turntable.

It was Jackson Browne. As the singer's clear mellow voice filled the room, Kelly felt herself relax. She had nothing to fear from Paul.

They spoke easily as they sat side by side on the high-backed sofa, sipping at their coffee. When the record ended Kelly put down her empty cup and looked pointedly at her watch. 'Well, I guess I'd better –'

'Kelly...'

His tone gave her warning and she felt her heart begin to pound. Slowly she turned to face him and Paul's arm, at rest across the back of the sofa, slid down to encircle her shoulders. Then he was pulling her close and Kelly could hear the force of his breathing as his face moved towards her own.

'No Paul!' She pulled sharply away and with one quick movement was on her feet. Her eyes were wide and fearful. 'I can't! Don't you understand. I can't!'

For a long time after the door had slammed behind her, Paul Shelton sat motionless, pondering the ambiguity and breathless despair in those words.

CHAPTER TWENTY-NINE

'I MUST say, Anthea, *Vogue's* write-up on you was most impressive; I read every word.' Harriet gave Anthea a quick smile. 'It took a woman, I thought to myself, to make all those tedious issues totally understandable.'

Behind her sunglasses, Anthea hid her surprise. It had never occurred to her that Harriet might have any interest in politics. Harriet's next words were ample proof of this.

'Of course I'd never have given it a glance if it hadn't been about you my dear!' She gave a low throaty laugh.

The two women were sitting on Harriet's sunny terrace with its sweeping views of Sydney Harbour. The remains of a light lunch lay on the table between them.

As if it were an afterthought, Harriet added quietly, 'Nan would have been delighted... She had such high hopes for you, Anthea.' Their eyes met; it was the only allusion to a past dead and buried for both of them long ago.

The two women saw each other rarely but for Anthea this was more than a social visit. She wondered how to approach the subject she wished to discuss.

Harriet made it easy.

Leaning back in her chair, Harriet closed her eyes and held her face up to the sun; a gentle winter sun of little threat to her pampered skin.

'God,' she sighed deeply, 'no doubt it's age but it seems to take me forever these days to get over the hell of jet lag.' Slowly she opened her eyes and turned her head towards Anthea. 'I've been home for a week and I'm only now beginning to feel human... It's this Saturday night I'm worried about. I want to look my best for the Madrigal Committee's big charity do.' She raised an eyebrow at Anthea. 'At your favourite ex-boss's place this year, as a matter of fact.'

Anthea was instantly alert. 'At the Crane's?'

'M-mm... the usual crowd of course.' Harriet's eyes gleamed in anticipation of the splash she'd make in the new Ungaro she'd picked up in Rome. A certainty to get her a full-length photo in the Sunday newspapers.

She turned to Anthea. 'You know Roy often turns up at the bigger functions these days.' Harriet gave a devilish chuckle. 'He's amazingly popular with some of the more naive of our society matrons. And of course it's all good for business, isn't it?'

Anthea nodded. 'Understandable...' But she had no intention of being side-tracked. 'Harriet... how well do you know Maxine Crane?'

Harriet smiled thinly. 'Darling, it's more a case of how well does one *want* to know Maxine... Not my favourite person by a long shot. But then,' she pursed her lips, 'neither is he.'

Anthea persisted. 'Would you say the marriage is a... solid one?'

Harriet raised a perfectly-arched, sceptical eyebrow. 'Well, the mutterings that have reached me from time to time seem to indicate that life is not exactly A-1 wonderful at the Crane mansion. The daughter married an Englishman – lives in some big baronial hall in Berkshire, I think – and Maxine and Julian just go on living their totally separate lives.'

Anthea picked her words carefully. 'Have you ever heard that Maxine –'

With an amused smile, Harriet anticipated the question. 'Has lovers?' She shook her ash blond head. 'Not a murmur. Which is not to say, of course,' her eyebrow arched higher, 'that dear Maxine is immune to the odd dalliance. She's away a lot – Europe, America – Julian rarely with her,' Harriet shrugged her very slim shoulders. 'Who knows what she gets up to then?' For a moment she was distracted by thoughts of Cara Peruggi and a sudden desire heated her thighs. With an effort, she brought her attention back to Anthea.

'To tell you the truth, Anthea, if I had to take a bet on it I'd say that whatever Maxine might get up to out of the country, she'd be too damn scared of Julian to try anything on closer to home.' Her eyes glinted. 'Julian's always given me the distinct impression that, if the occasion demanded, he could be utterly ruthless.'

Anthea blinked behind her sunglasses. 'You could be right, Harriet...'

Anthea left soon afterwards, but Harriet sat on a little longer in the afternoon sun, her thoughts on their conversation.

What, she wondered, was Anthea's interest in Maxine Crane? Anthea had never told her the details but she knew that the split with the Crane organization had been less than amicable. Not, Harriet was sure, that it had done anything to harm Anthea's career. She was as high-profile and fêted as she had ever been. And now it seemed she was headed for equal success in the political field.

Harriet's perfectly manicured fingers played with the stem of her empty wine glass. Well, she was delighted for Anthea's sake, and admired her for what she was trying to do.

Nan had been right, she thought, as she stood up and walked slowly back into the house. Anthea *had* been destined to achieve great things. And, Harriet looked thoughtful, she was glad that in her own way she'd once been able to help.

The house was cool and dim after the sunshine and, as her heels clicked across the marble floor, Harriet realized just how pleased she was to be home.

She had enjoyed the time away – the days at Ascot and the Derby renewing her acquaintance with the many friends she'd made in Mike's world, the delights of shopping in Paris and Rome. But it was good to be back in her own home, surrounded by her own beautiful things.

This was the third home she'd owned since Mike's death; and at over three million dollars it was her most expensive. As she climbed the broad curved staircase to her bedroom, Harriet mused on the unexpected pleasure she'd found dabbling in the property market. She enjoyed the search for something that could be made-over, transformed, and enjoyed too the challenge of hunting out the exact style of furniture, the precise colour of drapes or wallpaper to reflect her own taste and sense of style.

The large spacious bedroom on the first floor demonstrated Harriet's current preference for the clean sparse lines of Japanese design. Cream carpet, beige walls, the low, black lacquer bed.

She pushed a button on the wall and fine slatted blinds glided down to shut out the view from the large picture window. In the darkened room, Harriet threw off her clothes and slipped between the crisp sheets. Yes, the house was perfect. Exactly as she wanted it – yet the very fact of its perfection made her restless for her next project. Soon, she decided, she would look for something else. A new challenge.

For how else, she thought as her eyes closed, could she keep herself busy, fill the long empty hours until the next cocktail party, the next opening night?

KELLY'S EYES SHONE with delight as she checked yet again that every detail of the table setting was correct.

Against the richly polished wood of David's dining table the silver gleamed and the crystal shone; the white heavy linen napkins lay perfectly folded beside each place; and the low porcelain bowl of colourful winter blooms was the perfect finishing touch.

She smiled in satisfaction, glad that there was nothing of the usual bachelor 'making do' about David. He had a love of fine things and obviously saw no need, even on a temporary basis, to do without. Lalique crystal, Waterford bowls, Rosenthal silver – nothing but the best for David.

Placing a record in readiness on the stereo, Kelly checked the clock on the mantelpiece. Just after 4.30. Everything in the kitchen was under control, thanks to Mrs Vincent. All she had to do now was take a leisurely bath and get ready. There was no need to rush.

RELAXING IN THE warm scented water, Kelly congratulated herself once again on the ease of her plan. It had been simple enough once the idea had come to her.

A busy man like David was bound to have all his meetings, appointments, social activities, noted in his diary – a diary accessible, of course, to his secretary. On her visits to the network, Kelly had been introduced to the slender dark-haired Sandra and there had been little difficulty in discovering when David was next free to enjoy one of his usual Saturday afternoon sailing events. Of equal importance, the diary had also revealed that for the same evening he had no other plans...

THE NEXT STEP too had been easy.

Five days ago Kelly had called at David's home to speak with Mrs Vincent and remind the housekeeper that she was a close family friend of Mr Yarrow.

Her story was simple and near enough to the truth to be convincing.

'I want it to be a surprise, Mrs Vincent. I'm going home soon and I wanted to say 'thank you' to Mr Yarrow – but something special, you know? I only wish I could do it myself but,' Kelly gave a self-deprecating laugh, 'I'm a lousy cook – you'd better believe it.' With a smile she flattered the middle-aged woman. 'But from what David tells me you sure don't fall into the same category. Far from it...'

The woman blushed at the praise and Kelly added coaxingly: 'So please say you'll help me, Mrs Vincent... I'm really counting on you.'

The housekeeper was surprised, but Kelly's persuasive flattery, coupled with a tempting financial inducement, were enough to remove any doubts she might have had. How could she refuse to help this young American friend of Mr Yarrow's? After all it was rare enough these days to find any of the young ones even *remembering* to say thank you, wasn't it?

And so it was arranged.

When Kelly had arrived an hour ago, her arms full of fresh flowers, the meal was in its final stages of preparation.

'The asparagus just needs to be popped into boiling water for a few minutes, love – I've tied up the bunches to make it easy.' Mrs Vincent lifted the lid of a pot on the sink. 'And these are the vegies – cut and peeled.' She replaced the lid, walked over to the oven and opened the door. 'And the lamb's doing very slowly in here.'

'M-mm.' Kelly breathed in the tempting aroma of lamb and fresh herbs. 'Smells delicious.'

Mrs Vincent looked pleased. 'Should be ready just about when you wanted it, love. No fuss or bother. And then there's a nice light lemon crème for dessert. It's setting in the fridge.'

Kelly was delighted. 'Absolutely wonderful, Mrs Vincent! Thanks a million – you've done a brilliant job. Now,' she reached for her purse, 'let me give you this and I don't need to keep you any longer...'

And that's how easy it had been, thought Kelly, stepping out of the bath and reaching for a towel. When David came home – sometime around six, she guessed – instead of the dark and empty house, he would find her waiting, eager to pamper and please. A glass or two of Dom Perignon, a wonderful meal, and the whole night to be together...

The thought sent a shiver up her spine and instinctively she held the bath towel, David's bath towel, to her face. Breathing in the faint spiciness of his aftershave, she was at once overwhelmed by an incredible sense of intimacy: here she was, naked in David's bathroom, her clothes spread out over his bed...

'Oh, David...' she murmured the words aloud. 'I want you so much... I've waited such a long time. Please, tonight... please let tonight show you that I'm not a kid any longer... that nothing and no-one will ever take your place...' Her body trembled as the images spun in her mind.

FROM THE BALCONY of the Yacht Club, Anthea looked down on the marina in front of her. The afternoon sailors were coming into berth, folding their sails and securing their boats.

David shouldn't be much longer, she thought, finishing her drink and deciding against another. She would wait until he joined her.

Only yesterday Kelly had announced that she would be away for the weekend and her unexpected absence had offered Anthea and David the glorious treat of a whole night together. With a smile, Anthea leaned back in her chair, dreaming of the pleasures ahead. How wonderful to spend all night making love and sleeping in each others arms; and then to wake up together in the same bed.

Her thoughts returned to Kelly and her expression changed. The girl had been evasive when Anthea had enquired – casually – about her plans. Taking the hint, Anthea hadn't pushed it.

Wherever Kelly was off to, it was no doubt in the company of Paul. Anthea continued to ponder as she watched the sun's rays low on the water. Perhaps it meant that the relationship with Paul was becoming serious? To be truthful, she wasn't sure if that was for the best or not.

Kelly still had a year of college to finish. If she and Paul really were in love then it would be tough to be apart. She wondered too how Kelly's father would feel if his daughter decided to come back to Australia to live. An aging, lonely parent...

With a smile, Anthea dismissed her musings. Here she was feeling sorry for someone she'd never met, inventing scenarios about Kelly and Paul when, God knows, she had no real idea what was going on between them. But it did seem that at last Kelly had got over David...

'Darling.' She felt David's kiss on the top of her head. 'Did I keep you? I figured it'd be just as easy if I had a shower and changed here.' He sat down beside her and Anthea took in his fresh dry clothes, his neatly combed damp hair.

She smiled and a surge of excitement went through her at his closeness. 'A view like this makes waiting easy.' She nodded at the water. 'How'd you go out there?'

David gave a rueful smile. 'The better man won. Three of them in fact.' His smile broadened. 'I guess my mind was on other things.'

He pointed to her empty glass. 'Can I get you another?'

'Thanks – it's orange juice.'

Pushing back his chair, he kissed her on the cheek. 'I hope you're aware that you're in terrible danger tonight... you could be loved to death.'

Grinning, he stood up and crossed to the bar, while Anthea looked after him with shining eyes.

It was close to six by the time they left and in the car Anthea told David about the lunch she'd had in the interests of pursuing Alex's line. Without mentioning Harriet's name she said: 'This woman is an old friend of mine, and she certainly mixes in the same circles as the Cranes. In her opinion, Maxine'd be far too frightened of Julian to have an affair too close to home.

Keeping his eyes on the traffic, David said with deliberation: 'Well, it does seem to underscore the fact that if Maxine Crane *did* ever have a fling with someone, Crane would certainly do something about it if he found out. And he mightn't necessarily stop at Maxine.' David gave her a quick sideway glance. 'Alex's theory of a revengeful ex-lover still has some credibility.'

AT LAST!

From the front window, Kelly saw the headlights of the car turn into the driveway. As quickly as possible in the darkness, she made her way back down the hallway and into the living room to settle herself in the wing-backed armchair.

She felt as if she'd been waiting for hours in the pitch black for David to come home. But now he was here. Her heart pounded with excitement. She crossed her legs carefully and the clinging low-cut dress crept further up her thigh.

Footsteps on the front verandah.

Straining to hear, Kelly frowned. Surely...

The rattle of a key in the lock, the sound of the front door opening.

And next moment her whole body went rigid as she heard the voices in the hallway.

'Darling... how wonderful to have you all to myself.'

With a sharp intake of breath. Kelly heard the hall light being switched on, just as recognition of that voice filtered through to her reeling brain.

'God yes, Anthea – I'm so sick of hiding, pretending... but surely it won't be for much longer now.'

Anthea...

Anthea James!

Kelly felt the heat rush to her face and as quickly drain away, leaving her whole body icy cold. And then the shock started in the centre of her and worked its way out: a tingling numbness that reached to her shoulders, elbows, knees, the joints of her fingers...

'Let's sit in here, darling... We'll have another drink before we eat.'

A second later the room flooded with light to reveal Kelly, her face like a crumpled sheet of parchment.

*

For an instant it was like some frozen tableau: Anthea and David rooted to the spot, their arms still round each other's waists, and Kelly, her eyes wide in shock, staring at them from the chair. It was as if the three of them had been turned to stone. Then, through the open panelled doors to the dining room, Anthea caught sight of the formally laid table, and immediately she understood.

'Kelly! What the hell –' It was David who spoke, his confusion and annoyance patently obvious.

Suddenly the spell was broken. Kelly was out of the chair and on her feet. In a voice trembling with rage and humiliation she spat at him: 'No! Not Kelly! – Sucker! That's my name... Sucker with a capital S!' Tears filled her eyes and her lips twisted in a dreadful parody of a smile as she mimicked David's words: ' "Stay with Anthea, Kelly... She'll look after you..." Oh, yes – the cool, sophisticated, so understanding Anthea James... Only you forgot to tell me the important stuff didn't you, David!' Eyes blazing, she faced him furiously. 'That the oh-so-wonderful Anthea James was also your lover... Your goddamn lover!' Her face crumpled and the next words were a cry of pain. 'How *could* you when you knew –'

'Kelly – my dear –' Heart breaking for the shaking, anguished girl, Anthea moved away from David's embrace and took a step towards her.

'No!' Kelly wheeled on her. 'Keep away from me!' Her voice rose in pitch as her bitterness spilled over. 'I trusted you! I thought you were my friend! And all the time –' Her breath was ragged and fury choked off her words.

'Kelly...' David's voice was gentle now as he moved closer to the trembling girl. 'There are things you don't understand; I –'

'Oh, I understand perfectly, David! Believe me.' Kelly's voice was harsh with emotion and her mouth twisted in angry contempt. '... It just takes me that little bit longer when I'm dealing with two goddamn cheating hypocrites!' The final words rose to an hysterical pitch and with a gasping sob Kelly lunged for the door.

Moving quickly, David tried to block her way, but Kelly was faster. She slipped past him and was out of the room and halfway down the hallway before he could do anything to stop her.

'Kelly!' David bounded into the hall and was just in time to see the front door slam with a resounding crash. His limp slowed him down and, seconds later as he ran out of the house, he heard the sound of a car engine roaring into life and headlights appeared out of the lane next to the house. With a screech of tyres Kelly shot out onto the street, leaving David to watch hopelessly as the red tail lights disappeared into the night.

Tight-lipped, David walked back into the house. Closing the door behind him he turned to face Anthea, who was standing in the hall. 'No good. She's off... and driving like a goddamn maniac.' He shook his head. 'What the hell was she doing here anyway, Anthea? How did –'

Anthea interrupted, nodding at the dining room door. 'In there – take a look.'

With a frown, David pushed open the door and then stood stock-still as he surveyed the elaborately-set table. Turning back to Anthea, he shook his head in silent disbelief.

'And here...' Anthea spoke quietly as she led the way back down the hall. She pushed open the door that separated the kitchen from the rest of the house and David was suddenly aware of the aroma of food cooking.

Dazed, he took in the preparations Kelly had made for the meal.

'Jesus...' He shook his head again. 'But why? What's the point of it all?'

'Oh David – don't you see?' A terrible sense of pity overwhelmed Anthea as she looked around the kitchen at everything Kelly had prepared with so much care and love.

Her eyes came back to David. 'It's to prove that you need her... that she can be anything and everything you'd ever want...'

CHAPTER THIRTY

SHE was stunned and sickened. Her eyes blinded with tears, Kelly knew she was driving recklessly but she didn't care. All that mattered now was to get as far away as possible from that house; from the scene of that devastating revelation.

What a fool she'd been! Her hands held the steering wheel in a vice-like grip. What a blind and naive fool! And all the time she'd been living under Anthea James' roof! Her face burned with anger and humiliation as she sped heedlessly through the dark and unfamiliar streets.

Suddenly, with a scream of protesting rubber, she slammed on the brakes and abruptly reversed to the corner she had just passed. Frowning through her tears, she peered out of the window. Yes, she recognized the place and now she knew where she was: across the street was the bar where she had met Paul.

Something clicked in her pounding brain and she knew what she was going to do.

She pulled over and brought the car to a jolting stop. With the help of the street light and the tilted rear-vision mirror, Kelly did her best to repair her swollen and blotchy face. But not for a moment did the rage fade from her blood.

Screw David! She would prove he meant nothing to her now – as she meant nothing to him. And it was Paul who would help her prove it.

'Kelly!' Even over the intercom she could hear the pleasure in Paul's voice. 'Come on up. Third floor, remember.'

He was waiting, the apartment door open behind him, when Kelly stepped out of the lift. One glance at her white face wiped the smile of welcome from his own.

'Kelly! What's happened? What's the matter?'

She didn't answer as, with a puzzled frown, he closed the door behind them.

'Kelly, sit down. Tell me what's wrong.' His concern was obvious as he pulled up a seat opposite where she had perched herself stiffly and tensely on the edge of the sofa.

'Can I get you a drink?'

She shook her head and studied Paul's anxious face, his troubled green eyes. Only a split second before she had rung the bell had it occurred to her that maybe Paul Shelton too was part of the deceit; doing a 'favour' for his boss by distracting her from Anthea's lover.

But now, seeing his genuine concern and confusion, Kelly knew this was not the case. Paul was straight. And the way he felt about her was obvious.

He reached out and took her hand and Kelly looked down at their clasped fingers. She took a deep breath and forced herself to speak.

'Something happened to me tonight Paul... I... grew up. In a very important way.' She swallowed hard and went on. 'Not in a very nice sort of way, I might add – but then, loss of innocence is rarely joyful, is it?'

Her voice quavered but with eyes still lowered she made herself continue. 'I – I probably won't say this as well as I should, but –' her fingers twisted tensely in his, '– what I'd like to do now is – is grow up in another way as well... The way every woman does...'

She brought her glistening pain-filled eyes up to meet his. 'Would – would you make love to me, Paul? Now... here?'

The total unexpectedness of the request, coupled with the naked desperation of her need, left Paul Shelton, for the first time in his life, almost lost for words.

'Kelly, I –' He began again. 'Kelly – what *is* it? What happened tonight? Where have you been?'

She gave an odd smile, and her eyes grew glazed and remote. 'I've been to David's. To his home.' She gave a dry, choked laugh. 'But I wasn't alone. Oh no!' She shook her head. 'David was there too... and his close friend, Anthea.'

In his concern, Paul missed the heavy irony in Kelly's tone. 'Look, Kelly – do you want me to call Anthea and tell her you're here with me?'

Her piercing laugh, as she threw back her long slender neck, startled him. 'Oh, Paul! You don't understand, do you?' The words bubbled through her laughter. 'You just don't understand at all!' She shook her head wildly, her laughter growing louder and more manic until a moment later she was weeping uncontrollably.

'He didn't want me! He didn't want me!' The words, repeated again and again, were barely audible through her gasping sobs. 'And I'd waited, Paul. I'd waited just for him. There was never anyone else. I – I wanted it to be David – and only ever David.'

He was beside her now on the sofa and she was clinging fiercely to him as a terrified child clings to a comforting parent. 'But there's no point now... no point...'

'Kelly... Darling.' He stroked her hair and felt the warmth of her body close to his own. The force of her emotions shocked him, but at last he was beginning to understand. Her arms wrapped around his neck, she sobbed as if her heart were breaking.

'Kelly... Kelly.' Still stroking her hair, Paul kissed her gently on her damp cheek, her warm neck. 'Oh, Kelly...'

She pressed herself against him and he felt a tremor of response in his own body. This was the girl he'd thought so cool, so self-possessed.

And then she brought her tearful face up to his and with a soft moan pressed her lips against his own; and the kiss, long, desperate and burning, made his senses reel. Paul was left in no doubt of her need.

'Paul... Paul' Breathless, she drew back from him and her eyes, huge and tragic, looked into his. 'Make love to me, please. Prove that it doesn't matter... Please... Please...'

Something froze inside of him then and, moving away from her, he stood up, his body trembling with desire and the shock of her demand.

'Kelly!' His back was to her but he couldn't hide the tremor in his voice. 'Don't... don't talk like that. You don't make love – for the first time or the hundredth time – to prove something.'

Steadying himself, he turned and looked at her. 'I – I have some idea what happened tonight... and at the moment I think you're very very hurt. Yet in some destructive way you imagine that making love to me is going to ease that hurt.'

With sad knowing eyes he looked down at where she sat slumped against the sofa. 'Maybe I'm a fool to say no Kelly, but what

I was hoping might be between us will never be if I do what you want now.'

He moved towards her and sat down again on the sofa. With a soothing hand he stroked back the tear-damp hair from her stricken face and said gently: 'Let me be a fool, Kelly. Let me keep that hope.'

IT WAS NOT long afterwards that Kelly, drained and exhausted by the raw emotions of the night, fell into a deep sleep, her head cushioned in Paul's lap. Unwilling to disturb her, he sat in quiet contemplation of the mask that had been removed that evening from Kelly Delamar.

Her obsession was difficult for him to understand. How could a girl as bright, as intelligent, who had so much going for her, allow herself to suffer from the sort of blinkered fixation more usual in teenage girls? It was perplexing to say the least. As to the focus of her emotions – David Yarrow – Paul would never have guessed. And why should he have? Kelly had spoken of him of course – quite openly and with obvious affection – but to Paul it had seemed nothing more than a natural fondness for a life-long family friend.

He pondered too her revelation about the relationship between Yarrow and Anthea. With the gift of hindsight, he realized that he *had* noticed something different about Anthea when Yarrow was around. An added glow, a sparkle and vivaciousness, that he saw now could easily be the sign of love in a woman.

Kelly gave a soft moan and he looked down as she turned restlessly in her sleep. His expression softened. Poor Kelly. Even in sleep there was a tenseness in her face; her fair straight brows were drawn together in a puckered frown. Tonight had made him aware of a very different side of Kelly Delamar, one he'd never suspected. He knew now that the sophisticated, self-assured exterior belied an emotional immaturity; a naivety and vulnerability that was almost childlike. It was a knowledge that made Paul feel strangely protective.

With a sigh, he slid carefully away from the sleeping girl. Who was he kidding, he thought, as he reached for a cushion to place under her head. Any fantasies he might have had about himself and Kelly Delamar had been well and truly shot to pieces by what he'd learned tonight. He had seen for himself that Kelly's obsession with Yarrow, no matter how unfulfilling, left her blind to him or to any other man.

In his bedroom, Paul shut the door quietly behind him. He sat down on the bed and reached for the phone. He'd been crazy enough to agree to at least one request Kelly had made of him tonight. An exercise in masochism to be sure – but what else could he have done? Kelly had been adamant that she would never return to Anthea's; she had begged to be allowed to stay with him until she could arrange her flight home.

It was up to him to put Anthea in the picture. He didn't relish the task.

He looked up her number and dialled.

'Anthea? It's Paul – Paul Shelton.' He cleared his throat, annoyed by the edge of embarrassment in his voice. 'Look – uh, it's not really any of my business – about what happened tonight, I mean. But I thought you should know that Kelly's here with me. She wants to stay here until she goes back to the States.'

CHAPTER THIRTY-ONE

WITH a heavy sigh Anthea reached across her desk for the next batch of papers awaiting her attention. The events of the weekend were making it very difficult for her to concentrate on work.

The awful scene with Kelly had upset her very much. It left a sourness in her stomach that still lingered.

The mood in which Kelly had run out of the house had left David white-faced with concern. 'Christ, Anthea – if anything happens to her, driving crazily like that – I'll have only myself to blame... only myself.'

He was slumped in the sofa, holding his head in his hands while Anthea did her best to reassure him.

'Darling.' She sat down beside him. 'Kelly's no fool. It was a shock to her – as much as it was to us – but she'll calm down; she won't do anything silly.' As she spoke the words, Anthea prayed that she was right.

She put a hand on David's shoulder and added, 'Look, when she does come home, I think it's best that I'm there waiting for her. I think I should get back now.'

With a sigh, she stood up and looked down at David. 'What we've got to do now is get all this settled between us before she goes home.'

David forced himself out of the sofa. 'You're right of course – and if it's okay, I'd like to come back with you now. He shook his head. 'I should have listened to Oscar, you know, and had it out with her right from the moment she arrived.' He gave a short bark of mirthless laughter. 'Years ago would have been more like it.'

He switched off the light, his face grim. 'Let's hope it's not too damn late now.'

*

IT WAS OVER two hours later that they received Paul Shelton's phone call. David was just on the verge of contacting the police.

He waited impatiently for Anthea to replace the receiver.

'Well...?'

Anthea relayed what Paul had told her. 'It's probably for the best – she'll stay with Paul until she gets a flight home. But,' she bit her lip, 'we can't let her go without talking all this through, David... It's something we've got to lay to rest once and for all.'

Getting together with Kelly was not going to be easy – Paul had made that clear enough. He'd come into Anthea's office first thing that morning and, with the door closed behind him, had reiterated in more detail the events of Saturday night.

'She was pretty screwed up, Anthea. This is a real hang-up she has with – uh, Mr Yarrow.' He shifted uncomfortably in his chair; discussing such personal matters with his boss didn't come easily.

'I know, I know.' Anthea nodded resignedly. 'And thanks for your help in all this Paul – I'm sorry you had to be dragged into it.' Her frown deepened. 'But we can't let her go without talking through the whole issue. She's got to speak to David – or both of us – before she goes back.'

'Well...' Paul sounded dubious. 'She seems to have made up her mind pretty firmly on that point.' He picked his words carefully, remembering how adamant Kelly had been about never wanting to face either David or Anthea again. He shook his head sympathetically. 'You can try, of course, but I don't think much of your chances.'

He saw the look on Anthea's face and tried to sound more positive. 'Look, I agree, Anthea – even if she refuses to see either you or David, she shouldn't go home in the state of mind she's in at the moment. It'll colour everything about her trip to Australia.' He gave a cautious smile. 'That's why I'm trying to talk her into staying until next weekend at least – to come with me to the Madrigal Committee's function.'

He looked at Anthea and pulled an apologetic face. 'Yeah – it's at our competition's home, I know, but it's for one of the charities I've always supported. And, hell, they're only using the

Crane mansion as a venue. From what I hear Crane himself won't even be there; he's on some takeover junket in New Zealand at the moment.'

But Anthea waved aside his apologies. 'Of course, Paul. That's entirely your own business. And as you say it might be a good way to send Kelly home on a brighter note. Although' – she sighed and leaned back in her chair – 'I would appreciate it if you could try to make her see that it really would be for the best if she'd talk to Mr Yarrow or myself before she leaves. It is important.'

With an effort, Anthea brought her attention back to the work in front of her: ideas for future programs of 'Open To Comment'. The show was doing very nicely in the first round of ratings. The reviewers had agreed that Anthea James had made an easy transition from daytime to evening programming.

The show received bundles of mail from viewers. There was the usual small percentage of abusive and crank mail, of course, but the majority of letter-writers were overwhelmingly positive about the program and Anthea's handling of it. With only a short time to go till the by-election she was contesting, her success with 'Open To Comment' could, she felt sure, only help her chances.

The ringing of her private line disrupted her thoughts. She didn't need any interruptions right now. 'Anthea?' It was Alex and she could tell from his voice he was excited.

'Good news, my sweet. Remember our ex-Customs pal? Well, we've managed to dig up a number of accounts he held in different names – with some hefty unexplained sums in more than a couple of them. But the exciting bit is that the money was paid by cheques drawn on a company account. The same damn company that took out the lease on the house that we find so interesting!'

As she hung up, Anthea felt a warm tingle of excitement and anticipation spread through her body. Her eyes gleamed. They were so close, so close. There was no way Julian Crane could escape their net now.

'LOOK, PAUL, I'VE agreed to stay for this function, and that's okay, but *please* – lay off me about David. That's over. Finished. I have nothing to say to him – or her. So drop it.'

Kelly looked at him from the sofa, her face a stony mask. But there was something in her eyes that failed to convince Paul. He'd promised Anthea this morning that he'd try to tackle Kelly; and he'd kept that promise. Now there was nothing else he could do.

'Okay, okay – but it just seems to me that sometimes it's better to straighten things out rather than leaving them in an unresolved mess. Yarrow's been a friend of your family for a long time; it seems a shame –'

'Paul!' Kelly's voice was as cold as her eyes. 'Give me a break! I've said all I'm going to say about it, okay?'

Paul looked at her, then shrugged. What business was it of his anyway? Kelly'd be here just a few more days and then none of this would matter any more.

The thought made something suddenly hurt in his chest and, angry with himself, he switched his mind into that blank passivity he'd adopted since last Saturday night when Kelly had landed on his doorstep.

He looked at her, so soft and feminine in her pale pink sweater and blue jeans. Christ, why did he have to –

Abruptly, he stood up. 'Sure. Forget I ever mentioned it.' He forced a grin to his face. 'Can I get you another drink and tell you all about my action-packed day?'

With a sense of relief, Kelly managed a smile as she handed him her glass.

ANTHEA LAY CURLED in David's arms but the frown hadn't left her face.

'It's no good, David. She absolutely refuses to see either of us. Paul's done his best, I'm sure – but she won't be budged.'

She sat up and looked into David's face. In his dark blue eyes she saw a reflection of her own distress. 'Do you think I should just go round there? Turn up, and hope she'll talk to me?'

David thought a moment then shook his head. 'No, Anthea. If what Paul says is right, it won't do any good at the moment. Let's give her a few more days to cool off. Then, if she still refuses to talk about it, I've decided I'm going to write to her. Try to make her see that we weren't deliberately trying to cheat or humiliate her. I'll tell her exactly how it was. She deserves that, poor kid.'

With the problem of Kelly uppermost in their minds neither were in the mood for further lovemaking. A short time later David left. As she got ready for bed, Anthea pondered David's idea. It was probably the only way left to them now. But, how she wished she could just see Kelly, talk to her, take her in her arms and ease the hurt.

To see David so upset wasn't easy either. He felt guilty, she knew, but none of it was his fault. Life just played some dirty tricks at times – and didn't care who got hurt.

Switching off the light, she slipped into bed but her mind was too busy for sleep. Apart from discussing Kelly, she had also told David about Alex's discovery, and his excitement had matched her own.

'That's the biggest break we've had so far, Anthea. Now if Alex can just link the bogus company to Crane...'

They'd discussed the pros and cons of breaking the news in her newspaper column of Leard's financial aliases; of the large sums of money found in the various accounts.

In the end they'd agreed that at this stage it was still best to keep quiet. Why alert Crane and his associates to the fact that they were so close?

With a sigh, Anthea turned restlessly on the pillow. She had such a lot on her plate at the moment. Tomorrow was typical. First thing in the morning there was the regular taping of 'Open To Comment' and then in the evening she was addressing a group of businessmen within her would-be electorate. It was a small important meeting, one where she hoped to prove her concern for issues that affected the community at large; she'd spent a long time ensuring she was completely *au fait* with the relevant topics.

She tried to still her whirling brain. A good night's sleep, and she would cope with it all. Didn't she always?

CHAPTER THIRTY-TWO

MAXINE Crane stood in the marble-floored foyer alongside the committee president, Elaine Windham, as they welcomed the hundreds of guests into the Crane mansion for the Madrigals charity function.

If Maxine's smile was a little fixed, if she swayed ever so slightly in her too-high heels, no-one yet had seemed to notice.

Her eyes darted to the nearest bar and she licked her lips. Christ, how much longer? She'd barely managed two quick ones before her duties as hostess had called. She'd downed those two from the bottle she'd had the foresight to hide in her study; the thimblefuls they were serving out here could hardly be expected to get her through a night like this.

'Maxine... darling.' Lady Vera Milhouse floated her expensive-smelling cheek past Maxine's, her gleaming scarlet lips smacking harmlessly in the air. Vera, the widow of an ex-Prime Minister, had recently penned a book on Australian etiquette that had left Maxine gasping, with laughter. Now, Maxine's eyes followed Vera into the room. She watched enviously as the other woman's blood-red nails clutched the proferred brimming glass.

'Paul! Supporting us as usual – how wonderful!' It was Elaine Windham speaking to the next couple in the row of guests. 'And *who* is your gorgeous friend?'

Out of the corner of her eye, Maxine took in the girl being introduced as Kelly Delamar. She hated her on sight. Hated her flat belly, her narrow waist, her flawless complexion. Next moment, all false bonhomie, Maxine was welcoming the couple into her home. She was pleased that Julian was not here this evening. This little number would be just his type.

'We've got past the dragons,' Paul grinned as he took Kelly's elbow and steered her down the broad marble steps towards the nearest waiter. 'Only the crocodiles left now.'

'The society matron would seem to have a certain universality,' Kelly answered with a wry smile.

She was glad now that she'd agreed to come here tonight with Paul. He'd been kind to her this last week. Apart from that one occasion, he hadn't interfered in any way. She guessed she'd made it awkward for him. Anthea James was his boss after all.

Kelly felt uncomfortable when she remembered how she'd talked to Paul that night, how she'd begged him to make love to her. His rejection, on top of the humiliation she'd suffered with David, had been shattering.

It was only in the last few days, alone in Paul's apartment, that she'd had time to think about what he'd said to her that night. She realized now that he'd been right. Much as he might have been tempted to do as she'd asked, he'd found the strength to resist. Now, in a clearer light, Kelly knew that if they had made love that night they would have both regretted it.

She might hate the way David had let her down, humiliated her, but Paul was right: lovemaking was too precious to become an act of spite...

Paul handed her a flute of champagne. 'To the future,' he said enigmatically, raising his glass.

Harriet was enjoying herself immensely. Her photo had been taken for both Sunday newspapers and a leading fashion magazine. She'd known the Ungaro was perfect the moment she'd tried it on.

With the photographers gone she judged it safe to go to the bathroom. As she moved through the guests, returning their greetings, she suddenly spied Roy in the far corner of the room. He was talking animatedly to a very attractive young girl and Harriet raised an amused eyebrow. A belated mid-life crisis, after all? Surely not... She changed direction to say hello. Roy was always good company.

'Roy, how are you?' She kissed him on the cheek. For almost sixty, Roy looked remarkably well.

'Harriet! How nice to see you. That dress is stunning!' He gestured to the young woman smiling beside him. 'Uh – may I introduce Miss Delamar. Kelly Delamar, Harriet Maddern.'

'How do you do.'

Harriet heard the American accent, saw the hand outstretched in greeting, but could make no response. She felt as if she'd been turned to stone. A loud buzzing began in her brain and a blackness descended in front of her eyes.

'Harriet!' Thrusting his glass into Kelly's still outstretched hand, Roy caught Harriet just as she began to sway.

'Harriet! What's the matter?'

'I – I'm... sorry. I feel –' The words came out in a breathless gasp.

'Do excuse me – please.' Turning from his companion, Roy led Harriet away. They were far enough away from the body of the crowd to escape attention.

'In here.' Hurriedly he opened the door of the nearest room. A shaded lamp lit one corner of what appeared to be a small study-cum-television room.

'Sit down.' Gently Roy lowered Harriet onto the sofa and, pulling a handkerchief from his pocket, mopped at her beaded brow.

He watched her anxiously. 'Harriet, what is it? Are you ill?'

Ignoring the question, Harriet turned and stared at him with wild, shocked eyes.

'Roy! That girl! The one you were speaking to! Who is she?'

Puzzled, Roy looked at her. 'Kelly Delamar? Just an American visiting Sydney. We were only talking for a few minutes. Her father's some big-wig publisher in the States.'

'Roy!' Harriet's slender beringed fingers clutched like claws at the cuff of his dinner jacket. 'Roy, listen to me! If – if anyone finds out the truth...'

And she told him, in a trembling voice, the reason for her panic.

IN THE CORNER, hidden by a bookcase, Maxine Crane almost dropped the open bottle from her fingers as she listened to every amazing word. And then her plump lips spread in a smile of pure ecstasy.

'COFFEE, OR A nightcap, perhaps?'

'Coffee'll be fine.' Kelly smiled as she sank back into the sofa.

It was nearly one a.m. and they had just arrived back at Paul's apartment. 'It never keeps me awake.'

Paul left her, returning a few minutes later with two mugs of coffee. 'Well,' he grinned, 'Sydney by night – does it make Beverley Hills pale in comparison?'

Accepting her drink, Kelly raised an amused eyebrow. 'Hey – the Beverley Hills party circuit is not my scene. Coked-out actors with giantsized egos? No thanks.' She shook her head. 'When I'm home with dad we take it easy. Dinners at home with close friends, tennis parties, maybe a day on the boat. Dad has links with the studios, of course, but socially we avoid that whole phoney set-up.'

Paul studied her as she sipped at her coffee. She looked achingly beautiful in her off-the-shoulder sapphire-blue dress. And in two days from now she was due to leave, to fly back home. He'd probably never see her again.

That thought and the champagne he'd drunk that evening made him do what he did next.

He stood up, put a record on the stereo and turned the volume down low. When he sat down again it was beside Kelly on the sofa.

Tentatively, he laid a hand on the soft coolness of her arm. 'You've been a great roommate, Kelly. I'll miss you.' He tried for flippancy but the edge in his voice gave him away.

She turned and for a long moment looked at him with her soft hazel eyes. 'And I'll miss you, Paul.'

And then, to his utter astonishment and delight, her lips, warm and gentle, were on his.

Paul's response was instant. His arms went around her, drawing her closer as he returned the unexpected kiss. He felt Kelly stiffen, but then his tongue found its way between her teeth and gradually she relaxed, responding to his own passion.

Paul felt his mind go soft and weak and his heart thundered in his chest as their mouths joined. The scent of Kelly's hair, her skin, her perfume, the warmth of her breath against his cheek, all drove him crazy.

'Kelly... Kelly...' He breathed her name against the softness of her cheek as he moved her backwards across the sofa, his hands sliding down her neck to the barely concealed swell of her breasts.

He felt her shudder in response and his own pulse soared with the knowledge that her desire was every bit as great as his own.

But, a moment later, her body went rigid and she pushed against him, tried to force him away. 'No, Paul! No! I can't! I just can't!' Her voice shook as she turned her burning face away from his incredulous stare.

'Kelly...' The plea was obvious in his voice; his whole body trembled with excitement.

'No!' She tore herself free of his embrace.

Paul stared at her and then, in one quick movement, he was on his feet. Breathing heavily, his body still aflame with desire, he stood with his back to the girl still curled defensively on the sofa. At last he turned and looked at her again and when he spoke his voice was cold and low-pitched.

'You've been spoilt silly all your life Kelly, haven't you? Always got exactly what you wanted. Only now – for the first time – it hasn't worked out that way. And you can't handle it. You just can't accept it. Yet you're determined to act the martyr, to keep playing the game you've set up for yourself. But you know what, Kelly?' She was staring up at him now, eyes wide and shocked at the venom in his tone. 'Only children play games. Kids. Maybe you should ask yourself if it isn't time you grew up!'

Paul spun on his heel and, a second later, Kelly heard the front door slam.

For a long time Kelly sat quite still as she grappled with the wild array of emotions – anger, outrage, confusion, dismay – that Paul's totally unexpected outburst had awakened.

How dare Paul! was her first defiant thought. How dare he! Her eyes blazed with rage. What gave him the right to talk to her like that? What would he know? And he was wrong, totally wrong. She *wasn't* playing games; she *wasn't* a child. She loved and wanted David, had saved herself for him. Didn't that prove she was a woman?

But even as one part of her denounced Paul's bitter censure, something else stirred deep inside her. As her anger slowly evaporated, she realized that a new point of view had been forced on her. She had to admit that even though she had made her feelings obvious to David, his response had always been cool.

She had found excuses for that, of course. His doubts about

the difference in their ages, about Oscar's reaction. But now, with Paul's condemnation ringing in her ears, she was obliged, for the first time in her life, to look more rationally at the truth of her relationship with David. It dawned on her that she had still been counting on the fact that nothing would come of David's affair with Anthea, that all the time she'd continued to hope that when David returned to the States she'd eventually get her own way.

Her own way.

The words Paul had used. The way, he said, that children thought and talked.

Kelly's eyes grew dark and troubled. Surely there had been nothing childlike in the way her body had responded to Paul's mouth and hands just a short time ago; in her excitement which had shocked her by its intensity and suddenness? Only the thought of David had –

Kelly stood up. Her face was clouded with confusion as she walked into the bedroom.

But sleep would not come. Her churning thoughts saw to that. She was still awake an hour and a half later when she heard the front door open; then she heard Paul make up the sofa he'd used as a bed during the week she'd been in the apartment.

Lying quiet in the darkness, Kelly's heart raced as she hesitated just a moment longer. At last, anticipation and apprehension stirring her equally, she slipped out of bed and in bare feet went through to the living room. She could tell by Paul's restless movements that he was as wide awake as she was.

She moved closer so he could see her in the darkness – but it was impossible for her to read the expression on his face. Then, beside him, she knelt down and whispered: 'Please Paul, forgive me. You were right about a lot of things tonight. It's never easy to face up to the difference between ... between reality and dreams.' Her voice trembled. 'But the way I felt when you held me in your arms tonight – that's part of the reality that matters. It's something I can't ignore, or chase away.' She took a deep breath and her words faltered. 'If – if you still –'

Before she could finish, Paul's arms were around her, crushing her mouth against his own.

*

IT WAS AFTER two a.m. when at last Maxine was free to climb the stairs to her bedroom.

From the time she had overheard that amazing conversation in her study, the rest of the evening had passed in a blur. All she had longed for was to be alone; to be able to sit quietly and consider just how best she could use the information she had – so unwittingly – been made privy to.

Now, as she sat creaming off her make-up, she hugged that information to herself. It was almost too good to be true – although she had not the slightest doubt of its veracity. Harriet Maddern had been too emphatic for that.

Tired now, she would leave it till morning to work out her strategy. But of one thing she was sure – by the time she was finished, the smirk would be well and truly wiped off Anthea James' face.

CHAPTER THIRTY-THREE

THE call from Oscar Delamar's lawyers in L.A. came through to David at 1.30 p.m. the next day, Sunday.

In the kitchen where he and Anthea were just finishing a late lunch, David picked up the telephone beside him. It took him a moment or two to grasp what he was being told.

'Je-sus!' The oath burst from his lips. '*When*, for Chrissakes?'

Anthea, on her feet, an empty plate in each hand, stopped in her tracks. David's tone and the shock on his face told her there was something very wrong.

'Sure. Yeah.' He nodded into the phone. 'I'll tell her, Dean, of course...Yeah, it was best you called me first. It's one helluva shock.'

Slowly he hung up and stared at the receiver. Then, raising his head, he became aware of Anthea's anxious expectant look. He said tonelessly: 'It's Oscar. He died an hour ago in Cedars. A massive coronary this afternoon while playing tennis. He never regained consciousness.'

Anthea felt a cold heavy hand squeeze her heart.

'Oh my God! Oh poor Kelly...' Putting the plates down on the table, she sank slowly back into her chair, David, still pale, was shaking his head in disbelief. 'Sixty-one. Only sixty-one. Jesus, he should've had years left to him.'

He looked at Anthea. 'I'll have to tell Kelly as soon as possible. Will you – will you call Paul Shelton for me and make sure they're home?'

Anthea's phone call caught Paul just as he and Kelly were about to leave the apartment for a walk along the beach. Their tentative lovemaking of the night before had given way to an explosive delight in each other's bodies that had kept them in bed until less than an hour ago.

Paul was a glow with happiness as he reached for the receiver.

To fall from such a height, as he listened to Anthea's voice, was especially hard. Fewer than forty-eight hours left with Kelly and they were to be spoilt so tragically and unexpectedly.

'Don't say anything to her yet, Paul,' Anthea warned urgently. 'Just make sure you keep her there until David gets around to break the news himself. I'm sorry,' she added, 'that you've had to be involved.' She was unaware of the bitter irony those words had for her listener.

'Oh God! Oh no!' Kelly's face went the colour of marble and her hand flew to her trembling lips. The tears began to spill down her cheeks as gently, David told her the details. Then his arms were around her, and Kelly buried her face in his chest, weeping unrestrainedly.

'Wh – why, David? Why?' She choked on the question no-one could answer.

The girl's heartbroken sobs brought tears to Anthea's own eyes and she swallowed hard. It was too soon. Too soon to lose the father Kelly so obviously loved. And then, from somewhere deep inside her, came the unbidden memory of another young girl; and the death of a father which had brought not sadness, but blessed relief.

Kelly brought her tear-stained face up to David's and blew her nose on the handkerchief he offered her. 'I – I'm sorry. It's such a shock. I – I just can't believe –' Her voice broke as the tears began again.

With an arm still encircling her, David sat Kelly down on the sofa. 'I know honey, I know. It was a shock to me too. He was so goddamn fit, so full of energy.'

In the background Paul cleared his throat. 'Uh – can I get anyone a drink?' Anthea guessed he was feeling as useless at the moment as she was herself.

'That'd be a great idea,' David said over his shoulder. 'Something strong.' Paul left the room and David turned back to Kelly. 'Why don't you wipe your face, honey?' He threw Anthea a meaningful glance and she got the message.

Moving closer, she sat down and put a hand on Kelly's shoulder 'Come on, my dear. Let me help you.'

But Kelly pulled away from her touch, although the gesture

seemed more instinctive than resentful.

'I'll be okay,' she answered dully, her eyes dark with pain. She stood up and went through to the bathroom.

Alone in the living room with Anthea, David ran a weary hand through his hair. 'Christ, there's never an easy way to give that sort of news, is there? The poor kid. If only she'd gone home forty-eight hours sooner. Maybe she –' He broke off and shrugged hopelessly. With a glance at his watch he added, 'Guess I'll have to call Dean back at a respectable hour over there. Find out the details of the funeral, when I'll have to be there. But what I really want to make sure of is that everything will be straightforward with the lawyers. I don't want Kelly having more hassles than she can handle.'

'She'll need you, darling, I know.' Anthea's voice was gentle. 'I think you've got to make sure you get a seat on the same flight as Kelly.' She paused, then added quietly, 'And David – when it's over, I think the best thing you can do is bring her back. Here, to Sydney. Her studies can wait. She needs you now. Just to have you close by will count for a lot. You're all she's got now that her father's gone.'

In the bathroom, Kelly stood stock-still, listening. The apartment was small and through the open door she could hear quite clearly every word that Anthea spoke.

Confusion and bewilderment made her senses reel. First, the terrible thunderbolt of her father's death; the father she had thought so indestructible. And now, Anthea James – the woman who had 'stolen' David from her – actively seeking to keep her close to him.

In the mirror above the basin she looked at her puffy red-rimmed eyes and her mottled face. She felt sick with the torment of feelings that made no sense. A world that made no sense...

CHAPTER THIRTY-FOUR

KELLY walked slowly through the darkening empty rooms. She shouldn't have done it, she knew, but somehow she'd felt driven to return just one more time. To take a final look at the home where she and her father had been so happy together.

Since her arrival in L.A. ten days ago, she'd barely had a moment to reflect on everything that had changed in her life. First, there had been the arrangements for the funeral itself, and afterwards, the hundred and one things that needed to be seen to with her father's lawyers.

Thank God, she thought, that David had been beside her, overseeing and explaining as she signed document after document written in the obscure and baffling language of the legal world. David's presence had been infinitely comforting.

And now at last there was only the house to see to. The decision to sell the rambling Spanish-style home had been easy. Kelly could not contemplate living in the huge house, empty now of her father, yet filled with memories of their years together.

With the help of the Mexican caretakers, she had disposed of furniture, paintings, books until all that remained was to go through her father's wardrobe and his personal items.

It was a heart-breaking task to sort through dinner jackets, sweaters, handmade shirts; to pack away her father's beloved tennis racquets, his favourite sneakers.

And the tears had spilled down her cheeks when she'd found, carefully stored away in a cupboard in his study, a framed photo of herself at the age of six. A lock of her fine baby hair lay with it under the glass. On the mount had been written in her father's hand: 'My love, my future, my life.' Her father's love had been unconditional – of that Kelly had always been certain.

Now, as her heels echoed on the bare floors, Kelly pondered the mysterious nature of love.

She had loved her father deeply. She loved David too. And

now, with Paul, she had seen yet another face of love. In a strange way, she felt as if she were on the verge of immense change in her life – as if suddenly the world had tilted on its axis before steadying again and leading her in a new and very different direction.

Her feelings towards David were part of those changes. During those first awful chaotic days back home, it was David she had turned to. As she struggled to come to terms with her father's death, to face the endless demands of lawyers and business partners, David was always there: comforting her, protecting her, guiding her. She had needed him so much. But, it slowly occurred to her, there had been a subtle shift in the focus of that need.

Somehow, in stepping into the breach left by Oscar's death, David had changed for Kelly. In his role as her protector, her advisor, David had become a virtual substitute for her father. In some strange way sensual aspects of her feelings for him had been defused and diminished. She loved David; she cared for him as much as ever, but something fundamental had changed.

They shared a long talk together the night before David's return to Sydney and, in a crazy about-face, it seemed to Kelly that he was talking to her for the first time as a grown-up woman.

He had explained to her the depth of his feelings for Anthea: for the person she was, the ideals she held, the way she had given his life a sense of purpose and direction.

To her surprise, he had told Kelly of knowing Anthea 'a long time ago'. 'We lost each other for more years than I care to remember, Kelly. The miracle of finding her again is something I'll never stop being grateful for.'

There were no more details but Kelly had seen the depth of love and contentment in his face. For the first time she understood. David had never been hers and never would be.

She stood still for a moment and leaned her head against the frame of the curtainless window. Now at least she could find it in her heart to be glad for his happiness.

A small smile touched her lips. She was growing up. Paul would be pleased.

SYDNEY HARBOUR, BLUE and dazzling, came into sight below, and Kelly remembered the excitement she'd felt only a couple of months earlier when she'd had her first glimpse of it.

She was confident she'd made the right decision in coming back to Sydney. School could be put on hold for a year or two and anyway she'd learn more in the field than she could hope to learn in five years in a classroom. There were lots of good reasons for coming back to Australia.

She'd hesitated only a moment when David had offered her a position as researcher on Anthea's program. He'd noticed of course, and, looking her in the eye, had said gently: 'Say yes, Kelly. Anthea cares for you very much. It'd make her very happy to be able to set you on the road you're aiming for.'

With a soft bounce, the plane touched down. Half an hour later – Customs was still too goddamn slow, Kelly noted impatiently – she was throwing herself into Paul's outstretched arms.

ANY AWKWARDNESS OR unease Kelly might have felt at what had passed so recently between herself and Anthea was at once swept away by the older woman's relaxed welcome on the morning of her formal start at AMN.

'I'm very glad you made the decision to return to Sydney, Kelly. I hope you'll learn a lot from us while you're here.' In the same easy tone she added, 'And I know David is much happier to have you close by. He feels sure your father would have preferred it this way.' Standing up, Anthea stretched out a hand. 'Welcome to AMN Kelly.'

As she took Anthea's hand in her own, Kelly understood. Nothing of the past was to taint this new beginning. Something told her she'd learn a lot more than she'd bargained for from Anthea James.

Kelly settled in quickly. She and Paul had taken a larger apartment and gradually the sadness of her father's death was displaced by the growing happiness of her relationship with the bright witty man she now lived with.

When David dropped in to the busy office she shared with other members of Anthea's staff, he was delighted to see the shine in Kelly's eyes as she spoke of her work. 'Great – I love it,' she beamed at him.

David felt reassured. He had done the right thing. Not only were his own difficulties with Kelly resolved, but Kelly herself was obviously radiantly happy.

He had been giving more time lately to thoughts of his own future. The months he'd spent in Australia told him he liked it here; he felt at home in the country which had been the scene of his childhood. That would make everything easier, he knew, for Anthea's career, her whole future, was in her own country. He would never ask her to turn her back on all that for him. Instead, he planned to restructure his own interests and make Australia his future base.

Already he had discussed the matter with his lawyers and there seemed to be no sign of any problems in the proposed relocation. What he was waiting for now was for Anthea's campaign to be out of the way. Win or lose, he would ask her to be his wife.

CHAPTER THIRTY-FIVE

MAXINE'S spirits soared as she dwelt on the best means of creating havoc for Anthea James. It hadn't taken her too long to realize that the person most likely to act on the very interesting information she had acquired was Julian himself.

Whatever had once existed between them, Maxine knew that since Anthea's defection to the opposition, Julian had hated her guts.

But something told her that there was more to Julian's sudden change of mood. Anthea James had got under Julian's skin in a way mere mortals rarely did. As Maxine herself was brutally aware, whoever Julian could not control he was quick to destroy.

Since devising her plan, she had been in an agony of impatience for Julian's return from New Zealand.

He had arrived home yesterday. Tonight, Maxine judged, the time would be right to make her approach. She could barely contain herself as, drink in hand, she waited for the purr of the Rolls in the drive. Oh yes, she thought gleefully, that bitch was going to pay for making her a laughing stock in this city.

And while the information she had to impart would not destroy Anthea James in one fell swoop, it would certainly raise doubts among the more conservative elements of society about her credibility.

Maxine raised an eyebrow in wry amusement. For some unfathomable reason the world invariably expected those in public life to be squeaky clean.

She drained her glass. Yes, Julian would delight in what she had to tell him. But, – a little smile played around her lips – it would cost him of course. She had that all worked out.

After dinner she tapped on the door of Julian's study. He looked surprised at the disturbance. They spent most evenings in very separate pursuits: Maxine at some glossy social event, or slumped half-loaded in front of the television; Julian at work in his study, or attending one of the numerous business functions that crowded his diary. It was unusual for Maxine to seek his company on the rare occasions they were at home together.

'Yes?' Pen in hand, he looked up from the work in front of him.

Maxine heard the irritation in his voice but wasn't about to be rushed. Closing the door behind her, she walked slowly into the room and perched herself on the arm of the dark leather chesterfield. With a hard, tight smile she got straight to the point. 'I have some news that might interest you, Julian. It could cause a few nasty ripples for the person concerned if you choose to break it in the press.'

The teasing note in his wife's voice further irritated Julian Crane. Any gossip Maxine might have to tell him couldn't interest him in the slightest.

'What are you talking about, Maxine. I have things to do. Stop wasting my time.'

Maxine raised an eyebrow. 'I overheard some very interesting news recently, concerning your favourite ex-employee – Anthea James.'

Triumphantly, she saw she had Julian's full attention.

With a frown, Julian Crane put down his pen. 'What do you know about Anthea James?' He spoke with slow deliberation.

Maxine's smile widened. 'I can assure you it'll do a lot to screw up her chances of winning next weekend. Our national paragon won't be able to hold her head quite so high when the dirt comes out.' Her tone sharpened 'But there's a trade-off involved here, Julian.' She met his gaze and felt a sudden stab of nervousness now that the moment had come. 'A – A deal. Our marriage is finished. Dead. We both know that. I agree, divorce isn't an option. What I want in exchange for telling you what I know about Anthea James, Julian, is the right to an "arrangement". An open marriage set-up. I can promise you I will be totally discreet and –'

Her husband's open hand caught her a stinging blow across the face. On his feet beside her, Julian Crane hauled his wife from the seat by her soft plump shoulders and shook her like a rag doll.

'You crazy bitch! Who the fuck do you think you are – striking your lousy "deals" with me!' His crimson face was only inches from her own. 'You're going to tell me exactly what you know about that bitch – Now!'

The second blow knocked the breath out of her.

'YOU OKAY THEN, Mrs Maddern?' Harriet's chauffeur switched on the hall lights and turned to face her.

'Yes, of course, Ken, I'll be fine. Good night.'

She locked the front door behind him and, as she slowly climbed the stairs to her bedroom, Harriet could hear the faint sound of the car moving down the drive at the side of the house. Ken Perkins, her chauffeur and butler, had his own small but pleasant apartment above the garage where the Bentley and his battered Honda hatchback were kept.

In her bedroom, Harriet slipped quickly out of her clothes. It was almost one a.m., and not only was she desperately tired, but the sharp throb in her right temple told her she was probably in line for a migraine.

Tonight, as usual, Lisa Hunniford had produced an interesting mix of wit, charm, and beauty – as well as an excellent meal. But Harriet hadn't enjoyed herself. It was when the conversation had touched for a few moments on Anthea James' chances in the forthcoming by-election, that she'd suddenly lost her appetite. Her stomach had tightened with fear – for Anthea and for herself. Now, as she slipped on her grey silk negligee and went through to the bathroom to clean her teeth, Harriet kept conjuring in her mind the ghosts of all those years ago...

With a sigh, she bent and wiped her mouth on the towel. If only she had refused to be involved. Yet how could she ever have imagined –

Harriet straightened up and the hand clamped across her mouth. Her arms were wrenched roughly behind her; her head was forced backwards and she stared wild-eyed with shock at the ceiling.

Barely able to breathe, unable to see her attacker, Harriet felt the panic bubble in her throat. She tried to scream but the hand, coarse and stale-smelling across her mouth, was as effective as a gag. Dragged stumbling backwards into the bedroom, she struggled furiously against her unseen assailant. Her terror gave her a strength she'd never have believed she possessed.

The blow caught her viciously against the head and, dazed with pain, she felt herself flung across the bed.

'Keep that up lady and you'll really get hurt.' The words were spoken softly but there was no mistaking their menace.

Her head singing, Harriet blinked open terrified eyes and saw a broad heavy face close to her own. She felt the sharp sting of metal against her pounding throat. Frozen in terror she choked out the words from a bone-dry throat: 'Oh God! Please! Please don't hurt me!'

Her negligee had slipped to reveal her breasts but she dared not make a move to cover herself as the man's cold gaze travelled slowly over her flesh.

Pressing the sharp tip of his knife more firmly against her he said softly, 'You're going to answer a few questions, lady, about your good friend Anthea James. Understand what I mean?'

The sheer unexpectedness of the command from someone she had thought set on robbery, even murder, left Harriet bereft of speech.

'Under*stand*?' Harriet flinched as the blade dug deeper and she let out a strangled cry, 'Yes! Yes!'

The man smiled. 'From what I hear you know a lot more about Anthea James than most people. Right?'

Filled with terror and confusion, Harriet stared up at the blond-haired man who loomed above her. His lips twisted unpleasantly. 'All you've got to do is let me in on the bitch's dirty little secrets and maybe I won't have to hurt you.'

Heart racing, her breath coming in short shallow gasps, Harriet shook her head frantically, 'No! I don't know –'

The words dried in her throat. Numb with shock, she looked down in horror at the line of scarlet running across her right breast. Oh God! Oh God! Her prayers were an unheard scream in her head.

Again the man's face was close to hers and she could smell the sourness of his breath as he said with dangerous deliberation: 'Does that help your memory, lady? Those lovely little titties won't look so pretty in tatters, will they?'

Without warning, the man's hand moved swiftly again and now a shrill scream of terror burst from Harriet's trembling lips. A matching seam of red spurted across her other breast.

Her fragile control snapped. Gasping out the story between hysterical sobs, she told her attacker everything.

Everything... even the secret Anthea herself had never guessed.

Twenty minutes later, close to two a.m., Frank slipped in the open side door to Julian Crane's study. Drink in hand, he began to fill his boss in on the amazing story Harriet Maddern had felt compelled to reveal.

As Frank spoke, a slow grin of exhilaration and triumph spread over Julian Crane's fleshy features. He could barely contain his elation.

Everything Maxine had told him was true – and she'd known only the half of it. For a second Julian Crane felt an almost grudging admiration for Anthea James. For her gall, her coolness, her audacity in carrying it off. All these years no-one had come near to guessing the secret that could totally destroy her.

What Harriet Maddern had revealed, the whole incredible truth, was beyond Julian's wildest dreams. He almost laughed aloud. Oh Anthea baby, it's all over now. Finished. Totally and utterly finished.

THE SHARP BURR of the telephone beside his bed woke Roy with a start.

Heart pounding, he fumbled in the dark for the receiver while focusing sleepy eyes on the illuminated dial of his radio alarm. Jesus, a quarter to two in the morning. Who the hell –

Still dazed with sleep, the torrent of garbled words at first made no sense and, cursing under his breath, he was about to hang up when suddenly, through the hysteria and incoherence, he recognized the voice of Harriet Maddern.

Roy sat bolt upright in the bed as he began to grasp what Harriet was trying to tell him.

Moments later, his face grey, he was dressing as quickly as his trembling fingers would allow.

ASHEN-FACED, HARRIET OPENED the front door as soon as she heard Roy's footsteps on the drive.

'Oh Roy! Thank God! Thank God!' She closed the door quickly behind him, one hand still clasping a blood-stained towel against her chest.

'I couldn't call the police... My doctor... The explanations, everything I've managed to keep a secret for so long –'

She broke off. Her face crumpled and Roy could see how very close she was to collapse.

Gently he steered her into the kitchen and sat her down on one of the yellow-cushioned chairs. 'My dear, let me see. What have they done to you?' Carefully he prised her stiff fingers from the red, sodden towel.

The sight of the cruel slashes across Harriet's pale skin sent a spasm of nausea shooting through him.

'You see, Roy?' She stared up at him with brimming desperate eyes. 'You see what he did to – to my beautiful breasts?' Looking down again, almost in disbelief, her tears mingled with the bright blood that still oozed from her wounds.

Using the towel to clean away the worst of the mess, Roy saw with relief that the slashes were not as bad as he'd first thought.

'It'll be all right, my dear. There'll be no scars. I'm sure.' He forced the quiet reassurance into his voice. 'These are just fine surface cuts – lots of blood but no real damage. We'll get you cleaned up in no time.'

Twenty minutes later, dressed in a clean negligee, her breasts bathed and bandaged, Harriet sat propped up against a mass of pillows in her wide satin-covered bed. The two Valiums Roy had found for her, and the almost empty glass of Scotch she held in her hand, were beginning to take effect. Slowly, painfully, she told Roy the details of what had taken place.

'So I – I had to tell him, Roy. Everything... Oh God, I was so deathly afraid. I had to... I just had to.' Already her speech was becoming slurred.

Sitting on the bed beside her, Roy patted her soft ringless hand. 'You had no choice, my dear. I understand that. What we have to worry about now is how that information is going to be used – for used it certainly will be.' His voice was grim.

'But Roy,' Harriet turned heavy lidded eyes up to his, 'how did he know to come to me? And who – who would want to harm Anthea? Who's behind all this?'

A hard light came into Roy's eyes. He had no doubt who was the instigator of the attack on Harriet. He side-stepped the question. 'Anthea has a lot of power in this country, Harriet. And if she wins a seat in this election she'll have a damned sight more. Believe me, there are more than a few people who won't like that, who'd do their best to have Anthea James shut up once and for all.'

Harriet's voice was a whisper now, 'Then shouldn't we warn her? Tell her what's happened to me. Tell her the truth at last?'

For a moment Roy sat in brooding silence. 'I think we're going to have to take a gamble, Harriet, and sit tight on what happened here tonight. The election is less than a week away. Everything Anthea has worked so hard to achieve is at last within her sights. The worst thing possible would be for her to be unnerved or distressed by this sort of news. Later, we'll tell her. Everything. But when it's all over. When she's won.' A hard note crept into Roy's voice. 'Because she's going to win. No matter who's trying to stop her.'

Gently he took the empty glass from Harriet's slack fingers.

CHAPTER THIRTY-SIX

FRANK almost chuckled aloud as he pressed the buzzer by the front door. It was all so easy. So incredibly bloody easy. Julian had wanted it seen to as soon as possible and now, just four days later, Frank had got it all worked out.

Like the other mornings when he'd watched the apartment, Frank had seen the kid go on his morning jog. His only worry had been that today, Saturday, there might have been a change in the couple's routine.

But no. Relieved, Frank had watched Paul Shelton leave just five minutes before. He knew now that the red-hot little number would be alone for at least half an hour. Frank grinned.

'Hello?' The American accent was obvious even over the intercom and Frank heard the uncertainty in Kelly Delamar's voice. Why not: who came calling at seven o'clock in the bloody morning?

He went smoothly into his pitch. 'Hi! I'm the tenant from 9A. Sorry to bother you at the crack of dawn but it seems like I've got myself boxed in a bit downstairs. Any chance you could come and move your car so I can get out?'

'Uh... oh sure. No problem. I'll be right down.' Kelly Delamar's obliging tone made Frank grin again.

Upstairs in the apartment Kelly threw off her dressing gown and quickly pulled on a pair of pink tracksuit pants and a T-shirt. As she picked up her keys and made for the front door she smelt the coffee beginning to percolate on the stove top. No need to turn if off, she thought as she closed the door behind her, she'd only be a moment.

She gave a half-smile as the lift slowly descended. This was one way to meet the neighbours.

Her caller was nowhere to be seen when Kelly stepped out of the lift, but the usual congestion reigned in the dimly lit basement car park.

The parking arrangement was the worst feature of the large

and airy apartment, Kelly thought as the lift doors closed behind her. Too many vehicles for the allotted spaces meant an inevitable blocking of access on numerous occasions.

Kelly stood for a moment trying to recall where she and Paul had parked his third-hand battered Renault the night before. Then she remembered with a sudden frown that in fact they had had an early night and eaten dinner at home. And yes, there was the Renault, itself wedged in by later arrivals.

Her caller – whoever he was – had made a mistake, Kelly thought with a touch of irritation as she turned towards the lift.

Jolted savagely backwards, she barely managed a heavy grunt of surprise before the sweet sickly smell in her nostrils robbed her of consciousness.

'JUST ONE MORE photo, Miss James!'
'Hold it right there, Anthea!'
'That's it, Anthea – a big smile!'

Her professional smile in place, Anthea posed a moment longer for the assembled press before dropping the envelope into the ballot box.

It was three p.m. and, after a busy morning visiting as many polling booths in her electorate as possible, Anthea was at last lodging her own vote.

The overwhelming interest of the press in her campaign was more than she'd dared hope for. She paused to answer a few questions.

'How do you rate your chances, Miss James?' asked a tall, red-headed reporter from the Sydney Morning Herald.

'I have ensured that voters understand exactly where I stand on vital issues. Those people who appreciate my concern for this country and its future will, I feel confident, choose me as their representative.'

'Is this the beginning of the end of your media career, Miss James?' The question was put by a slight, curly-haired woman in the front of the bunch.

A sparkle lit Anthea's dark eyes. 'I can assure you that once I'm elected you'll all be seeing and hearing a lot more of me than in the last twelve years.'

'What you're saying then is that you have your sights set on becoming a major force within the party, Miss James?' asked another male reporter, a hint of chauvinistic scepticism in his voice.

Anthea looked him straight in the eye. She spoke clearly and emphatically. 'That is my ultimate goal, yes.' She left no doubt about her meaning.

A moment later, surrounded by supporters, Anthea was ushered into a waiting car. Her work for the day was far from finished.

PAUL WAS PUZZLED.

He'd returned to the apartment just before eight, to the sight and smell of the coffee pot bubbling furiously on the stove top – but there was no sign of Kelly. At first he thought that perhaps she'd made a quick trip to the corner store. But leaving the coffee on like that wasn't a risk he'd have taken himself.

He switched off the stove and went to take a shower, sure that by the time he'd finished, Kelly would be back.

But she wasn't and when he found the car still parked below, he was more confused than ever.

Back in the apartment, sipping abstractedly at his cup of coffee, Paul suddenly remembered.

Of course! Today was the day Anthea faced the polls. How could that have slipped his mind? Kelly had been discussing it for days, and tonight they were both invited to dine with Anthea, David and her supporters, while they waited for the results. That was it, Paul decided, the confusion clearing from his face. For some reason Anthea had called on Kelly, who had wasted no time in responding. Though it irked him that she hadn't bothered to leave a note.

He picked up the telephone and dialled Anthea's home number. Selena answered with her usual efficient courtesy. Miz James had left the house an hour ago. No, Miz Kelly had not been with her.

Frowning, Paul replaced the receiver. Had he got it wrong? He was sure Kelly had gone to help Anthea. There was no other explanation. No doubt they would be meeting somewhere along the route. Kelly would be delighted, he knew, to have some role to play on Anthea's big day.

For Paul could see that in the time Kelly had been back in Australia she had formed what was much more than a mere business relationship with the woman who was their boss.

Since her father's death Kelly had done a lot of growing up. It was as if suddenly she realized she was no longer someone's daughter; no longer a spoilt and wilful child intent on always getting her own way, but a woman who would have to discover a place for herself in the world. And in Anthea James, Paul could see, Kelly had found the female role-model she'd needed for so long.

He looked at his watch. Almost 9.30 a.m. With Kelly surely gone for hours, why waste such a great day indoors? Breakfast in the sun on Bondi beach would kill the time perfectly. After scribbling Kelly a brief note, Paul gathered up the morning newspapers and left the apartment.

THE ENTHUSIASM WITH which she was greeted throughout the electorate made the adrenalin pump in Anthea's veins. She was so close now to everything she'd ever dreamed of and had worked so hard to attain.

For a moment as she smiled, shook hands, accepted the good wishes of the ordinary Australians for whom she wanted to achieve so much, Anthea's thoughts flew back to Nan. Nan who had always encouraged and guided her, who had had such utter faith in Anthea's ability to 'be someone and get somewhere'.

A fleeting shadow crossed Anthea's face as she realized how different it all might have been if – if the child had not been still-born. Would motherhood have sapped her ambition, her strength? Diverted her from her goals? Pushing the thought from her mind, Anthea shook yet another eager hand. That was something she would never know.

CHAPTER THIRTY-SEVEN

PAUL was annoyed and upset when Kelly still had not put in an appearance by five p.m. He poured himself a second glass of beer. Surely she could have called by now? Told him what was going on? At seven they were expected at the Harbourside function room for what was intended to be Anthea's celebratory dinner.

But, by six, when there'd been no call, Paul decided to get ready. If he'd had no word by 6.30 he'd assume Kelly was expecting to meet him at the venue. Hardly like Kelly though, he thought, moving through to the bathroom. He'd have expected her to want to change into her gladrags for a night like this.

He shrugged and drew the razor up his throat. Better men than he had been floored by impossible female logic.

It was twenty to seven when David left home to join Anthea and the closest of her hard-working supporters to await the results of the by-election.

As he moved into the flow of Saturday evening traffic he felt a flutter of nervousness in his stomach. He knew how very important the next few hours would be for Anthea. Everything had been driving her to this crucial moment. The best he could do now was pray with all his heart for her success.

If she won tonight the entire base of her power and influence would be immeasurably extended. David knew that, in her new role, Anthea would be unstoppable in her desire to grapple with the problems and inequalities that so troubled her in their society. He was aware too that, with the political process on her side, she would at last be able to expose and destroy the machinery of corruption that allowed men like Julian Crane to operate with such immunity. That was Anthea's immediate goal.

He slowed down in the congested traffic surrounding the brightly-lit function centre. But what if Anthea were to lose tonight?

His hands tightened on the steering wheel and a look of implacable determination came over his lean dark features. Marriage to a woman driven by her obsessions would not be easy – but loving her would never be a problem.

At last he was here! Out of the corner of her eye Anthea had been watching the main entrance to the function hall for the last five minutes. Surrounded as she was by the Party faithful and its officials, she wanted David more than anyone else beside her now.

She saw him stand a moment in the doorway, gazing over the noisy crowded room. And then at last his eyes found hers and in their clear blue depths she could see reflected that intensity of love and passion which bound the two of them inexorably to each other.

David smiled: a slow secret smile. The message it sent made the breath catch in her throat. Then he was moving towards her, edging past the excited groups until at last he stood by her side.

They had deliberately chosen this night to confirm the rumours they knew had begun to circulate, to lay to rest press conjecture about the recent absence of Alex Volka in her public life. As Anthea made the introductions she was fully aware of the interest they were arousing in all corners of the room. Yes, she felt like announcing loudly and triumphantly, this is the man I love, have always loved, want always by my side. I will do everything I can for all of you – but I want this too.

Her heart soared. How much better could life get?

PAUL HAD LEFT it till the last moment to leave the apartment and by the time he reached the function centre the assembled guests were already moving into the dining room. He could see Anthea; he picked out David four steps in front of her – but there was no sign of Kelly.

He pushed his way through the chattering crowds until he managed to reach out and tap Anthea's shoulder. Glancing round, she recognized Paul and gave him a quick warm smile of welcome.

'Paul! I was beginning to wonder where you two were!' She looked past him. 'Is Kelly –'

With a look of real puzzlement on his face, Paul interrupted her. 'You mean she hasn't been with you all day? I thought...'

'No...' Anthea threw the word over her shoulder as she followed the flow of people into the next room. 'What made you think that?'

But Paul could see that any further conversation at this stage was useless. As he watched, Anthea was seated at the long table at the end of the room. On one side sat David, his attention already claimed by the overdressed matron next to him, while on Anthea's right, sat a thick-set, red-faced man in a pin-striped suit, whom Paul recognized as Party president, Harvey Minton. For the next hour or so at least, he could see there would be no possibility of talking to Anthea.

And now there was no denying his growing alarm. Something was wrong. What reason could Kelly possibly have for disappearing on Anthea's big day? For a moment it flashed across his mind that Kelly's disappearance might be motivated by jealousy; jealousy at the attention being focused today on the woman who had 'stolen' David from her.

He dismissed the thought as quickly as it had come. Kelly was over all that now. Her relationship with Anthea was based on real friendship and admiration; it was a relationship, Paul knew, which Kelly treasured and was proud of. He felt sure she would not willingly have ignored Anthea on this crucial day.

Nearly everyone was seated now. The television sets arranged around the room would very soon supply the election results they all awaited so eagerly. Irresolute, Paul stood by the two seats reserved for Kelly and himself. Was he panicking for no reason? Would Kelly turn up at any moment with a perfectly reasonable explanation?

From her place at the top table Anthea caught sight of the distraction and anxiety on Paul's face and wished they'd had time to talk. What had made him think that Kelly had been with her all day? And where was Kelly now?

Her face clouded when she saw Paul suddenly turn on his heel and hurry from the room. It took an effort to bring her attention back to Harvey Minton.

Less than half an hour later the reports on the nine o'clock news made it obvious that Anthea would win the seat she had campaigned so hard for. This was confirmed by Harvey Minton's short phone call to the tally room.

On his return to the head table, he called the noisy room to order. 'Ladies and gentlemen.' He paused. A broad smile lit his face. 'It is my very great pleasure to inform you that Anthea James has won the seat of Elwyn for the Action Party with what looks like being an overwhelming majority!'

The news brought a burst of spontaneous clapping and cheering from the packed gathering. In response to Harvey Minton's call for a toast, two hundred chairs were scraped back as Anthea's supporters rose joyfully to their feet. There was an unspoken belief among all present that their candidate would not remain long on the back benches of the Parliament.

Anthea looked at the rows of smiling faces turned towards her. She had waited a long time for this moment. Now, her heart skipped a beat, the blood pounded in her veins as she realized she had done it. She had won! The vision she had carried with her for so long was about to become reality.

Her eyes shining, she turned to look up at David who, glass in hand, was on his feet beside her. He smiled down at her, and the admiration and respect she saw in the clear blue eyes of the man she loved meant more to her than anyone would ever know.

Anthea rose confidently to her feet to give her victory speech.

PAUL'S GROWING SENSE of unease made it impossible for him even to consider staying at the function for Anthea.

Hurrying back to the battered Renault, he knew he could never have sat making small talk with those around him while every passing moment strengthened his conviction that Kelly's disappearance was now cause for serious alarm.

Kelly's name and picture had made the gossip columns of the Sydney press on more than one occasion. It was no longer any secret that she was heir to her father's massive publishing empire. But never in his wildest dreams had he ever imagined that in Australia she'd be in any danger.

Cursing the crowded evening streets that delayed his return to the apartment, Paul saw at once that Kelly had not been there in his absence. He began to look in earnest for clues to her disappearance.

A thorough search of the bedroom and bathroom made a cold hard knot form in his stomach. As far as he could judge, Kelly's wardrobe was as chock-a-block as always. In the bathroom her various jars and tubes lay just as she had left them, and, worst of all, he found her wallet in the side pocket of her briefcase.

His heart thudding, he moved slowly back into the living room. So what now? Where did he go from here? No matter how telling the evidence, his mind still balked at accepting the worst.

Hands in pockets, his face tight and grim, he paced about the spacious living room. An accident of course was another possibility. He clutched at the idea which seemed preferable to the unthinkable alternative. Maybe on her way to the store... and without identification...

At once Paul snatched up the telephone. Thanks to his work he had a network of contacts at Police Headquarters. Without asking too many questions, they'd soon tell him what he wanted to know.

Five minutes later that avenue had become a dead-end. Nothing. Slowly Paul replaced the receiver. It had been on the tip of his tongue to make a formal report of Kelly's disappearance. The only thing stopping him had been the thought that he must first tell Anthea and David Yarrow what he now so strongly suspected.

He checked the time. Almost nine. Somehow, though it'd drive him crazy, he'd have to be patient for another hour or so.

It was close to ten-thirty before Anthea was at last able to take her leave of the seemingly endless number of admirers eager to offer their congratulations.

'We *need* women like you my dear,' one sharp-eyed well-spoken woman in her sixties said emphatically. 'Maybe now I can believe that my granddaughters won't have to fight to prove that they're not Australia's second-rate citizens. And what's more' – she lowered her voice and nodded knowingly – 'it's taken a woman to poke her nose into the dirt that no-one else wants to admit exists in this country.' She patted Anthea reassuringly on the arm. 'Keep your courage, Anthea – there's plenty who want to see you make it all the way.'

Similar good wishes had come from many of those present – men and women – and it brought home to Anthea even more sharply the burden of responsibility she now shouldered. Yet, far from being daunted by her supporters' ambitious expectations, Anthea felt fired with her resolve and vitality. While she would never under-estimate the road she still had to travel, she felt more than equal to the task. She looked forward to it, in fact, with relish.

It wasn't until she was alone in the car with David on the way home that the subject arose of Kelly's non-appearance. Obviously annoyed, David declared: 'Did you see? The only two empty seats in the place. What's up with those two? They could have had the manners at least – if not the loyalty – to be there.' It was plain that he had not seen Paul arrive.

Frowning, Anthea looked ahead at the neon-lit streets. 'Paul did make it along – but without Kelly. We had hardly a moment to exchange a word but I got the impression he thought Kelly'd been with me all day; he was surprised, I think, to find that I hadn't seen her. He rushed off then, and didn't stay for the dinner.'

David wasn't appeased. 'Well, if it's young love at war, they could have sorted out their differences for a couple of hours on a night like tonight.'

'No.' There was a puzzled note to Anthea's voice. 'It didn't sound like that. I think I'd better give Paul a call when we get home.'

An obviously thrilled Selena had the front door open before Anthea could use her key. There was a broad smile on her dark attractive face as she exclaimed: 'You win, Miz James! I am very very happy for you!'

'Thank you, Selena. I'm happy too.' Laughing, Anthea and David made their way down the hall and into the sitting room.

Anthea barely had time to take her first sip of the iced tea Selena had prepared before the telephone rang. David watched in fond amusement as Anthea took call after call from excited well-wishers.

At last the phone fell silent. With a sigh of relief, Anthea slumped down on the sofa beside David.

'You're dog-tired, my love,' he said, pouring her a fresh drink. 'Enough's enough for one night.'

'God, I'm dying for that.' Gratefully, Anthea accepted the glass from David's hands. 'My throat feels like –'

The insistent burr of the telephone interrupted her yet again. Anthea groaned.

'That's it,' David announced firmly as she reached out a weary hand for the receiver. 'It's the answering machine after this.'

With the phone to her ear, Anthea listened in astonishment to the last voice she would have expected to hear that evening.

'Good evening, Anthea.' Julian Crane was as glib and smooth as ever. 'You've not been an easy person to reach this evening. No doubt the fond congratulations have kept your line running hot?' He gave a derisive snort. 'Well, forgive me if I feel unable to join in the apparent euphoria over your election to public office this evening. I –'

'What do you you want, Julian?' Anthea's tone was cold and exact. She had no intention of letting Julian Crane's mockery spoil her night.

'Since you ask so nicely, my dear. Your immediate resignation from the aforementioned public office.'

David, alert now to the identity of the caller, frowned as he saw the look of incredulity that came over Anthea's face.

'You're crazy, Julian. And I haven't got time to waste –'

Now it was Julian Crane's turn to interrupt and, as she heard the note of sneering triumph in his voice, a sudden warning bell began to sound in Anthea's brain.

'Your very good friend Harriet Maddern didn't waste any time either, Anthea. In telling me everything she knew about you, I mean. It's understandable now, of course, why you never chose to speak of your – very interesting past.'

Anthea was dumbstruck. The blood pounded in her ears. Harriet? Surely Harriet hadn't... No! No! Julian Crane was bluffing. He had to be.

But his next words proved it was no bluff.

'I know it all, Anthea. The brothel; the role you played in helping Nan Reilly; where the money came from to set you up in the first place.' Julian Crane chuckled. 'Oh it's a great story, my sweet;

front page news for days I'd say, wouldn't you?'

As she listened Anthea felt icy fingers probe into her every pore. Vaguely, she was aware of the expression of growing concern and puzzlement on David's watching face.

Fighting now for her life, her future, in desperation she forced out the words: 'I don't know what the hell –'

Julian Crane's snort of delight cut off her attempt at bluff. 'Come now, Anthea. Denying a friendship that goes *so* far back? Although,' he adopted a musing, taunting tone, 'Mrs Maddern may not have been quite as good a friend as you imagined. After all, she never told you, did she, that the child you thought was still-born, was in fact very much alive?

'Or that it was Harriet Maddern herself who arranged for its adoption – by Eve and Oscar Delamar?'

CHAPTER THIRTY-EIGHT

AFTER that everything else Julian Crane said seemed to Anthea to come from far far away. The threats, the demands, the instructions, sounded as if they were coming from the far end of a long dark tunnel.

'... twenty-four hours, Anthea, that's all. To get that tape to me and tender your resignation from the Party. I don't give a shit what you tell them, just get out. Do exactly what I tell you and the girl'll be all right.

'And,' Crane added spacing the words evenly, 'in case you're thinking of sticking around in the media scene a little longer – I wouldn't recommend it. Do that and I can promise you I'll make sure everything comes out. Every single filthy detail. You're no fool, Anthea. You know as well as I do how ruthless the public can be in disposing of its former shining idols. If that story breaks there'll be no place left in this whole fucking country for you to hide.' He made no effort to conceal his elation. 'Twenty-four hours, Anthea. Or it's your own flesh and blood you'll be condemning.'

The line went dead but Anthea made no move to replace the receiver. The blood froze in her veins. God...! Oh God...! Kelly... Kelly...

'Anthea! Darling, what's wrong?' On his knees in front of her, David stared fearfully into Anthea's grey sagging face. It was the face, he realized with a sudden shock, of an old woman. What the hell had Crane *said* to her?

He took the receiver from her clammy hands. He saw no response in Anthea's blank face. 'Darling... PLEASE... What *is* it? What did that bastard say to rock you like this?'

It took a supreme effort for Anthea to focus her gaze on David's deeply troubled face. How was she going to tell him? How?

'I – It's –' Her tongue, suddenly thick and clumsy, choked on the words in her throat.

'Darling.' David was on the sofa again, his arms holding her tightly. 'No matter what it is,' he said quietly, 'I'll always love you. And I'll never let anyone hurt you. I promise you that.'

The words, spoken with such total conviction, seemed to reach through the barrier of her shock. She turned her shattered face up to his. 'It's Kelly. He's got Kelly. He's kidnapped our daughter.'

In the utter silence that followed, David's eyes never left Anthea's face as the world began to roar inside his head.

When at last he spoke his voice was a hollow whisper. 'Anthea – what are you saying to me?'

In the intense blue pools of David's eyes Anthea saw an incredulity that matched her own. For a moment the room began to spin. How could she tell him? How?

'Anthea!' She heard the tightness of control in his voice. 'Tell me what Crane *said* to you!'

Forcing the words from her parched throat, she told him everything Crane had said; exactly what Crane wanted.

David felt as if he were slowly going crazy. Kelly?... Kelly?... His daughter. All these years. And now Crane... Clenching and unclenching his fists in a fury of frustration, he said, 'You never told me, Anthea. You never said a word.' His voice was faded and husky.

White-faced, sitting absolutely motionless on the sofa, Anthea whispered: 'There seemed no point. When it happened I – I never thought I'd see you again. But I was determined to keep the baby. It was part of you, all I had to remind me that you had existed. But Nan found out. She tried to make me have an abortion. But I couldn't. I just couldn't. And – afterwards, she told me the baby had been born dead.'

A sudden shrillness came into her voice as she stared up at him, her eyes huge and dark.

'I never saw it, David! Never wanted to. Can you understand that? I thought the child was dead. Nan *told* me it was dead. But she lied to me, David! She lied to me!' Then, covering her face with her hands, her shoulders shaking convulsively, Anthea yielded to tears. Tears of bitterness, anger, fear.

Then David was holding her again. 'Darling. Oh, my darling.' He stroked her soft gold hair as she buried her face in his shoulder. 'It's a terrible shock, I know. For both of us. But we've got to stay calm, darling, to get to the bottom of all this. And it seems as if it's only your friend Harriet Maddern who can shed light on everything that's happened.'

Gently he lifted Anthea's head and brushed the tears away from her mottled tear-stained face. 'Crane is dangerous, Anthea, we both know that. And he's given us just a short time to act. One of us has to speak with Harriet Maddern immediately.'

Fighting for control, Anthea nodded her head. 'You're right, David,' she whispered. 'And I'm the one to make that call.'

'I'M SURE YOU'LL agree, Harriet, that what we have to discuss can hardly be done on the telephone.'

The trembling edge in Anthea's voice had brought Harriet to instant alertness. 'I'll expect you here within the half hour. I think I've waited long enough, don't you?' With a click the line went dead.

Under the bedclothes, Harriet felt a sudden chill creep through her body. Anthea knew. Somehow she knew. Harriet's heart thundered in her chest. But surely *she* couldn't be blamed for something she'd done out of the goodness of her heart so long ago?

It had been a favour. A favour to Nan.

'You have the contacts, Harriet,' Nan had said. 'Mike must know those who'll be more than pleased to oblige. There's plenty I'm sure, who can't have what they want.' There had been a sharp note of command in Nan's voice. 'But not in Australia, Harriet. England or America. But not here. There'll be childless ones keen enough and with the means, I'm sure, to arrange these things.'

And there had been.

Mike had helped her there, discreetly inquiring among the ranks of the wealthy. Those who had everything except what they wanted most...

The names of Oscar and Eve Delamar had finally emerged.

Harriet would never forget that rainy afternoon in London over twenty years ago when, in the quiet elegance of the suite in the Ritz, she had placed the tiny sleeping baby into Eve Delamar's waiting arms. The sheer joy and love on the older woman's kindly face had tugged at Harriet's heart.

Yes, she thought at that moment, the child would be well looked after. And Nan's ambitions for Lenore would not be thwarted.

Now, tears of self-pity welled into Harriet's frightened eyes. All she had done was oblige an old friend. None of it had been her fault. Her face crumpled in despair. She wasn't a young woman any longer. She couldn't cope; couldn't face Anthea's bitterness and anger. Not so soon after... Her hand moved to the red welts on her breasts. No! Let Roy deal with this. After all, he'd been in on it too.

'ALEX?'

Alex frowned. He heard the American accent and guessed at once who it was.

'It's David Yarrow.' Jesus. Alex glanced at the time on the brass and leather clock on his desk. He'd been hard at work, shifting his way through the pile of briefs that awaited his attention. He'd taken a break only to watch the nine o'clock news. When he could see that Anthea was going to have an easy win, he'd called at once to leave a congratulatory message on her answering machine. She'd be busy all night, he knew. Tomorrow he'd call and get all the details.

Now he frowned. What reason could Yarrow have for calling him?

'Great news for Anthea,' he began. 'I –'

'Alex, there's a problem. An urgent problem, concerning our old friend. Can you get here fast?'

'It'll be all right, Anthea. Kelly will be all right.' The dullness had come back into Anthea's eyes while David was on the phone.

'Yes. Yes, she will be.' There was a hard flinty tone in Anthea's voice. 'Because I've decided I'm going to do exactly as Crane ordered. Give him everything he wants. When he's got that, Kelly will be safe.'

For a long moment David studied Anthea's shattered face. 'Believe me, Anthea – Kelly's safe return is what I want most in the world at this moment. But I'm not prepared to see you lose everything you've spent your life working to achieve. That son-of-a-bitch isn't going to –' He shook his head and smacked his fist hard into his palm. 'Jesus! If this had happened back in the States there'd be so much more I could do. At home I've got contacts, a network. But here –'

By force of will he restored the note of confidence to his voice.

'Listen, Anthea, Alex is on his way. I've only met him briefly but that was enough to give me faith in the guy. He's streetwise, and he's got his finger on the pulse of this town. Between the lot of us we'll be able to come up with something.'

ROY WASTED NO time in responding to Harriet's desperate call. Now, facing Anthea from where he sat on the wing-backed chair, his tired, guilty eyes pleaded for her understanding as he began the hardest explanation of his life.

'Nan thought it was for the best, Anthea – for you *and* the child. Maybe you were too young to realize just how stubborn Nan could be when she'd made up her mind on something. Believe me,' he leaned forward in his chair, 'I tried to talk it over with her, to let her see that maybe she was playing God with too heavy a hand this time. But,' he sighed heavily, shaking his head, 'she wouldn't listen. Harriet made all the arrangements – I never knew where or with whom – and Nan got her way.'

He looked imploringly into Anthea's pale stony face. 'Try not to blame Harriet too much, my dear. She did what she did as a favour. Nan could always twist Harriet around her little finger. In a way, you know, she made Harriet feel guilty for her own good fortune. Told her that she'd had *her* chance – and you deserved yours.'

'But it was *my* decision to make, Roy! Not Nan's, or yours, or Harriet's! I would have kept David's child. It was the child of the man I loved.' Once again Anthea's tears seemed threateningly, uselessly close. 'And now it might all be too late.'

From where he stood behind her David placed a hand on Anthea's shoulder. It was meant, she knew, as a gesture of comfort. But nothing, she thought, despair squeezing her heart, could comfort her now. To know that her child was alive and then to lose her; the reality was too terrible to contemplate.

She knew now how Crane had found out, knew the appalling cruelty to which Harriet had been subjected to force her to reveal the whole story. Roy had told her everything.

And if in turn he had been surprised by Anthea's revelation that the man who stood in front of him was the father of the child Nan had deprived her of so long ago, he hid it well.

She stood up. 'Roy, it's very late. There's no need for you to stay. We're waiting for Alex now. There'll be a lot to discuss.'

Roy understood. Pain and guilt flicked across his face. There was no place for him here; he was one of the deceivers.

Wearily, he got to his feet, murmured goodnight to David, and followed Anthea out into the hall. By the open front door he paused and looked with anguished eyes into Anthea's tight face.

'My dear, will you ever forgive me? I should have been stronger. I should never have allowed Nan –' His voice faltered. Leaning forward, he kissed Anthea quickly on her cold cheek and turned away.

Only moments later Alex arrived, his confusion and worry obvious.

'What the hell's Crane been up to now?' He looked from David to Anthea. 'What's happened?'

From where she sat Anthea raised her eyes to David. She knew he would leave it to her to reveal as little – or as much – as she wanted of the whole complicated story. Twisting her hands nervously in her lap, she took a deep breath. 'Alex, it's –'

The chime of the front door bell made her jump.

'I'll get it.' David hurried from the room and, awkwardly aware of the increasingly puzzled looks Alex was directing at her, Anthea said nothing while she waited for David's return.

It was Paul Shelton, distracted and breathless, who followed him into the room. Nodding at Alex Volka, whose acquaintance he had made on a number of occasions, Paul turned to Anthea: 'I had to come, Anthea. Something's happened to Kelly, hasn't it? You've heard something, haven't you?'

For a long moment Anthea looked in silence at the two men who had joined them. One, a close and comforting friend, the other someone who, she knew, loved Kelly without reservation.

Could she possibly bring herself to tell them everything? Could she expect them to accept and understand as David had accepted and understood?

Aware of their puzzled frowns, the tension in their anticipation, once more she looked at David. What she saw in his eyes gave her the courage she needed.

Taking a deep breath she said quietly, 'I think you both deserve to be told the whole truth.'

From the other side of the living room door, Selena heard every word.

*

Long after Alex and Paul had left, David and Anthea talked into the quiet silver hours of the dawn. They began at last to accept the full force of a reality that neither in their wildest dreams would have suspected.

But their joy in the knowledge of their child's existence was agonizingly blighted by their awareness of the peril she now faced.

'You know, David, nothing else seems to matter now,' Anthea said softly. 'The results of the election, my ideals, the goals I'd set my heart on achieving.' She shook her head. 'If anything happens to Kelly, it'll mean nothing. All I want now is the chance to know her, to hold her in my arms.' She struggled to fight back the tears.

Beside her, his hand clasping hers, David felt a tightness in his throat. He was remembering all those years of watching a little girl grow up; he'd never dreamt...

He recalled the happy seven year-old; the bright and enquiring eleven year-old; and the intense, determined teenager, whose devotion to him had already begun to crystallize into that overwhelming obsession which had endured for so long. Was it beyond comprehension, he wondered wildly, to imagine that some instinct had been at work, pulling Kelly relentlessly towards him?

Anthea's heavy sigh brought him back to the present. Her voice was a whisper, 'I tried never to let myself think about what had happened. The baby was dead, I told myself, it was over. But there were times when what I thought was so carefully buried would creep to the surface and I'd start to wonder how things might have been. If the baby had survived, I used to think, would the anger, the fight, have died in me instead? Would it have been submerged by the need to protect, to love and care for my child? It was always an impossible question to answer.'

For a moment David said nothing. Then he stood up and gently helped her to her feet. 'Come to bed, darling. Let's try to get some sleep. Nothing's hopeless yet.'

But, her mind on fire, Anthea watched the sky grow light through the gap in the drapes while, beside her, David's restless tossing told her he too was far from sleep. She moved closer to his strong warm body. Thank God, she prayed. Thank God she had him now.

CHAPTER THIRTY-NINE

THE first thing Kelly became aware of as she regained consciousness was the overpowering stench of petrol. It filled her nostrils, choking her as she slowly blinked awake.

Darkness... But the slit of light she could see out of the corner of her left eye told her it wasn't night. Gradually other sensations came crowding in: a gentle rocking motion, a soft slapping sound near her right ear. It felt like – what? A boat? What was she doing on a boat?

She shifted her stiff aching body, and felt a restraining roughness against her wrists and ankles, a strange muffling pressure against her mouth. Suddenly she became alert.

She remembered now! The call to the apartment, her trip to the basement, and then...

A wave of nausea swept over her, the combined effect of the stink of petrol, the movement of the boat, and her shocked understanding of what had happened.

Her mind spun. Not in Australia surely! L.A. was where the crazies hung out. Everyone knew that. It was the reason she and her father had lived in a house that resembled a fortress: hi-tech alarms, security patrols, electrified gates. She knew that her father had lived in mortal fear of some weirdo taking it into his deranged skull to get his hands on the heiress to the Delamar publishing fortune.

And now it had happened. Kelly had no doubt about that. And in the last place in the world where she'd thought it could happen. Yet, in retrospect, she could see her carelessness. The press had rooted her out, of course. The details had been there for the world – and the crazies – to see. It hadn't pleased her – the invasion of her privacy – but it certainly hadn't seemed anything to worry about.

As the full seriousness of her situation hit her, Kelly's heart began to thud against her ribs. Who were her abductors? What were they demanding? How long would they keep her here?

Moving gingerly into an upright position, the ropes chafing at her soft skin, Kelly felt the beginning of real panic.

SLEEPILY, JOSEPH TOOK the call. He checked the round-faced dial on the kitchen wall – it was not yet 6.30. Who, he wondered, could be telephoning to him? He was a stranger in this country.

'Hello?' Automatically he spoke the word in his native Tagalog.

'Joseph! – It is Selena.' She too spoke in Tagalog but softly and quickly, as if she were afraid of being overheard. 'You must forgive me for waking you but I have very important news. About the man, Crane.' Swiftly she told him what she had heard the night before. 'You must do something, Joseph. This time he must not go unpunished.' There was determination in Selena's voice despite the softness of her tone.

Joseph replaced the receiver. His suspicions had been confirmed. This was the evil one who surely had murdered Selena's cousin; who with equal certainty had hidden his sister, Philomena, where he could not find her. Now he had the daughter of Miz James. The Miz James who was such a good friend to Selena; who had tried to help him find his sister. He had been going to talk about Philomena on television but then the evil one had stopped him.

He hurried back into the dark cramped space under the stairs. It was his room and he was grateful for it. As he dressed, Joseph thought again how good his own people had been to him when they had so little themselves. He had much to thank them for.

'Who was your caller?'

About to slip quietly out the back door of the house, Joseph turned to the gentle-faced woman with the dark hair pulled starkly back from her face. It was she who had called him to the telephone.

He came back into the kitchen. Teresa Renaldo was one of those kind enough to give him shelter, help him in his time of need. He had to explain.

'A friend, *Ginang* Renaldo.' He addressed her politely. 'Someone who can help me in this evil matter.'

That seemed to satisfy Teresa Renaldo. She nodded solemnly. 'Stay safe. God's blessing, Joseph,' she said quietly as he turned to go.

Joseph started the protesting motor of the rusty battered car that had been lent to him by another of his countrymen, and prayed that at last his luck would change.

In all the weeks he'd been in Sydney he had found no trace of Philomena's whereabouts. But he hadn't given up. To give up would mean going home to the anxious faces of his parents. And he was not yet able to do that. In his letters he reassured them, explained that it was taking time, but he was sure that soon he would find his missing sister.

His mother had worried about how he would manage to live. Surely, she wrote, the money she had borrowed for his journey had long gone?

It had. It was used up in the first two weeks in this strange and frightening place but Joseph didn't tell his mother that. He wrote that he was getting by – and he was, thanks to the kindness of the Filipinos he had met here. They had been glad to help, angry at the growing number of young girls who came to this country and vanished without trace.

'Joseph, you must not give up.' Rafael Menza had been one of those who had encouraged him in his search. In his forties, he had left the Philippines ten years ago in the hope of finding a better life in Australia. It was Rafael Menza's car Joseph was driving now. 'We are afraid now for all our women,' his new friend went on. 'My own sister's daughter – a beautiful nineteen year-old – is always begging her poor mother to let her leave their village. She thinks that in Australia she will find a paradise. Ha!' Rafael Menza spat at his own feet. 'Look at me, Joseph! Do I look as if I have found a paradise?' He shook his head. 'And for a young girl it is even more difficult. And now, dangerous as well. We will help you, Joseph. You must find out what is happening here.'

A quiver of excitement shot through Joseph as he waited for the traffic light to change to green. His friendship with Selena had given him another chance. From those Filipinos whose assistance he had gratefully accepted, Joseph had heard about the terrible fate of Selena's cousin. At once he had felt it his duty to speak to this poor woman, offer his condolences, and find out if she knew anything that might help him.

A meeting had been arranged and, to Joseph's great surprise, he had discovered that Selena was employed by the gracious and important lady who had tried to help him tell his story.

At first Selena seemed to know little. But then:

'It was not that I was trying to listen, Joseph, this you must understand.' Selena was determined to make this point very clear. 'But since I am living now with Miz James I have been hearing many things. And it is one name I hear again and again. She speaks about this with her friends and she has a big suspicion of this person.'

Selena told him the name.

'He is very important, Joseph, very rich. The sort of man the police can never reach.' There was a bitterness in Selena's voice she could not conceal.

Joseph looked at her and frowned. 'But how can Miz James be so sure, Selena?'

Selena told him about the ring.

And now, thought Joseph, bringing the old car to a wheezing stop in the shade of a large fig tree, another innocent girl was at the mercy of the evil one. If only he could find her before it was too late... maybe he would be led to Philomena too. And, if not – he touched the sheath that lay tightly strapped against his shin.

His dark eyes fixed on the tall metal gates of the evil one's house, Joseph settled down to wait.

THE BURR OF the telephone woke Anthea with a start from a brittle and fitful sleep. Her eyes heavy with fatigue, she reached for the receiver and at the same time saw that it wasn't yet eight o'clock. She'd barely managed two hours sleep – and the sound of the shower told her that David had probably got even less.

'Anthea, it's Alex.' A spark of hope flared inside her – but the next moment it was gone.

'It's not a lot, Anthea, but it's a start. Ted spent what was left of Saturday night enjoying the company in some of the city's less salubrious watering spots; and with a little more pressure than was strictly legal he came up with something that might just be our best lead to date.

'Seems like Maxine Crane *did* have a lover, and a disgruntled one at that. Had his pretty face rearranged it appears, by one of Crane's henchmen. And when he's had a skinful, starts to sound off about how he's able to pin one on Crane anytime he feels like it. What I'm trying to do now is get a line on this bloke. Whatever he knows – or thinks he knows – I want to hear about it.' Alex's voice softened. 'Be brave, sweetheart, and pass all this on to David will you? Paul's going to be giving me a hand and I've just sent Ted off to put a tail on that bastard Crane the moment he's foolish enough to set foot outside the pile of bricks he calls a home.'

Alex hung up before Anthea could speak the words that trembled on her lips. In the cold light of day she suddenly felt she couldn't bear to take any risks with Kelly's life. There was an easy way, a safe way, to get her daughter back. She could do exactly what Crane had ordered.

As she slipped out of bed the memory of Crane's words pierced the soft tissue of Anthea's brain. 'It's your own flesh and blood you'll be condemning.'

CHAPTER FORTY

JULIAN Crane's feverish ecstasy had robbed him of a good night's sleep but, as he waited impatiently for the heavy ornate gates to swing open, he felt no tiredness. His success in outmanoeuvering Anthea James was more than enough to keep fatigue at bay.

He headed south, the sunroof open on the late model Mercedes. It wouldn't take him too long, he figured, in the light Sunday morning traffic. He was taking a risk he knew, but he would not deny himself the pleasure of watching the girl's face as he broke the news.

Oh, yes, he'd assure her with a smile. Anthea James. *Yes, your mother. But there was no way she could have had you hanging round then, sweetheart. Not when she was so busy whoring.*

Whore! Julian Crane's pale hairless hands tightened around the steering wheel. A slut who sold it to any who could afford the price. That had been the start of Anthea James' 'career'.

Harriet Maddern had tried to tell it otherwise, of course, but he wasn't swallowing that. Anthea James had been part of Nan Reilly's very successful little set-up. And there were no freeloaders under Nan Reilly's roof. He was sure of that.

Julian Crane's face hardened. He'd decided long ago that all women were whores of one sort or another. Anthea James, Maxine... They'd all sell themselves to get what ever it was they happened to want at the time. And for a short time they'd wield the only sort of power a woman could ever have over a man...

His eyes darkened behind his sunglasses. Only they didn't, would never, have that power over him. He was immune to their well-practised artifices, their deceitful languid eyes, their devious tongues. With him it was different. He was the master. It was he who exerted absolute control.

A sudden rage heated his blood. It was women like Anthea James who were the danger. Women who attempted to extend the power they assumed all too easily in bed, into other spheres of life.

But that was where Anthea James had made her biggest mistake. She'd been too blind to see that her success was due to him. That she had been nothing more than *his* creation, *his* employee, to direct, to command, to eliminate as he wished.

And to dare to challenge him! To lay down *her* rules, issue *her* commands... Crane's face twisted in contempt. He'd teach the bitch a lesson she'd never forget. As soon as he had that tape safely in his hands, he would set about destroying every last part of the myth Anthea James had woven around herself in this country. How much credibility would be given then to her incessant bleatings about crime and corruption?

Absorbed in his thoughts, Julian Crane paid not the slightest attention to the battered blue Holden that stayed always two cars behind him.

'AND ALEX SEEMS to think that if he can find this ex-lover of Maxine Crane's he may be able to help somehow. Anthea stared bleakly into the cup of black coffee that was growing cold as she spoke. 'But I really don't see how it can.'

'Darling, have faith in Alex. He knows what he's about, I'm sure.' David met Anthea's eyes across the table. They were taking coffee together – the only breakfast either of them had been able to face – on Anthea's sunny verandah.

'It's obvious Crane wouldn't have been personally involved in Kelly's abduction,' he went on. 'He'd hardly take that sort of risk. David shook his head. 'No, there'll be someone doing his dirty work for him, of that you can be certain. And if I'm on the same wave-length as Alex, then whoever beat up lover-boy is the same guy who abducted Kelly. If Alex can locate Maxine Crane's ex-lover then this guy might be able to provide a description of the hood involved; maybe even pinpoint him in a mug shot if the bastard's got a record already.'

He reached across the table and patted her hand. 'We've got to be patient, Anthea.' He studied her unhappy face and saw her obvious exhaustion. 'Darling, you look wiped out. Since there's nothing more either of us can do right at this moment, why don't you take a couple of sleeping pills and try to get some rest. For one thing the press'll be expecting a statement from you about the election result first thing Monday morning. You'll want to be on the ball for that.'

Anthea looked at him, her eyes dark and hard. 'What the hell does it all matter now?' Her voice was thick with bitterness. 'Even if we do what Crane wants and we get Kelly back safely, do you think for one moment he'll keep his mouth shut about what he knows?'

With a sigh, she got to her feet. 'That side of things is finished for me, I'm sure, David. But you're right. I'll try to rest.'

David watched as she walked back into the house and his heart went out to her. He wondered how long she had been aware of what he'd realized right from the start?

IT WAS TWENTY minutes later that Joseph saw the long sleek car turn off the main highway onto the narrow winding road that soon showed glimpses of the sea below.

He would have to be careful now. There was no other traffic in sight, and he allowed the car in front to disappear around the corners well ahead of him. He was not afraid of losing his prey. On one side the road dropped away to the sea, on the other it rose into steep rough bushland. The man in front of him, Joseph was sure, would have to stick to the road.

Ten minutes later he saw the arching bay below. A dozen or so small craft bobbed gently at their moorings on the sparkling azure water. A faded wooden sign pointed out the narrow path that led to the beach, but Joseph saw no sign of the evil one's car and continued cautiously on his way.

A few minutes later he braked suddenly. The long gold-coloured car was stopped at the extreme edge of the road, its nose sheltered by an overhang of dry dusty foliage that had found a foothold in the rocky terrain. Of the driver there was no sign.

His heart beating faster, Joseph continued around the next corner. Here the road petered out into a rough unsealed track. He drew Rafael Menza's car as far off the road as possible though, from what he could tell, this part of it was seldom used.

He ran back to where the gold car was parked and saw at

once that it was locked. Did the man expect to be some time? Pushing his way into the same bushes that sheltered the car he peered cautiously through the dusty leaves at the bay below.

The evil one had wasted no time. Already he was moving slowly across the water in the small outboard. From his hiding place Joseph could hear the muffled sound of the motor as it chugged towards the only vessel moored in this tiny rugged bay. A vessel as old and shabby, he thought with a frown, as those used by the fishermen at home. Hardly the craft he would have expected a rich man to possess.

With the warmth of the summer sun heating his shoulders through the sparse canopy of leaves, Joseph saw the man reach his destination. Securing the small outboard, he climbed onto the deck of the larger craft and, as Joseph squinted across the shining expanse of water, he saw the man unlock the entrance to the cabin on the deck – a cabin, which, even at this distance, Joseph could see had every window covered over.

Confused, he tried to make sense of the evil one's actions. What was his reason for coming to this remote place? Was this where he had taken his sister Philomena? Other young girls? The missing friend of Miz James? Joseph knew it was a very good friend of Miz James the evil one had taken away. In a serious voice Selena had explained it all to him on the telephone this morning. 'This man Crane knows Miz James is trying to help us, Joseph. To make her stop he has taken the friend she cares for very much!'

Suddenly, a scream came clearly to his ears across the water. Then another, and another. Joseph felt the blood drain from his face. It was a woman's scream! A scream of terror!

Bursting from his hiding place, Joseph moved closer to the very edge of the cliff face. He could see now the slippery winding path that surely led to the beach below. His eyes swept frantically up and down the narrow sandy strip. There was no way he could hope to get to the boat. The beach was deserted. Nowhere could he see any sort of craft in which to cross the water.

Joseph muttered prayers under his breath to the Virgin and tried to decide on the best course of action. He thought of the larger bay further back along the road. Would there be anyone there to help? To understand? To believe him?

As if hoping that some miracle would bring a saviour to his

aid, he looked over his shoulder at the road behind. It was then that his gaze fell on the instrument that sat between the two front seats of the gold-coloured car.

His eyes widened and his heart hammered wildly in his chest. He had heard that the cars of the very rich were equipped with a telephone. Surely he was looking at one now?

Joseph dug into the back pocket of his faded cotton pants and pulled out a small, well-thumbed notebook. Between its green covers he had kept every detail of his search for Philomena – the people he had spoken with, the places he had visited, the assistance he had been given. Names, addresses, phone numbers. And, amongst them, the number he now understood he must call at once. It was Selena he must tell what he had seen, what he had heard.

With fumbling fingers Joseph found the number and, stowing the book back in his pocket, he muttered it over and over, as he pushed his way back through the foliage. By the side of the road, he searched for and found a large heavy rock, warm from the sun. He ran over to the car and wasted no time in smashing the rock as hard as he could against the driver's window. The glass shattered with a noise like a thunderclap and Joseph prayed that the man had heard nothing. Trembling, he carefully reached in through the broken window and released the lever that unlocked the door. He brushed aside the shards of glass and, resting one knee against the soft leather of the car's front seat, he picked up the curved dark instrument. He repeated the number aloud and his fingers felt for the correct buttons. Twenty seconds later he felt a thrill of relief at the sound of Selena's voice.

As she listened to Joseph's frightened explanation, Selena understood at once what she must do. 'Do not leave that place, Joseph. I will send help but you must tell me exactly where you are.' A sudden shudder ran down her spine. Surely she had said those very words to Beatrice so little time ago... 'Tell me, Joseph,' she repeated tersely.

Joseph frowned. He had done his best to pay attention to the route the evil one had taken. But this city was so big, so unfamiliar to him. The main highway south... the turn off near the coastline... then the wooden sign, and the name with the familiar ring. Joseph screwed up his face with the effort of concentration.

Yes! Batana Beach! That was it! So much like the name of the Philippine city of Batangas...

'Selena! This is the way...'

As she wrote down Joseph's directions, Selena spoke quickly. 'You have done well, Joseph. Now you must stay and keep watch until help comes. We must pray it will be in time.'

A moment later she was running through the house to find David Yarrow.

BREATHING HEAVILY, JULIAN Crane sat on the upturned crate. He watched the unconscious girl. Why had she been such a fool? He'd had to do it but he wished now he hadn't hit her so hard. A hot ache grew in his throat. He wanted her conscious again, aware, her eyes glistening with the fear and panic he'd seen such a short time ago.

He'd entered the cabin and left the door ajar to lighten the gloom and provide some relief from the stifling heat. For a long moment he had stood there, staring silently at the girl who lay awkwardly propped up against the rough timber walls. Frank's crude, leering description had not prepared him for the beauty of the girl in front of him. He took in the firm young skin, the soft mass of hair, the long lithe body, and felt a sudden dryness in his mouth.

The girl's eyes gleamed with defiance as he stepped into the cabin. She was moaning furiously against the tape that bound her mouth. He picked up one of the plastic bottles of water Frank had left in readiness. Turning back to the girl, his face expressionless, he raised one eyebrow. The girl nodded wildly.

He bent down to remove the tape that covered her mouth. Merely a precaution. The bay was too shallow, too treacherous, to be popular with sailors, and it was unlikely anyone would ever get close enough to hear her screams. In any case, the girl would be here only a short time; he was sure of that. Anthea James had no option but to co-operate.

'You son-of-a-bitch!' The words exploded from Kelly's lips. 'What the hell –'

His hand, clasped like a vice around her chin, cut her off.

'Shut up! Or the tape goes back on at once.' He spoke deliberately as he pushed her head viciously back against the rough timber wall.

His face was close to hers and he was suddenly and agonizingly aware of her smell, of the feel of her flesh under his fingers, of the fear in her wide staring eyes. It was then that the heat started between his legs.

Sweat beading his upper lip, he reached out with his free hand and found the soft smooth swell of the girl's breast. Mesmerized, he stroked and squeezed. The girl's futile struggles added to his pleasure. For a moment he closed his eyes in sheer soaring ecstasy.

It was then, with a furious effort, that Kelly managed to tear her head free of her captor's grasp and, using the only means available to her, she sank her teeth deeply and viciously into the soft plump flesh of the man's palm.

With a howl of pain, Julian Crane snatched his hand away. His lust turned instantly to rage. He swung that same hand hard against the girl's cringing face. Again and again his blows found their mark as his victim screamed in pain and terror.

His breath heaving in his chest, he only dropped his hand when at last the girl slumped into unconsciousness.

CHAPTER FORTY-ONE

Hands in his pockets, his brow furrowed with worry, David paced restlessly back and forth the length of the verandah. He was frustrated and angry; such enforced inactivity was unbearable. Alex was doing his best, David was sure, but to be forced to stand by helplessly while others took over was driving him crazy.

The lines set deeper in his face. There had to be *some* way to beat that son-of-a-bitch, Crane; some way to get Kelly safely back yet at the same time ensure Anthea's future.

David's brain played with a dozen wild ideas.

The video tape. That was what Crane wanted most of all. If he could somehow do a deal... some sort of business shuffle that'd look good enough to tempt Crane in the short term. Just enough to buy them the time to get the rock-hard evidence they needed.

Jesus! He ran an exasperated hand through his hair. Who the hell was he kidding? Crane was too smart to fall for crap like that. He wanted to destroy Anthea and nothing short of a miracle was going to stop him.

David shut his eyes and felt a heavy throb in his right temple. Oh God, why did it all have to go so wrong? He loved Anthea so much; she filled his life in a way he would never have believed possible. And to discover there had been a child, that Kelly –

'Mr Yarrow!' The sound of Selena's voice broke into his tormented thoughts.

One look at her face told him something had happened.

Slamming down the receiver, David spun around to face the young Filipino.

'Look, Selena,' His voice was terse and clipped, 'I can't reach Mr Volka now and I haven't got a moment to waste. What you must do is wake Miss James, tell her what's happened, where

I've gone. If she can find Mr Volka, I want her to give him the same directions you've just given me... Tell him to get to the area south of Batana Bay as fast as he possibly can.' He looked piercingly into the girl's anxious eyes. 'Do you understand?'

Selena returned his gaze and nodded. 'Yes, Mr Yarrow. I will do exactly as you ask.'

IT WAS THE miracle he'd been praying for, David thought feverishly as he broke the speed limit through the light Sunday morning traffic. He'd get the details later, but somehow Selena had known everything and had set this guy on Kelly's trail.

He had located Batana Bay in his directory. The whole area was far from the busy popular marinas south of the city; a fact which only made him more certain that this was the place where Kelly was being held.

A perfect choice, he thought, grim-faced as he pushed his foot down hard to beat the next amber light.

And if Crane had harmed a hair of Kelly's head – David's stomach twisted at the thought of it – he'd kill the bastard. With his bare hands.

A GRIN FLASHED over Joseph's thin dark face. He knew there was one important thing he could do while he waited for help to arrive. Yet a moment later a frown took its place. How to ensure that the evil one could not escape in his absence? How to stop him leaving in his car? Then his smile returned. Like his father, Joseph knew about engines. The problem would not be a great one. He found the lever that released the bonnet.

WITH A LOW moan of protest, Anthea turned over. She wanted only to sink back into the dark numbing depths from which she had been disturbed. But her tormentor would not go away.

'Miz James! Wake up! *Please*. It is important!'

The urgency of the words penetrated Anthea's consciousness. Feeling as if she were struggling upwards through several layers of damp cotton wool she finally blinked open her eyes.

'Miz James!' Selena's face was close to her own. 'You must wake up. *Please*. Mr Yarrow – he needs help!'

David drove as quickly as he dared around the next tight corner of the rapidly deteriorating road. He caught a glimpse of the tiny cove below. He was sure it was the place he was looking for – and the sight of the Mercedes parked on the next bend told him he was right.

He pulled off the road as far as was possible. Leaving his own vehicle, he hurried to inspect the gold-coloured car. The shattered window and the car phone told him at once how the Filipino had made contact with Selena. The boy had acted smartly, David thought, although there seemed no sign of him now.

He pushed through the rough whipping branches of the bushes that lined the road and made his way to the edge of the cliff. One glance at the scene below made him curse his own shortsightedness: there was a solitary vessel – a battered, peeling Halvorsen – at anchor in the bay; a dinghy was tied to its stern, but he could see no sign of any other means of crossing the water...

Jesus! David clenched his teeth in frustration. How the hell was he going to board that floating wreck? He was a strong enough swimmer but the boat was a fair distance from the shore, and he had no time to waste.

'Mister...?' The word, whispered from somewhere behind him made David spin round, his senses on full alert.

'Mister?' A thin dark-skinned youth, whose nervousness was evident, suddenly appeared from the bushes. He eyed David warily. 'Selena send you here, mister?'

David answered quickly. 'Yes... I am a friend of Miss James.' He gestured towards the vessel in the bay. 'It was from there you heard a woman's scream?'

The boy nodded. He was relieved. He had been afraid that this man might be a friend of the evil one.

'And the man – is he still there?'

The boy nodded again and David's throat tightened.

'Listen,' he said rapidly, 'I've got to get a boat from somewhere – quickly. Is there –'

With a sudden grin, Joseph interrupted. 'No problem, mister. You come with me.'

David's surprise was obvious. 'You mean you *have* a boat?'
Still grinning, Joseph gestured for David to follow.

DESPITE HIS BAD leg, David managed to slither and stumble his way down the steep slippery cliff path behind Joseph. Moments later, he was pushing off in the dilapidated dinghy that lay hidden among rocks at the far end of the beach.

Pulling with all his might on the oars, David raised his head to see the young Filipino clambering back up the cliff face. He would keep watch for Alex.

David's eyes grew dark with smouldering rage. He wanted first shot at Julian Crane himself.

WITH STIFF FINGERS, Anthea punched out Alex's home number for what seemed like the hundredth time. Oh please, God, please...

But there was no reply.

Unable to sit still, she paced endlessly around the room, telephone in hand, trying the number again and again. And all the time the one agonizing question played endlessly in her burning brain. By not acting at once on his demands had she now placed David, as well as Kelly, at Crane's mercy? Mouth dry with fear, she tried Alex's number again.

CHAPTER FORTY-TWO

SWEAT glistened on Julian Crane's flushed face as he tossed aside the girl's tracksuit pants. His excitement was unbearable. It had been necessary to release her legs of course and now her furious writhing, her frantic efforts to hinder his advances sent the blood roaring through his veins.

'Yes' he breathed hotly, 'fight my lovely... fight.'

A shudder of exquisite anticipation ran through him. Slowly he unzipped his trousers, his glazed eyes never leaving the girl's bruised and blemished face. He was swollen, rock-hard, aching to take, to subdue, to control.

Her mouth bound by the tape that kept terror silent, Kelly stared with enormous panic-stricken eyes at the man who loomed over her. Bathed in perspiration, weakened by hunger and excruciating thirst, and by the beating she had taken earlier, she was as helpless as an insect trapped in the torture of a spider's web.

Julian Crane moved in on his tempting prey, feasting on the wild desperation in the girl's swollen discoloured eyes, on her frantic thrashing efforts to deny him his pleasure.

There was a sudden shuddering crash as the cabin door was thrown open.

'JESUS! YOU GODDAMN STINKING BASTARD!'

From the open door of the cabin, David stared in furious disbelief at the scene that met his eyes. Startled, the blood draining from his soft damp face, Julian Crane spun round to stare in amazement at the last person he would ever have expected to see.

Fumbling to refasten his trousers he drew back. His mind reeled as he tried to understand the sudden unexpected appearance of a man he knew only as a business rival.

The moment Julian Crane moved away from where Kelly lay wide-eyed with shock, David acted.

Launching himself across the space that divided them, he hit

Crane with the force of a cannonball, bringing them both crashing to the ground. Giving full vent to a fury that knew no bounds, he smashed his fist again and again into that pale bloated face. The sight of Kelly's injuries, the thought of what she had suffered at the hands of this animal, gave him an almost manic strength.

But, after the first shock of attack, Julian Crane reacted swiftly. Driven by a violent rage at the intruder who had robbed him of his ecstasy, he drove an almighty blow into his attacker's stomach. Winded, David momentarily slackened his grip. It was the chance Julian Crane needed.

He rolled away and, scrambling to his feet, made for the outer deck. If he could launch the dinghy and escape, he could deny everything. He was a name in this country. He was esteemed and respected. No-one could prove a thing.

His breathing was heavy as he struggled furiously to release the ropes that moored the dinghy to the peeling wooden rail of the Halvorsen. He realized now that Anthea James had put Yarrow on to him. She had dared to take the risk. And Yarrow, to keep things quiet, had been fool enough to handle it alone. Swiftly he tossed the mooring lines aside. That bitch would pay. By Christ she –

He cried out in pain as his right shoulder struck the raw timbers of the deck. And now he was staring up into the dark congested features of David Yarrow's face and feeling the hands tightening like a vice around his neck. The black weight of unconsciousness was descending upon him.

With a last surge of strength, Julian Crane jerked his knee upwards and struck viciously into the other man's groin. His assailant released his hold, grunting in agony. In one desperate movement, Julian Crane rolled free and scrambled to his feet. His hand closed around the heavy rusty grappling hook that hung on the exterior wall of the cabin.

David saw the blow coming but was powerless to escape it. As if in slow motion, he saw Julian Crane raise the grappling hook with both hands above his head and, face contorted with loathing, swing it downwards.

David shrieked, his head erupting in a searing, white-hot pain. But Julian Crane wasn't finished. He lifted the hook again.

Struggling against excruciating pain, the warm blood flowing into his eyes, David tried desperately to roll away. But his body failed to respond. Something in his mind seemed to freeze as he waited for the next agonizing blow to fall.

It was in the next split second that David heard the low moan that blew from Julian Crane's fleshy lips, saw the look of surprise that slipped the mask of violence from his features.

Then colours exploded in his brain and the last thing David saw was Kelly standing by the open cabin door, staring wide-eyed with horror as Crane fell heavily to the deck.

After that the world became still and white and peaceful and silent.

CHAPTER FORTY-THREE

FOR as long as she lived, Anthea would never forget the scene that greeted her as, her heart banging in her chest, she clambered aboard that decaying, dilapidated boat.

She would remember always the sight of her daughter kneeling white-faced on the hot timber of the peeling deck. The tears rolled down Kelly's battered cheeks, ran along the ridge of the tape that still bound her mouth and finally fell onto David's shockingly injured head which she cradled in her lap.

A foot away lay Julian Crane, face down and motionless. The blood oozed in bright pools around his bloated frame.

For a moment Anthea stood still. Greyness swept over her. She felt as if a thin veil had descended between herself and reality.

In front of her, the blood draining out of him, lay the only man she had ever loved, would ever love. And the daughter he would never have a chance to know was watching while her father died.

They made the journey back to the city by the same means in which they had arrived – aboard the powerful speedboat Alex had hastily commandeered from a friend.

And their return was every bit as nerve-wracking as the trip south – the temptation to open the throttle even further was always overcome by the need to keep David as still as possible.

With extreme care and gentleness, Alex and Paul had transferred the deathly pale, unconscious man from the deck of the Halvorsen to the vinyl seat cushions that were laid out in readiness on the bottom of the bobbing speedboat.

Squatting beside him, using a clean beach towel to staunch the worst of the blood, Anthea cradled David in her arms as Kelly had done a short time before. Now, as she looked down into that still white face caked with blood, she didn't dare to pray, to hope, to think.

Instead, nerve ends screaming, she experienced like a physical force, every precious second that passed; every precious second that kept them from efficient surgeons, steel trolleys, anonymous grey corridors...

Yet never once did she forget that on the narrow ledge beside her, wrapped in the comfort of Paul Shelton's arms, sat her daughter. Her daughter who had been terrorised and humiliated for reasons she might never completely understand. For there was nothing in Kelly's demeanour to suggest that Crane had revealed the truth to the girl he had kidnapped.

And now – Anthea's heart tightened in her chest – with David so close to death what moral justification could she find for telling Kelly the truth: that the man dying in her arms was in fact her father.

Anthea's eyes took on a haunted look as she thought of the unbearable price she would be forced to pay for her silence. To say nothing to Kelly would mean that she could never reveal the bond that existed between her daughter and herself.

Anthea reached out a hand and laid it gently on the young girl's arm.

ALEX ARRANGED EVERYTHING. The media knew nothing of David's admission to hospital, the source of his injuries, or Anthea's anxious presence at his bedside.

As soon as he had seen David Yarrow into the hands of the discreet and capable medical staff, and assured Anthea he would return as soon as possible, Alex hastily convened a meeting in the privacy of his chambers. It was attended by two leading judges and two senior police officers all of whom, Alex knew, could be trusted absolutely.

It was then he told the whole story of the private investigations into the activities of Julian Crane by Anthea James and himself. It was a story he could support with the evidence now at hand.

He provided his listeners with details of the widespread corruption among Customs officials that ex-Customs officer Leard had told him about; he explained how the ownership of a house, where it could be proved Filipino women had been held captive, had been traced to a company owned by Crane; he described the abduction by Crane of Kelly Delamar, 'a close personal friend and employee' of Anthea James, in an attempt to short-circuit Anthea's investigations. And, looking into the grim faces of the men present, he informed them too of the discovery of a witness willing to testify in court to the murder by Julian Crane of the Filipino woman whose body had been washed up a short time ago on one of Sydney's northern beaches.

It was while his listeners were still coming to terms with the whole amazing story that he quietly informed them of the death of one of Australia's wealthiest and most prominent citizens.

THE FIRST TWO hours that David was in the operating theatre, Anthea stayed with Kelly. Sedated, the wounds on her face and arms now cleaned and dressed, Kelly lay sleeping in her private room.

The lacerations to her wrists, inflicted during her repeated attempts to sever her bonds against the blade of a rusty fishing knife, would heal soon enough. It was the very same knife she had used on Julian Crane.

But the shock at what she had done had set in as soon as they reached the hospital.

'Oh, God, Anthea! Oh, God! What else could I do? What else?' Sobbing convulsively, she gasped out the words again and again, clinging frantically to Anthea in the small treatment room where they sat.

'He was going to kill David! He was going to *kill* him! I had to –' She buried her swollen blood-caked face into Anthea's neck.

'Darling...' Anthea forced herself to speak soothingly as she stroked the frantic girl. 'It'll be all right. I'm sure of that. No-one could possibly bring charges in the circumstances.'

Raising her head, Kelly looked with stricken eyes at the older woman. 'But Anthea,' there was an edge of hysteria in her voice, 'I *killed* a man! I *killed* another human being!'

'No, Kelly.' Anthea's voice went suddenly hard and cold.

'Not a human being. An animal.'

As she held her daughter's soft hand in her own, Anthea felt as if she were breaking up inside, piece by tiny piece.

Crane was dead but her career, her future, her life, everything she had striven for was over.

Despair flooded her heart. If she lost David now, lost the promise of a relationship with Kelly, how could she find the spirit, the strength to carry on?

Eyes brimming, she looked at Kelly's poor savaged face against the pillow. She would recover. She would be all right. But what then? Would she marry Paul? Stay in Australia? Or would the terrible events of the last twenty-four hours send her running back to the States?

Whatever Kelly's decisions, Anthea knew that they would be taken with no knowledge of the fact that she had a mother, a mother who was ready to love her child with every breath of her being, to comfort and guide her in the years to come.

With a soft moan of utter despair, Anthea could hold back her tears no longer.

Five minutes later there was a knock on the door of Kelly's room. It was Paul. He had things to do he'd said when he'd left earlier, but now Anthea realized he had understood her need to have time alone with Kelly.

He walked quietly into the room and shook his head in sympathetic reply to Anthea's fearful, unspoken question.

'Nothing yet. He's still in theatre,' Paul said softly.

IT WAS ANOTHER two hours before Anthea was told that David was now in intensive care.

She searched the surgeon's eyes for any sign of hope. Still dressed in his creased green gown, the tall, thin-faced man sighed heavily as he spoke to her in the small waiting-room.

'I'm not going to give you false hope, Miss James. Mr Yarrow's condition is very serious. There is acute pressure to the brain which we have done our best to relieve but you have to know that his chances are very slim.'

He rubbed a weary hand across his brow. 'The next twelve hours will be crucial – he'll be monitored every second, but there's nothing more that can be done now.' He seemed suddenly to notice Anthea's blood-stained clothes, her smeared exhausted face. 'Why don't you go home? We can call –'

'No...' Holding her hands against her face, Anthea whispered the word.

Alex found her half-an-hour later sitting with her head bowed, her eyes blank, in the small green room with its grey metal chairs. For a moment he was loathe to disturb her, so intensely concentrated did she seem on her own thoughts.

But then she raised her head.

'Alex...'

He entered then, taking a seat beside her and began to tell her what had occurred. Again her head was bowed and Alex wasn't sure how much she took in, but he told her everything.

'We've pulled off the big one, Anthea. Maxine Crane's ex-lover picked out Crane's hitman from police files. A Welshman named Frank Carter. Twice had assault charges brought against him but thanks to some fancy footwork by his lawyers – retained no doubt by Crane – he's managed to get off. But not this time. Loverboy was more than keen to bring charges of assault but Carter knows that's just the beginning. He'll talk, Anthea – no doubt of that. We've put the fear of death into him. If he insists on protecting Crane, the murder of that Filipino girl will be hung fair-square on his own filthy shoulders.'

There was grim satisfaction in Alex's tone as he went on. 'We're going to pick this whole operation apart. Peel back every dirty layer of it for public scrutiny. There'll be no way then that the government dare not act. They'll know that if they don't their chance of retaining office at the next election will be next to nil.

'As far as Crane's death is concerned – a boating accident is how it'll be reported. Ill-timed of course in the circumstances. But there'll be nothing for Kelly to worry about – and I'll assure her of that myself as soon as I can talk with her.'

He patted Anthea's hand but still she didn't look at him. Lowering his voice, Alex went on: 'As far as Crane's henchman is concerned you have nothing to worry about, my dear. I had a long talk to him – alone. He won't be opening his mouth about what he knows; I can guarantee you that. And I can tell you now how Crane found out, how he got on to Harriet Maddern. It's so amazingly simple. Harriet panicked when she met Kelly at the function at Crane's house. She realized at once who she was, what a threat she posed. It was when she was telling Roy about it that Maxine Crane overheard.'

He squeezed Anthea's ice-cold hand. 'Maxine won't be a problem Anthea, I promise you that. The police have already informed her of Julian's "accident"; while she's still coming to terms with that shock I want to speak with her. By the time I've explained a few things to Maxine Crane she'll see that it'll be in her best interests to keep a very low profile in this country for a long long time.'

Anthea nodded but said nothing and a moment later Alex stood up. Only when he put a hand gently on her shoulder did she finally raise her head. He looked down into her white exhausted face and when he spoke his voice was charged with feeling. 'I – I understand now, Anthea. After what you've told me, I understand everything a lot better. I see now why things had to change so suddenly between us. What – what I want you to know now is that I'm hoping with all my heart you get the chance for the happiness you so dearly deserve.'

Abruptly, before she could see the tears in his eyes, he turned and left the room.

As he drove away from the hospital, Alex was planning his next move. He had no intention just yet of facing Maxine Crane. His first step was to use the legal grapevine to reveal the facts that would soon stun Australia.

Back in his study he made a number of phone calls and then leaned back in his chair, a look of grim satisfaction on his face.

Within the hour Julian Crane's lawyers, already reeling at the news of the media baron's death, would then have to deal with the prospect of Crane's criminal activities providing sensational front page copy for the country's papers.

Maxine Crane, Alex felt sure, would have more pressing matters to concern her than the exposure of Anthea James.

AT SEVEN P.M. they brought her tea and sandwiches but Anthea left the food untouched. Once or twice her thoughts strayed to the following day: the press who would, no doubt, be clamouring for her comments on her election win, the direction she would be taking in the future. But none of that seemed to matter any more, the claustrophobic room, the relentless ticking of the standard issue clock set high on the wall, the piercing agony of losing what she had possessed for such a short time: these were the only things that existed for her now.

By eight she could bear it no longer. Getting to her feet, she went off in search of the ward sister.

'Please...can I see him... just for a moment?'

The plea in Anthea's voice, the pain in her gaunt face and hollow eyes, did not surprise the dark-haired girl who sat writing by the shaded night light on her desk. She knew by experience that, faced with tragedy, the famous, the wealthy, the celebrated, are every bit as vulnerable as the plain, the poor, the anonymous.

Pushing the chair back from her desk, she got to her feet.

'Take your time, Miss James,' she said quietly, leading the way out of the room, 'You won't be disturbing him.'

And there he lay, so white and still, surrounded by the paraphernalia of modern medicine, the magical tools in which Western civilization puts its faith at moments like this.

Though his head was heavily bandaged, though tubes and wires criss-crossed his body, David's face was miraculously unmarked. It was the face Anthea had never forgotten through the years, and would never forget in the years still to come when the memories of the last few months would have to last a lifetime.

How she longed to touch him, to hold him close to her for one last time. A tightness gripped her throat and her eyes burned with tears. 'Oh, David.' She barely realized that the words had escaped from her lips. Like an incantation, a prayer, she went on: 'David, don't leave me... Please, my darling, I love you so much.' The tears were falling freely now. 'We've found our daughter David, we've found Kelly... after all these years. Oh my darling, there's so much for you to live for.'

The slight noise behind her made her spin round and through brimming eyes she saw Kelly. She was dressed now and her bandages were almost hidden under the long sleeves of her blouse. The bruises on her face were only faintly visible in the dim half-light as she stood motionless in the doorway.

Kelly stared at her without speaking, shock and confusion etched on her face.

Anthea felt herself begin to sway and then, at once, Kelly was by her side, holding her, supporting her, in her bandaged arms.

'Are you telling me...?' Kelly's voice was a tremulous whisper.

Heart flopping crazily, Anthea nodded as she looked into that incredulous young face. 'Yes, my darling,' she said softly, her voice breaking. 'This – this is your father lying here.'

CHAPTER FORTY-FOUR

THROUGH that endless night the two women sat close together in the quiet solitude of that small green room and Anthea told Kelly of another life and of another young girl. It was this girl's love for the boy she had known such a short intense time that had brought Kelly into the world.

About her life with Nan, Anthea was equally candid. She held nothing back, hoping only that Kelly would understand that the things she had seen and experienced at that time had given her the drive and the desire to change the status quo. 'So many of those girls were driven into that way of life, Kelly. They had few other choices. After seeing that, I knew I wanted to do everything I could to change things.'

Watching Anthea intently, Kelly listened in silence until finally the story was at an end.

Exhausted, drained by an emotional outpouring that was cathartic in its intensity, Anthea leaned back against the hard metal chair. She had made no excuses. Now it was up to Kelly to judge her on the facts.

For a long moment Kelly was silent, her face clouded with the struggle to absorb the amazing story she had just been told. Then a strange light came into her soft hazel eyes.

Anthea's apprehension was swept away in a wave of utter joy: in Kelly's expression she recognized the understanding, the acceptance, she had prayed for.

Her tearful daughter threw her arms around the mother she had found at last and Anthea was made aware that it was more, much more, than that. 'I love you,' Kelly sobbed into her neck. 'It meant going to hell to find you but none of that matters now. Only having each other, knowing David will get better; that's all that counts now.'

For what seemed like an eternity they clung to each other.

*

At seven a.m. the surgeon found them asleep, slumped awkwardly together.

He touched a hand to Anthea's shoulder and she woke, instantly aware of her surroundings. As Kelly stirred Anthea looked up with hollow eyes at the man in front of her and heard the sweetest words of her life.

'It's been touch and go, Miss James, but I think now we can say he's going to make it.'

His eyes fluttered open and slowly, very slowly, the two people in the room came into focus. They were bending over him, smiling, and though he tried to speak, the effort of moving his lips sent the pain slicing through his head.

'Don't speak, darling.' The voice was soft and tender. He felt a hand close gently over his own. 'We're here – Kelly and I – and we'll never be far away. We both love you very much and everything's going to be all right.'

He closed his eyes and the vague movement around his lips told the women who loved him that he understood.

CHAPTER FORTY-FIVE

SLOWLY, painfully, Maxine turned her head on the pillow. Her brain exploding with blinding lights, she fought to focus her vision on the bottle she knew stood somewhere on the bedside table.

With a superhuman effort she raised the deadweight of her bare fleshy arm and felt around for the welcome comfort of the Smirnoff.

Just another mouthful, that's all she wanted. Her heart pounded crazily in her chest with the effort of her search.

She smiled weakly. Vodka and Nembutal. Solace, comfort, oblivion. The shame and humiliation that Julian had dumped on her – she could leave it all behind. The fascinated horror she would see on the faces of those she had once called 'friends' – none of it would matter any more.

Her clutching fingers touched something hard and smooth. She had it! But then, a heavy thud. And past the buzzing noise in her ears, Maxine heard the soft gurgle of liquid losing itself in the thick woollen carpet.

A bubbling sob escaped her lips and tears of frustration rolled down her bloated, sweaty face into the corner of her slack open mouth.

A moment later her scrambled brain forgot the reason for her tears.

CHAPTER FORTY-SIX

DURING the month it took David to make a complete recovery from his injuries, the Australian media went crazy with a series of sensational reports detailing the full extent of the empire of vice and corruption that had been established so successfully by Julian Crane.

As Alex had predicted, it was Frank Carter who eventually provided the information that enabled the Crane operation to be exposed.

Widespread corruption among Immigration and Customs officials had facilitated the illegal entry of hundreds of Filipino women into Australia for employment in a network of brothels established by Crane in each of the East Coast capitals. When these were located and raided by police, the enormous scale of the operation was revealed to an outraged public.

Nearly a thousand young girls, among them Joseph's sister, Philomena, had provided a captive work force for Crane's highly profitable set-up. Intimidated by threats about the consequences of their illegal entry into Australia, the girls had been too frightened to do anything about their plight.

In addition to the huge profits generated by the brothels, there had been another equally lucrative side to the business. Files confiscated by police during a search of Crane's premises had revealed a wide scale blackmailing operation involving certain leading public figures foolish enough to patronise the establishments in question. Pressure brought to bear against the various individuals involved, had assured Crane of especially favourable outcomes in more than a few important business deals. A number of well-known citizens reached fearfully for their newspapers every morning as the revelations continued.

The extent of the operation, the huge cover-up by corrupt members of the police, public service and judiciary, resulted in a violent public outcry, and an uproar in Parliament.

Despite the coroner's verdict of 'death by misadventure', rumours continued to circulate concerning the death of Julian Crane. The general belief was that, faced with imminent exposure and disgrace, suicide had provided Crane's only means of escape. The subsequent death of Maxine Crane merely added credence to the rumour.

When the roles played by Alex Volka and Anthea James in the destruction of Julian Crane's operation were revealed, public admiration for both reached new heights. It was an admiration that enhanced formidably Anthea's political position.

Yet, despite the public acclaim, for a short time Anthea felt plagued by a nagging sense of guilt about the cover-up of Crane's death. Had she and Alex also been responsible for abusing their powers for their own ends?

Finally though, reason had prevailed. Justice and the law Anthea knew, did not always protect the victims. And that Kelly had been a victim, she had no doubt...

In those first few weeks Anthea kept a close eye on Kelly, looking for signs of delayed emotional reaction. There had been nightmares at first, a sense of burdening guilt and self-doubt, but Paul had helped and between them they had done everything in their power to restore Kelly's peace of mind.

Anthea felt certain that Kelly's recovery had been assisted by her daily presence at David's bedside. Witnessing his slow though steady progress must have done a lot to help her justify what she had done. There had been a choice – Crane's life or David's. No choice at all.

KELLY SPENT MANY hours alone with her father. While David grew stronger they talked together as they now needed to talk. Sitting next to him on the bed, Kelly sometimes felt overwhelmed by the reality that faced her. It was then that she recalled the strange obsessional pull she had always felt towards this man.

EPILOGUE

'PAUL! Will you please keep your daughter under control...' Kelly grinned as her husband, scrambling to his feet, set off across the lawn after the gleefully squealing toddler.

The child retrieved, the family again settled themselves on the rug spread over the lush springy grass.

'Right, I think we're all set to go.' Roy smiled as he made a final check of the focus.

From the verandah Harriet looked fondly at the scene on the lawn. She and Anthea had made their peace: the past was behind them now and Harriet felt sure that in her heart Anthea had extended forgiveness to Nan as well.

Roy's voice broke into her thoughts. 'Right everybody, this is going to make a great shot. Steady now.'

But before the photograph could be taken, Catherine Shelton began to wriggle furiously in her father's grasp.

'Okay.' Kelly shook her head in amused exasperation and stretched out her arms. 'Hand the little demon over.'

David and Anthea looked on in patient delight as their boisterous granddaughter was coaxed into sitting still for the camera.

'Happy darling?' David, his arm around Anthea's shoulders, whispered the question in her ear.

'Unbelievably so,' she answered softly, turning shining eyes up to his.

And she was. A feeling of utter contentment swept over her as she sat amongst those she loved most dearly. This was her family, the family she had never dared to dream of, but now was proud to acknowledge.

The fact that Anthea James had admitted to an illegitimate daughter had caused a three-day-wonder in the country's press. But times were different now, and for the minority who condemned her, there were plenty who applauded Anthea's courage in admitting to the child she'd given up at birth. The public had taken to their hearts the romance involved in Anthea's reunion with her child's father, the man she had loved so long ago.

Anthea's career had not been impeded in any way. Slowly divesting herself of her media interests, she threw herself wholeheartedly into the political arena. She was working hard, harder than she had ever worked in her life, but the rewards were enormous.

From the moment she had become an elected member of Federal Parliament, she had exerted relentless pressure on the Government to shake off its appalling political apathy concerning the expansion and entrenchment of organized crime in Australia. Now there was confrontation and action, and Anthea took satisfaction in the knowledge that she and Alex had played an important role in giving impetus to such vital changes. Alex's book too had done much to assist in the implementation of new policies.

In time, Anthea's promotion to a portfolio had led to other victories too. In holding true to the principles that had driven her so long and so far, she had overseen legislation that had done much to eliminate the discrimination, prejudice, and sexism that had oppressed women for so much of Australia's history.

The rough and tumble of political life hadn't been easy, but Anthea had proved she was a survivior. It was the Action Party's defeat in the last Federal election that had opened the way for her run to the top. In the uproar and shuffle that followed, her popularity, her achievement and drive, had been formally recognized. The Party leadership was hers.

Anthea smiled into the camera as Roy prepared once more to take the photograph. There was much to celebrate. Today was her granddaughter's second birthday and in twelve days from now, as Leader of the Opposition she would take her Party for the first time into an election. At last she would get her chance to prove it could be done: that a woman could make it to the highest office in the land.

With her popularity ratings running high in the polls, Anthea knew it was a very real chance she was being offered. If she was successful the ground would have been broken. Those women who followed after her would not be seen as the few who had somehow 'slipped through the net'. Anthea felt sure that in ten years time, a woman Prime Minister in Australia would arouse no particular comment. She would merely be the best person for the job.

As the shutter clicked and the moment of family happiness was captured at last, Anthea felt a joy inside her that knew no bounds. She had set out on a long hard road to achieve her goals – in the end she had gained more than she'd ever dreamed of.